Wildfire

Content Warning:

<u>Wildfire</u> *is intended for adult readers only*

It contains ...
is not in...

Also by Hannah Grace

Icebreaker

Wildfire

HANNAH GRACE

SIMON &
SCHUSTER

London · New York · Sydney · Toronto · New Delhi

First published in Great Britain by Simon & Schuster UK Ltd, 2023
First published in the United States by Atria,
an imprint of Simon & Schuster, Inc. 2023

5 7 9 10 8 6

Simon & Schuster UK Ltd
1st Floor
222 Gray's Inn Road
London WC1X 8HB

Simon & Schuster Australia, Sydney
Simon & Schuster India, New Delhi

www.simonandschuster.co.uk
www.simonandschuster.com.au
www.simonandschuster.co.in

A CIP catalogue record for this book
is available from the British Library

Paperback ISBN: 978-1-3985-2571-9
eBook ISBN: 978-1-3985-2572-6
Audio ISBN: 978-1-3985-2573-3

Printed and Bound in the UK using 100% Renewable
Electricity at CPI Group (UK) Ltd

MIX
Paper | Supporting
responsible forestry
FSC® C171272

For younger me,
who wanted to be his first choice.

Playlist

SPARKS FLY (TAYLOR'S VERSION) | TAYLOR SWIFT	4:20
WILDFIRE | SEAFRET	3:43
MOONLIGHT | ARIANA GRANDE	3:22
ALONE WITH YOU | ALINA BARAZ	3:45
CHRONICALLY CAUTIOUS | BRADEN BALES	1:59
BEST PART (FEAT. H.E.R.) | DANIEL CAESAR	3:29
SWEAT | ZAYN	3:52
NAKED—BONUS TRACK | ELLA MAI	3:17
LATE NIGHT TALKING | HARRY STYLES	2:57
HARD TO LOVE | BLACKPINK	2:42
PEACE | TAYLOR SWIFT	3:53
YOU | MILEY CYRUS	2:59
NONSENSE | SABRINA CARPENTER	2:43
SLEEPING WITH MY FRIENDS | GAYLE	2:48
PRETTY PLEASE | DUA LIPA	3:14
DID YOU KNOW THAT THERE'S A TUNNEL UNDER OCEAN BLVD | LANA DEL RAY	4:44
WHILE WE'RE YOUNG | JHENÉ AIKO	3:56
BIGGEST FAN | MADDIE ZAHM	3:01
THE ONLY EXCEPTION | PARAMORE	4:27
EVERYTHING | LABRINTH	2:15

"To love is to burn, to be on fire."

—Marianne Dashwood, *Sense and Sensibility* (1995)

Chapter One

RUSS

HENRY'S EYES ARE BURNING INTO me from across the living room. "Your summer is going to suck."

There's an echo of snorts from my teammates, the loudest coming from Mattie, Bobby, and Kris, who all told me something similar when I said no to joining them in Miami this summer.

"Inspiring words, Turner," I shoot back at my unimpressed roommate. "You should become a motivational speaker."

"You'll be sorry you didn't listen to me when you're stuck doing manual labor and team-building activities at staff training next week." Henry continues to flick through the Honey Acres brochure, his forehead creasing with a frown the further he gets into it. "What's night duty?"

"I have to sleep in a room attached to the campers' cabin twice a week in case they need anything," I say casually, watching Henry's eyes widen in horror. "The rest of the time I sleep in my own cabin."

"It's a no from me," he says, throwing the brochure back onto the coffee table. "Good luck, though."

"Could be worse," Robbie muses from across the living room. "You could have to move to Canada this summer."

Nate groans loudly, burying his head in his girlfriend's hair, sinking further into the recliner they're sharing. "Fuck off about fucking Canada."

"You brought this on yourself," Stassie mutters just loudly enough for us all to hear. "Stop being such a crybaby. Nate, you want to play for Vancouver."

"I'd rather move to Canada than look after twenty kids for nine weeks." The genuine disgust on Henry's face would make someone think I'm going to work in a slaughterhouse, not spend the summer as a counselor at a sleepaway camp. "You really didn't think this through, Callaghan."

I really did.

Honey Acres' main clientele are busy and rich parents who need to keep their kids occupied for the full summer while they work. Thankfully, the fees are expensive as hell, which means the facilities are better than every other camp I looked at, and given the work keeping multiple kids in check, the job is well paid with multiple full days off. Something I know is a luxury and definitely not the case with most camps.

Kris and Bobby suggested I apply after I turned down their vacation offer, explaining I needed to get a job. They went to Honey Acres one summer ten years ago, and swore it was the best camp in California, and I was willing to apply for anything. Money has been tight since the bar I worked at was shut down by the cops. Unfortunately, its reputation for suspicious activity and serving underage students finally caught up with it, and there's no sign of it reopening.

So even though Henry thinks my judgment is seriously flawed, the alternative is hanging around Maple Hills, unemployed, being hounded by my mom to visit her.

It was a very easy choice.

"What I'm hearing, Hen, is you still don't want to come with me," I tease.

"It's still a no. Thanks. But if you need a fake emergency to be able to leave, let me know. I'll make a call."

JJ leans closer to Henry from beside him on the couch, nudging him with his shoulder. "The only emergency you're going to have for the next two years, Captain, is drowning in too much p—"

"JJ!" Stassie squeaks, cutting him off.

"Get your mind out of the gutter," he chastises. "I was going to say paint."

Stassie rolls her eyes at him, giving him the finger as he blows her a kiss. Lowering her hand, she focuses on me, a soft smile on her lips. "You'll have fun, ignore Henry. We'll miss you around here, though."

"You don't even live here anymore," Mattie says, eyebrow raised.

"You've never lived here!" she counters, starting off an argument about who spends more time at this house.

As grateful as I am to have a job this summer, it does kind of suck to be heading off when I've only just moved in with Henry and Robbie. Plus our unofficial roommates Mattie, Bobby, and Kris, who magically appear whenever food is mentioned.

It's weird having my own room after two years of sharing in the fraternity house, and before that with my brother, Ethan, but I'm already so much happier here.

Aside from the obvious things like having my own space and living with people I like, it feels good not to have to strategically plan when I can jerk off or, on rare occasions, get laid. Henry had the courtesy to let me know that after six months of living next to Nate and Stassie, he can confirm with absolute certainty that the room is not soundproof.

"Are you two going to argue all afternoon or should we get ready for the party?" Robbie shouts over Stassie and Mattie bickering.

Tonight we're throwing a party to say good-bye to the guys graduating, or a "farewell and fuck off" party, as Robbie calls it. He's staying at Maple Hills for grad school and is happy to retain his title as party planner.

That said, no one looks particularly enthusiastic about preparing the house for the horde of Maple Hills students descending on us in a few hours. I know it feels like the end of an era for the guys; four years is a long time to spend every day with someone. For Nate and Robbie, it's even longer; they haven't ever lived in different towns, never mind different countries.

For me, it feels like the start of one. I joined a fraternity at the beginning of school because I wanted a family that wouldn't let me down like my real one does. I thought my frat brothers would be there through the good and the bad, that I'd finally have people I could rely on, but it didn't happen. I sensed I'd made a mistake freshman year, but I persevered, thinking it'd take a while to feel like family. I knew I'd made a mistake when all the shit happened with the rink at the start of the year and the only people who were there for me are in this room.

It was the worst time of my life, which says a lot, and I was bottling up how embarrassed I felt. Then one day Henry asked me if I was all right and I told him I was fine. I expected that to be the end of it, but he told me he knew I was lying and he'd be back when I was ready to talk. Every week we had the same conversation, until I bumped into him over winter break.

I'd tried to go home, but only lasted twenty-four hours with my dad's post-casino-loss drunk, incoherent bullshit, and my mom's borderline professional inability to hold him accountable for his actions before I was on my way back to campus. Henry was heading to the hockey house to get his art supplies, and when he saw me, he asked me if I was all right, and for the first time, I told him no.

After spending so many years too ashamed and angry about my dad's gambling problem to tell anyone, it all came tumbling out like word vomit. Not even Coach Faulkner or Nate know the full extent of my home life, but I told Henry fucking everything.

He stood there, a canvas tucked under his arm, listening.

When I was done, feeling like a ton of bricks had been lifted from my shoulders, he asked me if I wanted to get Kenny's wings and hang out with him over the break. He didn't ask me questions, he didn't offer advice, he didn't judge me. That's why I immediately said yes when he asked if I wanted to live with him and Robbie.

The room has descended into chaos like it always does when everyone is together, with multiple conversations overlapping, the next louder than the last. People mistake me being quiet for being shy, but I'm not shy. I don't think I'm even that quiet, it just looks that way because of how loud everyone else is. I prefer to sit and listen than be the focus of everything, unlike my teammates. There's too much pressure with being the center of attention, too many opportunities to fuck everything up. I'm much happier being an observer, watching from the outside.

Making my way into the kitchen, I grab a water from the refrigerator, taking another when I sense someone behind me.

"You ready for your official first party?" JJ says, accepting the bottle from my hand.

We both lean against the kitchen counter, looking into the living room. "I think so. Don't piss Robbie off is the only rule, right?"

JJ snorts as he unscrews the lid of his drink. "It happens to be my favorite pastime, but it depends how hard you want to be worked next season."

"I think I'll stay on his good side."

"Feel like home yet?" he asks, taking a sip of the water.

I've spent a lot of time with JJ over the past few weeks and have discovered that beneath the joker persona, he's very brotherly. After using my savings to buy myself an old truck a couple of months ago, I became the unofficial moving guy for everyone's boxes. It was nice to feel useful, so it didn't bother me until Lola was worried her stuff would accidentally get shipped to Nate's new place in Vancouver and she drew dicks on the boxes that weren't hers or Stassie's.

JJ and I drove to his new place in San Jose with a truck bed full of the decorated boxes, getting funny looks from other drivers for the entire journey. You learn a lot about who someone is when you're stuck in an enclosed space with them for ten hours. Ironically, JJ joked that I give hardly anything away.

"Getting there," I admit. "Big change from what I'm used to."

"Remember, you belong here. Everyone wants you around, you hear me?" he says quietly.

I've never voiced my insecurities to any of the guys, but somehow JJ knows I keep myself on the outside of things. I called him perceptive once and he said it's because he's a Scorpio. Whatever that means.

I appreciate it anyway, and for the first time in a long time, I feel understood. Which is a strange feeling to accept, since a lot of the time I don't understand myself.

"I hear you," I confirm. He slaps me on the shoulder before heading back to his seat in the living room. I follow slowly, throwing myself into the seat beside Henry.

Robbie claps his hands once, giving us all hockey flashbacks as we instinctively give him our immediate attention like well-trained dogs.

"Such a mini-Faulkner. Jeez," Nate grumbles, shuffling uncomfortably in his seat.

"You know I flinch during rounds of applause now," Bobby adds. "I think it's an actual trauma response."

"I hear that clap when I'm alone," Mattie says, nodding in solidarity.

"Nah," Joe snorts. "That's Kris next door. Just the one. Clap her cheeks, singular."

Robbie hisses something under his breath as Kris launches a couch cushion at Joe, which he catches and throws back, chaos ensuing.

"Where were these defensive skills when you played hockey, Joe?" Henry asks, catching him off guard long enough for one of Kris's cushions to smack him right in the face.

"For fuck's sake," Robbie grumbles. "This party isn't going to happen if one of you clowns ends up with a concussion. Come on, one last time."

A natural silence settles over the room as everyone reluctantly lines up to be told what to do by Robbie, and there's a weird moment where I think it occurs to everyone that this is the last party the guys are going to throw together in this house.

I'm lost in my thoughts when JJ starts laughing and shouting. "Five bucks! You all owe me five bucks!"

"What?"

"Stas is crying!" He wraps his arm around her and kisses the side of her head. "And it's before she's had any alcohol! I win."

Wiping her tears away with the backs of her hands, she looks around bewildered. "You guys bet on me?"

The guys all reach for their wallets, plucking out bills. Mattie shrugs as he slams it into JJ's awaiting palm. "We technically bet on your tears."

"This is unbelievable. Nate, did you kn—" She turns to her boyfriend, who's discreetly pulling money from his pocket. "You're such a douche bag! You're all douche bags."

Nate hands his five-dollar bill to JJ and tugs her into a tight hug, kissing her temple affectionately. "You didn't even try to last. I could have bought you chicken wings with that money."

"Unbelievable. It's just so sad. You guys are all going your separate ways and there's just an atmosphere."

"If I told you Russ didn't bet on you crying today, would that make you feel better?"

Her watery eyes meet mine and she grins. "Thanks, muffin. You're not on my shit list."

I give her a nod of acknowledgment, letting her think it's because I thought she wouldn't cry—which I knew she would—instead of saying it's because I don't gamble.

"Excuse me," Henry interrupts. "Neither did I."

Henry also knew she would cry, but decided he doesn't gamble anymore in solidarity. JJ is still counting his money when Lola strolls in with bags full of red cups. She looks along the line and scowls. "She cried, didn't she?"

"Yup," the room echoes.

"Goddamn it, Anastasia." Lola drops the bags into Robbie's lap, bending to kiss him, before reaching into her purse and pulling out some cash. "This is the last time you're ever getting my money, Johal."

"Until I fail at hockey and follow my true calling in life," JJ counters. "Stripping."

"Until then."

"Now that everyone's debts have been paid can we please get this shit show started?" Robbie groans.

The silence from earlier returns, the same shared thought running through my teammates' minds one by one. Nate clears his throat, nodding. "One last time."

The weird atmosphere disappears as soon as Lola burst out laughing. "All right, Alexander Hamilton. And I'm supposedly the dramatic one, jeez. Bunch of fucking drama queens."

Chapter Two

AURORA

I'm not supposed to be here right now, but there's something about basketball players that messes with my ability to exercise self-control.

I said I wasn't coming and Emilia is already waiting for me at the hockey house, so I don't know why I let Ryan freaking Rothwell convince me to abandon my plan and swing by. What is it about tall, muscular men who are good with their hands that makes me weak? It's one of life's great mysteries. One that half the women at Maple Hills are trying to figure out, judging by the crowd at this party.

With several of the team's players graduating, tonight is their final party. Ryan and I said good-bye to each other four times last week and, as great as he is, we both know he's not going to keep in touch. He has the NBA draft next month and I'm under no illusions I'll be invited to sit courtside anytime soon. But that didn't stop me from coming by just because he asked me to, which says more about me than it does about Ryan.

I'm minding my business, questioning all my life choices and nursing my drink in a quiet spot in the kitchen, when someone I wish was leaving slides along the counter beside me. My eyes instinctively roll the second Mason Wright's mouth opens, but that doesn't stop him from bothering me.

He steals my drink from my grip—an act he knows I detest—and takes a sip. "Looking for your next victim, Roberts?"

God, I hate him. "Isn't it your bedtime, Wright?"

His eyes roam up and down my body and he smirks, making me internally gag. "Is that an invitation?"

Thankfully, I have no problem exercising self-control around this particular basketball player. "An invitation to fuck off and leave me alone? Yeah."

He chuckles, and the idea of him finding joy in anything irritates me. I don't know where this kid got all his confidence, but he should bottle it and sell it. I've never known anyone, especially a freshman, as arrogant as this boy.

Returning my drink to me, he leans in a little closer. "You know playing hard to get turns me on, right?"

"I'm not playing, Mason. You can't get me."

"And why's that?"

"Other than the fact I cannot stand you? You're a freshman."

"You're four months older than me." His eyebrows pinch together in frustration because God forbid a woman doesn't immediately fall to her knees in his presence.

"You're. A. Freshman," I repeat.

He'd never believe any woman not being interested in him. Partially because he is very attractive, but mainly because he's overconfident as hell. He looks more like a stereotypical rock star than a basketball player. Tall, black hair, piercing blue eyes and pale skin with detailed tattoos decorating his arms and back. Sighing, I down the rest of my drink. "I don't like people who are younger than me."

"Careful, princess." He smothers a laugh with his hand and my eyes narrow. "Your daddy issues are showing."

"The only issue I have is you." I want to strangle him, but knowing Mason, he'd probably assume it was foreplay. "But speaking of daddies, how is Director Skinner?"

As arrogant as my archnemesis is, he does have one weakness: his dad. Nobody knows that his father is head of athletics at Maple Hills, and he wants to keep it that way, which is why he uses his mom's maiden name. You'd think both of us having issues with our dads would help us bond, but Mason and I have never gotten along, and a friendship will never develop over time. I can safely say I always will be patiently waiting for his downfall.

"Nice to know I'm the topic of yours and Ryan's pillow talk." His signature smirk sinks into a scowl instantly and he reaches for the nearest liquor bottle. "I'm moving into Ry's room; did he tell you? I won't even change the code so you know how to get in."

This kid does not know when to quit. "Aren't you cute. But seriously, Mason, can you give your dad my number? He's hot." He's not. "And I want to be handed a position on the basketball team."

"Oh fuck off, Aurora," he grunts, slamming the bottle back onto the counter and stalking off toward the garden.

"Careful, princess!" I shout after him. "Your daddy issues are showing."

Arms wrap around my waist from behind and I'm preparing to start throwing punches until I hear a deep voice I'm very familiar with. "I'm not bailing you out of jail if you kill him."

"He told me I have daddy issues." Ryan looks confused as I turn in his arms to face him, like he's not quite sure where this conversation is going. "It's only okay when I say it."

He nods, finally understanding. "Gotcha. What did you say to piss him off?"

"I asked him for his dad's number so I could be given a spot on the basketball team."

"Rory . . ." He drags out the *ry*, so I know I'm in trouble. "You know that's supposed to be a secret. He's a sensitive little bean beneath that broody bad boy act."

It isn't my fault that Mason has a bad relationship with his dad. It doesn't exactly make him special and I never said the word *nepotism*. "Well, if it was a secret, why did you tell me?"

Ryan leans down and kisses my forehead tenderly. "Because I know you hate him and I was trying to get into your pants."

"Hmm. I would have let you in anyway."

I would let Ryan Rothwell into my pants any day of the week. I have let Ryan Rothwell into my pants many days of the week, in fact. Ryan's a great guy, which is probably why I'm choosing to face Emilia's wrath for the sake of seeing him one last time.

My expectations for men are so low they're in the pits of hell, but Ryan is one of the good ones, and our friends-with-benefits situation over the past couple of months has been fun.

He has a bit of a reputation for string-free fun, and I firmly believe he should be awarded by the college for his services to women's happiness during his four years here.

They should erect a statue in his honor.

Maybe I'll ask Mason's dad about it.

His finger nudges under my chin, tilting my head up and dragging me from my thoughts. "I'm going to miss you, Roberts."

A response is stuck in my throat. Something like, "I'll miss you, too," or even a simple "thanks" would be enough, but the words won't come out. I hate that a few affectionate words, a simple gesture of friendship, a sign that the times we've spent together meant something to him, is enough to make me spiral.

Our relationship has always been purely physical. Not that he hasn't tried to make me stay over after hooking up, but hearing he'll miss me feels good, even if he does have a dozen other women to tell that to.

He sighs, almost like he can hear my racing thoughts, and pulls me into a hug, sinking his face into my hair. "I'm gonna be jealous of the guy who gets to hear what happens in your head when you have that look on your face. Bring him to a game so I can launch a ball at his head."

"I don't think either of us needs to worry about that happening."

He laughs into my hair, still not letting go. "I'm just the stop gap. I'm the guy you fuck right before you meet the love of your life."

"Statistically, that's going to happen if you fuck everyone."

"Trust me, Roberts. I should start a money-back guarantee scheme. You'll get your happy ending."

"God, Ryan. Don't make me emotional when I'm about to head to a hockey party. You know being sad makes me horny."

He laughs as we reluctantly untangle and take a step back. "If you say being sad makes you horny two more times, Mason will appear like Beetlejuice."

I roll my eyes as I search out my nemesis, finding him inconveniencing someone else across the room, out of earshot. "Can you take him with you? I can't deal with him without you."

He tucks my hair behind my ear. "You told me you want to change this summer. Maybe you'll come back from camp and be able to tolerate him. You'll be more experienced with dealing with children."

"I said I wanted to grow out of all my toxic self-sabotaging habits. I did not say I would change enough to stop hating Mason."

"Maybe you should switch out some of those contemporary romance choices for self-help books."

My eyes narrow. "You complete one English degree and you think you're qualified to start handing out book recs?"

"You're right, Roberts. Let me just stay in my lane."

The good-bye is hanging in the air, but I can't quite force myself to say it. "You'll let me know how the draft goes, right?"

Kissing my forehead one last time, Ryan nods. "You bet. Stay out of trouble."

"Don't I always?"

"Literally never," he laughs. "That's the problem."

EMILIA MEETS ME AS I step out of my Uber, sporting the un-impressed scowl I know and love. "You're late."

It's hard to be intimidated by her when she looks so angelic—literally. Her mousy brown curls have been braided into a halo, and the tip of her nose and cheeks are still red from sunburn after falling asleep in our garden yesterday. The rest of her has remained her normal shade of ghostly white, so I'm not sure how she managed to just fry her face. Something I won't be bringing up right now. "Would it help if I told you how pretty you are?"

It doesn't help and I lose her the second we walk through the door of the hockey house and past what appear to be life-size cardboard cutouts of the hockey team.

We tend not to visit these parties despite their campus-wide reputation, due to Emilia's preference for events that end before midnight and my preference for basketball, but JJ, one of her friends from the LGBTQIA+ society, is heading up north to play hockey professionally and she promised to say bye.

So naturally I agreed to tag along because I'm a great friend, but also because she promised me a veggie pizza on the way home later. I am slightly worried that being late is going to mess with her willingness to buy me pizza.

Despite the hordes of people, it feels oddly homely for a college house occupied by hockey players. There are pictures in frames on the walls featuring a group of guys and two girls, couch cushions that don't look like they're harboring enough germs to start a biological war, and, unless my eyes deceive me, someone has dusted in here.

Is that a coaster?

Fighting my way through the crowd, mainly confused that my

feet aren't sticking to the floor, but definitely thirsty, I head toward my favorite place at any party: the kitchen. The huge island is already covered in various half-empty liquor and soda bottles. My eyes scan the various cupboards trying to guess which one seems the most likely to hold glasses.

Party or not, I've watched too many documentaries about the sea to use plastic cups. I tentatively sneak a look in one of the cabinets to find nothing but shot glasses.

Literally.

Not one thing other than shot glasses in an entire kitchen cabinet.

The second cabinet has bowls, and as I'm about to find out if the third cabinet is the right one, feeling a lot like Goldilocks, someone clears their throat beside me. "Are you a burglar?"

Looking around the cupboard door, knowing my face is definitely the color of a stoplight, I take in the guy who just caught me red-handed. I'm five foot seven, even taller in my stilettos, but he still towers over me. However, there's something decidedly unintimidating about him. His biceps are fighting to escape the sleeves of his black T-shirt, the fabric tight across his broad chest. But his features are soft, and there's only a hint of stubble along his jaw; it's like the delicacy of his face doesn't quite match the rest of his body. His light brown hair is styled off his face and, when I finally settle on them, his sapphire-blue eyes stare back at me, something unsure but intrigued swimming in them.

This is probably the most awkward way I've ever met a hot guy.

I give him my most innocent smile. "Is it a burglary if it doesn't leave the premises?"

"Oh damn, I knew I should have studied law." His lip quirks up in the corner, dimples appearing beside his mouth as he fights a laugh. "I think burglary is taking something that doesn't belong to you."

"What if the owner never finds out?"

"Well, if the owner never finds out then surely that's just negligence on their part," he says, rubbing a hand against the back of his neck. I try to keep looking at his face, not his bulging arms, but I'm weak. "What're you looking for?"

He takes a step toward me, the strong smell of sandalwood and vanilla reaching me. He presses his hand against the door I'm still clinging to, closing it gently.

What am I looking for? "Glasses."

"There are only plastic ones, sorry."

"Do you know how much plastic ends up in the ocean? No one who lives here will know." This is the longest conversation I've ever had about glasses. It's possibly the longest conversation anyone has had about glasses, but I find myself thinking about what other kitchenware I can bring up to keep this going.

"So, this crime is for the sharks?"

"Well, not just the sharks. Fish, turtles, whales are all included." His eyes close as he fights a smile, shaking his head. "Maybe an octopus or two. My good deeds don't discriminate."

Reopening his eyes, his hand lingers on the cabinet door for another few seconds before he takes a step around me and heads to cabinet six, opening it to reveal shelves of various mismatched glasses. "Don't throw it at anyone or we'll both be in trouble."

Stretching onto my tiptoes, I take one with a Maple Hills emblem on it and one for Emilia that says "My friends went to LA pride and all I got was this glass."

"You found those quickly. Have you burgled here before?" Stop talking, Aurora.

Placing them on the counter, I reach for the nearest liquor bottle, pouring its contents into what I'm calling my victory glasses. The helpful stranger laughs and opens a bottle of soda, sliding it in my direction. He waits until I'm about to pour to answer me. "No, I live here."

Oh shit. His words catch me off guard and the soda bottle misses the rim of the glass, covering the counter in fizzy, sticky liquid. Double shit. "Sorry, sorry, sorry!"

Before I even have a chance to react, he's mopping up my mess with a dishcloth. "I'm s—"

"Don't worry," he says softly, stopping me before I can apologize again. "It's just soda. Stand over there so you don't get wet."

I do as I'm told and watch as he produces a disinfectant spray, cleaning the counter properly among the drunk and oblivious people still trying to make their own drinks. When he's done, he grabs the soda bottle and carefully fills both glasses, handing them to me.

"So you're the one who dusts," I mutter.

"What?"

"Nothing. Thank you . . . and sorry again."

He leans against the counter "Sorry for breaking the stay-out-of-our-cabinets rule or for trashing the kitchen?"

Folding my arms across my chest, I purse my lips playfully. "I don't see a sign."

This time he really laughs. A deep rumble in his chest that seems genuine. I notice the way he watches me, discreetly looking me up and down. His attention makes my body buzz and I immediately want more of it. "You don't strike me as the type of woman who would pay attention to a sign anyway."

"And why is that?" It's a loaded question. I know it. He knows it. The guys, who I assume are his teammates hovering close by trying to listen in, know it. "Answer carefully, we've got an audience."

He pulls his eyebrows together as he turns to check behind him, and by the time he turns back to face me, the tips of his ears have turned pink. Our spectators scurry off, but it's enough to have killed this guy's confidence. I find his sudden shyness endearing. I'm used to being hit on, but I don't think anyone has ever blushed in front of me. I want to find out what his first impression of me is. I want him to keep looking at me like he did thirty seconds ago. I want to murder his friends a little.

I'm about to come right out and ask him, when a warm hand settles on my arm and Emilia appears from behind me. "I'm so thirsty." She takes one look at Mr. Helpful and me and grins at him. "Hi, I'm Emilia."

He gives her a polite nod. "Hey, nice to meet you. I'm Russ."

"Are you Jaiden's Russ?" she asks, grabbing her drink and rolling her eyes at me when she reads the slogan.

He looks almost bashful as he registers what Emilia just said. Why are you so cute? "Uh, yeah. I think so anyway. I don't think JJ knows anyone else called Russ."

He rubs the back of his neck again, the hem of his T-shirt showing the tiniest sliver of suntanned skin, and my horny brain malfunctions a little. "I'm Aurora," I blurt out, borderline aggressively.

Emilia turns to look at me, her expression a mixture of confusion and embarrassment on my behalf. I opt to ignore it and guzzle my drink, letting the harsh bite of the vodka sting away the pangs of humiliation. Russ's eyes are locked on to me as my cup lowers and he comes back into view.

His dimples are showing again.

Emilia clears her throat and I force myself to look at her. She's staring at me like she's definitely going to torment me about this later. "I came over to tell you that a game of drunk Jenga is starting in the den if you want to play."

"Drunk Jenga?"

"They put dares on some of the blocks," Russ explains. "Robbie and JJ like to make things interesting."

Emilia tuts playfully. "I knew he'd be involved somehow. God knows what the dares are. Rory, I'll see you in there?"

I nod and she disappears again, leaving me with my new friend. "How interesting are we talking?"

His lips quirk up again and, my God, there is no reason for me to want to make out with someone because of how their lips tug up, but the way he flits between confidence and uncertainty is doing something to me.

Russ takes a long sip of his beer while he considers my question and I just wait. I should be more embarrassed about shamelessly hanging on the words of a man, but this one is hot and a little awkward, and those concerns feel like a problem for my future therapist.

"Why don't you come with me and find out?"

Chapter Three

RUSS

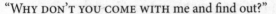

"WHY DON'T YOU COME WITH me and find out?"

It sounded good in my head, but now that I've said it out loud I can't help but internally cringe. This woman is far too hot to be talking to me and I have no idea how I've managed to land myself in this situation.

JJ caught me watching her snoop around the kitchen and gave me a "success with women" pep talk worthy of an Oscar before pushing me in her direction with the instruction to offer her a drink.

While I'm not *totally* useless with women, I'm far from the best, which I proved when my first conversation with the attractive stranger in my house was about burglary. I usually need a bit of time to relax before I feel comfortable, which isn't ideal at college parties. Alcohol sometimes bridges the gap long enough for me to ask for someone's number, but I don't drink often, which is why I'm chronically single.

Even though I'm buzzed from my drink, Aurora is just too fucking pretty, which is my excuse for why my brain is scrambling for some engaging conversation. I couldn't even see her face when I approached her, just long legs and curves covered by a tiny skirt and top. Then her head popped out from behind the door, blond waves framing her face, cheeks flushed pink, emerald-green eyes glaring up at me innocently, like someone who got caught with their hand in the cookie jar. And then she smiled, something she's probably done a million times in her life, but I forgot about my lack of skill with women. I forgot about everything.

I promised myself earlier I would talk to someone if I thought they were hot and, technically, I am doing that even if she's about to politely reject me. I'm trying hard to channel the artificial confidence my beer is giving me and not crumble beneath her inquisitive gaze as she considers my offer.

She holds out her hand and I have to stop my eyebrows from shooting into my hairline from the surprise. "Lead the way."

Threading my fingers with hers, I navigate us toward the den, silently repeating *fake it till you make it* and *you're a hot hockey player* and *the only person who knows you're not confident is you* in my head like JJ told me to.

I never expected his advice to work, but he looks totally unsurprised as I walk toward the Jenga setup hand in hand with Aurora. He looks a little smug, in fact. I keep her body close to mine, careful to stop drunk people from bumping into her until we reach the crowd around the dining room table.

"You ready for this?" I say, although I'm not sure if I'm talking to myself or to her.

As she looks up at me, her eyes soften and her hand squeezes mine gently. "How much trouble can one game of Jenga cause?"

"My friend Joe is heading to Yale Law School and they asked him what's considered a felony in California." Joe didn't even look surprised. After he read out a list from his cell phone, Robbie and JJ wouldn't let anyone else see what they were writing on the blocks, giggling to each other like schoolkids.

"Nothing says college spirit like posting bail. I'm sure we've both done worse. Come on."

She doesn't let go of my hand as she moves confidently through the crowd, head held high, hair dancing across her bare shoulders with every step. I'm not sure how I ended up as the one being guided, but I follow her toward the gap between Stassie and Emilia.

Stassie waves at me enthusiastically as I come into her view, patting the table beside her. "I saved you a spot, muffin."

It's clear she's already drunk by the fact she pats so hard the Jenga blocks and shot glasses wobble.

"Okay, Godzilla," Lola snaps from across the table. "Let's not take down the tower before everyone's naked. Jeez."

Stassie mouths an *oops* and gives me a dopey, drunk smile as she cuddles into Nate's side. Her eyes flick down to my hand joined with Aurora's before flicking up to Aurora, her jaw slacking slightly before giving me an awkward thumbs-up.

How am I supposed to fake being confident with women in these conditions?

"Muffin?" Aurora asks as we slot into the space between our friends, letting go of my hand to rummage through her purse for her cell phone. I want to do something with my hands instead of standing awkwardly beside her, but checking my phone is my least favorite thing to do, so I settle for pushing my hands into my pants pockets instead. I watch as she swipes across at her notifications, huffing slightly before pushing it back into her purse and looking up at me.

"It's a really, really long story." My hour-long fake relationship with Stassie feels like a million years ago now, and I'm not even sure I could describe the weird but wholesome bond we now share. Even though she says my poor communication skills give her a headache.

Say something interesting, Callaghan.

Aurora doesn't say anything further to my nonanswer, instead turning to talk to Emilia on her other side. Blowing out a sigh, I turn my attention to my friends. The guys are hammering Robbie with questions and I can see him getting more and more irritated. "Where's Hen?" Robbie asks, eyeing each of my teammates. "This was his fucking idea."

"I'm here!" Henry shouts, pushing his way through the crowd, a woman with mussed hair following him closely. "Sorry, I'm here."

If this was hockey and Henry was late because he was getting laid, Robbie would tear into him. Robbie takes party games as seriously as he takes hockey, but he's desperately trying to prove he's not as uptight as Faulkner after being compared to him all day.

Becky, Henry's latest fling, whispers something into his ear, kisses him on the cheek, then disappears back into the party. Henry's smirk is annoying Robbie more, which is great for every player on a secret countdown, waiting for him to go off.

Robbie stops staring everyone down and his arms lift slightly, like he's about to clap, and everyone holds their breath, but one arm lowers and the other wraps around Lola's hips. "Oka—"

"Do I have time to go to the bathroom?" Kris asks.

"No, you fucking don't," Robbie snaps. "Just fucking stand there and listen to the rules of the game before I lose my goddamn mind!"

There's an echo of sighs as everyone besides me and Henry reaches for their wallets and piles bills into Kris's outstretched palm. Robbie waits with his arms folded tightly across his chest, and when all the money has changed hands, he starts again. "The next person to piss me off isn't playing next season." Everyone waits silently, biting their lips trying not to laugh. "You pull out a Jenga block: if it's blank, the turn moves to the next person, then you stack it on the top of the tower."

"So like regular Jenga then." JJ grins.

Robbie ignores him, probably because he can't bench JJ anymore. "If you get a dare, you either do it, do the forfeit on the back, or drink the two shots. If you're not a two-hundred-pound hockey player, you only need to do one shot to make things fair. Whoever knocks the tower over has to streak down Maple Ave. Lola, you go first."

"Wait," Joe interrupts. "Why are there shots if there are forfeits on the back of the blocks?"

Robbie pins him with a look that sends a chill down my spine. "Because I made the rules and I say there are shots and forfeits."

The game starts, and in typical Titans fashion it's chaos. Mattie has to send the last photo on his camera roll to his family group chat—he won't tell us what it is, but he does step away from the table to take a call from his grandmother. Henry and Bobby have to switch clothes. Joe pulls a block that reads "Give your underwear to the person opposite you," and Aurora's friend Emilia argues with Kris that she's definitely not opposite Joe; he is. By the time the game reaches our side of the table, Kris is wearing Joe's boxers over his clothes and he takes two shots instead of making out with Emilia, who has a girlfriend and threatens to punch him if he even tries. Emilia pulls a blank block, followed by Aurora doing the same. It's hard to miss the disappointment.

I'm distracted by her cute pout when I hear a "Hurry the fuck up, muffin" from one of the guys. I push the block through the center carefully.

SHOW THE LAST MESSAGE YOU RECEIVED TO THE PERSON BESIDE YOU

I try not to drop the block as my hands start to sweat, flipping it over because whatever my forfeit is won't be as bad as that.

SEND FAULKNER AN "I LOVE YOU" TEXT

Wrong.

People are asking me what it says, but my mind is running, working out how to get out of this without explaining why I need to. Aside from having no desire to get on Coach's bad side again, my last-received text message was from my dad asking me to send him money. My stomach sinks with the weight of the ugly truth that he finds a way to snake his way into every situation and spoil it. I didn't even read it fully before closing the conversation; it's always the same shitty excuse anyway.

I'll pay you back. I'll pay you double back. I know a guy who knows the trainer and the race is a sure thing.

Or, once he's had a drink: *You have everything because of me. You've turned your back on this family. Won't even help your own flesh and blood, you're not my son. You think you're better than us because you go to a fancy school, you'll just fuck it up anyway.*

Impatient for a response, Stassie plucks the block from my hand and reads it out to the group, who understandably laughs. I'd laugh, too, if the message was from anyone else. I take a shot in each hand, downing them in quick succession.

"Wow, you really didn't want me to see those nudes," Aurora says as I wipe a stray droplet with the back of my hand. "I'm kidding, don't look so serious. It's nice."

"Nice?"

She nods. "That you're not flashing around your private stuff. Private is nice."

Private. Something I'm good at. Shame it's for all the wrong reasons.

The game continues, around and around, shots are taken, dares done, insults flung in the direction of Robbie and JJ. Nate ends up having to send his sister money for not kissing the person to his left: Robbie. Bobby sends an "I miss you" text to Faulkner, Henry has to shotgun a beer, and I end up shirtless for not kissing the nearest redhead, who happens to be Lola. Kissing the girlfriend of my roommate and coach doesn't feel like the best way to make it through the rest of my college career.

Emilia leans across to the tower, which is looking significantly more unstable than earlier. A grin spreads across her face as she reads from the block. "Nominate two people to kiss. You guys are so childish," she mumbles, turning the block around to face us, lips tugging into a mischievous grin. "Well, since they're the only people I know . . . I suppose . . . I'll just have to choose Aurora and Russ."

"What am I? A ghost?" JJ shouts from the other side of the table, throwing his arms up dramatically. "Our friendship is clearly a joke to you."

I hear her say something, but it doesn't immediately register that she's said my name until I sense Aurora looking up at me. She really is gorgeous, Jesus.

The only person who knows you're not confident is you.

Her cheeks are more flushed than earlier, eyes glossy. "Are you sober enough to be okay with this?"

She nods, grinning. "Are you?" I gently slip my hand beneath her hair to cup the back of her neck, rubbing my thumb beneath her jaw as her pulse hammers against my palm.

"Yep." She stretches up on tiptoes as my head lowers, her hands finding their place on my neck, and then my mouth meets hers. Soft at first, hesitant, until she moans softly and for a minute, I forget that we have an audience.

The audience doesn't forget us, though, and when I pull her body closer to mine, they whoop, bringing us both back down to earth with a crash. She takes a step back, hand shooting to her lips as she turns to Emilia and mutters something that makes her grin.

Fake it until you make it.

The game moves on, blank block after blank block around the whole table, making people question if Robbie and JJ just gave up writing dares, to which they're incredibly insulted. Aurora pulls another blank block and a disappointed groan from the table follows.

"This tower is holding it together better than I can," Aurora mumbles, putting the block on the top of the wobbling structure.

I pull mine and immediately spot Robbie's untidy scrawl on the wood.

CHANGE DIRECTION

"Change direction?" I read out loud. "I don't get it."

"It means it's my go again," Aurora says from beside me, and Robbie nods to confirm.

She picks her block, which—speaking strictly from an engineering standpoint—is one of the worst ones she could've chosen if she wants the tower to stay upright. It occurs to me that she might just want to see it fall over, but the thought stops there when she starts to laugh. And it's fucking magical.

She spins the block to face the group.

GIVE YOUR NEAREST HOCKEY PLAYER
A LAP DANCE FOR 2 MINUTES

"That was the one I wrote!" Lola shouts happily. "You're welcome, muffin."

If looks could kill, I'd be dead. Every player is looking at me with pure jealousy after appraising Aurora for a little too long. I clear my throat loudly and they all snap out of it.

Oh, man. I'm going to get a boner in front of all my friends.

Bobby rushes off to find one of the chairs we stored earlier as Anastasia asks Aurora her musical preferences. I know it isn't a big deal, but it low-key feels like a big deal. I'm pretty sure my face is bright red. How the fuck am I supposed to fake confidence through this?

Bending to her height, I move close to her ear so only she can hear me. "You don't have to do this. Don't let them pressure you."

"It's a silly dance," she says, squeezing my arm. "But thank you. If you're not good with it, I'll just do the shots."

"I'm good with it." I'm so fucking good with it.

"Anything you don't want me to do?"

"You can do anything."

There's something about already being shirtless that makes this whole thing feel more intimate. Thankfully, having multiple people staring right at you while you sit in a dining room chair is enough to wipe that feeling away.

Nice to know this is what I'll think of next time I sit to eat.

Aurora reaches for her shots, doing two. "I'm not forfeiting," she confirms quickly. "It's for courage."

I feel like I need courage, and all I've got to do is sit here and let a woman who is so far out of my league we're not even playing the same sport dance on me. The music changes from the upbeat chart song that was playing to Zayn's "Sweat," and Lola holds up her phone with the timer set.

It's easy to forget the rest of the room when Aurora walks over, smiling as she positions herself behind me. Both hands start at my shoulders and slowly trail down my chest and abs until she's bent over enough that her head is level with mine. She pecks my cheek and laughs lightly, and that's the moment that I know this is about to be the best kind of torture.

Moving in front of me, she starts to sway her hips slowly in time to the music. Nudging my knees a little wider, she steps between them, turning, and lowers herself down onto me.

Thirty seconds of Aurora's ass rubbing right against my dick pass by in a flash. Her back is flush with my bare chest, the smell of peach wafts under my nose as her hair swishes around. I start reciting dead presidents in my head, but it's no use. Her hips change rhythm and her body vibrates as she chuckles, looking up at me. Yeah, she can definitely feel my hard dick digging into her ass.

My knuckles are white from gripping the seat of the chair; I don't even need to be touching her, apparently. She lifts herself from me and I don't need to panic about everyone spotting my boner for long because she turns and lowers herself back into my lap, straddling me.

This is worse, so, so much worse.

Worse in a better way, that is. Since she's fucking hot and now I get to watch her face as she grinds into me, looking wholly pleased with herself. "You can touch me," she whispers, her eyes dark.

George Washington, John Adams, Thomas Jefferson . . .

My hands grip her hips as she continues to move, my thumbs gently grazing an exposed sliver of skin between the band of her skirt and her top. Her hands sink into my hair, breasts pressing against my chest as her face gets closer to mine.

And then the timer blasts and I want to commit a murder for the first time in my life.

The spell lifts and we're both instantly aware that we're not alone. She sits back, breathing heavy as, thankfully, JJ suggests everyone takes a break to get new drinks and use the bathroom, saluting me as the area begins to clear.

My hands are still on her hips, her eyes are still locked on mine, and there's something there beneath the surface, something uncertain. Like she's waiting for something, but I don't know what. "Uh, good job."

It's clear she was waiting for some form of praise because her smile increases as she starts to stand, but I tighten my grip, keeping her on my lap. "Can I have a minute?"

Her teeth sink into her lip as she fights a laugh, nodding. "Sure."

James Madison, James Monroe, John Quincy Adams . . .

Chapter Four

AURORA

STRADDLING THE LAP OF A hockey player is not the action of a woman trying to turn her life around.

To be honest, sitting on the boner of a total stranger is not how I saw tonight going. Well, maybe, but in a way that would involve no clothes and certainly no audience. I forgot all about my summer self-improvement efforts the second I stepped foot in this house, and that lack of commitment to the cause is exactly why I need time away from the temptations of Maple Hills.

I shouldn't be this happy about doing a good job, but what can I say, I'm a girl that likes feedback. More than anything, I needed the reassurance I didn't just make a fool of myself in front of most of the hockey team. It's not my first rodeo, lap dance–wise, but it's the first time with someone who now isn't making eye contact with me. If I'm not looking at his face, I have to look at his body, and the guy is essentially a slab of muscle.

"You won't burst into flames if you look me in the eyes, you know," I say softly, feeling a little insecure. Time seems to move slower in this house, and while there's nothing unusual about two people being this close in a dark corner of a college party, the minute that's passed feels like a lifetime. I can feel his steady breaths under the palms of my hands, his skin hot.

As expected, color rushes to the apples of his cheeks as his eyes meet mine again. He clears his throat and rubs the back of his neck, a nervous tic he's done several times since I met him earlier. First in the kitchen, then when he had to take his T-shirt off and everyone cheered at his perfectly sculpted body, and now while we wait.

"Listen, this isn't working. You're too fucking hot and the presidents aren't helping, I've moved on to Stanley Cup winners, but with you just here"—he gestures to my thighs spread across him—"looking like that," he says, gesturing up my body, "it's going to take forever."

You're too fucking hot.

The compliment floods my system, melting me, and the vulnerability from ten seconds ago dissipates into nothing as the validation seeps into my system like a drug. It's not that I've never been told I'm hot before, I have, but this guy seems tortured by it. Like he'll never recover from it. Like I'm the tipping point of his sanity, and that is a feeling I could get addicted to.

My lips quirk as I desperately try to ignore my brain seeking more attention; it's unreliable in the presence of men since it's so easily impressed by mediocrity. "Presidents?" The blush spreads to the tips of his ears, something else about him I find incredibly endearing, like he wasn't planning to share that little snippet of information. "How about you stand behind me until you're good?"

"You're an angel," he sighs. "Sort of. That wasn't very angelic, but you know what I mean. Thanks."

He holds my hips, guiding me as I stand, the bulge in his pants unmissable even beneath the dark lighting in the den. I feel my skin flush as it registers quite how much I like his tight grip on me.

There isn't the same energy when the game restarts and I'm too

distracted by the man behind me to pay attention. It's hard to concentrate on which block to pull when his arms are caging me in and
he quietly whispers which ones to avoid in my ear. I particularly like
when I bend toward the tower and my ass brushes against him, I
swear I hear him groan.

Thanks to Russ's guidance, my turn doesn't pull down the tower,
but I can't pretend there isn't a small part of me that wishes it would
fall. The round passes by us without incident, and although there's
no reason for Russ to hide himself behind me anymore, he doesn't
move. I lean back, head resting against his chest, and when his posture stiffens, I immediately start to move away from him. But his
hands find my hips again and he pulls me back gently, his body more
relaxed this time.

The sound of crashing blocks makes me jump, and when I drag
my attention back to the game, one of the guys is holding a block and
staring at the pile on the table.

"Henry, you can't just knock over the tower when you get bored,"
one of the guys shouts.

"I didn't," Henry says. "Maybe I'm just not very good at Jenga."

Russ scoffs behind me. "You're never going to be good at it if you
pull the one block keeping the foundation straight."

"Not everyone is an engineer, Russ," he says. "It isn't my fault."

"Time to face the consequences!" the redhead across from me
squeals. "Get naked!"

"If you wanted to see me naked, Lola, you could have just asked."

"Watch it," Robbie snaps.

Emilia nudges me, interrupting the argument between what are
obviously very close friends. "Bathroom and drink? I have no interest in watching a naked man scare the neighbors."

As much as I'd like to see someone streak down a road, I don't
want to leave her alone. "Sure."

It takes all my willpower to give Emilia my hand and let her drag me away. "I'll be back" I mouth to Russ, and fight my way through the crowd with the heat of his hands still on my skin.

How do you lose someone in their own house?

"Maybe he's hiding from you," Emilia says, muffling her snicker with her drink.

"I thought he was interested . . ."

"I think he's really shy, y'know," she says, leaning against the kitchen counter. "I'm sure he's the guy JJ said just moved in. Quiet, keeps to himself. Not your usual type at all."

I roll my eyes as I reach for a soda bottle. Not because she's wrong—she isn't, shy isn't who I usually bring home—but because Emilia likes to regularly remind me how terrible my taste in men is. To be fair, I give her an opportunity to remind me every time a guy turns out to be the asshole the red flags told me he'd be. The red flags I ignored in favor of string-free sex. Emilia thinks liking men is a poor choice to begin with, and I have to remind her that, unfortunately, you can be attracted to men and not actually like them as a species.

"If I wanted to be rejected by a man tonight, I'd have called my dad." An awkward not-quite-a-laugh bubbles out of me as I fill up our glasses, careful not to spill the soda this time. "God, I can't wait to get away from Maple Hills."

Before I can say anything else, Emilia's cell phone lights up in her hand. "I'm gonna step outside and take this call from Poppy. It's breakfast time in Europe, you good for five minutes?"

"I'm sure I can keep myself out of trouble for five minutes, go. Give my love to Pops, please."

Emilia kisses my temple affectionately. "You say that, but I'm not convinced. I'll be back. Text me if you're about to go missing."

She looks genuinely excited as she makes her way toward the

backyard to talk to her girlfriend. I love their love, I really do, but God they make me feel single. It's hard being the official third wheel to two people disgustingly perfect for each other, especially because I've never had a real relationship in my life. I haven't even had a first date. For the most part, I'm happy single, but sometimes, when they're curled up together under a blanket at home, for a tiny moment that I'd never admit to, I do feel a little jealous.

When faced with two people so well suited, I find it impossible not to wonder what my own version of that might look like. But then I remember how fun being traumatized by my parents' relationship was, and the desire for my own evaporates as quickly as it arrived.

For all the romance books I've read and all the happy endings I've enjoyed, I can't imagine my own. I'd like to hope I'll have one, but hope can be dangerous.

Someone much smarter than me once said something poetic and clever about love being when you give someone the power to hurt you but trust them not to, but I can't imagine ever trusting someone that much. If I want my feelings hurt, I am more than capable of doing it to myself. It's a skill I've honed over many years, and arguably my best one. I'd like to trust someone one day, though, maybe.

Pulling my cell phone out of my purse, I decide to wait for Emilia by pretending to look at what people are saying about qualifying for this weekend's Grand Prix. My aimless scroll lasts ten seconds before I give in to the real reason I got my phone out: snooping on my dad's latest girlfriend from my fake account.

It's my current favorite way to hurt my own feelings and, luckily for me and my masochistic tendencies, Norah loves updating every second of her life on her stories, like she's a thirteen-year-old on social media for the first time, and I love being unhappy watching it.

I also love reporting the pointless lives she does for bullying and harassment.

At least 90 percent of the impulsive decisions I've made in the past month have been triggered by her posting about how wonderful my dad is—and yet here I am again, watching it. Her face fills the screen, far too close and terribly lit, and then, in a move that makes my heart stop beating, she pans around to film my dad packing boxes in what appears to be her daughter's dorm room.

I'm not sure my dad would even know where I go to college if he didn't pay my tuition.

I hate watching it, but I can't stop. My entire life has been a fight for my dad's time, so to watch him give it away so freely is like a punch to the gut.

When I spoke to his secretary to see if he would be at my leaving breakfast, she said yes and that he didn't travel to Spain for the Grand Prix this weekend because he had "important plans." The foolish part of me that still hopes her dad isn't a total jackass questioned if I was the important plans, and he wanted to say good-bye to me before I leave for the summer. Now I know who he really considers to be important, and, once again, it isn't me. I hate the type of person it's turned me into, one desperate for attention and validation, and I hate that I've let my life become one shaped by kneejerk reactions to feeling forgotten.

For once I want to make a decision because it will make me happy, not because something has triggered me into acting out.

I lock my phone screen and push my phone back into my purse as soon as the body in my peripheral vision gets too close. It's not that Emilia doesn't know I snoop, but it's still embarrassing, particularly because her dad is actual perfection, and as much as she tries, she'll never understand.

It isn't Emilia.

"Hey," Russ says carefully. "Are you okay?"

Forcing a smile, I look up at him with as much enthusiasm as I can muster. "Yeah, I'm great. Are you?"

He watches me closely before responding. "Are you really okay? Did someone bother you?"

"He's been bothering me for twenty years, it's totally fine."

His mouth forms an O as he nods, apparently understanding immediately. "What can I do to make you feel better?" My brain wants me to tell him to take his T-shirt off again, but that feels like the wrong move. So I shrug, because I don't have the answer to what will make me feel better yet. "There must be something."

"Tell me a secret."

"A secret?" he repeats.

"Yeah." I don't know why I said it, but I can tell he's thinking about it. It's a silly thing my sister and I started asking each other when we were kids. We've never been the closest siblings, but our middle ground has always been doing things we shouldn't, and it was our way of sharing.

"You make me nervous," he says eventually, immediately taking a swig of his beer.

"That isn't a secret," I laugh. "That's very obvious."

He blows out a sigh and rubs his hand against his face. "I think you're stunning."

His admission catches me off guard. Stunning. I shake my head anyway, and my hair dances in front of my eyes. "That isn't a secret, either . . ."

"You're impossible." He chuckles. His hand reaches out slowly, cautiously, tucking my hair behind my ear, hovering a little longer than necessary. "My secret is I don't really like parties, but I'm glad I came to this one and met you. And when I couldn't find you I was sad when I thought you'd left."

Oh shit. "That was smooth."

"Was it actually? Because I tried really fucking hard. I was really close to confessing to a crime I didn't commit because of the pressure." There he is.

"You did a great job."

"Thanks, I don't do this a lot. I'm, uh, I'm not good at it."

"You don't go around telling strangers your secrets?" I hide my smile with a sip of my drink. A real smile this time.

"I don't tell anyone usually, but I meant I'm not good at talking to people I'm interested in."

I don't know what it is about his uncertainty that I find so charming. Maybe it's because even though he's not sure of himself, he's sure he wants to talk to me—and I'm clinging to those slivers of certainty with both hands. "You said you live here."

"Because I do."

"You have a room."

"Is that a question? They don't make me sleep outside if that's what you mean." This fucking guy. "Yeah, I have a room."

Painful. Actually painful. "Are you going to . . . show it to me? You said you don't like parties. We could get away from it."

I practically see the lightbulb appear above his head when he realizes what I'm asking. "That depends. Are you drunk?"

"A little buzzed, but definitely not drunk. Are you drunk?"

He shakes his head, trailing his hand across my shoulder and down my arm until his fingers thread through mine. "Buzzed, but not drunk."

Russ's hand makes mine look tiny and our linked fingers are what I watch as he leads me through the crowd toward the stairs. Drunk people are draped over the banister watching the events in the living room, presumably waiting for a bathroom or something, but they all turn to look at us with interest. I keep my head held high and try to not let it show that I know this will be on the UCMH gossip page tomorrow.

I pull out my cell phone as he taps the door code, pulling up my chat with Emilia, and follow him into the room.

EMILIA BENNETT

Bedroom at the top of the stairs

Door code is 3993

Russ?

Yeah he's awkward

It's charmed me

I knew I shouldn't have left you unattended

You sober enough to be making
good choices?

When do I ever make good choices?

But yes

Remember we have breakfast
with your parents tomorrow

And a flight to catch

Do you have condoms?

Yeah

Please manifest him knowing
what he's doing

The universe doesn't care about
your orgasms, Aurora

Be safe

Remember to share your location

"Sorry," I say to Russ, putting my cell back into my purse and setting it down on the bedside table. "I was just letting my roommate know where I am."

"Responsible." He smiles and sits on the edge of the bed. "My old captain made us use a tracking app, but it was mainly in case anyone's location pinged at a police station."

"You don't seem the pinging-at-the-police-station type . . ."

"Uh, thank you . . . I think." He laughs, deep and warm; it tugs at my stomach in a weird way.

I finally take in the room, wandering aimlessly, looking for picture frames or something about him, but finding nothing. I'm not joking when I say this is the tidiest bedroom I've ever been in, mine included. Even the empty cardboard boxes have been collapsed and lined up next to his wardrobe. His bed has more than one pillow. And they even look like nice pillows. They all have pillow covers on them and don't look like they've been run over by a sixteen-wheel truck, unlike many of the guys on this campus.

I reach his desk, and other than some engineering books, there's nothing personal. No signs that it's him who lives here. He watches my tour of the room quietly, eyes following me from corner to corner. Turning to face him, I slide myself onto his desk, pushing his textbooks out of the way. "Do you have a girlfriend?"

My question catches him by surprise, and his mouth twists in confusion. "No?"

"Your room is really clean. There's nothing about you in here: no pictures, hobbies . . ." I wouldn't even know he played hockey if he didn't live here. There isn't one piece of dirty, smelly equipment littering the floor. "And you have pillows. With covers."

The last one makes him snort, and he stands, strolling over to the desk. "Is the bar really that low? Pillows with covers makes you think I have a girlfriend that I'm cheating on?"

He finally stops right in front of me; I widen my knees and he steps into the space they create, his body dangerously close to mine. My heartbeat speeds, heat prickles at the nape of my neck as he leans over me. He doesn't touch me, though; his hand travels past me and toward a shelf above the desk.

Much like everything else in here, the picture he hands me is pristine—not even a slightly bent corner. It's him and several of the guys I met downstairs, trying to hold up a trophy. They look like they're all jumping on Russ and he has the biggest grin I've ever seen.

"A picture and a hobby."

I gaze up at him, a small smile on his lips. "You look really happy."

Putting the picture back on the shelf, he nods. "Best day of my life."

"Why?"

"Tell me about the best day of your life."

His redirection is odd, but there's no point in me pushing him because it's not important really, and emotional baggage isn't really well suited to the whole onetime hookup thing anyway.

"I don't think you brought me up here to hear about my life, did you?" I shuffle closer, legs widening to accommodate his huge frame, and lean back on my hands. "Or do you need a Jenga tower to want to touch me? Should I find a board game? What about seven minutes in heaven? Should I set the timer?"

"Aurora," he says softly. His hand finds my chin, nudging my face up to look at his. The moonlight peeking through his half-cracked blinds illuminates him, making him borderline ethereal. "If a timer goes off, I'm smashing your phone."

Chapter Five

AURORA

I EXPECT HIS MOUTH TO crash into mine. For him to tug my skirt up around my hips, for him to grab and pull and fumble, but he doesn't.

His mouth is soft, gentle, testing. His hand moves from my chin, tracing my jaw until his fingers skim the sensitive area beneath my ear, continuing until it's entangled in my hair at the nape of my neck.

Our mouths break apart and his forehead rests against mine for a moment. "I'm not expecting anything from you, y'know. We can stop at any time."

My heart has no right to be beating as hard as it is. "You know the same applies to you, right?"

"Yeah, of course."

It's the bare minimum we should expect from each other, but it still makes me feel relieved. He's the same man he was downstairs; he didn't change as soon as he got me alone. I didn't let myself get played by pretty words and an even prettier face.

His lips meet mine again, but this time he's all in. He helps me pull off his T-shirt, taking a sharp breath when my hands trail his abs and reach for the buckle of his belt. Discarding his sneakers, then his socks, he shimmies his jeans to the floor, stepping out of them so he's left in only his boxers.

He starts at my feet, carefully unbuckling the tiny strap around my ankle, pulling off each heel, sliding his hands along the backs of my calves and thighs, until he's high enough up to lift me from the desk.

It's not a long walk to the bed, but it's long enough for my brain to register how perfectly my legs fit around his waist, how he isn't clumsy like I thought he might be and that, maybe, I don't care that much about not getting my veggie pizza with Emilia on our way home if this is the alternative.

He's careful as he lowers me onto his bed, immediately moving to kneel between my knees. "You're so fucking beautiful," he murmurs, helping to take off my skirt as I pull off my top. It makes me feel dizzy, the way he compliments me. Like he's unsure how to say something, but he means it wholeheartedly. His eyes lock on to my face and I suddenly feel twice as naked.

My eyes travel up his body, shamelessly scanning every hard ab and inch of suntanned skin until they're back on his face and his dimples appear.

I'm not shy. I don't think I've ever had a moment of feeling shy in my life, but the way he touches me so tenderly, the way his breath hitches as he pulls my panties down my legs slowly, and the way he looks at me when I let my legs rest open is making me feel freaking shy.

He leans over to kiss me, harder this time, keeping his body hovering above mine so I don't get any satisfaction from feeling his weight on me. I can't decide if he's purposely teasing me or if he's just really enjoying taking his time. There's something polite about it, respectful, not something I've ever labeled a random hookup.

His kisses move lower, sparking a fire in every place he touches. Neck, breasts, stomach, hip bone, until his head is right between my legs. He keeps watching me as he finally, finally, puts his mouth on me, moving my legs over his shoulders, and after that I don't know what he does, because my eyes roll to the back of my head.

There's nothing polite or respectful in the way he goes down on me. My heart is thrashing against my rib cage, breathing erratic, body writhing so much he uses an arm to pin me to the bed while he licks and sucks and—

"Oh my. Oh fuck. Yeah, like that."

With one hand in his hair and one hand clinging to the duvet, my back arches while my feet dig into the muscular planes of his back, pressing myself further into his face. I'd be embarrassed if my actions weren't met with satisfied moans. My stomach tightens, his fingers and mouth keep the same pace. "I'm going to . . . oh my God."

He keeps going as I squeeze around his fingers, crying out his name, and when the orgasm finally subsides, I'm pretty sure I'm goo.

Russ collapses next to me on the bed and my brain knows I want to be near to him, but my body doesn't even know what planet we're on. Shuffling closer, he kisses me softly, the taste of me on his mouth. "Are you okay?"

"Yeah. Feeling like I should have put more effort into the lap dance. Didn't know you were going to put on the performance of your life, jeez." My brain and body finally start communicating again, allowing me to climb on top of him, straddling his thighs. "Do you have condoms?"

The expression that settles over his face is like something out of a horror film. It's funny really, the moment he realizes he fucked up. "Sorry, I've just moved and haven't had a chance to get some and I wasn't expecting to . . . I'm sorry, I didn't think." He looks down at the erection pressing against his boxers and blows out a sigh. "I'll check Henry's room."

"As much as I'd love to see you try and hide that from a houseful of people, I have some in my purse."

By the time I've retrieved one and thrown it onto the bed be-side us, the look of panic has disappeared. He sits up, leaning back against one hand, cupping my face with the other. I'm waiting for him to say something, again. Nervousness floods my system as he strokes his thumb across my bottom lip. "So perfect."

I want to fill the silence with every thought in my head for rea-sons I don't understand. I think his awkwardness has rubbed off on me a little.

Pushing him back down, I pick up the condom and tear the wrapper with my teeth, lifting myself up to let him move his boxers down until his erection springs free. I release less of a gasp and more of a surprised hiccup when I realize what we're dealing with here. He takes the condom from my hand, rolling it on while I evaluate.

"There's no way that's going to fit. I mean I love a challenge, but I can only be challenged so much, y'know?" He pulls me down to him, our mouths aligning, my stomach moving with his as he chuck-les at my crisis.

He still tastes like me when his tongue moves against mine; he groans into my mouth when I roll my hips against him. His eyes close, voice strains. "We'll make it fit."

Oh Lord.

Carefully, and while kind of wishing I took another shot for courage, I push myself up from his chest and sink down onto him slowly. "Holy fuck." Russ's hands grip my hips tightly. "Is this okay?" he whispers.

I nod as I lift myself up and sink down a little more, then again, until I'm finally taking most of him. My nails dig into his chest, his fingers sink into my skin, and the sound of our bodies slapping together echoes around the room.

Why did I think I had the stamina to go on top?

"You're taking it so well, sweetheart." I work a little harder, clearly motivated by words and moans. "That's it, good girl."

Who knew Mr. Helpful and I would be so compatible. I like it when he praises me and he really likes it when I swirl my hips on the end of his dick. Dream team.

One of his hands travels between my legs, rubbing exactly where I need him to, and my body moves instinctively, grinding and chasing the building feeling.

"Russ . . . Yes, yes." He keeps praising and rubbing and letting me take what I need until my entire body tightens and I collapse on top of him, crying out. Rolling me onto my back, he takes his weight on his arms while I pant beneath him.

He brushes my hair out of my face, slowly moving in and out of me again. His head falls to my neck, kissing my skin lightly as I wrap my arms and still shaky legs around him. "You feel so good, Aurora," he whispers. "I want to feel you come around me again."

Where the fuck did this man come from?

The sweet way he talks to me, kisses me, even the way he looks at me, is totally contradicted by the confident way he freaking pounds me into the bed. I'm exhausted, satiated—and yet I don't want it to end. My hand slips to where we're joined, frantically working to finish when he does. His body falls out of rhythm, breathing gets heavier; I'm nearly there.

A few more thrusts and I'm falling off the edge again, dragging him with me. We're loud and sweaty and so freaking satisfied.

Holy shit.

Who cares about basketball when hockey players exist?

WELL, I WASN'T EXPECTING THAT.

He rolls off me onto his back, and we both lie staring at the ceiling trying to catch our breath.

"Do you need anything?" he asks softly.

My arms cross over my face, covering my eyes as I shake my

head, attempting to work out how to ask for that, like, twelve more times. "No. I'm good."

I feel the bed shift as he stands, various noises of him shuffling around the room filling the silence, before I eventually hear the bathroom door close. My body feels like it's made of Jell-O, and it's a mental battle to convince myself to find my underwear.

Reaching toward the bedside table for my cell phone, I bring up my chat with Emilia.

EMILIA BENNETT

Live location shared

You coming home or staying over?

Home

He's in the bathroom. I'll leave soon

Do you want pizza?

YES

He's been so long

Is he waiting for you to leave?

Maybe

Okay I can hear him talking to someone

He's gotta be waiting for me to go, right?

I'm getting dressed now. Be home soon

Weird

Pizza is ordered

I'm not taking it personally that Russ went into the bathroom to wait me out. The prolonged trip to the bathroom so the other person gets the hint to leave is something I've done many times. I once had to spend so long in my bathroom before the guy understood that I rearranged my entire skin-care collection into alphabetical order.

I don't need to be forced out the door, I'm more than happy to sleep in my own bed tonight. Normally I wouldn't wait so long, but

I just assumed he wasn't a hide-in-the-bathroom-post-hookup kind of person.

My legs tremble as I stand from the bed, a sign I put in a lot of effort and, more important, that I need to start working on my legs or something because I feel like a newborn deer learning to walk. Switching on the lamp on the table beside the bed, I'm immediately drawn to the small stack of books now visible in the light: *Engineering Thermodynamics*, *Addicted to the Game: A Story of Recovery*, *Roll of the Dice* . . . I reach for the book on the top of the stack, picking it up to inspect it. He's reading *The Beautiful and the Damned*. What the hell?

The English major in me cringes at the cracked spine and folded page corners, but the soft girl in me is squealing at the idea of him lying in bed at night reading. The superhot, kind of awkward, great at sex, full-set-of-bedding-using, Division One hockey player reading in bed after getting laid. It kind of makes me wish I wasn't about to go, but the idea of his face dropping when he eventually leaves the bathroom and sees I'm still here is not one I can stomach.

I mean, worst-case scenario, he comes out of the bathroom when I'm half dressed and we have a really great conversation about how my deep-rooted abandonment issues mean I'll never expect more than the bare minimum from a man, and how my father's blatant disinterest in my existence has given me a stifling fear of rejection, which has shaped every romantic interaction I have, so I'm not judging him for wanting me to leave.

Or, alternatively, I can bottle that up and make a therapist really rich one day.

I put the book back where I found it and scan the floor, which is suspiciously free of clothes. I look around the room and my gaze lands on his desk, and the shuffling around when he got out of bed suddenly makes sense.

He was folding my clothes.

I don't take long to dwell on the unfamiliar, fuzzy feeling that floods my stomach at the realization before quickly pulling my clothes back on and heading toward the door. At this point, I'm ready to be in my own space again. I back out of the room slowly, holding down the handle to close the door as quietly as I can so he doesn't think I'm storming out of here.

I'm satisfied with my efforts to leave, maybe feeling a little smug, since Emilia and her ballerina friends tell me I'm about as quiet and graceful as a drunk hippo. Well, feeling smug until I turn around to leave and two pairs of inquisitive brown eyes are staring right at me.

"Why do you look like you're fleeing from the scene of a crime?" Russ's friend Henry asks at a volume I'd prefer him to lower.

"I don't." The girl he's with gives me a sympathetic look that says you do, without her saying it out loud. "I gotta go, sorry."

They both step out of the way as I rush past, hoping with everything I've got that it's not going to be difficult to get a ride and I'm not going to be forced to do the walk of shame.

"He's a good guy," Henry says. "A really good guy."

"I can tell," I mumble. "I really do have to go."

The party is in its final stages. The only people around to potentially witness my disappearing act are too wasted to care, and by the time I reach the front door my shoes are back on my feet. I can't get an Uber to accept my request, so I set off on foot in the direction of home.

EMILIA BENNETT

omw

You good?

Yeah

You getting the feeling scaries?

Yeah

You wanna sleep in my bed?

Yeah

The feeling scaries is what Emilia calls the moment of clarity you get after you've left a situation you were wrapped up in. It's the sinking feeling in your gut when the anxiety sets in and you consider whether you did the right thing. It's a moment like now, when I'm alone with only my thoughts to keep me company. When I weigh whether what I just did made me feel better or worse. Whether I'd have done that if I'd stayed off my phone and minded my business. And how long that hit of validation and feeling wanted is going to keep me going before I'm looking for the next place to get it. Then finally, whether any of this really matters either way when nobody cares what I do.

The feeling scaries isn't necessarily regret, it's reflection, and I prefer to be distracted rather than reflective.

EMILIA BENNETT
Why are you moving really slow?
Are you in a car?
Aurora are you walking!!!
Don't you dare get murdered
I'm so mad at you

I'm almost home

"You're a clown," Emilia says as I climb into bed beside her. "Stop playing chicken with your safety because you're too impatient to wait for a ride."

"Noted." Maybe if I'd managed to get a ride I wouldn't have spent the entire walk home thinking of the guy I just left.

"Your pizza is in the kitchen."

"I'm not hungry anymore."

Emilia sighs heavily. "Go to sleep. You'll need the energy to break up your parents' brawl."

"Are you sure you want to go for breakfast?" I don't get a response, just a pillow launched in my general direction. "We could just fake our own deaths."

"Your mom would know. You really need to sleep, Ror," she says through another yawn. "Just think, a whole summer without sharing your location in the middle of the night. Just weeks and weeks of keeping small children alive and uninjured, and self-development."

"The dream."

Chapter Six

AURORA

NOTHING ON THIS EARTH INSPIRES the same pure, unadulterated despair as having to spend any prolonged length of time with my parents in the same location.

It sounds dramatic, but honestly, Chuck and Sarah Roberts are the poster couple for "sometimes divorce is a blessing." There's just something about them being within six feet of each other that turns them both into monsters.

With that in mind, I should probably count myself lucky that Dad hasn't shown up to the good-bye breakfast he promised he'd be at before I head to Honey Acres sleepaway camp to work for the summer with Emilia.

The most annoying part isn't being consistently let down by a man who is supposed to be one of the stable pillars in my life; it's the effect his absent-parent bullshit has on Mom, who, if anything, I could cope with being a little more absent.

"Why don't you try him again?" She watches me over her orange juice with a sad pout. "Have you tried his assistant? Or Elsa? Your sister can always seem to reach him."

"He's not going to answer; it's fine." It is fine, because you can't be disappointed by someone you have zero faith in. "Our plans clearly weren't his important ones. What were you saying?"

Reaching for my glass, I gulp down my water and free the metaphorical brick lodged in my throat. The one that gets slightly bigger every single time I say the words *it's* and *fine* in the same sentence.

"I was about to ask if you thought any more about moving home when you get back." Give me strength. "Don't look at me like that, Aurora. I literally made you."

You'd think after twenty years I'd be used to the incessant probing and the not very discreet attempts to remind me that she's the reason I exist, and yet—here we are. "I, uh, Mom, you know we've signed the lease for next year already. Dad already paid the full year upfront . . ." What's a polite way to say, "Hell will freeze over before I voluntarily live with you again"? "You can't expect me to commute from Malibu every day when I have a perfectly nice home right next to college . . . I'd spend half my day sitting in traffic."

"There are children in other cultures who live with their parents forever," she says in a hushed tone. "Your sister is in London. You take three days to return my calls. Don't act like I'm the unreasonable one for wanting to see my daughters regularly. It's not even far."

God forbid Sarah Roberts ever be accused of being the unreasonable one.

"I think my parents' worst nightmare would be me moving home," Emilia interjects, forcing a chuckle to lighten the increasing tension.

Emilia Bennett is the perfect roommate, best friend, and occasional human guilt shield. Two years studying public relations and six years playing emotional babysitter to my mom and her turbulent moods has turned her into my own personal crisis manager.

"I'm sure they would love it if you moved home, Emilia," Mom sighs dramatically. "I'm sure their house feels huge and lonely without you."

The only reason Mom's house feels huge and lonely is because she sold my childhood home and used the divorce settlement to buy a huge "fuck you" house on the beach.

Her eyes land on me and it's a look that I recognize: expectancy.

She expects me to want to be home as much as she wants me to be home, and she can't understand why I'd rather work all summer than spend it with her. It was never a problem when I was the one sent to camp; the problem started when she realized I was much happier there than with her.

We traveled around a lot when I was a kid, moving from country to country depending on where Fenrir, the Formula 1 team my dad owns, was racing that month. Following the team around the world was always Dad's top priority, never stability for his daughters and wife.

Elsa and I have always joked that Fenrir is the only thing he's ever helped create that he actually loves.

I love my sister, but even with the same complex web of mommy and daddy issues, our six-year age difference was too big to overcome for two kids looking for connection. I was acting out worse than ever, and that's why my parents started sending me to camp every year when I was seven.

It was everything I didn't know I needed. I had routine, I was able to spend time with kids my age, and I could begin to build the foundations of who I was without constantly being surrounded by adults and a moody older sister.

Honey Acres was the first place that ever felt like home. Even when my parents eventually split up and Mom moved us back to America full time and enrolled me in school, I still insisted on going to Honey Acres every summer. I loved how happy the staff was to see me every year, and it's my first real memory of feeling wanted.

I want to get those feelings back, which I'm hoping to do by rebuilding the foundations I've broken. I love college and the experiences I've had there in the past two years, but I feel lost. I make choices I don't understand in the moments where my feelings get too big, and because there's nobody there to tell me to stop, the little voice in my head tells me, "Fuck it." I'm becoming someone I don't recognize and I need a factory reset. I want to feel at home again. I want to feel at peace.

Emilia's foot making contact with my shin drags me from my train of thought, and even after I apparently zoned out, Mom still has that look on her face.

If I wish hard enough, do you think I can summon my dad for a distraction?

Unsurprisingly, my father doesn't materialize, but thankfully the server arrives with our breakfast and interrupts the growing tension slowly building beneath the surface of Mom's sadness. It feels like a cruel twist of fate to have one parent who doesn't give a shit and one parent who cares far too much.

I can't remember a time when she wasn't like this, which means I can't decide if this is who she is as a person, or if this is the result of her spending her life feeling like she has to love me twice as much.

I say love and not parent because she's never parented me. For every inch my dad has pushed me away and favored his job, she's tried to pull me closer twice as much. For every time he's let me down, she's made allowances because it's easier to blame him for my behavior than it is to risk driving me away. She's never cared about anything I've done unless it directly affected her.

When I was younger, I always strived to be the best, to know the most, like somehow the validation of being the perfect daughter would give me the type of attention from my parents I craved so desperately, but it never came.

So I stopped striving for the best. I achieved validation and attention through other means and became my own person, but somewhere along the way I've found myself in this limbo of happily doing whatever I want because people don't care, and then being hurt that I can do whatever I want because people don't care.

I worked my ass off to get into Maple Hills because I wanted to prove to my teachers I was more than the girl who cut class and didn't pay attention. Instead of my achievement, all Mom saw was my impending departure. When I got my acceptance letter she acted like I was going to war, not a college in our state, and she didn't talk to me for three days. It didn't matter that I'd stayed close by, unlike my sister who moved to our dad's place in London when she graduated high school.

The balance between being the perfect daughter and my own person is like walking a tightrope.

Except there's a hurricane.

And the rope is on fire.

I've fallen down more times than I can count and I'm really fucking exhausted.

"You can visit us at camp if you want to, Mom." I push a strawberry around my plate, waiting for her response, because with a mother like mine, whose self-worth is so heavily intertwined with the title of mother that it becomes exhausting, every word is a chess move. "Visiting day is in July. I can text you the date."

"You clearly don't want me to visit, Aurora."

I've never been very good at chess. "Mom—"

"Ms. Roberts, did I tell you about the camera Poppy bought me to take pictures at camp?" Emilia interrupts, reaching for her purse. "As you know, I didn't get to go to sleepaway camp when I was younger, and I was so happy when Aurora finally gave in to me begging her to be a camp counselor with me. She says you picked the best camp, so I'm really excited."

I begged Emilia to be a counselor with me, not the other way around, but my mom doesn't need to know that. She'll be too distracted by the praise.

Like mother, like daughter.

"Aurora has always had the best. Not that you've ever appreciated it, have you, darling? You'd have been happy rolling around a pig farm when you were younger. You just wanted to play somewhere there weren't any tires."

Emilia grabs the camera from her purse and hands it to my mother. Mom's face lights up as she clicks through the pictures, murmuring about what a beautiful couple Poppy and Emilia are and how great Emilia looks wearing blue.

"And where were you when the girls were hiking?"

I was sitting on a basketball player's face. "Studying."

"You were studying? After your finals?"

"Yeah." Shit. "I was studying ropes and stuff for camp." I was tied to a bed. "Plus they're a couple, Mom. They don't want me third-wheeling on their date."

"That's true. Will you not miss her, Emilia? Ten weeks is such a long time." She's talking to Emilia, but I can feel her eyes on me, waiting for me to react to her subtle dig. "Trust me, it feels like forever."

"I'll miss Poppy, but it's fine, we'll both be super busy. She's in Europe with her mom until school restarts."

Emilia knows what she accidentally did before I even have time to flinch. Her big brown eyes meet mine and she gives me a look that says, "I'll fire myself, don't worry."

Crisis manager, my ass.

Mom's lips pull into a tight line as she focuses on neatly folding the napkin from her lap and placing it on the table. "Poppy must really love her mother to want to spend the whole summer with her, isn't that nice. Excuse me, girls, I'm going to use the restroom."

It's amazing how one woman can suck all the oxygen from the room with one sentence.

"Ow," Emilia cries, placing her hand on her forehead over the spot I flicked as soon as the door to the restroom closed behind Mom. "I deserved that. It just came out!"

"You could have said anything."

"I'm sorry! God, I wish your dad was here. He's better at being in the firing line than me. Maybe I need to change majors; I'm terrible at this."

"You really are."

"I wonder if Elsa's friends were ever put through the Emotion Olympics with your mother," she muses, mopping up the last of her syrup with a piece of French toast.

"Like Elsa would ever agree to breakfast. Or have real friends."

"That's true. When do you think we can politely say peace and leave?"

I can't help but snort. "She might keep us here until we miss our flight."

"Are you good? She's been even more intense than normal this morning."

"She's just spiraling because Dad's girlfriend and Elsa are competing to see who can spend the most time in the tabloids and I'm leaving. It's fine."

"Your dad's girlfriend the florist?"

"No, he broke up with her, remember? I'm talking about Norah. The ex-weather woman. Or was she a Real Housewife of somewhere?" I shake my head as I mentally try to recap my father's long dating history. "I can't remember. Anyway, whatever she did she loves a photo op."

I hear Mom's heels hitting the tiles, which gives me enough time to force a smile back onto my face. Her hand gently brushes over my hair as she passes and she twirls the end around her fingers. She always says it looks like hers when she was twenty and how happy she is that I'm all her. Same light blond hair and green eyes, same freckles that appear after too long in the sun, same everything.

Unlike my sister, who is a carbon copy of my dad, with me there's not a Chuck Roberts gene in sight.

Taking a seat across from me again, she sighs. "I'm going to miss you girls. Should I get the check? I'm sure you want to get to the airport with plenty of time."

"That'd be good. Thanks, Mom."

It's funny how the moment Mom acts reasonable I start to feel bad about leaving when she so clearly would love me to stay. There is nobody on this planet who can get under my skin like my mother, which only fuels my complaining about her, and yet the moment she shows a shred of humanity I crumble. The guilt begins to creep into my system like venom burning its way through my blood, but the universe delivers me the antidote in the form of my cell phone buzzing in my pocket, quickly reminding me why I so desperately need to get away from this place and everyone in it.

MAN WHO PAYS THE RENT

Got delayed helping Isobel move out of her dorm
so won't make it to breakfast.
Safe travels.

I discreetly tilt my phone screen toward Emilia while Mom hands her credit card to the server, thankfully keeping her distracted. I don't need to be looking at my best friend to know she's rolling her eyes hard. It's not a surprise to me after I saw him moving Isobel out of her dorm on Norah's story last night. It's nice Norah's daughter gets the caring dad treatment; perhaps one day Isobel can let me know what it's like.

The easiest thing for me to do is convince myself it's just who he is as a person. That it isn't anything to do with me. The disinterest, the broken promises, the cold and aloof parenting method is because he wasn't ever cut out to be a great dad, and that's not my fault. But then I see him with someone else's kid and I'm back to thinking maybe it is me.

I'd be upset if it wasn't so fucking predictable.

I'm tired more than anything. Tired of feeling like I don't fit into my own family. Tired of questioning my every choice. Tired of wanting to do better but feeling like I can't manage it.

Emilia keeps Mom chatting the whole drive back to the house, which gives me the opportunity to stew in my anger and feelings that are most definitely not disappointment, rejection, and hurt. I'd have to care to feel rejected, and I don't care anymore.

It's clear the universe has no intention of giving me a fucking break as we idle in traffic in front of an ice rink. Russ has been on my mind since I woke up this morning, which is not a problem I'm used to having after a one-night stand. He wasn't what I'm used to, in a good way, and I can't get him out of my head. I'm trying not to feel bad that things ended without so much as a good-bye, but it's hard to forget about him when his fingerprints are still decorating my hips from where he held me.

Pulling into the driveway beside my car, the impending good-bye hangs awkwardly in the air as we all climb out. The guilt floods me again, because for all of Mom's faults, she'd never bail on me for someone else's kid.

She'd never not call. I've never had to beg, cry, or fight for her to love me.

The hug I pull her into catches her off guard at first, but she wraps her arms around me tightly and nuzzles my hair, whispering so only I can hear. "Don't forget to call."

"I won't."

Emilia waits until Mom is a dot in the car mirror before daring to speak. "You good?"

"I'm fine. I just need plane snacks and to manifest both Fenrir cars spontaneously breaking down midrace."

Chapter Seven

RUSS

I HATE MYSELF FOR DRINKING last night.

Why I decided that was the night finally to relax a little and do what I want I'll never know. I never quite reached being drunk, but the consequences of slow, constant drinking to stay buzzed is almost worse. It means this entire drive has been even more tiring, and even longer than it needed to be with a small, low ache in the base of my head. If I'd gotten blackout drunk I would have gone to bed alone and I might have had a good night's sleep for once.

Not sleeping isn't anything new for me, and after years of sporadic, light slumber, my body operates pretty well on empty. This drive has been rough, though, and I'm seriously regretting driving instead of flying.

If I'd flown, I could have had several more hours in bed, instead of having to get up and get on the road first thing. Henry and Robbie waved me off, both red-eyed and practically still asleep, mumbling something about rescuing me from horses and cows if I needed them to, but it meant a lot anyway, and for the first time in forever, I feel excited to come back to Maple Hills at the end of summer and see my roommates.

Maybe if I'd flown, I wouldn't have spent the past four hours thinking about the woman in my bed last night. Well, in my bed until she wasn't. I should accept it for what it was: a one-night stand between two consenting adults. Not something I usually do—generally it takes more than one night for me to get the confidence to make a move—but she was so confident and I wanted to match it.

I'm kicking myself for not saying more to her while I had the chance to. Although, maybe her leaving and telling me without any words that she wasn't interested in anything more is easier in the long run. I spent so long in the bathroom hyping myself up with one of JJ's silly pep talks to convince myself to ask her if she wanted to go on a date when I get home from camp that if she'd rejected me to my face, I'd have probably locked myself back in the bathroom.

Yeah, it was a blessing she left without saying good-bye.

Message received.

One night only.

I probably made a fool of myself, but there was something in her gaze, in her smile when I looked at her. Maybe she pitied me; that would make more sense, to be honest. Pity or not, I've spent the past several hours torturing myself with the memory of her soft skin beneath my fingers and her moans in my ear. I know I won't see her again, and I should probably just forget about her, but sometimes it's not that easy.

If I remember how fucking unbelievable she felt maybe it'll dull the feeling of disappointment that I didn't get to ask her out.

THE STONES CRUNCH UNDER MY tires as I turn into the large dirt track adjacent to the huge Welcome to Honey Acres sign. Anticipation drowns all the other feelings in my body and it hits me that I'm finally here after so much waiting. I didn't go to sleepaway camp when I was younger because my family couldn't afford it. Mom was reluctant to commit to anything so far in the future, never knowing whether Dad's paycheck was going toward the bills or a bet.

She wouldn't look at places for kids in families with financial insecurity because she was too busy pretending things were fine. I didn't get it when I was younger, which I'm thankful for in many ways, because for a long time I just thought she liked having me and my brother home.

But like everything else, I've gotten myself here. I might not be a kid anymore, but I'll get to see what I was missing all those years and, even better, I'll get paid for it.

In the distance, a huge log cabin appears, and as I get closer, parked cars and a bus decorated in Honey Acres branding come into view. Pulling into an empty space, I take a deep breath and give myself a minute to adjust. It looks exactly like the brochure, even down to the people wandering around with their bags looking excited.

Grabbing my things from the backseat, I head toward the people lining up to register their arrival. Pulling out my phone, I see a string of messages in the group chat Stassie set up last week.

PRETTY BEST FRIENDS

STASSIE
Let us know when you get there safely, muffin
Drinking before a big drive wasn't the best idea

KRIS
He'll be fine. He had an early night ;)

MATTIE
I'm not fine in case anyone cares

BOBBY
How early?

KRIS
According to the UCMH gossip page he took Aurora
Roberts up to his room and they did not reappear

LOLA
I can't believe you read that shit. They posted
that I might be pregnant two weeks ago because
someone told them I was crying in Kenny's. I
literally had hot sauce in my eye

MATTIE
Nobody cares then? Okay cool cool cool

BOBBY
Why does Aurora Roberts sound familiar?

STASSIE
She's friends with Ryan

ROBBIE
You watched her give Russ a lap dance last night, genius

BOBBY
No I know that but her name sounds familiar

MATTIE
"Friends with Ryan" has never worked out well for any guy

STASSIE
Nate told me to tell you to fuck off

KRIS
That was Aurora Roberts???

LOLA
Am I the only woman at this school Ryan Rothwell hasn't stuck his dick in?

ROBBIE
Yes, and I thank the stars for that daily

STASSIE
Nate told me to tell you to fuck off as well

KRIS
Her dad owns Fenrir. The F1 team with the wolf

BOBBY
Oh shit

STASSIE
Nate is excited by that news for some reason

LOLA
She was hot. Congrats muffin

HENRY
You guys are annoying.
I thought someone had died.
There's no need for people who see each other every single day to text this much.

ROBBIE
The only person who's gonna die is muffin when he realizes he's gonna have to pretend to like F1 if he ever wants to get laid again

JJ
At least it isn't something boring like tennis

ROBBIE
Who let you in here? This group is supposed to
be for the people actually staying in Maple Hills

JJ
I'll be there in spirit
And I get FOMO

KRIS
It was Stassie, wasn't it?

STASSIE
Excuse you

JJ
Nah, I negotiated with Hen

BOBBY
"Negotiated"

HENRY
He hid my paintbrushes.

JJ
You'll be glad of my presence when one of you
asks for advice from a real-world adult

LOLA
I'll be sure to never, ever do that

                                              RUSS
                                      This was a lot
                      I'm here but the cell service sucks

I always wondered what it'd be like to be in the inner circle when I was on the outside. Now that I'm in it, I realize it's mainly chaos, but in a kind of wholesome way. By the time I'm done catching up, I'm at the front of the line, which gives me the perfect opportunity not to dwell on the fact I am once again on some shitty college gossip page, the girl I'm with on there has a super-rich family, and there's absolutely no way I'm going to be able to fake knowing anything about race cars if I ever see her again.

It doesn't take long for me to be given my welcome pack, told a meeting starts in an hour, and find my cabin. Pushing my way through the stiff door, I immediately spot my new roommate for the summer.

"What's up, man," he says coolly, nodding from the bed he's taken on the other side of the room. "I'm Xander."

"Russ." I swear I nearly say muffin. "Good to meet you."

"You, too." His eyes drop to my T-shirt, where the white Titans logo stands out against the navy-blue material. "You at UCMH?"

Part of me dies a little bit, because I didn't think when I put this shirt on. I hoped there wouldn't be Maple Hills students here, since it's so many hours away, but it was silly of me to assume they wouldn't be attracted to the same things as me. You'd think familiar faces would be a comfort, but as soon as I mention hockey they bring up the rink, which I fucking hate talking about. I reluctantly answer Xander. "Yeah, you?"

"Nah, man. My mom's husband is faculty and I don't need that in my life. Plus, my stepbrother is there and we'd probably kill each other if we played on the same basketball team. I'm at Stanford. You play?"

Dropping my bags to the floor and emptying the things from my pockets, I sit on my bed and brace for the normal reaction. "Yeah, ice hockey."

"Sweet." He gestures toward the keys. "Was it a long drive?"

It takes me longer than it should to answer him because it wasn't the question I was prepping for, and the more small talk we make, the more relaxed I become because he doesn't mention the rink at all.

I'm sure it's an anxiety thing to assume that every single person with links to Maple Hills knows about the situation I caused at the start of the year. It's my biggest shame, the first time I thought, "Yeah, Dad's right, I am a fuckup," so it isn't as easy as choosing not to think about it like my teammates suggest. Stassie says that over time it won't be the first thing I worry about, but I'm still waiting for that to happen.

An hour flies by so quickly I don't even get a chance to open my welcome pack before we have to head over to the main hall for the meeting. This place is huge but, thankfully Xander worked here last summer so he knows exactly where we're going.

We grab two empty seats in the front row and wait for the rest of the room to fill up. Xander passes me a sign-in sheet being sent around the room, and at the top is the Wi-Fi password.

"The Wi-Fi fucking sucks, by the way," he groans. "It's not too bad if you're in the main buildings, but in our cabin it's nonexistent. You'll get random service and all your messages will come through at once and scare the shit out of you."

"No service is good for me, to be honest." I sign my name and connect anyway, passing the sheet on to the people beside me. More messages from the group chat come through, along with some other notifications and messages from my mom.

MOM

I've been trying to reach you all week and so has your brother

I hope you have a great summer at the camp

Please visit when you're back

Missing you, sweetie

Me and your dad both do

I check the other notifications and the one that stands out is the one from my dad.

DAD

Request from kcallaghan19

$50

I lock my phone quickly in case anyone is looking over my shoulder and put it back into my pocket. I feel bad for ignoring Mom's calls, but it's always the same excuses I'd rather not hear. My brother, Ethan, only calls to give me shit about not visiting, despite the fact he fled to the East Coast with his band as soon as he possibly could, leaving me to deal with it all alone.

I've always been second choice: to my dad's addictions, to my mom's excuses for him, to Ethan's desire to move away far enough that he can pretend nothing's wrong.

I love my family, but I hate what we've become. Tiptoeing around the things that keep us divided, making excuses for Dad, refusing to work toward a solution in favor of pretending there isn't an issue. I've reached the point where it's easier to ignore them and keep my distance both physically and emotionally. Thankfully, now that I'm here, that distance I'll be keeping is four hours north.

An older woman taps a live microphone at the same time a fluffy golden head lands on my knees. Xander immediately reaches for the dog, scratching between its ears in a way that makes the dog's eyes close and tail wag. "Hey, Fish! I've missed you and your hair all over my clothes," he coos. He looks at me to explain. "She's Jenna's dog; you'll meet her, she's a director. Jenna works in the office mainly, so Fish just roams around the camp, getting attention from everyone. She usually picks a favorite and sticks with them. Looks like you're a contender."

"Welcome, everyone!" the woman calls from the front. "For our newbies this year, my name is Orla Murphy and I'm the resident dinosaur here at Honey Acres. I'm the camp executive director and owner and I oversee everything and everyone here. My family founded Honey Acres and I'm so happy to welcome you to our family this year."

I'm half trying to listen, half trying to fuss over Fish when Xander grabs me suddenly. "Oh my God," he whispers, squeezing my arm tightly. Following his line of sight, my eyes land on the cutest two—equally as golden and fluffy, but much smaller and chubbier—dogs trotting toward us. "Baby Fishes!"

I realize I'm not listening to anything Orla says about the camp as the puppies reach us and Xander scoops them both up under his arms. Twisting the shiny aluminum name tags hanging from their collars, I try to suppress a laugh when Salmon and Trout are staring back at me.

Laughter coming through the speaker drags me back to the present, and when I look back to the front of the room Orla is staring at us. "I see the dogs are doing their usual trick of outshining me. For those of you who have been with us before, Fish had puppies and she's very proud of them. Fully expect you may get back to your cabin one day to find them in your bed."

There are murmurs around the room as others on the front row lean forward to catch a look at the fluffy bundles currently boxing each other in my roommate's arms.

I commit to paying attention as Orla explains a lot of the things I already know from the brochure about a typical day, expected behavior, days off, and what to expect until the campers arrive in a week.

There's something about the idea of team building that makes me shiver. Icebreakers are my least favorite thing to do, and I've basically signed myself up for a week of them.

Orla continues with her introduction and a puppy crawls into my lap, right beside its mom's head, and falls asleep. "Onto the important stuff. I'm sure it won't come as a surprise to you, but alcohol and drugs are strictly prohibited, even if you are of legal age . . . which most of you aren't. You are here to give our campers a magical summer; if you wanted to spend your summer under the influence, you should have gone on vacation instead."

Kris, Bobby, and Mattie's faces immediately pop into my head. They said something similar when I countered their offer to go to Miami with working at camp with me.

"For many of our kids, this summer will be the highlight of their year, so keep that in mind when you think about showing up with a hangover. And finally, everyone's favorite topic: romance. Here at Honey Acres we have a zero-fraternization policy, which if breached will result in contract termination. This is, of course, for the well-being of our campers, but also for your sanity. You have ten weeks together, and trust me, it goes very slowly when you desperately wish you could escape someone who seemed like a great idea when you had your camp goggles on."

I lean toward Xander, lowering my voice. "Camp goggles?"

He chuckles. "You'll see. Everyone is attractive after a month."

She finishes by explaining that all staff can hang out together in the shared staff areas, but not in each other's cabins, and a few other perfectly reasonable rules I'm going to have no problem keeping. The last thing I need is to be sent back to Maple Hills midsummer because I fucked up. Again.

Today is a settling-in day, since so many people are tired from traveling, and the final step of our welcome is meeting the group of people we'll be working with for the next ten weeks.

The kids are separated into one of four groups: Raccoons, Brown Bears, Foxes, and Hedgehogs. Each animal represents an age group, and each group has six counselors who work on rotation to make sure there are always four counselors available each day and two overnight.

I put my preference as Brown Bears, which are kids aged eight to ten, because they're old enough not to be totally needy, but young enough that I'm not potentially going to be fighting an attitude for just over two months. Unlike a lot of other summer camps where campers stay for a week or two before heading home, our kids are here for the entire summer.

One of the staff starts calling out names, and people head toward their groups. I try to put the puppy back on the floor in preparation, but it squeaks until I give up.

"Brown Bears, you're up . . . Clay Cole . . . Alexander Smith . . ." Xander stands, opting to take the puppy with him after watching my failed attempt. ". . . Emilia Bennett . . . Russ Callaghan . . ."

I stand to join my group, Fish close behind my feet, as more names are called. My group is busy getting acquainted with the puppy still in Xander's arms, and as I approach, one of them turns around.

My heart sinks as I immediately recognize the girl staring back at me.

I don't need to calculate the probability of who Emilia might be here with—it's written on every bit of her shocked face. I know she's here, because the universe loves nothing more than to drag me to hell and back for fun.

Emilia's eyes look past me and I turn instinctively, immediately spotting the same blond hair that my face was buried in less than twenty-four hours ago.

It takes her an extra second for her to spot me, but when she does, she stops abruptly, her jaw slacking slightly, her eyes widening as she takes me in. "Oh shit."

Chapter Eight

AURORA

"Oh shit."

I don't mean to say it out loud. I was looking at the puppy. Why didn't I just keep looking at the puppy?

Russ doesn't say anything as we stare at each other. The easy, friendly smile from last night gone, replaced with something cooler, more guarded. I'm scrambling for something to say, something that says, "Hey, I know we've seen each other naked and we thought we wouldn't see each other again, but now we're in the same group, so let's not think about it again? Cool? Cool."

I have thought about it, though, even when I didn't want to. My mouth starts to open, to say what, I don't know, but slams shut before I have the opportunity to embarrass myself when he turns to face the rest of our group without uttering a word.

The silence stings.

And the irony isn't lost on me, since I have ignored several one-night stands while passing by them on campus, but I'm not sure I'd truly be my father's daughter if my biggest talent wasn't hypocrisy.

There's nothing nasty about Russ's reaction; I'm not sure there's anything nasty about the guy who whispered how beautiful I am into the dark or folded the clothes he peeled off me into a tidy pile. I'm just surprised, I suppose, since he was so sweet last night.

I let the uncomfortable feelings linger, unwilling to push them away or attempt to soothe my growing unease. This is what you get for seeking comfort from strangers, Aurora.

Lesson learned.

"Hi, everyone. My name is Jenna, or as I'm more commonly known, Fish's mom. I'm the Brown Bears senior this summer, which means, as well as my responsibilities as one of the camp directors, I oversee your plans, make sure everyone is happy and healthy, and help you navigate any tricky stuff that might come up with your campers."

Taking a spot beside me, Emilia links her pinky with mine, her signal of solidarity and what-the-fuck rolled into one because of the brooding hockey player standing to our right. I'm trying to concentrate on Jenna's introduction, but Russ keeps drawing my focus because he won't even look in my direction.

"I'm going to give you all a tour of the main grounds. I recommend you fill your water bottles before we head out. When we're done, we'll have dinner together, then the rest of the evening is yours to enjoy before the hard work starts tomorrow."

Everyone heads to the water machines in the corner of the main hall. When they're all gone, Jenna's professional smile slips into her real one and she lunges at me, pulling me into an oxygen-stealing hug. "I've missed you so much!"

"Can't breathe, Jen."

She releases me, taking my face in her hands instead. "I want to cry. I feel like my baby has come home; you're so grown up now."

My words catch in my throat and the overwhelming urge to sob floods me. Jenna was my counselor when I was a camper, and as I aged and moved into different camper groups, so did she. She swore it was a coincidence, but I liked to tell myself it was because she wanted to hang out with me, and as a kid who just wanted to be wanted, it was bliss.

I felt like I could breathe again when we drove down the dirt road earlier, like I was finally where I'm supposed to be.

Jenna was eighteen when we first met, but unlike my actual big sister, Jenna was the one I'd always needed. She was the tooth fairy when I lost my first tooth here, my savior when I got my first period, and my shoulder to cry on when I had my first kiss with Todd Anson and a day later he was kissing Polly Becker by the volleyball court.

"I spoke to you two days ago and it hasn't been that long since we had a sleepover," I laugh, freeing myself from her grip and taking the spot beside her. "When did you become so needy?"

"Yes, but it's been so long since you were here. Too long, in fact." I love her being needy, she knows I love it, but she plays along all the same. "Sorry, it's the puppies. They're making me maternal. Now I'm going to have to look at tall, muscular guys carrying them around all summer." She sighs as she nods toward where Russ and the others are playing with the trio of golden retrievers. "It looks like Fish has picked her victim for the summer. She has good taste."

If Russ can feel our eyes on him, he doesn't look up. I shouldn't be staring at him, but he looks as good as, if not better than, he did last night. I turn so my back is to him. "About him . . ."

Jenna's eyes narrow like she's trying to see into my brain, and she might have achieved it because her face sinks into disgust. "You've been here two hours! Aurora, please tell me you haven't managed to break cardinal rule number one already?"

"What? No! Of course not. What do you take me for?"

"Thank goodness. I can't be your boss if you're going to break the rules."

"I haven't!"

She mutters something that sounds a lot like "phew" and puts her hands on her hips. "Good."

"It was last night."

"Rory!" Jenna exclaims, dragging a hand down her face. "Do not make me regret accepting your application by messing around all summer. You promised me you'd work hard. You strutting around here like you owned the place was cute when you were a sassy nine-year-old, but if you're going to be in charge of campers, I need to know your head is in the game, not in some basketball? Football? player's bed."

"He actually plays hockey . . ."

"I'm glad you're diversifying your roster, but I really mean it, Ror. You promised me an entire summer. No throwing in the towel because you're bored of camp life. I need you to show up for the kids, not show up for some random guy."

"Have some faith in me, Jen. Jesus. I didn't know he was going to be here! Funnily enough, he didn't ask me about my summer plans when he was pounding me into his bed," I say, folding my arms across my chest.

"First, I never want to hear about your sex life in that much detail again," she groans, scrunching her face in repulsion. "And second, I do have faith in you, Rory. I'm your biggest supporter, but I also know you. Let's not make both of our lives harder, please. Focus all your energy into the kids."

"I know, Jenna," I drawl. "Like I said, didn't know he was going to be here."

She looks around me quickly, then back at my face. "When you woke up this morning, did neither of you say, 'Got to go, have to go to Honey Acres'? or, 'Thanks for the sex, but gotta get to camp'?"

"No, of course not. I left last night while he hid from me in the bathroom, and when he saw me a couple of minutes ago, he pretended he didn't know me. Like real adults."

"Oh, to be in college again."

I move to stand beside her, looking at my group mates chatting around the water machine. There are two guys with Russ, both good

looking, and if I'm hearing correctly, they're talking about basketball, something that under normal circumstances would pique my
interest. "Besides, I'm not even interested in Russ, the other two guys
are cuter." Lie. "You don't need to worry." Big, fat lie.

"No funny business with any of them . . . No, don't give me that
look, Aurora. I mean it. You don't get a free pass because I love you
and you think the rules don't apply to you. You told me you want to
find yourself this summer."

"Because I do."

Jenna might be five inches shorter than me, but even at five foot
two, she still manages to move me a couple of inches to the left when
she bashes her shoulder into me. "Well, if you have sex with someone on campgrounds, the only place you're going to find yourself is
buried in the woods when I murder you."

"You're not going to murder me. I'm not interested in him and
he's clearly not interested in me." I retake my place and wrap my
arms around her, resting my head on hers, something I started doing
when I overtook her in height, which I know annoys her. "Tell me
you love me again."

She huffs, a sound I've missed during our time apart. Jenna becoming exasperated by me doesn't quite have the same effect on a
video call. "This feels like a HR complaint waiting to happen."

"Tell me," I tease, dragging out the *me* until she attempts to elbow
me, her short black bob tickling my face in the struggle. "Please,
please, please."

"I love you, Aurora Roberts. Welcome home. Now get off me, I
have a tour to conduct."

"My feet feel like they're going to fall off."

I shoot Emilia a disbelieving look. "You're a ballerina. Your feet
have been through worse."

"Being a ballerina has not stopped my sandals from shredding my feet because I was wearing the wrong shoes on a freaking hike."

"Typical city girl," I tease. "Should have read more small-town romances to prepare yourself for the country."

The short-and-sweet, sandal-appropriate camp tour Jenna was planning to give was hijacked by Cooper, the senior in charge of the Hedgehog counselors, who I suspect has a soft spot for her and asked to combine tours. That's sweet and all, but thanks to Cooper and his enthusiasm, our tour took two hours longer than everyone else's and I feel like I've seen every blade of grass at Honey Acres.

The long walk gave us the chance to talk to the other counselors, except Russ, who stayed up front, talking to Xander, the same guy he was with earlier.

"Yes, that's where I went wrong. Not enough small-town romances." She wiggles her toes in the sand that borders the shore of the lake, commonly referred to as the beach, where we've commandeered two deck chairs. "I'm going to sit on the dock and dip my feet in the water; do you want to come or guard the seats?"

"I'll stay here." Our seats are the perfect spot to people watch, and it's fun seeing who is drawn to each other and make predictions on who will get close. It was funny listening to Orla talk earlier about how fraternization is prohibited, knowing nobody is going to listen to it. When I was a camper here, we would all speculate who was secretly kissing after hours. Then annoy the hell out of our counselors to tell us the adult gossip.

My favorite thing to do now that I'm a counselor myself is to watch the dogs inspect everyone, occasionally sitting down to be petted, before moving on. I love dogs, which is exactly why I'm watching one of the puppies sleep on Russ as he laughs and chats with Maya from our group, while Fish and the other puppy sleep at his feet.

"Anyone sitting here?"

Looking behind me, I find Clay, the third guy in our group

standing barefoot in the sand, holding two beers. "Not right now, but she'll be back soon." I point in the direction of Emilia, chatting with someone on the dock. "Take a seat."

Sitting beside me, he holds out one of the beer bottles. "Beer?"

Although Orla does her best to enforce the no-drinking rule, short of inspecting everyone's bag when they arrive, there isn't a way for her to stop people sneaking it in for training week. I assume she knows, but is less strict as there are no children around currently. What she does take very seriously is campers sneaking in alcohol, which I found out the hard way when I was fifteen. "No, thanks. I'm, uh, I'm trying not to break all the rules on day one." Or massively piss off Jenna.

Clay shrugs as he puts the spare beer in the drink holder. "We never get caught. I've been here before. But you're right, we have plenty of time to break the rules."

He launches into a tale about being a counselor and I'm struggling to follow along. Not because I'm not smart enough, just because it's really, really boring. By the time he's moved on to talking about playing basketball at Berkeley (or was it USC?), he's totally lost me.

It's not his fault that my mind is elsewhere and I'm sure he's not used to women zoning out when he's trying to talk to them. He's attractive by conventional standards: tall, sharp jaw, nice eyes and smile. Not a huge fan of the amount of gel he uses to slick back his hair, but mainly because there's so much I'm concerned there's going to be a pollution incident if he jumps into the lake. And I could do without the way his eyes drop to my chest when I'm talking, but he's not the worst guy who's ever tried to befriend me.

Normally I'd take the attention he's showing me and run with it, but I find his confidence off-putting and his bragging hard to listen to. I hook up with one quiet guy and suddenly I don't like confident basketball players? The matrix is glitching.

My eyes wander across the beach and the dogs look super comfortable as Maya brushes something from Russ's shoulder, smiling at him sweetly. The puppy on his lap doesn't even stir when he shuffles in his seat and rubs the back of his neck with his palm.

"I will have that beer actually," I say, interrupting Clay telling me how much he can bench.

"Oh, sweet. Here . . ."

At least it's still a bit cold. "Thanks. Nice chatting with you."

I don't hear if he responds as I stand and rush over toward Emilia on the dock. Her eyebrows pinch together as she sees me approach. "What happened to our seats?" She spots the beer in my hand. "And becoming a changed woman?"

She accepts it from me, taking a sip as I sit beside her, dipping my feet into the water. "I'm starting tomorrow. Too many things to be irritated about today to overhaul my life."

"He's just shy, Ror," Emilia says carefully, handing me back my beer.

I turn to look at her, confused. "Clay is not shy. Shy people don't talk to your breasts."

Her eyes roll. "You know who I'm talking about. The one you keep staring at."

Looking over my shoulder back toward the beach, I see Russ is still talking to Maya, and Xander has joined them. "I'm looking at the dogs," I say. "But if you're talking about Russ . . . well, he's not too shy to talk to other people, is he?"

"Just go over and talk to him."

"And let him ignore me with an audience? No, thanks."

"Maya is homesick, he's probably just trying to make her feel better."

"I know, I chatted with her while you were on the phone to Poppy. She lives near the Fenrir UK base, but a few of her friends from home are here, too. Look, it's not important, he can talk to whoever he wants, I'm not trying to be that person. It just sort of sucks that I seem to be the only person he doesn't want to talk to, y'know? I'm beginning to think maybe I got played and he's not as nice as he seems."

"You didn't. But if you did, who cares? You hooked up, you'll move on like you always do." Emilia wraps her arm around my shoulders and pulls me closer, resting her head against mine as I swallow a glug of the now warm beer. "If you make me listen to you complain about a man all summer, I will tell your mom you're moving back home."

"I won't. I told you, starting tomorrow I'm going to be a new woman."

Chapter Nine

AURORA

WHY IS SAYING YOU'RE GOING to work on yourself easier than working on yourself?

I want to leave my self-destructive habits behind and yet here I am—day one of Project Aurora, cell phone in hand, watching Norah's story knowing it's going to upset me.

And it is upsetting me. My manifestation technique requires some work because Dad's team smashed the Spanish Grand Prix and he's super happy about it. Which I know from the sweet videos Norah posted of him celebrating with her daughter at his house.

Stuffing my cell phone into the back pocket of my shorts, I try to forget about the perfect family I'm not part of and speed walk in the direction of the fire safety training, which I'm already running late for.

While the team-building exercises take place in larger groups across roles, all our specific training is done in our group of six, making it impossible to sneak in undetected.

"You are"—Jenna looks at her watch—"six minutes late, Rory."

Normally I wouldn't care about being late, but feeling everyone's eyes on me is making the blood rush to my cheeks. Well, all but one person. I mutter a "sorry" quietly and keep my head down as I fill the empty seat between Emilia and Clay. He leans in, lowering his voice. "You haven't missed anything. Basically, fire is bad."

"I'll try to remember that." I fight the urge to chuckle and try to concentrate on Jenna starting with the evacuation drill procedure. He offers me a grape from the bag in his hand, which, after yesterday, feels a little like a gesture of goodwill.

Jenna is busy explaining the campfire rules when I feel a tugging on my foot. Looking to the floor, there appears to be a ball of fluff chewing on my shoelaces. Picking up the chubby puppy, I turn the tag toward me. "Which one are you?" Salmon. "Where's your brother, little girl?"

As soon as I look up, I spot Trout cradled like a baby, snoozing on Russ's chest. Oh man, this is not fair. I can't drag my eyes away from the cuteness, which is a mistake, because when Russ finally glances up from the sleeping dog, he looks right at me.

We stare at each other, and it's as awkward and weird as it sounds, right until Salmon decides to chomp on the ends of my hair, distracting me. When I look back at him, he's focused on whatever Jenna is saying.

The rest of the training flies by without any further staring contests, and by the time we're all walking across the main lawn on our way to our team-building activity, I'm feeling better than I was a couple of hours ago, snooping where I shouldn't be snooping.

"I've decided I don't care," I announce to Emilia.

"That's good," she says nonchalantly, trying not to trip over Salmon, who's weaving around our feet as we walk, trying once again to eat shoelaces. "What are you talking about exactly?"

"Everything."

"That feels healthy and definitely not like it'll backfire on you in the future."

She expertly dodges my elbow when I try to poke her in the ribs.

"I'm going to delete my spam account and lock my cell phone in my suitcase. If I don't see it, it doesn't exist."

"I support it. I've said it before, nothing good can come from putting your faith in a man. Let Chuck and Norah play happy families online and you concentrate on you."

"Jesus, it was like being with my mom for a second," I tease.

Tired of dodging her, Emilia bends to pick up Salmon, tucking the puppy under her arm. "You're so annoying," Emilia groans.

The dog's tongue lolls out of her mouth as Emilia struggles with the deceptively heavy golden retriever. I reach over to scratch behind Salmon's ears as we continue toward the activity. "Aw, she's not annoying. She's a baby."

Emilia's brows knit as she looks over at me. "I was talking to you."

We finally reach the rest of the counselors standing around several planks of wood and platforms arranged in groups of four. "I don't know what the hell we're going to have to do," Maya says.

I've seen this activity before, but I've never done it. "You have to get your entire team from the first platform to the one at the end, but it gets harder to move between them because the gaps gets bigger and the platforms get smaller. Nobody can touch the floor."

"Bedlam then." She smiles. "I'm going to say hi to my friends, I'll be back in a sec."

"I wonder if you'd annoy me less if you still had a British accent," Emilia says quietly, watching Maya as she walks away from us.

"I never sounded like Maya. I still sounded mostly American. It got stronger depending on how much time I spent hanging around at Dad's work."

Xander, Russ, and Clay finally stop whispering to one another, turning to face Emilia and me. "Okay, game plan," Xander says seriously. "We're going to jump between the platforms."

Emilia bursts out laughing and I immediately shake my head. "No, we're not."

"Why not? It'll be the easiest way," he immediately counters.

Emilia is still laughing at the idea of us trying to make those jumps. Xander looks genuinely surprised, while Clay is trying to fight a laugh, too. Russ is . . . observing. "Maybe for you, Mr. NBA hopeful, but for the rest of us mere mortals, jumping that far isn't possible."

"We'll help you. You'll be fine."

Xander's mouth doesn't move, and that's when I realize the person talking to me is Russ.

"Oh." Say something, Aurora. "Cool."

I hate myself.

Russ does that nod thing guys do, without saying anything more. It was nice to hear him speak, so now I know he is real and not just a figment of my imagination haunting me like the ghost of hookups past.

"Is this thing on?"

We all turn our attention to Orla, standing at the last platform with a megaphone. She's had that megaphone for as long as I've known her, and every time it breaks, she gets the maintenance team to fix it for her instead of investing in one from this century.

I stole it once. Used it to scare the shit out of Jenna when she was flirting with one of the other counselors and ended up in a time-out for the rest of the afternoon, but it was worth it.

Orla goes over the rules, explaining that you can't start moving to the next platform until your entire team is together. If anyone in your team falls off, your team has to start again from the beginning, and whoever makes it to the end, managing to stay on the platform for thirty seconds without falling, is the winner.

Maya wanders back to our group and Xander immediately turns to her. "We're jumping."

"No, we're not," Emilia and I say in unison.

"You're tall—" Maya says, looking him up and down.

"Thank you for noticing . . ."

"If you're so confident, why don't you just lie down between them and we can all walk you like a plank?"

"Yeah, Xan," Russ says, grinning. "Why don't we just walk you like a plank?"

"I don't think I'd like being crushed by a hockey player, funnily enough."

"Don't knock it until you've tried it," I say quietly without thinking.

Thankfully, most of the group didn't hear my little admission, but Russ and Xander did, and Russ's cheeks flush pink.

Xander's eyes flick between us quickly, but the whistle blows, putting an end to anything he might be about to say. The six of us rush toward the first platform, only just fitting on comfortably.

"We are at a distinct disadvantage because the three of you are so massive," Emilia groans into Clay's back, which is pressed up against her face.

"Aurora, I'm really sorry my hand is touching your bum, but I can't move it," Maya says.

"It's touching mine, too," Xander adds.

Russ sighs. "No, that's mine."

The platform creaks as Russ jumps to the next one, followed by Clay and Xander. There's enough room for the three of us to maneuver now that the boys are gone, and we coordinate moving our plank to the next platform to walk along it.

"Just jump!" Xander shouts.

Maya holds her arms out to keep her balance as she walks to the next platform. "I am not bloody jumping when there is a walkway!"

"Come on, Mary Poppins," Clay says, holding his hand out to Maya, helping her to take the final few steps. It's easy to follow, and when we're all together on the next platform we start the whole ordeal again.

"Xander, you're going to push me off!" I cling to Clay behind me, and his hands immediately land on my waist. I switch to holding on to Emilia beside me, looking up at him over my shoulder. "It's okay, you don't need to hold me."

We realize that the wood hardly reaches the next platform, which is farther away than the last, and the guys work out a plan that has one of them jumping over last, then they'll help those of us who aren't part kangaroo get across. The sound of all the other teams shouting instructions at one another is flooding the air, and realizing that we're slightly in the lead kick-starts the competitive part of me.

Xander easily jumps to the next platform, kneeling and reaching to accept the end of the plank that isn't long enough to rest against the edge of where he's standing. He keeps it steady with his hand, and we all pat his head as we climb over him, keeping as close to the edge as we can to let Russ and Clay jump over, too.

"Oh my God," Emilia squeaks. "Someone jump before we lose our balance."

The guys all spring across, making it look ridiculously easy, but as soon as they're all on the final platform together it's immediately clear that there is not enough room for six people. Even if there was enough room, there's no way we're making that jump.

"How the fuck are we supposed to do this?" I'd put my hands on my hips, but there isn't enough room without nudging Maya off.

"Is anyone concerned about the weight limit of these platforms?" Clay says, looking at the creaking box beneath their feet.

"Was anyone a cheerleader?" Xander asks.

"This isn't the type of team building we're supposed to be doing right now, buddy," Emilia says sarcastically.

Rolling his eyes, he points at the distance between us. "Two of you can launch the other across the gap. We can catch." We're all silent. "You're telling me nobody was a cheerleader in high school?"

"Yeah . . ." Maya says. "That's not a thing where I live."

"Aurora got kicked off the cheerleading squad freshman year,"

Emilia says. "And as for me, ballet and human pyramids aren't a good mix."

"You also aren't very cheerful," I mutter under my breath.

"What did you get kicked off for?" Clay asks immediately.

"Not importa—"

"She stole the other team's mascot and lost it."

"Emilia!"

Xander peers over to the other teams, his face twisting in concern. "Guys, we really need to get moving . . ."

"How do you lose a mascot?" Russ asks, looking right at me.

"I, um . . . It ran off." That gets his attention. His eyes widen and I immediately feel the need to clarify. "It was a pig, not a person. They found him a few hours later; he was totally fine. He was hanging out with the janitor's dog, but, um, they felt my actions did not align with the team's core values. Anyway, can we get on with this? Who are we throwing?"

"Guys, if we lose because you're all short and Aurora is a pig stealer, I'm going to be so pissed," Xander snaps.

"Everyone's short when you're a freaking giant. Maya, you're up," I say, linking my fingers together and bending for her to put her foot into the cradle my hands have made. Emilia copies me and Maya holds on to us both as she tentatively steps into our hands.

"For the record," she says quietly, "I think this is a terrible idea."

"Be ready to catch her! Three . . . Two . . . One . . ."

It feels like we're playing human bowling as Emilia and I launch poor Maya in the direction of the guys a little too enthusiastically. Thankfully, they catch and squish her against them to keep her on the platform. There is physically no more room for people, and I'm not sure how we're supposed to do this.

"Get on someone's shoulders, Maya!" Emilia shouts. Russ and Clay hold Maya's arms and help Xander move her onto his shoulders, once again creating a tiny bit of space for another person.

Emilia nudges me lightly, something she can do now that there's a tiny bit more space. "You next."

"Absolutely not. You next."

Xander is once again looking at the other groups. "Aurora, as much as you think you're not, you are tall enough to jump." If he thinks I'm more qualified because I'm five foot seven to Emilia's five foot three, he clearly doesn't know she's capable of leaping across a stage like a freaking gazelle. "Emilia, I have an idea, do you trust us?"

"Not even a little bit," Emilia calls back. I shake my head, too, trying not to smirk when Xander immediately looks irritated.

"Can you learn to trust us in the next five seconds? Jump forward with your arms out. Like you're diving to catch a baseball."

"Do I seem like the type of person who knows anything about baseball?" she snaps.

I'm laughing before I've even said what I want to say. "You know a lot about third base . . ."

"No! No! No!"

I manage to stay on the platform by clinging to Emilia, even though she's the one trying to push me off, much to the horror of our teammates and their screams.

"Jesus Christ this is stressful," Clay groans. "Arms out, Emilia. Me and Russ will grab your hands and pull you over; you just need to get far enough for us to reach you."

"I hate you for convincing me to come here," she mumbles before setting herself at the edge of the platform with her arms out. To Xander's credit, it works perfectly, and within a few seconds Emilia is across and sitting on Clay's shoulders.

There's no way that Clay can help pull me across with Emilia on his shoulders, which means I'm really going to have to jump. The urge to just step off the platform and make us lose is overwhelming. "I'm scared," I yell, trying and failing to visualize myself being able to cover the distance. There's a lot more room now that I'm over here on my own, but it's not enough for me to run before jumping.

"You can do it, Rory," Emilia shouts from above Clay. "Please do it quickly, though. I think I'm developing a fear of heights."

"I don't think I can . . ."

"Aurora," Russ says softly, shuffling so his body is the one closest to the last space on the platform. "Look at me. You can do it, you just need to jump toward my arms and I'll catch you, okay?"

"What if you fall?"

"Then we'll fall together." He smiles at me, and my heart bashes brutally against my chest like the traitor it is. We're not supposed to be caring about anything, remember? "And Xander can be pissed at both of us."

"I will be pissed at both of you," he grumbles.

"Ignore him, just look at me," Russ says. "I believe in you. Take a deep breath. I'm going to count down from three and then I want you to jump as far as you can."

"And you'll catch me?"

"I promise I'll catch you. Three . . . Two . . ."

He leans forward with his arms out and I zone out when he reaches one, instead concentrating on launching my body toward his. His hands are on my arms almost immediately, dragging me forward until I hit his chest.

"Brown Bears! Thirty seconds to be the winners," Orla announces through her megaphone.

"Nobody fucking move," Xander snaps.

I wiggle my arms free from the position they're locked in against Russ's chest, but he doesn't loosen his grip on me, and my body stays flush against his, keeping us both on the platform. He smells like clean laundry, sandalwood, and vanilla, and when I look up toward his face, his eyes are shut tight and he's quietly muttering names of hockey teams.

And then I feel it against my stomach and his hold on me finally loosens, but it's too late.

It's the slowest thirty seconds in history, as Russ desperately tries to lose the boner pressing into me.

"Brown Bears win!" Orla announces, much to Xander's delight.

I step off the platform and away from Russ. Thankfully the other guys are distracted by getting Maya and Emilia off their shoulders, and when Russ looks at me, I can't help but wink.

His blush reaches his ears this time.

Chapter Ten

RUSS

"Are you going to say something, or are you just going to stare at me?"

JJ doesn't change the smug look on his face, and it's making me want to disconnect the video call. "I'm just honored, although not surprised, that you're calling me for life advice. What can I do for you, buddy? You need to know how interest works? What a 401(k) is?"

"Yes, I called you from camp to find out about retirement plans," I say sarcastically, rolling my eyes. "I should have called Nate."

"Take that back right now." JJ, who was lying on his couch, sits upright. "You have my full attention. What's up?"

I'm in the main building during our lunch break because it's the only place to get Wi-Fi. I check around me to make sure I'm still alone. "Aurora. The girl I hooked up with on Saturday night. She's here."

"Sweet. I love a summer romance," he says cheerfully.

"No. There's no romance here. She, uh, she left while I was in the bathroom." I sink farther into my seat, embarrassed to be admitting I was walked out on to my friend. "And also staff isn't allowed to mess around together, but even if we were, she isn't interested."

JJ sits in silence and I'm busy waiting for him to react. "Russ, you're going to have to explain it to me like I'm five, because I'm not following what the issue is here."

"I was hyping myself up to ask her out, and when I came out of the bathroom she had already gone. Embarrassing, I know, but now it's awkward because we're both here and I've been staying away from her, an—"

"Back up, Callaghan. You like this woman and you're staying away from her why?"

"I don't want to make her feel uncomfortable. She didn't want to see me again and now she can't escape me. We're in the same group."

JJ sighs heavily. "Did she tell you she didn't want to see you again?"

"I haven't actually talked to her. Like I said, I've been staying away. I don't wa—"

"Want to make her uncomfortable, yes, you said that. Oh, Russ. You are so hopeless, but I love you anyway."

"Thanks? I think?"

"It's not true unless she said it. Unless she actually tells you she doesn't want to see you again, then you're just making assumptions."

Fantastic. "So what now?"

"Well right now you look like some guy who got what he wanted and is now ignoring her, and you're not that guy. You're the good guy who doesn't realize sometimes people leave after hooking up and that doesn't have to mean anything dramatic. You're not going to have a chance with her if you ignore her, genius."

I really am hopeless. "I'm not looking for a chance with her. I don't want to get fired."

"So why are you calling me about the girl you don't want a chance with?"

"I just want to know how to be around her, since we have to work side by side for weeks." I scratch my jaw, feeling pretty clueless about women right now. "She was pushed up against me yesterday—stop looking at me like that, it was during a team activity—and she was so close to me I could smell her shampoo and, well . . ."

Quickly turning down the volume on my cell phone, I check once again that I'm still alone, while JJ does what can only be described as cackle. He eventually calms down and I feel like my entire face is on fire. "It happens to the best of us, buddy. Does she know?"

"Well it was digging into her stomach." Sighing, I run my hand down my face as I prepare for the cackling again. "When she moved away, she winked at me."

I count all the way to thirty-three before JJ finally stops laughing. "The real reason you wanted to talk to me."

"What do I do?"

"You accept that you completely misjudged the situation and you talk to her instead of avoiding her like a dick. Be around her by doing just that, being around her. It's easy."

The doors open behind me and I look over my shoulder to spot Xander walking in with the dogs. "I gotta go, but I appreciate you, man. Thanks for hearing me out."

"Bye, lover boy, keep me updated," JJ says, disconnecting the call.

Now that my phone has service again, my notifications have come through while I've been talking to JJ. The last thing in the group chat is a picture of Mattie, Bobby, and Kris at the beach in Miami and one of Lola, Stassie, and Joe on their flight to New York.

I take a video as Trout scrambles up the outer side of the beanbag chair and slides down into my lap and send it to the chat. I'm about to close my messages when I spot more from someone I was hoping to avoid hearing from.

DAD

How are you?
Did you see my request??

Then a few hours later.

Too good to text back now?
Think you're better than me do you
Too good for this family

"I'm fucking beat, man." Xander groans, throwing himself into the giant beanbag chair beside me, causing me to lock my phone immediately and put it into my pocket. "This sun is a killer."

It takes me longer to process what he's said because my heart and brain are racing after seeing the messages from my dad. "Yeah, it's brutal. Where is everyone?"

He kicks off his sneakers and stretches his legs out fully. "Tanning, I think. I need to cool down before I melt."

Sharing with Xander has been a great arrangement so far. Other than being very competitive, which I learned yesterday, he's usually super chill, tidy, and seems to have this radar for when to stop before his questions go too far. When he realized Emilia, Aurora, and I go to the same college and I shrugged when he asked if we knew each other, mumbling, "Sort of," he didn't push.

We sit in a comfortable silence, another thing I appreciate, and Xander scrolls on his phone. I'm too scared to get mine out again, so I give Trout all of my attention and think about what JJ said.

"You excited for training?" Xander asks, looking up from his phone.

Even though there are camp nurses, we all have to do basic first aid training. Anything is better than the harness safety training this morning where I spent the majority of my time eye level with Xander's dick. Don't even get me started on all the icebreakers, which are now my least favorite thing in the world. "At this point, anything that's not an icebreaker is a win in my eyes."

He groans, throwing his head back against the bean bag and Trout jumps at the noise. "Someone should tell them the ice is officially broken. I saw Clay naked this morning by accident; you don't get more broken than that."

I was attempting to herd my dog shadows out of our cabin this morning when Xander practically crashed into me looking mortified. "Walked into the wrong cabin," he spluttered, smothering a horrified scoff with his hand. "Wasn't paying attention. Oh my God."

"Maybe we need to refreeze the ice a little, in that case," I joke. "You want me to fill up your water bottle before we head out?"

He nods, handing it over. "Thanks, bro."

I'm walking toward the water machines when someone turns the corner, colliding with me. Dropping the bottles to the floor, I catch the arms of the person stumbling away, keeping them upright.

"I'm so sorry. I wasn't looking where I was go—" Aurora finally looks up after finding her balance. "Oh, hi."

"Hi." She moves and that's when I realize I'm still holding her and her eyes are puffy. "Are you okay?"

"I'm great," she says immediately, giving me a bright smile that looks entirely pretend. I've seen her real smile before—making her smile and laugh is ingrained in my brain—but this isn't it. "Everything is wonderful."

Everything doesn't feel wonderful. I pick up the bottles I dropped and take the few seconds without her sad, green eyes looking at me to rack my brain to work out what could be wrong with her. I overheard her say to Maya this morning that she dislikes being paired with Clay because she doesn't like the way he looks at her body when they're working together.

I also don't like the way he looks at her body when they work together, or the way his hands stay on her a little bit longer than necessary. But I put that down to jealousy, not substance in my concerns. Aurora and Maya agreed he's harmless, just annoying, which made me feel better and a little less like I should push him into the lake or into the path of a bear.

"I'm just getting some water for me and Xander."

"Water is good," she says far too enthusiastically for the topic of conversation. "Water is, uh, hydrating."

Tucking the bottles back under my arm, I clear my throat. "Aurora, did something happen?"

"Nothing that I shouldn't expect at this point. It's fine. I'm fine. Everything is peachy," she says. I'm not sure whom she's working hardest to convince, me or herself. Before I can ask anything else, she takes a big step back, fake smile still in place. "See you at training."

She's gone before I even have time to respond.

THE SOLAR-POWERED FANS POINTING TOWARD the six of us as we wait for our instructor are useless in the face of the exceptionally hot afternoon sunshine.

"I can't live like this," Xander groans, fanning himself with his hand. "Why couldn't we have done this inside?"

"How do you think I feel?" Maya says, wafting her Brown Bears staff T-shirt. "We don't get sun in England."

"I'm more worried that the resuscitation dummies are going to melt," I say, nodding toward the pile of plastic.

"Hello, hello. I'm here. Sorry, everyone, I'm Jeremy and you should be"—he checks his clipboard—"Alexander, Aurora, Clay, Emilia, Maya, and Russ? Yes? Perfect."

I'm a fan of Jeremy straight away because he immediately complains about how hot it is and moves us and the equipment into the shade. He also doesn't pick me to do the demonstration, which also scores him points.

Emilia is fully sweating and panting by the time she manages to get Xander into the recovery position, but when she's done, she sits back and admires her hard work with her hands on her hips, like a proud dad.

"The rest of you pair up and practice, please," Jeremy announces. "I'll be watching; please shout up if you're struggling with anything."

Clay immediately moves toward Aurora, but I'm closer to her. "Come on," I say, gesturing toward one of the empty practice mats. "I'll do you first."

"Oh, okay." I think this is the quietest I've seen her since we arrived a few days ago. I know I shouldn't expect anything better after avoiding her for forty-eight hours, but I still don't know what upset her earlier and it's bugging me. "Thank you."

We both get into position, her on the mat and me beside her, and I suddenly can't remember how to do this. I've done first aid training before, because Coach Faulkner makes us do it every year, telling us we'll never know when we'll need it—and yet here I am once again, clueless.

I watch Xander moving Emilia and it suddenly comes back to me. Gripping the back of her thigh, I start to lift her leg into the correct position. "You should tell him you don't like it when he touches you."

Thankfully the task at hand gives me the perfect opportunity not to look at her face, but I can feel her eyes burning into me. "And you know that how?"

"Your entire body language changes when he's near you."

She scoffs. "You seem to have noticed a lot about my body for someone who's barely looked at me since we got here."

Her words make me freeze, but only for a second before I push through it, gently moving her arms to the right angles and rolling her onto her side into the recovery position. "Just tell him, Aurora."

"Are you jealous?" she asks, rolling onto her back and moving into a sitting position. She's leaning back on her hands, her hair ruffled from the mat, light freckles beginning to decorate her cheeks. She's fucking beautiful, but there's something different about her today. Of course I'm jealous of it being so easy for Clay to just talk to her and touch her without caring about any potential consequences. "No, I'm not jealous."

She looks sad. "Then you don't need to worry, do you?"

"Aurora, I—"

She stands before I can say anything else. "Excuse me, I'm going to use the restroom."

I nod and watch her walk away, lying down on the mat so I don't have to see everyone else getting along and moving onto the next task. Five minutes pass before she reappears, dropping down onto the grass beside me.

She tucks her hair behind her ears and hugs her knees close to her chest, offering, "I'm sorry for being weird. I'm having a bad day. It's my dad's birthday and, well, we have a really shitty relationship. To call it a relationship at all is actually a huge stretch . . . *aaand* now I'm officially oversharing. Can we start over? I really want to recovery-position you."

"I'd really like to be recovery positioned."

It's cute watching how hard she's concentrating. She tries to lift my leg, just like I did to her, only to huff and try with two hands. "Do you want me to make it easier for you?"

"No!" she says, tugging my leg up to the correct position. "If you were passed out you wouldn't be making it easier for me."

"Okay, then . . ."

"Jesus Christ, I feel like I'm working out. Why are you so big?" She's going to kill me while trying to save me. "Oh, I forgot to check if you were breathing!"

Before I can reassure her that I'm definitely breathing—for now— I'm drowning under a sea of blond hair that smells like peaches as she puts her ear to my face. With all my limbs eventually in the right positions, she pulls me toward her, rolling me into the final pose.

"Well done, Aurora," Jeremy says somewhere behind me. I hadn't even registered he was there. "You guys can move onto the bandages now. There's a step-by-step guide to follow; I'll get you a pack and then you can tell me when you're done."

"Good job, partner," she says, holding up her hand for me to high-five. "We're a good team." I slap my palm against hers. "You're really good at . . . recovering people."

My lips quirk as I listen to her go on and on, looking more confused with every word out of her mouth. "You're good at recovering people, too."

"The sun is melting my brain. Let's get the bandages. You can tie me up first." She shakes her head, pressing her hand against her forehead. "I made it weird, didn't I?"

Embarrassed Aurora is adorable. "Yeah. Good job, partner."

Chapter Eleven

RUSS

AURORA IS REALLY, REALLY DRUNK, which means I'm back to keeping my distance.

While Xander has assured me that people drank alcohol when he was here last year and nothing happened, I'm still choosing to stay away from the chaotic drinking game that appears to be half Truth or Dare, half Never Have I Ever, depending on which side of the campfire circle you find yourself on.

Our cabin is one of eight counselor cabins that borders the lake, giving me the perfect vantage point to watch what all the other staff are doing, while also mind my business with my book.

My love for reading started when I was a kid and my dad would be in a bad mood because like most gamblers, he's shit at gambling. Reading was the most fun I could have while making the least amount of noise, and I always wanted to avoid drawing attention to myself when he was likely to start an argument over something.

It feels full circle to be the thing keeping me out of trouble as an adult.

I know to everyone else it makes me seem boring, but so far I love being here, and aside from the obvious reasons, that's something else that makes me want to not be sent home. I can try not to worry about what people know or think about me, which is something I struggle to put to the back of my mind when I'm at college. I probably won't see half of these people again, and that's what I keep telling myself when I'm trying to be myself and get involved.

There's one person I might see again, though, and she's currently drinking directly out of a liquor bottle and laughing loudly. It doesn't feel authentic, though, but more like for show. That's a recurring thought about Aurora, about how happy she portrays herself to be, with big smiles and bigger laughs—and yet sometimes it seems forced.

I felt like the world's biggest asshole earlier when she walked toward me, presumably to get me involved, and as soon as I saw the tequila bottle in her hand, I walked in the other direction toward my cabin and away from her. I've caught her looking over here a few times, but when she spots me looking back at her, she quickly focuses back on the game.

Grabbing my water bottle from the railing beside me, I stretch my legs and head to the water machines near the main lawn. It's weird not having to worry about accidentally falling over a dog, and I miss my little shadows when they're not around.

Jenna says I should feel honored to be the chosen one, and I do. I haven't ever been anyone's first choice, so I'm grabbing on to it with both hands. Even if they are dogs.

I'm walking past the empty kids' cabins on the side of the main lawn when I hear footsteps on the gravel path. Aurora's cheeks are pink when she catches up to me, eyes glassy. "I freaking hate running," she pants, supporting herself against her knees as she tries to catch her breath. "What are you doing?"

"I'm getting a drink. Is everything okay?"

She nods, standing up straight before immediately starting to sway. "Everything's great. I love my life." She doesn't look like she loves her life; the way she says it is slurred and high pitched, un-natural and uncomfortable. I don't know what happened between work this afternoon and now, when she looks one drink away from being the drunk girl who cries.

"Are you sure you're oka—"

"You're not joining in." She stumbles forward, regaining her balance quickly and walking toward me until she's close enough I could touch her if I wanted to. The smell of the fire lingers around us and it's a welcome change from being assaulted by my own memories of her shampoo. Her lower lip wobbles as she takes a sharp intake of breath. "Is it me? Did I do something wrong?"

"No. I don't want to get into trouble by drinking," I explain honestly. "And you're really, really drunk. You should probably go to bed; we have water-safety training tomorrow and it's late."

She's still swaying and I can practically hear the cogs in her head turning while her brain wades through the tequila she's tried to drown it with.

I recognize the familiar sounds of dog collars jingling and paws against gravel. Deciding not to wait to find out who they're with, I grab Aurora's arm, quickly pulling her toward the darkened space between the cabins. "Someone's coming," I say when she looks up at me alarmed.

This would be a really bad time to discover some of the less cute creatures that no doubt roam this camp at night.

I move us into the shadows as quickly and quietly as I can, practically carrying Aurora as she giggles. Yes, she thinks it's funny. "Stop laughing," I whisper. She leans forward, burying her face in my T-shirt in an attempt to smother the amused noises escaping her. It's not enough, and when she lets out a little snort, I put my hand over her mouth gently. "Shhh."

Fish stops at the spot Aurora and I just vacated, staring toward the darkness and, therefore, us. I'm holding my breath, my heart hammering so hard I'm surprised Aurora can't hear the thud, thud, thud. I'm mentally running through all the excuses I could possibly give, realizing that being in a dark corner of the camp alone with a drunk girl is far more alarming than talking to one. Then Fish barks and I swear my heart stops beating all together.

"Stop it, noisy girl," Jenna chastises, clicking her tongue at the puppies to follow her. "Fish, come on," she says, and whistles. I wait until I can no longer hear the gravel before finally letting myself breath properly again.

"Ow, fuck!" I snatch my hand away from Aurora's mouth. "Did you just bite me?"

"You forgot I was here." Like that could happen. "You're good at that."

How did I end up here when I was purposely trying to stay out of the way?

"Come on, Edward Cullen. Back on the path before something bigger and scarier than you decides to bite me." It's like guiding a toddler as I hold both her arms to lead her through the dark and back into the lit-up path.

"Russ, I feel sick," she mumbles.

"Do you need some water?" She nods, and there's a very real possibility she's about to barf on me. Leading her toward the porch steps of the cabin labeled Raccoon, I sit her down and jog toward the water station. It doesn't take me long, but she's paler when I get back. "I don't feel good," she moans into her hands.

"I'm not surprised. You drink like a fish. Here," I say, handing her my water bottle.

She looks up, her green eyes fixed on me between slow, long blinks. "I drink like a dog?"

"What? No, I didn't mean—never mind." She guzzles the water, wiping the excess from the corner of her mouth with the back of her hand and offering the bottle back to me. "Do you want me to walk you to your cabin?"

Nodding, Aurora holds out her hand and I gently tug her to her feet; her fingers intertwine with mine and she begins to lead me toward her cabin, which is in a different section from mine.

We're halfway there when she suddenly stops, pulling me to a stop, too. "Do you want to go skinny dipping?"

Jesus Christ. "You need to go to bed."

"I don't want to go to bed." Her bottom lip juts out and she reminds me of Stassie and Lola when they're drunk. It'd be cute if I weren't so stressed.

"Well, you have to," I say, dragging her along.

"Make me."

"I'm not going to try and make you."

"You've gotten me into bed before, it shouldn't be that hard for you."

I should have stayed reading my book. "If you don't go to sleep, you're going to feel like death tomorrow and you'll have no one to blame but yourself."

"My dad is to blame for all of my problems, so that's not true, is it?" As drunk as she is, there's something clear and certain about the way she says it. It's a feeling I can relate to, but I think trading daddy issues is the exact opposite of what I need this summer. It's definitely the exact opposite of what I need right now, dealing with a drunk person. "You don't get to tell me what to do, mister. You're not the boss of me."

"But you *just* told me to make you. I know I'm not the bo—" I stop talking because I'm arguing with someone who probably isn't going to remember any of this tomorrow. "Is that why you're so drunk? Your dad's done something?"

"It's his birthday." She looks at her watch, squinting. "Is that a twelve or two? Was his birthday. I arranged for a gift to be delivered. Silly, silly Rory, always expecting too much and trusting the wrong people."

"And he didn't like it?"

"He didn't open it. I spoke to his assistant, Sandra, no, Brandy? Brenda. I spoke to Brenda because he didn't answer my calls and it was still in his office." She shrugs and her whole demeanor changes again. It's like every time she talks about something that makes her unhappy, she forces herself to look happy. "His girlfriend and her daughter took him to Disneyland as a surprise. He fucking hates Disneyland. He never went with us when my mom took me and my sister. But anything Norah and Isobel want they get, and I just have to exist in their shadow."

"I'm sorry." I don't know what else to say, but we reach cabin 22 and she begins to climb the steps. Thinking back to Xander and Clay's wrong cabin accident, I keep hold of her hand. "Is this definitely yours?"

"Yup." She points to the fairy lights decorating the porch. "Cabin two-two. Angel number."

I stop on the bottom step, letting go of her hand. "Angel what?"

She spins around so quickly she almost loses balance, but the walk here, the water, and the short period without a tequila bottle in her hand has helped sober her up a tiny amount. "Why have you stopped?"

"We aren't allowed to go into other people's cabins."

She huffs, her hands landing on her hips like somehow I'm the one in the wrong here. "Nobody cares about those rules. Nobody cares enough to punish me."

"I care about them, Rory. And you'd understand that if you weren't so drunk."

She drags me up the steps, and I reluctantly follow. "Come in, please."

"I'll stand in the doorway," I say firmly, which is a waste of breath, because she pulls me over the threshold anyway. "Aurora, I can't be in here. I need this job."

"I liked it when you called me Rory."

"Rory, get into bed, please. Lie on your side in case you're sick." To my surprise, she kicks off her shoes and throws herself down onto her bed. "Good girl. Okay, good night."

"Wait!" she shouts as I turn to leave. "I'm hungry."

It really is like being with Stassie and Lola. "I can't do anything about that right now. I'll get you breakfast in the morning."

"No, you won't." She wiggles under a blanket, and while her sleeping fully clothed isn't ideal, it is not something I'm prepared to tackle. "Tomorrow you'll go back to hating me."

My mouth opens and closes, but no words come out at first. "I do not hate you."

She yawns and begins to lose the fight to keep her eyes open. "Will you wait until I fall asleep, please? It won't take long."

I'm still stunned she thinks I hate her, even though it's probably drunk babble. "Sure, why?"

"Because it's easier to wake up and you're not here than it is to watch you leave me."

I sit on the edge of her bed, mulling over her words, scrambling for a plan to untangle the mess I've created for myself starting tomorrow. It doesn't take long for her to fall asleep and I'm instantly jealous, because I know I'm going to be up all night wondering if it would have been easier to watch her leave after we hooked up. Or was it easier to find her gone?

BREAKFAST IS QUIETER THAN NORMAL with Aurora missing, and I hate it.

She's practically a Honey Acres expert, after coming here as a camper for so many years, and she spends so much time during meals when we're all sitting together answering questions about what it will be like when the kids are here.

Emilia sits down with her food and gives a vague answer about Aurora feeling sick and not wanting breakfast, not revealing that she's definitely hungover.

I wait until everyone is deep in conversation about the pros and cons of semester-abroad programs before slipping away and setting off toward cabin 22 with a bottle of orange juice and some granola bars.

Aurora is already standing on the porch when I get there, and the way her face drops when she sees me stings. I hover at the bottom of the steps. "Hey. I brought you breakfast like I promised."

She accepts reluctantly, looking at my offering like I'm a cat that just dropped a dead mouse at her feet. "Thanks."

"I wanted to see how you're feeling. Emilia said you're feeling si—"

"Russ, what are you doing?" she asks, cutting me off.

"I said I'd bring you breakfast last night. You probably don't remember, you were pretty drunk."

"No, I mean here. Now." She shakes her head, dragging her hand through her hair. "You're either super nice to me or you avoid me. And now you're here, being sweet, and I don't know if you'll be like this all day, and I'm tired of wondering what I've done to make you not like me."

"I do like you. I'm sorry, Aurora. I do like you."

She sits on the top step, setting her breakfast beside her. I can sense her frustration growing. "You're nice all the time, but it's with everyone but me, Russ. Everyone. I'm so tired of being treated like that when I'm at home—"

The guilt fucking sucks. The last thing I want to do is make things harder for her, especially when she's totally right. I have made an effort with everyone but her. The first thing I should have done after my call with JJ yesterday was apologize to her. Instead, I sort of hoped it'd just blow over and we could both ignore it. I should have known it wouldn't work like that. Spending all your time with a group of people in an isolated place makes everything feel bigger and more intense, even after only a short time, and I know that's only going to increase as time goes on.

I know I need to be honest with her, so she realizes I'm the problem not her, but the words just won't come because I'm a coward.

"—and I came here to escape those feelings and work on myself. I don't know what I'm doing, but whatever it is I'm doing a totally shitty job so far, so I don't need you making it worse by blowing hot and cold for the rest of the summer. If you only want to try to be my friend some of the time, I'd prefer you to just, I don't know, just don't try. Ignore me all the time; it'll be easier to cope with."

Taking a deep breath, I force myself to start talking. "Rory, I messed up. I'm sorry. When you walked out and didn't leave your number or say bye, I thought that was your way of telling me you didn't want to hear from me again," I say calmly, trying to suppress the feelings of embarrassment. "Then we were dropped into this situation together and I didn't want to make you uncomfortable. I get that I shouldn't have assumed and I didn't mean to hurt your feelings."

Her jaw is hanging open as she looks at me from the step. "I know I'm hungover, but did I just hallucinate and hear you say the reason you've been like this since we got here is because I left? When you wanted me to leave?"

"I didn't want you to leave. What are you talking about?"

She stands quickly, the steps making us about the same height, giving me the perfect view of how confused her face is right now. "You were in the bathroom for so long. You were waiting for me to go. I heard you talking to someone so I left."

"I was talking to myself, Rory. I was hyping myself up to ask you out, which is something I hoped to never have to admit out loud to you. But I'd rather embarrass myself than have you think I'm the type of guy who would wait in a bathroom for you to leave."

"Oh my God."

"I never do the one-night stand thing and I thought we had fun. I wanted to see you again, but you're so out of my league and—"

"Oh my God." She drops back to the step and this time I crouch down in front of her as she hides her face in her hands. "Miscommunication. Russ, we did the miscommunication thing. You made me a miscommunicator!"

This conversation is too much to process. "A what?"

"We could have just had a conversation. This is not the kind of main character moment I'm looking for in my life!" She groans loudly, peeking at me between her fingers.

Reaching forward, I wrestle her hands away from her face so she has to look at me. Her head tilts to the side as she takes me in, her expression falling somewhere between frustration and relief. "I'm sorry, Rory. I always fuck everything up. I mean it when I say I didn't mean to hurt your feelings."

"If you hadn't avoided me last night, drunk me would have probably asked why you were acting weird during Truth or Dare, loudly and with an audience, so we'd have gotten to the bottom of it one way or another." Her left hand is still holding mine, but her right is drawing patterns across my palm. I know I should stand up and leave now that we're both on the same page, but lack of self-control is clearly a Callaghan trait.

"Drunk you nearly got us caught by Jenna last night." I sigh. "I can't promise I'm going to be around when you're being reckless, Aurora. I really need this job and I can't risk being fired, so if it happens again, please don't think I'm avoiding you."

She groans again, this time accompanied by a dramatic eye roll, but her fingers keep dancing across my skin. "I don't think I'm going to drink anymore anyway. But nobody ever actually gets fired, Russ. People break all kind of rules while they're here and nothing ever happens."

The memory of how soft Aurora felt beneath me invades my brain.

Think with your head, not your dick, Callaghan. "I don't want to test that theory."

"But testing the theory is the fun part." She smiles at me, a real one that makes a little line appear at the corner of her eyes. "And the trick is to not get caught."

Her eyes burn into me and I should look away, but I can't. They travel down to my lips, then back to my eyes, her teeth sinking into her lip.

I want to kiss her.

She looks like she wants to be kissed.

It takes every shred of restraint not to lean in, especially when she's looking at me like that. Sighing, I force myself to remember why I'm here and what I'm avoiding. "I just want to peacefully co-exist with you and stay out of trouble, Aurora."

She shrugs, dropping her hands into her lap as I stand. "That's fine. I'm supposed to be working on myself or something anyway. It was really clear in my head, now it's kind of fuzzy. I should probably get back to doing that."

"I need to go before someone comes looking for me. I don't want them to think it's weird we're here alone. I'm sorry again, I'm glad we've cleared this up." It's an oddly formal response to a personal revelation, but the longer I'm around her the easier it becomes to want to test her theory.

Thankfully she doesn't call me out. I watch as she unscrews the orange juice and holds it up to me. "To our peaceful coexistence."

Chapter Twelve

RUSS

"Why do you look like the golden retriever that got the bacon?"
Xander says suspiciously, scrutinizing every inch of me.

"The what?" I watch Salmon's and Trout's ears twitch at the mention of bacon and it immediately becomes clear why Xander is their favorite this morning.

"It's like the cat that got the cream, but relatable, y'know?"

"It's just my face." And the relief of not having to avoid someone I don't want to avoid. "Grab that paintbrush for me?"

My roommate does not look convinced as he hands me the brush.
"You were gone a long time taking Aurora breakfast this morning."
I imagine him adding, "And now you're in a good mood," and even though he doesn't say it, the smug look on his face is enough to assume that's what he's thinking.

"I don't think I was that long."

"She's so hot. I might see if she wants to pair up at the swimming training later," he says carefully, in a way that tells me he's baiting me.
"What do you think about that?"

Not looking at him, I concentrate on making sure I have enough paint and paintbrushes, knowing I'll immediately give myself away. "I think that's a great idea."

"You're such a fucking liar, Callaghan." He laughs. "Fine. Have your secret summer of fun. I'll just be lonely in our cabin with my dogs."

"Our dogs."

He leans against the wall beside me. "It's always the quiet ones."

"I haven't even done anything." Don't look at him. "It's all in your imagination."

"Oh cool, my bad. I'll let Clay know he's got a shot with her then."

The words almost refuse to come out of my mouth. "Yeah, you should."

Xander snorts, punching me in the shoulder gently. "Your secret is safe with me. They don't call me an unproblematic king for nothing."

This time I can't help but look at him as my eyebrows pinch together. I take the bait. "Who calls you an unproblematic king?"

"I do."

"Okay, unproblematic king. I'll be near the tennis court if you want me." Collecting my equipment, I head to my project for the rest of the morning. One of our responsibilities this week is getting the camp ready for the campers, and this chill morning activity is a nice change of pace from the constant training and icebreakers.

Nobody has asked me to share about myself, I don't have to remember which order to tie something together, or what to do if someone stops breathing. I'm painting fence panels and dragging furniture and wiping stuff down and, other than Xander, nobody has been bothering me.

I feel good after my talk with Aurora earlier and I'm less worried about how I'm going to get through the summer with her.

"Birds are gross." Turning toward the voice, I lower the hose I'm using to wash down a picnic table some birds have made their personal toilet. Aurora looks more alive than she did earlier, carrying a thermos in each hand, with a shy smile on her lips. "I brought you coffee. If you want it, obviously."

I've watched her do sweet gestures for people since we got here—filling up everyone's water bottles, being the first to help people struggling during training, distracting Maya from her homesickness. Now I've earned the same treatment. "Coffee is good, thanks."

"You're welcome," she says, handing it over. "I thought you might need it. I saw you running super early this morning; I forgot to mention it earlier. You don't sleep much, huh?"

I hate running, but it's one of the only things I can do to clear my head. Like Xander said when we arrived, occasionally your phone comes to life and messages come through. This morning, my mind was already working overtime after dealing with drunk Aurora, so when it started buzzing in the early hours I checked it.

The first thing I saw was a message from my mom with a picture of her and Dad out for dinner, smiling into the camera like nothing's wrong. That triggered my curiosity and I started to scroll up, eventually piecing together that Dad had won big somewhere and they were celebrating. The frustration was enough to have me running before anyone was awake.

Dad's addiction issue has never been with alcohol; it's gambling. The alcohol consoles him after losing, and like most gambling addicts, he loses a lot. It's the alcohol that turns him nasty, and that's when his texts start to change into something harsher. When he's on a winning streak, he's a different man, but streaks are what gamblers say is happening to make it seem like some kind of skill is involved and not purely a series of lucky occurrences.

Aurora is still waiting for me to answer.

Talking about my parents feels like opening Pandora's box. I sometimes wonder if the load would feel as heavy if I had someone to confide in, but I can't bring myself to tell anyone. Even though

Henry knows my history, I still find it difficult to tell him as stuff happens. It's embarrassing to admit that my own dad doesn't care about me as much as he cares about betting slips.

I settle for my default vague answer. "Not much, no. I'm used to it, though, don't worry. I can't believe you were up early enough to see me."

She takes my thermos back, her hand brushing mine ever so slightly, just enough to send sparks up my arms, and places them both on the now clean table. I watch her as she methodically unscrews and presses buttons until she's poured me a cup. "Would you believe me if I told you I was meditating?"

"No." I accept the coffee cup, watching her over the rim as I take a sip.

"I was sick. That's why I was awake so early," she says, laughing awkwardly as she pours herself a tea from her own thermos. "I like to think it was food poisoning and not the excessive amount of tequila I drank last night. You may remember it; I was the one making a fool of myself in front of you."

"I do vaguely remember having to decline your skinny-dipping offer."

Her cheeks flush pink, eyes widen. God, it feels good not to be the one blushing for once. "If you'll excuse me, I need to find a hungry raccoon and feed myself to it. Bye."

I grab her hand as she tries to turn to leave. "It was funny, in a very stressful I-don't-want-to-be-alone-with-this-drunk-girl-wanting-to-get-naked way."

When I realize she's not leaving, I let go of her hand. She clears her throat and sips from her cup, watching me carefully as she lowers it. "Do you need any help today? Emilia banished me from the dance area."

"Why?"

She kicks out her leg, the darkening purple indicator of bruising spreading across her shin. "I was bored because she's a control freak and I tried to hurdle the freestanding ballet barres."

The laugh that rips out of me is so loud I don't realize it's me until she starts laughing, too. Dragging a hand down my face, I shake it off. "If I let you help me, can you be good?"

"Usually, with the right motivation."

I sense I shouldn't ask further, but I can't help myself. As much as I don't want to be, I'm the moth and Aurora is the brightest flame. "What's enough motivation for you?"

Her teeth sink into her lip again while she pretends to think and my brain flashes back to a very different scenario where I watched her do that. "You thinking I'm good."

I'm going to get burned. "All right then, grab a paintbrush."

AURORA HAS HER LEGS OVER my shoulders. Again.

This time she's sitting on them to paint the highest point of the storage shed, but the same inappropriate thoughts remain. My hands cling to her thighs, which are warming my ears, and her hand is intwined in my hair while her other swishes the paintbrush against the wood.

"Have you ever seen *Ratatouille*?" she asks, running her fingers through my hair again.

It's hard not to physically react to goose bumps spreading down my body. "Of course I have, why?"

"I feel like the rat." She tugs on my hair gently. "Should we see if I can make you cook?"

"Excuse you." I squeeze her thighs playfully and her hand tightens in my hair. "His name is Remy."

"My apologies, I didn't realize I was in the presence of a *Ratatouille* expert. Okay, I think we're done up here."

The shed looks ten times better than it did when we started, and while it probably wasn't necessary to spend so long working on a random structure, the lack of interruptions has been nice.

"Russ?"

"Yeah?"

"Which bit of your hair do I need to pull for you to let me down?"

"Oh shit, sorry." I crouch low enough for her to climb off, and it's pathetic that my first instinct is to work out if there's anything else we can paint together. "You did a great job."

Her eyes brighten at the praise, and slowly, the tiny pieces of what I know about her are beginning to fit together. "I couldn't have done it without you. Literally."

There's a smudge of brown paint decorating her jawline; I instinctively reach out, thumb rubbing against it, but it doesn't vanish. "You're so messy."

"You have no idea," she says quietly.

Now that we're alone, I want to ask about what she said this morning. I'm curious about why she thinks she needs to work on herself. From the snippets of information she's shared during the icebreakers we've done and our first interaction at the party, it's hard to believe she's anything but the confident woman she comes across as. Yeah, she can be a little awkward occasionally, but so can I. The problem I have is that asking questions tends to invite questions back—and that's something I'd selfishly rather avoid.

Aurora takes my silence for what it is, a closed door, and we both stand on the outside of this thing hanging between us. She drops the paintbrush into the tray and reaches for the hose I was using earlier, pressing the lever down as she points it directly at my chest.

My jaw drops as the cold water drenches me and a surprised laugh bubbles out. The look in her eyes is the exact same as the one she gave me when I found her in our kitchen: mischief.

"Au—" The spray hits me again. "Okay, you asked for it . . ."

It's more of a squeal than a scream as I close the gap between us with a couple of strides. She tries to cling to the hose, turning her back to me to protect it. Her body is flush against my wet T-shirt, vibrating as she laughs, attempting to fight me off. It's not hard to grab it from her and point it downward over the top of her head.

"It's freezing!" she cries, fighting to redirect it at me. "Okay, truce! Truce!"

I let it fall to the ground and step back. The wet material is clinging to my body and she's right, it is freezing. Grabbing the back of my T-shirt, I pull it over my head, wringing out the worst of it. "We didn't think this through."

She squeezes out the water from her hair, watching me. Her clothes are relatively dry. "I dunno, doesn't feel like a bad choice to me."

I don't have the chance to ask what she means before I hear the signature jingle of dog collars—Xander must have run out of bacon. Fish, Salmon, and Trout find me no matter where I am, but this time, they've brought a friend.

"Do I want to know why you have no T-shirt on?" Emilia asks as she approaches us. She turns to Aurora. "You look like a drowned rat."

"Rude," she mumbles. "His name is Remy."

"I—wait, what?" Emilia says. I'm still trying to make my T-shirt dry enough to put back on and Aurora still seems to be trying to concentrate on Emilia, not me. "I've come to free you from your exile. Jenna asked me to take the truck and pick up the egg order from the farm near the mini golf. It wasn't delivered or something and everyone else is too busy."

"Why can't Jenna go?" Aurora asks, squeezing out water from the ends of her hair. I sit on the ground cross-legged and both puppies immediately settle in the gap between my thighs while I stroke Fish.

"She said the farmer is a dick and she hates him with the fire of a thousand suns. I think they had a fight when she called him about the delivery. The truck's a stick, so I need you."

"You know how to drive stick?" I ask, quietly impressed.

She nods, doing a double take when she spots me with my furry fan club. "My dad owns a car company, well kinda, and I've spent a lot of time in Europe. Are you going to be okay on your own?"

I don't ask any follow-up questions about the "car company" because then I would have to admit I've talked about her with my friends and I know her dad owns a Formula 1 team. I want to offer to go with her instead of Emilia, but I think that'd be weird. "I'll be fine. Go get the eggs."

"See you at the lake later," she says, walking toward Emilia.

Emilia waves as she turns, wrapping an arm around Aurora's shoulders before heading back the way she came. "That looked cozy," I hear her say.

JUST WHEN I START TO think coexisting will be easy, Aurora takes two tiny shreds of material decorated with daisies and calls it a bikini.

"It's so cute," Maya tells her. "I love the cut."

The cut? How can Maya concentrate on the cut when most of Aurora's ass is out?

"Stay strong, brother," Xander whispers beside me. I ignore him, still attempting not to feed into his suspicions. There's nothing to be suspicious about, but I still don't need to tell him about what happened before we got here.

"Rory," Jenna sighs as she approaches the six of us waiting at the end of the dock. "Where's your one-piece?"

"It's drying in my cabin because butterfingers over there spilled orange juice on it," she responds, gesturing to Emilia with her head. Jenna folds her arms across her chest and Aurora mirrors her. "Nobody is going to die if they see my stomach for an hour. I know not to wear it when the kids arrive."

Jenna pinches the bridge of her nose between her thumb and forefinger, shaking her head. If I didn't already know otherwise, I'd assume Jenna and Aurora were sisters. They don't look alike—Aurora is tall and blond while Jenna is short with black hair—but the way they bicker and love each other reminds me of siblings. "I only came to share that your instructor is running late. He won't be long."

The camp has multiple fully trained and properly qualified lifeguards, but for additional safety, counselors are also given basic water safety training to keep themselves safe, as well as any campers.

Emilia waits until Jenna is heading back to the shore before pushing an unsuspecting Xander into the water, instantly triggering a power struggle between the rest of us. Small hands dig into the base of my spine, but the force is only enough to move me an inch. I can hear Aurora huffing and puffing behind me as she tries to push me, which is why it's so easy to grab her hands and pull her in with me as I jump from the dock.

The water is colder than I was expecting, but it's a welcome change from the heat, and when I kick myself back to the surface, I'm greeted with pouty lips and bright eyes. "That was cruel," Aurora says, splashing me with her hand as she treads water beside me. "I wasn't ready!"

I push back the wet hair stuck to my forehead, laughing at how pissed she looks, which doubles when I send a wave of water in her direction with my hand. The laugh that erupts out of her is goddamn magical. Unfiltered, loud, raw. Her eyes pierce me as she smiles, droplets of water clinging to her eyelashes, freckles dusting the bridge of her nose.

She's so fucking beautiful it hurts.

Oh, man. I'm not supposed to be this attracted to her.

Why do I love to make myself miserable?

Her hand rises out of the water and I preemptively brace, waiting for her to drench me again with water, until the horrified squeal she lets out has me grabbing her hand and pulling her toward me.

"Something touched my foot!" Her legs wrap around my waist and her chest presses flush to mine as she clings to me. "I'm going to cry."

I'm pretty sure this isn't the survival training anyone had in mind.

I'm pretty sure I'm not going to survive having her wrapped around me.

"It'll be a plant or something, don't worry."

Aurora leans back, putting some distance between our bodies so she can look at my face, but keeping her legs crossed at the bottom of my back. "It could be a shark."

I can't help but snort. "It's not a shark. We're in freshwater. We're also in California."

"Bull sharks are diadromous, they can survive in freshwater." My eyebrow quirks. "What? I watch *Shark Week*."

"If it's a bull shark, sorry to be the one to tell you, but you're screwed."

She grins as her hands link at the nape of my neck. "If it's a bull shark, we're both screwed because I'm dragging you with me. You're bigger, you'll taste better."

"Trust me, you taste incredible."

I stun us both. I didn't mean to say it out loud. Her eyes flick to my lips, then back to my eyes, and her breathing slows. "Oh," is the only thing she says, and that response is enough to pray it is a shark and it's about to save me from myself.

Chapter Thirteen

AURORA

TWO SUMMERS AWAY HAD MADE me forget how much I truly love Honey Acres.

After we completed our week of training with minimal further incident or embarrassment, our campers arrived a few days ago, full of excitement and trepidation, but mainly sugar, and I feel like my feet haven't touched the ground since.

I've traveled to so many different places with Formula 1, experienced some of the best the world has to offer, and this dot on a map in the middle of nowhere in California is my favorite place on earth.

It makes me feel so content, watching the people I've gotten to know become comfort counselors for kids, some of whom are away from home for the first time. It's only been a few days, but I finally feel like I'm doing something with purpose. I've been so tired and busy it hasn't occurred to me to check my cell phone, and after Russ and I finally cleared the air, I spend my time thinking about how to make things the most fun and not overthinking.

I've already replaced Emilia with two new best friends, Freya and Sadia, two eight-year-olds in our group, because they said they liked my freckles and I'm really tall. That's nicer than Emilia has ever been to me, so she's out. She totally understood when I told her, and she confirmed she's also replaced me with Tammy, a nine-year-old fellow ballerina who in the few days she's been here has not attempted to hurdle the ballet barre.

Xander and Russ watched Emilia and me argue playfully for five minutes, heads moving between us like they were watching a tennis match, until Xander finally wrapped an arm around Russ and declared he'd never replace him.

Russ has been the most relaxed I've seen him in the past few days. He's amazing with each and every kid in our group, knowing exactly what to say or do to get them involved or bring them out of their shell. I'm careful not to stare in awe too much because kids at this age notice absolutely everything, and the last thing I need is to be hounded about whether he's my boyfriend.

There are twenty campers, aged eight to ten, in our Brown Bears group, and what I apparently didn't consider before asking for this age group is eight- to ten-year-olds are really fucking nosy. It's tricky territory for me, a chronic oversharer desperate for any kind of acceptance she can get, but I've managed to keep my mouth closed so far. Plus, Russ has no intention of being my boyfriend given his love of rule keeping. Not that I want him to be my boyfriend, but an only semi-celibate summer would be nice.

Only eight and a bit more weeks to go.

The kids are currently having an hour break after lunch to keep them out of the sun at the hottest time of the day and give them a chance to wind down after a morning of horse riding, archery, and volleyball. Making my way across the camp, I immediately spot Russ and Emilia watching something near the Brown Bears' cabin.

"What're you doing?" I ask as I approach the two of them. I'm immediately greeted with shushing. Russ points toward a shaded area beside the cabin, where several of our campers appear to be coordinating a routine of sorts. Blocking the sun from my eyes with my hand, I watch in silence with them for two minutes before asking again, "What're you doing?"

"We've been trying to work out what they're doing for five minutes," Emilia says. "But we can't decide if they're playing together or plotting to take over a small country."

"Maybe it's a ritual," Russ clarifies, shrugging when I glare at him, confused.

"You two should not be left in charge of children. They're clearly practicing for the end-of-summer talent show. They must have been here before. Smart to get a head start. We should have done that."

"Sorry, back up," Russ says, stepping in front of me, eyebrows pinched together. "Why should we have done that?"

I lower my hand. "My favorite thing about you is you're big enough to block out the sun," I say, referring to his six-five frame.

Emilia shuffles closer to me, standing in the shade Russ creates. "Oh, you really are."

"Aurora, why did you say we should have been practicing? Practicing what exactly?"

"Did Xander not tell you about the talent show? Everyone has to do something, including the counselors. They'll announce it on Sunday most likely; that's what they used to do when I was here."

I've never seen him so distressed, and I've just spent a week watching him awkwardly stumble his way through compulsory sharing about himself. His jaw is tight as he chews the inside of his cheek, and I struggle to stay focused on his concern as my mind begins to wander to the image of him dancing on a stage.

"Are you gonna throw up?" Emilia asks, taking a step away from us.

"I have no talent," he says.

I want to tell him that's not true, since I've personally witnessed what he can do with his mouth, but that is counterproductive to our fledgling friendship.

"I'm sure you do," I offer. "What about hockey?"

"I can't play hockey at a talent show. Can I cheer you on from the audience? It's better for everyone if I'm not involved."

"No, you have to do it. I love the talent show. I look forward to it all summer. The kids do, too."

He sighs, tilting his head back to the sky before looking at me again. "It's really important to you?"

I nod. "I was tutored when I was younger because we traveled with my dad's job. I didn't have school plays and talent shows. This was the only chance I had, and it made me feel less lonely."

"Fine. I'll do it."

"Promise?" I ask, holding out my pinkie. "You have to come to all the rehearsals."

He links his pinkie with mine. "Promise."

"That was Aurora's really wholesome way of emotionally blackmailing you into participating, Russ, and you fell for it," Emilia says. "Have you considered showing hockey through the medium of contemporary dance?"

"You're the goalie, right?" His reaction switches to surprise and he nods. "I'll throw stuff at you and you can block it. There. Talent."

Dragging a hand through his hair, he slides it to the back of his neck, digging his fingers into his skin to ease out tension. "Why does this feel like you just want to throw stuff at me?"

"You know her so well," Emilia jokes, turning her back to us to watch the kids dancing around again.

Russ smiles, the dimples of his cheeks making me lose my train of thought until he speaks again. "Maybe that's my talent."

"You don't need to feel nervous," I say quietly so only he can hear me. "Promise?"

"I promise."

AFTER A WEEK OF SETTLING in, camp is in full swing and my soccer elective sign-up sheet is almost full. I'm buzzing with excitement.

Following lunch and break time, the campers get to pick how to spend their afternoon by signing up for different counselor-led activities. After having their morning decided for them, the kids have a chance to do things more suited to their personal preferences.

The only thing I've ever been good at is getting myself into trouble, but Jenna said I wasn't allowed to put that down as an option. I thought about doubling up with Emilia to offer dance, but she immediately told me to get my uncoordinated body away from her studio. So I'm teaching soccer because it's pretty hard for me to screw that up.

It's near impossible not to have a good understanding of it when you spent your childhood around as many English men as I did. I just need to act confident and the kids will think I'm actually good at it.

I know my nearly full sign-up sheet doesn't really mean anything, but there's something soothing about knowing you're offering an activity they like and are excited about. And I know it's not about me, it's about the fact they want to play soccer. But it feels a little about me, and I'm happy they like me enough to choose to spend time learning from me.

Even if I'm about to make it up as I go.

Russ approaches as I'm spacing the colorful markers across the grass. "You need help?"

"You're supposed to be enjoying your day off."

Cool and calm. Don't get distracted by how pretty he is.

"I am enjoying my day off." His lips tug at the side, dimples appearing. "And I'm excited to learn about soccer."

He picks up a handful of markers from the stand and begins copying me, placing them on the ground at the right distance for kids to dribble a ball between. I repeat *cool and calm* in my head as he picks up the agility ladder and begins to spread it next to where I've already put the others. I'm making a conscious effort not to fill silences with nonsense because Russ is a quiet guy and I'm scared he'll get tired of me, but every quiet second feels like a missed opportunity to open him up a bit.

Plus, when I'm around him, I truly have no idea what's going to come out of my mouth.

I have nothing of value to say, so I settle for small talk, which some would argue is worse than rambling. "Where's your lover?"

"She's asleep in my cabin. It's too hot for her, but it's pretty cool down there."

My head whips up so quickly my neck crunches. "Wait, what?"

Russ stops what he's doing and there's a moment where we just stare at each other. He's trying to understand why I'm confused and I'm trying to work out if he's really telling me what I think he's telling me. Jumping to conclusions is silly, but I don't exactly pride myself on my levelheadedness.

He moves closer, until he's standing right in front of me, the soft smile from earlier still there. "Rory, I'm talking about Fish. Were you talking about Xander?"

Okay, see? This is a learning experience. "Yeah, I thought . . . I was trying not to jump . . . yeah. Yeah, I was talking about Xander."

He's trying not to laugh at me, which I appreciate because I'm trying to think of the best hiding place on site; I've found tons of great hiding places over the years, he'd never find me. I could live peacefully with the animals, like Snow White.

"He's having a nap with the dogs. I didn't change my entire personality and start fucking random women I work with in the middle of the day."

The way he says *fucking random women* makes me feel strange; it sounds alien coming from his mouth.

"I thought you might be ready to say fuck the rules. It's hard work being good all the time." It's not that hard now that I'm trying. It took getting drunk and hearing how committed Russ is to keeping this job to make me realize I needed to uphold the commitments I made to myself when I got here.

Continuing the same cycle of getting hurt and acting out doesn't benefit me, and it's not why I wanted to come back to Honey Acres. This is the longest I've stuck to anything that doesn't involve being petty.

"I'm not there yet, but you'll be the first to know if I feel like getting into trouble."

He's flirting with me. I'm 99 percent—okay, more like 87 percent—sure he's flirting with me. Where is Emilia when I need her? I need a second opinion. I need to respond with something smart and funny, and more important, something that tells him I am not above having sex in the woods.

I've got to stop forgetting about the universe's intention to mess with me because not even ten seconds later, I spot Clay and Maya walking toward us, followed closely by a crowd of eager soon-to-be soccer players. Maybe it's not the universe, maybe I just keep forgetting that I'm here to look after the kids and not just to stare at Russ's massive thighs in his shorts.

Either way, it's not the second opinion I was looking for.

The class goes by without a hitch, the flirtation percentage certainty reducing every time I think about it. By evening, I've survived another round of dining hall chaos, a dance, and making sure everyone gets ready for bed. The day is over and I'm totally exhausted, which significantly reduces my chances of getting into mischief. Emilia went to bed an hour ago after her nightly phone catch-up with Poppy, and I've been trying to summon the energy to get out of this very comfortable chair beside the campfire for twenty minutes.

Salmon is snoring on my chest, the heat of the fire is keeping us both warm, and there's a chance I could just fall asleep instead. My eyes are trying to close and I'm fighting to keep them open, knowing if I fall asleep here, someone will definitely draw on my face.

"Are you asleep?"

Opening one eye, I spot Russ standing over me, looking as fresh as he did this morning. "Yes, go away."

He chuckles, and it's annoying how great he looks all the time. I know how little sleep he gets, and I know how hard he works all day, and yet here he is—bright-eyed and bushy-tailed. "Come on, I'll walk you to your cabin. You can't fall asleep here. Xander said he's going to draw a dick on your face if you do."

"But I can't disturb the puppy," I groan, gesturing to my fluffy stomach warmer. "I think she's doubled in weight in, like, a week, so I'm not sure I could get her off me if I tried."

"Xander taught her to do tricks for turkey bacon. I'll pick her up, come on."

"Can't you pick both of us up? I'm asleep."

I try not to shiver when his hands brush my stomach as he scoops up the golden retriever, positioning her on his chest like you would a baby. I don't manage it, but he's polite enough to pretend not to notice. "You have legs and you don't have a bellyful of bacon."

He holds out a hand for me, pulling me to my feet gently. "How do you know that? Rude presumption."

"You're a vegetarian, Rory," he laughs. "If you're learning tricks for turkey bacon we have bigger problems than you having a dick on your face." He makes it so easy. There are so many things I could say, but I bite my tongue to keep them in. Russ shakes his head, ushering me away from the fire pit and in the direction of my cabin. "Don't say a thing."

"It's fine. You've made it clear who your favorite is. Salmon has legs, too, but whatever. Just know if I manage to befriend a real brown bear, you're dropping to second choice like that," I say, clicking my fingers.

"I—" he starts, then stops, and as we continue the walk to the cabin, when I look over at him, I can't read the look on his face. My watching snaps him out of whatever daze he was in and he laughs, but it sounds forced. "I think I can cope with being your second choice, but we don't have brown bears in California. I haven't been able to figure out how it fits in with Hedgehogs, Foxes, and Raccoons, since I read the brochure."

"Orla introduced the animal names for age groups when she took over from her dad. She thought it was more fun than being named for ages or something, and she let Jenna pick the names when she was like five or six. I can't remember the full story, but, yeah, baby Jenna doesn't know her bears apparently."

"Jenna came here as a kid, too?" he asks, running his palm down the puppy's back. "It's pretty cool she works here now."

"What? Jenna is Orla's daughter. Did you not know?" I say. "I thought everyone knew that, sorry."

His expression is hard to pinpoint, somewhere between amusement and despair. "Of course my boss is the owner's daughter."

We finally reach the cabins and I wish there was a reason to keep walking and talking. He stops as I reach the steps. I take the first one and stop, too, reluctant to say good-bye.

He takes a step closer and lowers his voice, presumably not wanting to wake Emilia, but I'm closer to his height on this step and his body is dangerously close to mine. "Jenna said we have to stop carrying the puppies everywhere, because soon they'll be too big, but they'll still expect it. She also said they're dogs not babies, but I can't help it."

My jaw drops. "I'm sorry, are you telling me that you're breaking rules?"

"It was more of a suggestion . . ."

"It's a rule and you're rebelling. Oh my God."

"I'm not. I'm ju—"

"You're out of control, Callaghan. That's how it starts. One minute you're carrying a puppy, the next minute you've crashed a boat you weren't supposed to be on into the rocks and are being threatened with deportation." His eyes narrow at my far-too-specific example. "Theoretically. Anyway, I'd invite you in, but unlike you, I respect authority and apparently there's something about cabins and not dragging men and their comfort animal into them."

"Who knew you could be such a good girl."

I almost choke. "Good night, Russ. Thanks for walking me."

I step backward up the remaining steps onto the porch of my cabin. Space between us is good. Space means I don't lean forward and kiss him. Or attempt to climb him like a tree.

"Good night, Aurora," he says softly. "Sweet dreams."

Turning my back to him, I quietly open the door, careful not to wake my sleeping roommate. When I look over my shoulder, he's still standing next to the steps. "What're you doing?"

"I'm watching you go in so you don't have to watch me leave."

My heart is in my throat as I close the door gently behind me, and when I finally get into bed, I decide that it was definitely flirting.

Chapter Fourteen

RUSS

I DIDN'T THINK THERE WOULD ever be a time where I'd voluntarily apply JJ's advice to my life and actually benefit from it, and yet here I am.

"The only person who knows you're not confident is you" is something he said to me to be confident with women, but I'm currently applying that to everyone, and surprisingly, it's working. Unnecessary worry is a mentally exhausting process, and by definition, there's no logic to it. All it does is make me feel alone, even when I'm surrounded by people.

The team has settled into a comfortable routine with all our campers, and Aurora and I have settled into a comfortable routine when we're not with the kids. Every time I walk her back to her cabin it gets harder not to kiss her good night, especially when she looks like she's thinking about it, too, but I'm grateful for her making an effort to keep us out of trouble.

I think I'm grateful.

I'm enjoying breakfast with Emilia when the woman always on my mind comes stomping toward us. She sits down beside her best friend and huffs. "Never again. I mean it. I will pay. I will fake my own death. I don't care about the consequences."

Hiding my laugh with my coffee mug, I check over my shoulder to make sure there are no listening ears from the kids still eating breakfast. Xander sits down beside me, his plate suspiciously loaded with bacon. I lean in, whispering, "Stop feeding the dogs."

He keeps looking at his plate as he shakes his head. "You're not my mom. I don't have to listen to you."

"Surely it wasn't bad," Emilia says to a still scowling Aurora, also fighting a laugh.

All our campers sleep in one cabin and we each take turns sleeping in there to supervise overnight a couple of times a week. There's always a senior like Jenna available overnight for emergencies, so as long as your kids aren't acting up, it's easy.

Maya was feeling sick yesterday, so Aurora volunteered to cover the night shift, incorrectly thinking she would be with Xander. When she realized she would be with Clay, she looked like the world was ending.

Yeah, petty me was happy about that.

"Sure it was bad, Emilia," she grumbles. "He told me he doesn't mind cuddling if I'm scared of the dark. I know he's joking, but he's so much funnier when he's not trying to be funny."

Emilia's eyes roll. "What did you say?"

"I told him I sleep stab." I almost choke on my coffee. "Which I thought was the end of it, but he started telling me it sounded like there was something under my bed and for me to wait on his while he investigated."

"You gotta admire the creativity," Xander says. "Being a douche bag is difficult in this day and age, but here he is, hustling."

Aurora's eyes lock on him murderously. "Jessica was coming to ask me to get her teddy that'd fallen down the side of her bed and overheard Clay joke that it could be a murderer under there and she started screaming. Then everyone else started screaming. I'm surprised you didn't freaking hear it. My ears are still ringing. It took, like, two hours to get everybody back into bed and calmed down."

"I slept like a baby," Xander says, taking a bite of his toast.

"I didn't. You snore," I grumble into my coffee.

"Damn," Emilia laughs. "I just thought the kids were all tired and gloomy because of how long the line is to call home for Father's Day."

My shoulders instantly sag; it's Sunday.

Aurora looks like she was told she has to pair with Clay again and I feel the same. It's a day. I know it's just a day, but it's one that feels extra loud and extra in your face when you don't have a good relationship with your dad.

One of the activities earlier in the week was making Father's Day cards for the kids to send home, and even though I knew it was coming, I still feel caught off guard.

Xander starts laughing. "Easiest way to work out who has daddy issues. Tell them it's Father's Day. What a bonding moment for us all."

"Speak for yourself," Emilia quips. "My dad is the best guy I know."

"And I, just this second, decided not to spiral today, so share your misery with someone else, thank you very much," Rory adds, giving him a sweet smile. "I will spiral later, alone, like a regular person. Or if I'm feeling really adventurous, I'll bottle it up and bury it deep down, letting it erupt at a much later, more inconvenient time."

"What can we do today with the kids?" I ask, changing the topic to avoid being dragged into this conversation too much. "What do they love the most?"

"Paint dodgeball," Xander and Rory say in unison.

Her eyebrow raises as Xander whispers, "Did we just become best friends?"

Aurora grabs herself breakfast while we work out what we need and Clay and Maya join us, immediately on board with our plan. Sundays are usually pretty chilled out; after a week of constantly scheduled activities everyone's tired, so we plan more low-key days and it means everyone has energy for the Sunday barbecue and evening event, which is usually movie night or a show.

Nothing sounds low-key about paint and dodgeball being in the same sentence.

When everything's arranged, Xander and I take the kids back to their room to clean up for the inspection. Brown Bears are currently in the lead in the camp rankings, which my colleagues have attributed to me and my need to keep things tidy.

Cleaning is more of a habit than a hobby. My dad's moods were often unpredictable when I lived at home; his gambling losses made him irritable and it often felt like he was trying to pick an argument. I hated getting into trouble, so I did what I could to prevent those arguments from happening.

I did my homework as soon as I got it, sometimes even during breaks at school. I constantly had odd jobs around our neighborhood so I never had to ask him for money. I kept everything spotless so he never had a reason to complain about things being untidy.

None of it ever mattered. After a loss and a drink, my dad could find an argument in an empty room, but the habits have stayed with me. Now they're going to help win some pizza. Go figure.

The morning moves at its usual Sunday slow pace. We set up five-aside soccer for the kids with energy, and puzzles and crafts for the others. I spend more time watching Aurora excitedly run around cheering on her players than I do trying to make the origami dove I'm supposed to be working on.

"You have a big, fat crush on Rory," Michael, a ten-year-old who apparently doesn't know how to read the room, says. "You keep watching her."

"That's inappropriate," I reply, suddenly very focused on my origami. "Rory is my friend. I'm watching the game."

"You didn't say you don't have a crush on her."

"I also didn't say I did."

He lets it go for now and I quietly breathe a sigh of relief that Michael's parents are actors and not lawyers, like some of the kids here who are really good at debating.

When it's time to usher everyone back into the dining hall, my dove is finally folded. Maya and Xander start leading the group for lunch, but I hang back to tidy up the various half-completed games and craft projects littering the table.

"Let me help you," a soft voice says, coming up behind me.

"I'm good, don't worry. Take a seat," I say to Aurora. "You must be tired."

She sits down in front of the half-finished jigsaw, staring down at it before starting to disconnect the pieces. "This is how I feel about you sometimes, y'know."

I'm looking at her; the apples of her cheeks are pink from running around all morning, her hair pinned back out of her face, showcasing the extra freckles decorating her nose after three weeks in the sun every day. She keeps taking the puzzle apart bit by bit, putting it back into the box. "Like you want to put me in a box?" I joke, unsure what she's talking about.

"No, like you're a jigsaw puzzle and I have all the outside pieces but I haven't worked out how all the inside ones fit together yet."

"I made something for you," I say, changing the subject quickly. "It's not very good. I was distracted watching you miss the goal every time."

Her shoulders shake as she laughs. "I'm so bad. I'm literally a goalie's dream."

"You are." She finally looks up as I put the paper dove down in front of her. "Speaking as a goalie, that is."

She picks up the dove, holding it in her hand like it's the most precious thing in the world even though it's terrible. "I love it. Thank you, Russ."

THE RULES OF PAINT DODGEBALL are the same as regular dodge-ball. The difference is your ball is actually a sponge, which you dip into one of the many paint mixtures dotted around the grass before launching at your opponents. Each round has a color to make it clear who's in and who's out.

Given the fact my opponents are mainly children, coupled with my long history of athletics, it didn't occur to me to be worried about getting covered in paint. But as the sponge hits me square in the chest, green paint spraying out from the impact, I realize my certainty was misplaced.

Aurora's expression is victorious as she shakes the excess green paint from her hand. The girl has an arm on her, which is fucking hot. I'm not ready to explore how her ability to beat me turns me on.

"I thought you were good at blocking stuff," she yells from the other side of the centerline.

"I told you I have no talent!"

"I can think of a few things you're very talented at."

I'll take her thinking I'm good in bed over being good at paint dodgeball any day of the week.

Leaving the court, since she knocked me out, I take a seat next to Maya, who's also covered in various paints. "When did eight-year-olds get so competitive?"

We watch everyone continue the game. My eyes close for a second as I turn toward the sun, loving the heat on my face. That's when something wet hits my leg. Snapping my eyes open, I immediately spot Rory smiling.

Maya laughs, handing me a towel. "She's gonna give you two away."

My stomach sinks. "We're no . . . There's nothing to give away."

"Sure, mate. Sure."

THE COMMUNAL BATHROOM IS BIG enough for both me and Aurora—several more of us in fact—and yet we're standing so close to each other I can feel the heat radiating from her body.

"It's no use," she groans, wiping the wet cloth across her neck over and over. "I'm destined to look like a colorful dalmatian forever."

"Come here." Lifting at her waist, I sit her on the counter and take the cloth from her hand. Her knees slide apart, letting me step between them as I gently tilt her face upward, giving me access to the parts of her painted different colors. "They really got you good."

As soon as the kids realized how good Aurora was, she became their biggest target. She hums as I slowly clean along her jawline, and when I move down her neck, she shivers. Her cheeks flush pink, but we both ignore it and whatever it might mean. "How are you today?" she asks, ending the silence between us.

"You don't like silence, huh?"

"You don't like answering questions, huh?"

"Okay, you got me there. Today was, uh, honestly easier than I was expecting. Being distracted helps, I think. What about you?"

"Same. I think all I've ever really wanted was for people to want to spend time with me. Because my dad just doesn't, no matter which way people sugarcoat it, and my mom wants to spend time with me but—" I move her face slowly, tilting it to get the other side of it. "I can't describe it without sounding horrible. Like, I don't know. She suffocates me sometimes and it's too much. But the kids want me around because they think I'm nice, and as pathetic as that sounds, it means a lot to me."

"It's not pathetic."

"And they can't leave." She forces a laugh. "So that's good."

"You deserve people in your life who make you feel good, Aurora."

"You make me feel good."

She turns back to face me, her pretty green eyes staring up at me through her long eyelashes. I want to rub my thumb along her bottom lip, kiss her, see if she tastes as good as I remember. She hesitates, but I recognize the look on her face. The one she gets when she wants to ask me something, but doesn't know how to.

"Just ask me, sweetheart. I promise I'm not going anywhere."

"It doesn't matter. We should get back to the barbecue before someone gets the wrong idea. I don't want to get you in trouble."

Aurora slides forward until her body is flush with mine and I take a step back, a few seconds later than I should have, but I deserve credit for doing it at all. My hands link with hers as I help her hop down, but then I let her walk past toward the exit.

"Rory," I call, turning and leaning against the counter she was just sitting on. She stops by the door, watching me with interest. "You make me feel good, too."

Chapter Fifteen

RUSS

MY RINGING PHONE INTERRUPTS MY running playlist for what feels like the millionth time in the past hour and my brother has officially irritated me to the point that I'm willing to answer just to tell him to stop fucking calling me.

"What do you want, Ethan?" My loud voice is a jarring addition to the tranquil Honey Acres morning. The horses grazing in the field beside my running route look at me wild-eyed, letting out a displeased neigh before scampering away from the fence line, spooked.

The best part about this place is the terrible reception, but there are certain patches that have pockets of service just long enough for my family to invade my peace.

"You're a piece of shit for never answering anyone's calls." It's a strong start, not unexpected. "You need to fucking grow up."

No matter where I am, no matter what I'm doing or how closely I follow the rules and pray that it'll be enough, the universe finds a way to humble me.

"What do you want, Ethan?" I ask again, the frustration from earlier diluted by the prickle of his words.

"Dad is in the hospital. Mom's asking for you; she wants you there. So stop burying your head in the sand and pretending you're not part of this family, like a selfish prick, and support her."

You'd expect my reaction to finding out my dad is in the hospital to be more emotional, but my first thought is I wonder how he landed himself in that situation. I've been here before, so it's not much of a surprise: When he pawned Mom's jewelry and the guilt made him drink so much he needed to get his stomach pumped. When he was in a fight at a casino and ended up needing stitches. When he crashed his car, but swore he hadn't been drinking.

"I can't. I'm working."

"Grow the fuck up," he says harshly. "If you don't get your ass on the road in the next hour, I'm going to come to that camp you're at and drag you home by your hair."

"Which state are you going to travel from to do that? You're going to interrupt your tour for this?" Ethan and I have never had that close brotherly connection people talk about. Our seven-year age gap was too big to overcome when coupled with his never wanting to be in Dad's verbal firing line. I've always been angry he left me alone, but I'm not sure I would have made a different choice if I were the older one.

"I'm in San Francisco right now. I'm not bluffing, Russ. Ignoring your phone isn't going to work this time. Show up for your family. You don't get to bow out because shit's difficult sometimes."

I don't know whether to laugh or scream. I want to tell him that bowing out is exactly what he did to me when he moved across the country and left me to navigate everything alone. Ethan says I'm stubborn and closed-minded. That I don't truly understand what it's like to deal with an illness so corrosive and that he understands better than I do because he's in the music industry.

He told me once that he has more memories of when things were good and that's why he isn't as angry as me. It's easy to say you understand and you're not angry when you're on the other side of the country most of the year.

"I don't want to talk to him, Ethan. You don't get it. He's so unpredictable. He can be nice as pie or he's awful and I hate it."

"He's sedated. Do it for Mom, Russ. It isn't her fault."

"Fine," I snap. "I'll see you later. You'll be there, right?"

"You're doing the right thing. Drive safe, little brother."

The familiar sense of dread fuels my run back to my cabin. It's early so there's nobody around and the kids won't be awake yet. Xander did the night shift, so he's in the Brown Bears cabin with Maya and I don't want to risk going in to explain.

After a quick shower, I throw a few things into a backpack and head toward the main building. It takes five minutes for me to work up the courage to knock on the door for the overnight leader's door. Jenna is half asleep when she pulls the door open and I'm standing there, backpack slung over my shoulder. "I'm really sorry to wake you up," I say when I can't find the words to explain why I'm going.

"Don't worry about it. Is everything okay?" she says carefully.

I wipe my sweating hands against my shorts and force myself to focus. "If I tell you something, will it stay private? Because you're my boss?"

She nods slowly, tightening her dressing gown around her waist and leaning against the doorframe. "It can stay confidential if you need it to. As long as it's not a safeguarding issue. What's happened, Russ?"

"My dad is in the hospital and I need to go home for a day or two. I can work back the missed shifts or something. I'm really sorry, Jenna. Is that okay?"

"Oh my God. Of course it's okay. Are you okay to drive? Is home far for you? I'm so sorry! What's happened?"

That's the moment it occurs to me I was so busy arguing with Ethan that I didn't even ask. When there's always something, sometimes asking about specifics gets lost in my order of priorities. I'd feel bad, but I could probably think up a handful of scenarios and be close to the real reason.

"No, my parents don't live far from Maple Hills. But I don't really like to talk about my family, is it okay if this just stays between us? I'd rather the team don't know I'm going to the hospital."

She nods and I instantly feel better.

"Can you just tell them there's a personal emergency or something? But that I'm okay. I don't want anyone to worry." It's not that I don't want my fellow counselors not to know I'm going back to Maple Hills, but there are tons of excuses I can come up with that don't involve my dad being the topic of conversation.

"Sure thing. I hope your dad is better soon. If you're going to be any longer than two days, can you call me?"

"Yeah I'll call, but I'll definitely be back soon. Thanks, Jenna."

MY STOMACH SINKS THE SECOND I see Maple Hills appear on the highway signs, and now that I'm taking the exit, I'm not sure it's even still in my body.

The gas station coffee I've been sipping on is burned and bitter, the perfect representation of how I feel right now. I ignore the signs I normally take to campus, instead following the ones toward the hospital.

As the building comes into view, I consider that I could turn around now, turn my phone off, head back to Honey Acres, and play pretend. I want to run away from this, not have whatever conversation I'm about to have, avoid the people I work so hard not to speak to—but I don't. I park my truck in the short-stay lot, like the action alone will manifest a quick visit and I'll be able to head back to a life I'm actually starting to love.

I spot Mom before she notices me in the family waiting area.

She looks more tired than the last time I saw her, whenever that was. Four months ago? Five? The bags under her eyes are dark and striking against her pale skin, her hair grayer, face more gaunt. She's clinging to the coffee cup between her hands as she stares into the distance, and once again I'm wondering if I should turn around and leave.

My feet keep carrying me forward until I'm standing in front of her. No part of me on the long-ass drive here considered that I'd have to say something when I arrived, and now that I'm facing her, I don't know how to start.

She doesn't say anything as she stands, throwing her arms around me. With her face buried in my chest, she begins to sob.

"What happened?" I ask, keeping my voice steady.

"He'd offered to pick up some groceries for dinner and he was hit by a drunk driver," Mom says, wiping her eyes on her sleeve.

"He was hit? Was he drunk, too?"

"No! He wasn't!" She sounds appalled, like it's totally unbelievable I could ever suspect he might be in the wrong. She gives me a full play-by-play and I know from where the crash happened that he was on his way home from the track. There isn't a grocery store near that intersection. "You can go in and talk to him in a minute, the doctor shouldn't be much longer."

"Talk to him? Ethan said he's unconscious. Also, where is Ethan?"

"He was unconscious but now he's awake. And your brother is on tour somewhere in the Midwest I think. Why? Did you think he was here?"

I'm going to strangle Ethan the next time I see him.

"I don't want to talk to him, Mom. I don't want to be here."

She sighs and takes a seat, gesturing for me to do the same. There's no one else with us in the room and I've never wanted to be surrounded by strangers more than I do right now. "You need to move past this delayed teenage rebellion phase, Russ. I don't know what to do with you. You're an adult but you're part of this family, whether you like it or not. You need to start putting us first."

I don't realize the noise is coming from me until the chair begins to shake because I'm laughing so hard. There's nothing funny about this situation; there's never once been anything funny about it, but the laughter continues to bubble up until it feels like it's choking me—and I stop. "You've never put me first, ever."

"How can you say that, Russ? Have you ever gone without a meal? Without clothes you needed? Gas in the car to get you to school? And hockey practice? A roof over your head?" Her eyes water as she stares at me, waiting for me to respond. "Do you think I worked extra hours for fun? Your father is sick, Russ. You don't turn your back on people because they're not perfect."

"You're enabling him. Every time you do nothing, you're making it worse. You know he wasn't going to the grocery store. You know that if he was, none of us would be here right now."

"You can't claim to know what it means or what it takes to keep a marriage together," she says, brushing her hands against her skirt. "When you love someone so much, you'd give your life to make them better. I really don't think the hospital is the right place for this conversation, Russ. Let's talk about it at home later."

"I'm not going home. I don't want to talk about it at all. I don't want to be here."

My mom has never talked so candidly about my dad's issues before. I feel her pain in her words, even when she delivers them calmly, but it doesn't erase mine. It's a fight in my head where no one else can weigh in, where no one else really gets it and, really, where absolutely no one wins. Where logically I understand it's a sickness, that it's a disease that takes hold. That he never stood a chance and the odds were against him, which, when talking about a gambling addict, is ironic, I know. I can say that and I can understand it and mean it, but it doesn't stop it from fucking hurting.

"Then why are you here, honey? If you don't want to talk about what's happening in our family, why did you come?"

I could tell her that Ethan lied to me to get me here. I could explain that the idea of him turning up at Honey Acres and making a scene in front of my new friends makes me feel physically sick. That having Aurora look at me with pity when she learns that while her dad prioritizes the billion-dollar industry he's part of, mine prioritizes a very different kind of race track.

"I didn't want you to be alone, but I didn't drive four hours to fight with you," I say, rubbing my fingers against my temples.

She reaches over, taking my hand in hers. "I wouldn't have married him if he was a bad man. People don't wake up one day and decide to become addicted to something. They don't choose to hurt the people they love."

My entire body is aching from the adrenaline of being here and I'm exhausted. Every feeling, every resentment, every sliver of hurt is on the surface like an open wound.

"Did you know he asks me for money?" I know before she opens her mouth the answer is no. She's never had a good poker face, much like Dad, ironically. "And when I don't give it to him, he tells me I'm a fuckup and I'm not his son."

Tears fill her eyes instantly, but she doesn't let them fall. "I'm so sorry, Russ."

"He makes me feel like I don't deserve the good things in my life." It's something I've never said out loud before and the words practically hack their way out of my mouth. "He makes me feel like no one could ever want me, because if my own dad won't pick me over a poker game, why would someone else?"

"That's the drink talking, the desperation. He loves you so much. We both love you so much."

I know her words are supposed to soothe me, but all she's doing is making more excuses for him. I don't think she even knows she's doing it.

"I don't know how to fake it like you, Mom. I shouldn't have come, I'm sorry."

"Tell your dad how you feel."

"Sorry?"

Mom stands, brushing herself down and fixing her hair, preparing herself to head out there and pretend things aren't a fucking mess. "You don't think he can get better, right? You want nothing to do with him. Us." Her voice cracks. "So go in there and tell him how you feel. What do you have to lose?"

I'm in a daze as I walk slowly toward Dad's room under Mom's instructions. I've never talked to her so honestly before; I don't think I've talked to anyone like that before. The doctor is leaving as I reach the door to Dad's room. "Family?"

"Son."

"Your father is very lucky," he says, patting me on the back as he passes.

Lucky.

Dad doesn't say anything as I enter the room and sit beside the bed. The machines he's hooked up to beep rhythmically, letting me know that somewhere in there, there is a heart.

The silence is deafening. It makes me think of Aurora and how she'd never stand for it. She'd fill it with something ridiculous and her cheeks would flush pink and I'd watch her, soaking up every single drop of her sunshine. I wish I hadn't answered Ethan's call. I wish I were playing tetherball or football or something, anything, in a place where I don't have to deal with this.

"You look like you have something to say," Dad says, his voice hoarse. He looks like shit; he's bruised and scratched, wires everywhere.

I have so much to say. Every bad thought I've ever had about myself. Every risk I didn't take because I was scared. Every conversation I cut short, too anxious for people to see the real me. Every relationship I didn't chase because I didn't want to mess up and let someone down.

"You've broken our family and I don't know how we can fix it."

He doesn't say anything for a long time, and the man I know to be angry and bitter looks small beneath the harsh hospital lights. "I know."

"For a really long time I hoped that the dad I loved was in there somewhere, trapped, but there. I don't think he is anymore. You're not the man who taught me to skate or ride a bike. I don't know you."

"I know."

"I'm scared to have the things I want in case I fuck them up, because you've made me believe I'm a fuckup—and I hate you for that. I hate you for being everywhere and nowhere all at once."

"I understand."

"You're like a weed. There isn't one aspect of my life you haven't invaded and ruined. I couldn't even get through the summer without you corrupting it. I don't speak to you. I don't even read your messages anymore and you're just there in my head constantly."

It comes out fast and frantic, but I mean every word and I'm pissed at myself for holding them in for so long. My chest eases with every syllable, the weight holding me down for so many years lightening.

"You deserve better, son."

He looks so weak in the bed, listening to me vent. "Yeah. I do. So does Mom. Sort your shit out."

Dad doesn't shout after me as I stand and leave. My body works on autopilot, muscle memory kicking in to get me as far away from him as possible. Ethan can say I'm burying my head in the sand, but I've been more honest with Dad in one conversation than anyone has been with him in years. Our family is broken right now, and papering over the cracks doesn't help any of us.

I don't register what's happening or where I'm going until my truck stops in front of my house on Maple Avenue. The familiarity is an immediate comfort and I decide to take a break and process before getting back on the road to camp.

The door isn't locked when I try it, and when it swings open, the last thing I expect to find is Henry's bare ass while he's balls deep in someone on the living room couch.

Chapter Sixteen

RUSS

THE FRONT DOOR SWINGS OPEN, revealing a now fully dressed Henry. I push off from my truck, avoiding eye contact as I walk past my friend into our house.

I've seen Henry's ass before; it's kind of a given when you're on a hockey team. Locker rooms and sharing hotel rooms; it's nothing new.

That was new.

"I'm sorry, man," I say, throwing myself into the recliner and not onto the couch I'll never be sitting on ever again. "I should have given you a heads-up; I didn't think you'd be here. Is your *guest* okay? I didn't see her if that makes her feel better."

"Why are you apologizing for coming to your own house?" he says, grabbing us both a bottle of water from the refrigerator. "She's fine, just a little embarrassed. She's taking a shower and I found her a moisturizing face mask thing to relax. I'll check on her after you tell me why you're in Maple Hills."

"Family shit. I've only arrived today; that's why I didn't text to say I was back. I want to shower before I head back to camp."

"You can't drive back today," Henry says. "That's too much driving for one day. Stay tonight, head back in the morning. You want to talk about the family thing?"

I shake my head, dragging my hand through my hair, realizing how tired I am now that I've stopped running on adrenaline. "You're right. I'll leave first thing. Don't feel like you've gotta hang around for me, though. I'll go into my room out of the way, just don't fuck in this chair, all right? This one is my favorite."

He gives me a strained smile as he stands and moves toward the stairs. "I feel sorry for you if you think any of the surfaces in this house are safe. I'll spare you the full description of what I walked in on Lola doing to Robbie when he was sitting there."

"Yeah, I'm sure I can guess."

"It was a blow job."

Maybe I'll sit on the floor. "Fantastic. Listen, I'm pretty beat, I'm going to shower. Maybe have a nap. Is Robbie still in New York?"

"Yeah, he gets back next week. I'll try and keep the noise down."

"You're a good friend," I laugh.

He nods and heads up the stairs, looking at me over his shoulder. "So are you."

NAPPING HAS NEVER BEEN MY strength, even when I haven't got a head full of noise. I put my phone on do not disturb after my brother started with the calls and the messages. Being without consistent reception for a month has killed any dependency I had on my cell phone; if I can hear it now, it irritates me.

I don't know how long I've been staring at the ceiling of my bedroom, but I know that it's long enough for me to be annoyed at the sleep that won't come. Maybe it's because I can't hear Xander snoring or there isn't a dog trying to starfish in my already limited space.

"Honey, we're home!"

At first I think I'm hearing things, but then I hear a laugh so loud and ridiculous I know that there's no way I could imagine that. Henry is a few steps behind me as I make my way down the stairs to the living room. Kris, Mattie, and Bobby are dropping pizza boxes and beer bottles onto the kitchen counter by the time I get to the bottom step.

"There he is!" Kris yells excitedly. "The prodigal son returns."

"I'm too jet-lagged to explain to you all the ways you don't understand what that means," Mattie says.

"Ignore him," Bobby says, slapping his palm against mine and pulling me into a hug. "He just likes saying he's jet-lagged so people ask him where he's been."

"Can you even get jet-lag from three hours?" Henry asks, immediately opening one of the pizza boxes.

"How was Miami?" I ask, accepting the beer Kris hands me.

"Wild, dude." Mattie hands me his cell phone, showing the three of them outside the Miami branch of The Honeypot. "Next time, you're both coming."

"I'm good," Henry says instantly.

Bobby hands out the pizza boxes as we all congregate around the kitchen island opening them. I suppress the urge to groan as I bite into the pepperoni slice, realizing it's the first thing I've eaten today. "What're you guys doing here anyway?" I ask, washing down the pizza with my beer.

"Hen said you'd turned up and unintentionally edged him," Kris says.

Henry groans in protest. "I didn't. It's in the group chat, did you not see it?"

"No, sorry," I pull my cell phone out of my pocket, turning my notifications on out of guilt. "I haven't really been on it since I left."

"We missed you, buddy," Mattie says, "and we're nosy fuckers. We want to know why you're back from camp because Turner is too nice to press you for it."

"But we did miss you," Bobby adds. "Which is more important than whether you got fired or not."

Henry mutters something under his breath I don't quite catch. I know I can trust Henry and he'd never share my business. "A drunk driver hit my dad. He's fine. I was visiting him but I'm going back to camp in the morning."

I nod through the echo of well wishes, thanking them and saying nothing more about Dad. They might not know exactly what the situation is, but they know there's something not right with my life outside of college. As much as I love my teammates, I don't think I'll ever be in a place to explain how embarrassed and frustrated I feel about the whole situation.

"Does Jenna still work there?" Bobby asks with a weird smirk on his face. "Everyone was obsessed with Jenna."

"You were obsessed with Jenna," Kris says through a mouthful of pizza. "He was convinced he'd have a chance as soon as he turned eighteen. We only went for one summer but he talked about her for, like, three years."

"Yeah, she's my boss. She's great, super nice. She kind of hates being in charge of people, so as long as you're not doing something wrong she stays out of your way."

"Is she still hot? I don't know why I'm asking because I know she definitely is," Bobby says. "Shit, maybe I'll work there next year."

"What's your group like?" Mattie asks, rolling his eyes at Bobby.

"Honestly, they're pretty great. There's one guy, Clay, he's a bit of a douche, but he isn't unbearable. Xander, the guy I share a cabin with, is really cool. Maya is great, she's on one of those Camp America international work things with her friends. She tends to hang out with them when we're not working, so I don't know her well yet. Emilia and Aurora are nice."

"Back up," Kris says.

"Aurora?" Henry follows. "That girl who left you in the middle of the night?"

I rub the back of my neck to ease the nervous prickling happening as I nod. We need to come up with a new way to identify her, because things have changed a lot since she was that Aurora.

Cheering erupts, jumping and hugging, a few high fives as they celebrate . . . I literally don't know what they're celebrating. "What're you guys doing?"

Mattie is the first to stop jumping. "She's the F1 girl, right? Can you get us paddock club passes?"

"There's no way you two have been together for a month and haven't fucked," Bobby says expectantly.

"We haven't." They all stop celebrating. "They've got this no-fraternization rule, and to be honest I pretty much avoided her the first week. We're fine now, though; we're friends."

I have an audience of confused faces staring back at me. They look among themselves, silently nominating a leader, who turns out to be Kris. "You know no one will be sticking to that rule, right? A bunch of twenty-year-olds stuck together for two and a half months with a rule not to do something? Screw that."

"I wouldn't last the week," Mattie mumbles, taking another bite of pizza.

Henry scowls at him. "Because you have no respect for authority."

"Let's see about that, Captain." Mattie grins.

Henry's eyes roll, like they do every time his newly appointed title is referenced. "Russ is following the rules."

"Fuck the rules," Bobby counters. "We could all die tomorrow."

"I need the job, guys. Sorry to disappoint. She's fucking great, though, like as a friend. She's . . . great."

"Swallowed a whole dictionary," Mattie laughs, dodging the napkin I throw at him.

I'd need a whole dictionary to describe just how great Aurora is. My mind wanders back to camp and what they're doing. The kids will have eaten dinner by now; they're probably drinking hot chocolate by a campfire. Aurora will be complaining her mug isn't big enough to fit the excessive number of marshmallows she adds, and Xander will be daring her to try and beat her record for the amount she can fit in her mouth.

I wonder if anyone will walk her back to her cabin tonight and if they'll wait to watch her go in.

Kris downs the rest of his beer, shrugging nonchalantly as he puts it back on the counter. "You won't be the only guy crushing on another counselor, buddy, and they can't fire you all."

IT'S BITTERSWEET LEAVING HOME FOR the second time.

After the guys gave up trying to convince me to start living my life to the max, they moved on to telling us about Miami and all the wild shit they got up to. I stopped after the one beer, but by their fourth, Bobby and Kris were reenacting the moment Mattie was mistaken for a famous movie star and they all ended up in the VIP area with Tristan Harding, the guy from all those romance films Stassie and Lola love.

We reminisced about games from last season, our championship win, and predictions for the new season. When I called it a night, knowing I had to get up early, they were genuinely gutted I was leaving again, which made me not want to leave at all.

Mattie and Bobby crashed in Robbie's and JJ's rooms, with Kris losing five consecutive games of rock paper scissors and ending up on the couch Henry violated.

They were awake, albeit slightly hungover, before the sun was up to make breakfast and coffee so I could have something decent to eat before getting on the road. Having real friends has shown me I don't need to quietly blend into the background anymore. Telling my dad exactly how I feel has freed me from whatever has been holding me back this entire time. Don't get me wrong, nobody changes overnight, but I'm arriving at Honey Acres again feeling like a brand-new guy.

I don't look like a brand-new guy, though. I hardly slept and it shows on my face. I feel it in my tired body when I move; I'm stiff from so much driving.

Signing back in at the reception at the front of the camp, I find Jenna in a meeting, which means I can wave to her through the main office door's glass panel and don't have to answer any of her questions. It's just before lunchtime and I know that Emilia or Aurora will be covering me. As tired as I am, more than anything I want to take over so they can enjoy the day off I stole from them.

Brown Bears are scheduled for swimming, and the lake is right by my cabin, so it gives me a chance to put my staff T-shirt on and leave my backpack before taking over.

Walking down toward my room, I spot Aurora coming toward me, looking down at the ground.

"Hey," I call when we're six feet from each other.

Her head snaps up, eyes widening as she takes me in. I realize I'm holding my breath, waiting for her to say something back, to give me the smile I've become accustomed to seeing when I see her, but it doesn't come.

"Are you okay?" she asks, hugging her arms around herself.

"Yeah, I'm fine. I'm sorry you had to cover for me. I'm heading to the lake now so you or Emilia can have your day off back."

"It's Emilia, I did yesterday. She won't let you take over, so leave her. We switched dance and swim around because we thought it looked like it was going to rain, but obviously it's still hot and dry as hell. You look like you need to sleep."

"I really am sorry. I'll cover you so you can have an extra day off or something. I'll make it up to you."

"You missed the talent show practice," she says softly. How disappointed she sounds fucking hurts. Her forehead creases as she frowns. "I don't care about covering for you, Russ. You disappeared. Jenna told us you had a personal thing and said it was no big deal. So I don't get why you didn't tell me you were leaving." Her voice cracks. "You just left me. Us. All of us have been worried. Me and Jenna had an argument about it because she kept saying he's fine and it was pissing me off."

"Aurora, I'm sorry." I take a cautious step toward her, then another, until I pull her into a hug. We fit together perfectly like this, with her arms wrapped around me, my head buried in her hair.

"Where were you? What happened?" she mumbles into my chest. "You can tell me."

"I don't want to talk about it," I say honestly. "I'm sorry I missed practice. I'm sorry I made you worried. I won't do it again, I promise."

Something I said causes her to untangle herself from me and take a step backward. "It's fine."

It isn't fine and I'm gutted to be on the receiving end of that smile she forces to make people think she isn't upset by something. I don't want the wall to go back up between us. The words come tumbling out of my mouth before I really know why. "Tell me a secret."

"Seriously?"

When I nod, she takes a deep breath and starts. "I'm sad you left without telling me. Not telling everyone, telling me. I think—thought—I might mean a little more to you than everyone else. That you might trust me the most because we have history, or whatever."

"You do."

"I thought about flirting with Clay last night just to feel wanted, how weird is that? I didn't. I called my mom, I went to bed early and spent all day lurking around Emilia, trying to keep myself out of trouble."

The idea that disappearing would drive Aurora toward Clay makes me feel like shit. "You're not weird, Aurora. I'm sorry I hurt your feelings. Again."

"It's not about me, you're the one who clearly has stuff going on. I'm just trying not to be the person that acts out because of other people. That's something I do a lot, and I don't want to. It's probably the only thing I do better than oversharing." She presses her lips together as she stares up at me. I wish I could put everything out there like she does, but even after the past twenty-four hours, something is stopping me. She shrugs, arms wrapped around herself, protecting her. "I want to be there for you because I care about you. I feel like I could be a better friend to you if you communicated with me."

"I made us miscommunicators again."

She nods. "Kinda. It doesn't have to mean baring your soul, Russ. We're getting to know each other; you're allowed to have boundaries and things you keep for yourself. Some people are good at sharing, some people aren't. We just have to find a middle ground."

"I'm really sorry I missed practice. I know how important the talent show is to you and I wouldn't have missed it if I'd had a choice."

Aurora unfolds her arms, her posture relaxing the longer we stand near each other. "It's okay. There will be a dozen more. Emilia and Xander were very intense."

I notice the backpack on her shoulder. "Were you going somewhere? Before you saw me?"

"I was going on a hike to this place I love, but I wasn't sure about the weather, so I was going to find my raincoat. I'm not even sure there's going to be rain. I think Xander might have made it up because he didn't want to swim."

"Can I come? I'm not going to be able to relax, so there's no point me trying. I'm okay with getting caught in the rain."

She smiles and the relief floods me. "If we get caught in the rain, we'll just enjoy the rainbow."

Chapter Seventeen

AURORA

I woke up this morning and told myself to forget Russ Callaghan. That he was just another man whose attention I'd become fixated on and he wasn't the guy I was turning him into in my head. Emilia says I get attached too easily, or not at all, and that I don't do the happy medium like most people.

I have to really question if someone is worth it when their actions make me call my mom just to hear her tell me how much she misses me.

I'd made my choice and I was sticking to it, which worked until he strolled back into camp and stopped in front of me. It's hard to be mad at someone when they look like total shit. It's hard to know that if he'd walked in smiling and looking his usual, beautiful self, I would've had the same reaction.

I was heading to grab some stuff for my hike when I overshared all my feelings with the man I constantly force my bullshit onto. I don't know what it is—the softness of his face or the way his eyes make me melt when he's giving me his full attention, or those freaking dimples—that makes me want to word-vomit my insecurities all over him.

He must be totally exhausted being stuck around me.

Not exhausted enough to make me carry my backpack, though.

Now freshly showered, Russ is matching each of my steps up the steepening trail path and making it look easy. "I can carry my own backpack," I repeat for the millionth time through strained breath. I really need to start exercising more. "I feel like you're one of those little donkeys in Greece."

"I like helping," he says, not even a hint of panting. "And I'm used to carrying shit around. Not used to being called a donkey, though; thanks for that one."

"How are you not even breaking a sweat? You can carry me if you want, my legs hurt."

I don't even have time to say I'm kidding before my ass is in the air and my nose gets buried in my backpack. Russ's hand grips the back of my thigh, keeping me in place over his shoulder as he continues, not even breaking his stride.

This was not what I was asking for.

"Aurora, every time you wriggle, you rub your ass against my face," he says casually.

Give me strength. "I didn't really mean carry me. I was being dramatic for sympathy!"

His fingers dig into my thigh, and a part of me that has been severely neglected starts to throb. How thick my thigh is versus how much of his hand can cover it is not something I should be obsessing over right now.

"This is my version of being sympathetic," he teases. "We're nearly at the top anyway. Definitely feel like a donkey now, though."

"I take it back. You're Shrek and I'm Princess Fiona."

He laughs and I jiggle as his shoulders shake. "Well, green is my favorite color."

"What type of green? Ogre green?"

"Whatever shade your eyes are." He starts to lower me to the ground again, but my legs are jelly. "Holy shit, this is nice."

I'm too busy reeling from what he said about my eyes to realize we've reached my favorite spot. I'm not sure what the official name for the type of water source this is, but the water is crystal clear and warm and we're far enough from anyone else to ever be disturbed. The rocks lining the edge were my favorite when I came here as a kid, but now I appreciate how quiet it is. Russ helps me spread the picnic blanket out on the grass next to the water and I unpack our water bottles and energy bars.

"This is the first time we've been totally alone since we got here. Not one person to disturb us," I say, kicking off my sneakers. He watches me, eyes dancing across my skin as I start to pull down my shorts.

He copies me, undressing slowly, watching me pull my T-shirt over my head as he does the same. I'm giddy with anticipation, my heart rate speeds up, and I can't keep the smile from my face.

He throws his socks onto the growing pile of our clothes. "So, we're doing this?"

I nod, counting down from three. The nervous energy rattles through me, and when I say go, my body takes on a mind of its own as I sprint away from Russ toward the rocks.

Sprinting in a bikini is possibly the worst idea I've ever had—and I've had so many terrible ideas. If I get a concussion from being hit in the face by my own breasts, I'll never recover from the embarrassment.

The rocks are hot under my feet as I climb to the top. It's not hard or high, but I'm very aware of the man behind me, the one I suspect slowed down to let me win and who definitely has my ass in his face for the second time today.

Our race was for the first person into the water, but now that I'm up here it feels higher than it did when I was younger. Russ doesn't give me the chance to spiral as he reaches the top, scoops me up into his arms, and throws us both into the water.

The cool water is relief against the hot sun, but it does nothing to make Russ look less hot. He pushes back his wet hair, his biceps peeking above the water, and floats backward soaking up the sun. He looks brighter than he did earlier somehow; I'm glad I brought him here. This is the most peaceful place I know and I feel like he needs it.

Maybe I should have sent him alone with directions, because the silence is making me itch, but I'm doing my best to not fill it like I normally do.

"How did you discover this place?" Russ asks, eyes closed, still floating on his back and, my God, the relief to be able to talk again.

I float closer to him, like somehow if I'm too loud it'll ruin things. "One year we had a counselor who wasn't really into team sports, so he would organize walks all over the land that Orla and her family own. This was my favorite spot."

"It's beautiful."

"It is."

"Chance of sharks?"

"Slim."

His eyes open and he smiles right at me, making my heart race. "What a relief."

"You look better already," I say cautiously. I want him to tell me why he had to suddenly leave, but I'm trying not to bulldoze into his life and make him uncomfortable after he told me he didn't want to talk about it.

God, it's exhausting trying to think about what you do before you do it.

"I feel better. Thank you for bringing me here."

"If you . . . Do you, um . . ." Great start, Rory. "If you change your mind and do want to talk about anything to do with where you've been, that would be okay with me. We could try and find that middle ground."

"I don't want to burden you with my baggage."

"I don't mind. It isn't a burden. You just carried my actual baggage and me up a hill. I can take whatever you throw at me, Callaghan."

"It is. You have enough of your own, you don't need other people's."

I hate me and my big mouth. I said that weeks ago when we first started working here, when someone asked me why I don't have a boyfriend. I didn't know how to say, "Little to no trust in men, especially when I'm a train wreck," in a nice way to the people I'd just met, including Russ. So I said the first thing that came to mind, which unfortunately happened to be about not wanting other people's baggage.

"I want your baggage."

"Aurora," he says more firmly this time. "I promise you, you don't."

He isn't listening to me and I'm growing frustrated, but I know I'm just dealing with the result of my own words. I can feel myself becoming flustered as I struggle to verbalize my thoughts. "I do. I want it all. Pretend I'm the airport. Give me everything."

I should be gagged, truly.

Russ's eyebrows pinch together, showing he's as confused as I am. "What are you talking about?"

"Airports? Baggage? I have no idea. I have no idea what I'm doing or saying most of the time, but I meant what I said earlier, Russ. I can take it."

I'm in such unfamiliar territory and I hate it. He reaches out and tucks my wet hair behind my ear, his hand lingering a little longer than necessary, and my entire body hums happily. "We should probably get out before we start to prune."

I scream internally.

He doesn't say anything as he helps me climb out of the water and we walk back toward the blanket. I throw myself onto the soft fabric, feeling a little defeated, and lie back to dry off.

I block out the sun with my hand, watching Russ awkwardly shuffle around, trying to get comfortable. "Put your head on my stomach."

"I'll be okay, I just need to fi—"

"You'll be comfortable, I promise."

Reluctantly, he maneuvers himself, leaning back and gently settling on my stomach. "If it becomes uncomf—"

"Emilia uses me as a pillow all the time. You're gentler than she is. I'm good, I swear."

I'm not sure when I finally become comfortable with the silence between us. But without the noise of my babbling, I get to listen to the sound of his breathing. Fifteen minutes of quiet passes before he starts talking.

"My dad was hit by a drunk driver." I freeze as the relief and panic that he's finally sharing both hit me at once. "I don't see or speak to my family very often because . . ." He pauses and I wait, stroking the top of his head gently so he knows I'm listening. "Well, because my dad doesn't make me feel very good about myself. He was my hero when I was really young. Never missed a hockey game, school fair, parent-teacher conference. By the time I graduated high school we barely talked."

"What changed?" I ask softly.

"He did. It wasn't an overnight change. It was little things, gradually getting more and more frequent over time, making him harder and harder to talk to. He got meaner and meaner, and now I can't stand to talk to him."

"That really sucks. And I'm sorry about the crash, too. That's a lot to process on its own. Was your dad okay when you got there?"

"He'll make a full recovery. I've had to visit him in the hospital a few times and it's always been his fault. This one wasn't technically his fault, but I still feel like he's to blame, y'know?" My hand is still moving through his hair and I'm scared if I stop, he'll stop. "Like if he wasn't doing what he was doing, he wouldn't have been where he was and then the car wouldn't have hit him."

"Yeah, I understand."

"I didn't want to go, but my brother told me he'd come here and drag me back to Maple Hills if I didn't go voluntarily. I didn't want to bring my home drama here; I came here to escape it. Turns out Ethan lied and isn't even on this side of the country. Smart, really. He knows I'd have ignored his threat if I thought he was far away."

"You guys aren't close?"

"Ethan is mad at the world and I don't understand why. My anger is because I feel like I can't escape. He escaped years ago, so what does he have to complain about? Makes it hard to bond when it seems like he's constantly yelling at me about something. He reminds me of Dad sometimes. I should tell him that the next time he's shouting at me. We just handle things differently, I suppose. He thinks I'm selfish for stuff and I think he's selfish for stuff and, well, it isn't a great foundation for a good relationship."

"I'm not close with my sister. We handle things in pretty similar ways, actually, not exactly a compliment to either of us, but we live very different lives. So I sort of get it."

"I was honest about how I feel for the first time yesterday. It felt good to finally say what I needed to say. It feels good to tell you this stuff, so thank you for being patient with me."

"You're really brave, Russ."

"I'm the opposite of brave. He's told me that enough times for it to be imprinted on my brain."

Word by word, who Russ is gets clearer and clearer to me and I feel honored that the man who shares so little is sharing with me.

"You are brave. We live in a society that tells us our parents are the greatest thing we will ever have and will ever lose, and you just—I don't even know. You're putting yourself first anyway. That's brave."

"I learned a long time ago that if I didn't put myself first, nobody else was going to. Forgiving people who repeatedly let you down is like sticking your hand in a fire over and over and expecting it to not keep burning you."

"Sounds like me and my dad. Except I'm singed to a crisp."

"What's the deal with you two?"

"Elsa thinks he hates us because we're both terrible drivers, but I think it's because I look like my mom and he really hates my mom."

He moves onto his elbows and looks at me over his shoulder. "Hold up, your sister is called Elsa? Are your parents Disney adults?"

I can't count the number of times I've been asked something similar. "Shut up. I'm named after the northern lights. Could have gone my whole life thinking I was named after a princess, but my mom decided to traumatize me by sharing where I was conceived instead."

He's laughing as he lies back against my stomach. "And Elsa?"

"Predates *Frozen*. It's a really popular name in parts of Europe. My dad likes to pretend he backpacked around Scandinavia when he was younger, but in reality he stayed in fancy hotels and ate in fancier restaurants every night—not a hostel or backpack in sight." Mom loves laughing at that one. "He owns a Formula 1 team called Fenrir, which is from Norse mythology, so there is a theme. Elsa used to tell people we had a brother called Thor."

"Would it help you to know that I am named after a dog my mom had when she was a kid?"

"Yes. I feel silly telling you about my dad after your dad has been so cruel to you. My dad isn't cruel. He doesn't outright say horrible things to me; he just makes me feel like his life would be easier if I wasn't around. He's always put work first, which I get because he's got a lot of responsibility on his shoulders, and because of it, I've had opportunities and been to places that people would kill for."

"Nice things don't make the bad stuff acceptable, though," Russ says.

"I'd give all that up to feel like he loves me. We've been stuck in this cycle where he ignores me, so I do something silly to get his attention. When I was a teen I shoplifted, knowing I'd get caught. I got a fake ID and went to places I was too young for. Pissed off my teachers. Posted a picture of myself on race day wearing the merch of his main rival, Elysium. The F1 pages reposted the shit out of it."

"Jesus, Rory."

"And it works, but only for a short time because he's annoyed; but at least he calls and sees me. Nothing ever happens. I'm not punished, he doesn't try to understand. My mom justifies it because of course I'm like this, it's his fault. Then his anger wears off and he goes back to pretending that I don't exist. And every time, I'm, like, this is going to be the time where he proves he cares—but I just end up hurting my own feelings." I know I'm rambling. I know I'm oversharing, but when I think about stopping he reaches up and squeezes the hand I have resting in his hair, urging me to continue.

"I repeat the cycle. He has a girlfriend named Norah, and she has a daughter, who's our age, called Isobel. Norah posts about Dad like they're the happiest of families. But I'll never be part of it, and it makes me sad and it makes me do things like drink excessive amounts of tequila and ask you to skinny-dip with me."

"That feels like a million years ago."

"That's why I loved this place so much growing up. It was a couple of months where I felt wanted and valued. I didn't have to worry about what was going on at home. I knew coming back here was the only thing that would break the cycle. So that's my trauma dump. How fun. We're quite the pair, aren't we?"

"A walking advertisement for daddy issues."

"Do you hate them? I don't hate my parents, even though they're definitely the root of all my problems." He doesn't say anything, so neither do I. I might have pushed him too far, so I keep twirling the ends of his hair around my fingers and pressing them gently into his scalp. "I'm sorry, you don't have to share anything you don't want to. I didn't mean to go too far."

"You haven't. I told my dad I hated him yesterday, but I was hurt. I'm not sure I do, though. I think I hate the way he makes me feel. If he stopped doing the things he knows he shouldn't and started acting like the person he was when I was a kid, then I could have him in my life."

"What about your mom?"

He hums, long and low. "I love my mom. I've just always been mad at her for enabling my dad. After talking to her yesterday, I think she's realized she doesn't know everything. So yeah, that's my trauma dump."

Knowing the type of difficult relationships he's dealing with makes me understand him so much better and I'm giddy that he's trusted me with something clearly so raw. "Thank you for sharing with me."

"Thank you for comparing yourself to an airport."

I try to stop the laugh so I don't give him motion sickness, but I can't help it. I cover my face with my hands, like that'll block out the embarrassment. "I swear I'm not this much of a disaster normally. You make me nervous, I think. It comes out and I can't even stop it. Sometimes I lie in bed awake at night cringing. Emilia has done nothing but bully me about it since we got here."

"I love it, Aurora." He rolls onto his stomach, resting his chin in the palm of his hand. I peek at him through my fingers. "You make it easier for me to be myself because you're so . . . you. I overthink everything I say and do and you just—"

"Don't think before I speak?"

"—you say what's in your head." He brushes my hands away from my face, so I have nowhere to hide. "It's great. You're great."

"You really know how to make a girl feel special, Callaghan." I might be about to combust. "Remember, you enabled me next time I start rambling."

He laughs, shaking his head as he lies back down, this time placing his cheek on my bare stomach. "Is this okay?" he asks cautiously.

"Yup." My hand settles against the nape of his neck, drawing patterns and trailing my fingers up and down the hard muscles of his shoulders. "Is this okay?"

"Yup."

And I'm not sure exactly which animal I'm doodling against his skin when it happens, but somewhere between a hippo and a penguin, he falls asleep. So I keep doodling, until eventually my hand slows and I fall asleep, too.

Chapter Eighteen

AURORA

"Rory, the smell. I can't do it."

Emilia's hands cover her mouth as she tries to smother the sound of her retching. I can't help but roll my eyes at her as she takes a cautious step back from the vomit-soaked bedding I'm bundling into a laundry bag. "You're such a baby. It isn't that bad."

"You can't make me do this during Pride. It's a hate crime, Aurora."

We started sneaking alcohol from our parents when we were freshmen in high school. I've held Emilia's hair back while she vomits more times than I care to remember, but the idea of dealing with someone else's sick is apparently abhorrent to her.

I tie the laundry bag tight at the top and hold it out to her. "Can you please get rid of this and send the nurse over?"

Snatching the bag from my hands, she nods and runs out of the cabin, shouting, "Love you," over her shoulder.

"*Auroraaaaaa!*" The sound of my name echoes from inside the bathroom block attached to the kids' sleeping area, but is immediately followed by the sound of barfing.

My name being called in that exact way was how I was first alerted to vomit-gate.

We'd spent the day celebrating Pride. I have glitter in places no woman should have glitter, which isn't a surprise after Xander was put in charge of it and he spread it on every surface. When we did our diversity and inclusion training, Orla explained we wouldn't be doing our Pride event until after the Fourth of July. One of the campers' moms manages up-and-coming singers and they were going to do a performance for the kids, but wouldn't be available until today.

You lose all track of days in this place anyway, so they could have told me it was still June and I'd have believed them.

I thought I had an easy night ahead of me when Jasmine told me she didn't feel well and wanted to go to bed straight after dinner. Maya and Clay are on night duty, but I said I didn't mind hanging out with Jasmine until they brought all the other kids to bed this evening.

Her temperature was fine when I checked it, so I told her to sit on her bed while I retrieved some face wash to get the glitter and rainbows off her cheeks and that's when I heard her call my name.

I don't know how she managed to cover her bed and herself, but she did. I sent her for a shower while I stripped her bedding, which is when Emilia swung by to see if I wanted a soda.

Poking my head into the cubicle, I find Jasmine sitting on the floor looking miserable. Her eyes fill with tears as soon as she spots me and her bottom lip begins to wobble. "I'm sorry."

"You have nothing to be sorry for, sweet girl." Crouching behind her, I pull her now-wet hair out of her way as she puts her head over the toilet again. "You'll feel better when you're done."

"I think I had too much candy," she mumbles.

"I think you did, too."

"I want my mom."

"I know, sweetie. But let's get you cleaned up and then we can get your mom on the phone."

Eventually, her body has had enough and I help her from the

floor just in time for Kelly, the camp nurse, to show up and check her over. As suspected, there doesn't appear to be anything wrong with Jasmine other than overindulgence and overexcitement. When it's the two of us again, I sit Jasmine on the counter while I head to grab her toiletry bag.

It doesn't take me long to spot him considering how hard he is to miss, but I'm still surprised. "You stealing teddy bears now, Callaghan?"

Russ looks up from his position bent over Jasmine's bunk, bedsheet in hand. "Yeah." He points toward a laundry bag behind him. "I particularly like the ones that smell like death."

"I don't know how one little girl can cause so much destruction. Thank you, you didn't have to remake her bed. I could have done it."

"Your hands are full. Emilia couldn't tell us what had happened without gagging, so I thought it was better to investigate."

I grab the toiletry bag and another pair of pajamas from the drawer under Jasmine's bed and get back to her quickly. She has the same queasy look as earlier, but the color is returning to her cheeks a little. She climbs down and changes into fresh pajamas; I brush and braid her hair while she brushes her teeth.

There's a knock on the bathroom door, and when I answer, Russ is on the other side of it with Jasmine's water bottle. "She's probably dehydrated."

Why are you so freaking cute? "You're right, thanks."

"The bed is done and I'll take the bear to the laundry room. Do either of you need anything else?" I shake my head. "All right, I'll get out of your way then."

"Thank you."

I watch him walk away before closing the door, turning back to Jasmine and handing her the water bottle. She frowns. "You're acting weird."

"No, I'm not."

"You are. You're being shy. You're never shy, you always talk and talk." For a kid who just barfed everywhere, she's surprisingly astute. "Leon said Russ is your boyfriend."

I ignore the immediate panic and instead concentrate on wiping the glitter from her face, because apparently even a shower wasn't getting rid of it. "Leon is wrong."

"Leon says you two look at each other all day and you always stand next to each other."

Leon is getting pushed into some mud tomorrow. "We're friends. I'm friends with all the counselors. If you stand next to Leon does that make him your boyfriend? No."

"Leon said you'd deny it."

What the hell is this face paint made of? "I think maybe Leon needs to spend less time gossiping and more time playing with his friends."

"He knows everything about everyone. He told us Mona's big sister is in the Raccoons and cried because she has a crush on Russ."

The rainbow finally begins to rub off and freedom from this conversation is so close I can taste it. Leon's dad owns an intrusive paparazzi-driven tabloid, which I have sadly been featured in, so it does not surprise me that Leon doesn't know how to mind his own business.

I sigh, suddenly feeling guilty for all the years I terrorized Jenna. "Mona's big sister is fourteen and is far too young for any of the counselors. She should crush on someone her own age."

"Are you jealous? You sound jealous."

Give me strength. "Adults don't get jealous of children, sweetie. But I'm assuming all these questions mean you're feeling well enough to be more than six feet from the toilet. I think it's time to get you back into bed. You still wanna call your mom?"

"No, it's okay."

Jasmine climbs into her now-clean bed as Jenna walks into the room. "Hey, honey."

"Hey," I respond.

"Not you," she grumbles at me, crouching down beside the bed. "I heard you're not feeling great."

Jasmine gives Jenna a recap on how she's feeling, kindly complimenting my hair-holding skills, and Jenna nods along until Jasmine is done, eventually declaring she's going to stay with her and will check on her regularly, but to get some sleep.

Jenna mouths, "You're welcome," as I leave.

The party is still going when I head outside, the unmistakable sound of karaoke in full swing, but I know I smell disgusting so I head back to my cabin for a shower. I've been to Pride events every year since Emilia came out to me when we were fifteen, and this is the first one I've ever had to leave to get rid of the smell of sick.

As much as I want to climb into bed, I head back toward the evening activity to help out my team with our kids. I'm halfway there when Clay shouts to me from the other side of the path. "How's Jas?"

"She's fine, just too much candy and excitement."

He sticks his hands into his shorts pockets and nods in the direction of the main building. "Can you help me find the marshmallows? We've run out of the gelatin-free ones."

I fight the urge to sigh, because it isn't him, it's me and my desire to sit in front of the fire with a dog or three, surrounded by graham crackers. But if he doesn't find them, I won't be eating, so I nod and cross the grass to join him.

"How're you enjoying camp? I can't believe we're halfway already." I smile up at him and his attempt at small talk, which he catches immediately. "That was a boring question. Sorry, I never get a chance to talk to you on your own."

I've been actively avoiding any one-on-one time with Clay since our night shift together because I'm not interested in him at all, not even as a friend. I'm not totally clueless; I know he was just trying to nail me. Normally I'd have been drawn to the attention, but his lingering gazes make me feel uncomfortable. I think spending time with people who want to spend time with me because they like my company is helping. Clay looks at me like he's undressing me. Russ looks at me like I'm telling him the world's most interesting story.

It's good to feel like I can offer something more. It feels good to feel like I deserve something more. My era of self-development and personal growth might have had a rocky start, but I'm getting there.

I've noticed Clay getting close to one of the lifeguards in the evenings after the campers are all in bed, so hopefully he's found someone new to chase.

"I love it here. I'll be sad when the summer is over. What about you?"

I immediately zone out when he starts talking about all the things he could have done this summer instead of coming here. By the time he mentions his budding modeling career for the third time he may as well be talking another language. As I push my way into the pantry, he follows me closely, telling me about the trip to Cabo he's going on with his buddies before school starts again.

"You could definitely come if you wanted to," he says, leaning against the shelves, offering zero help as I scan them looking for the marshmallow box.

"That's kind of you, but my passport is expired." It's not. "Thanks anyway."

Beans, canned tomatoes, beans . . . Why do we have so many beans?

"Well, we're not totally set on Cabo. We might go to Vegas."

Corn, hot sauce, more beans . . . "I'm sure you'll have a great time with your friends, wherever you end up. Oh! They're here." Stretching onto my tiptoes, I strain to reach the box of marshmallows so I can get the hell out of here.

"Let me help." Clay's body gets super close to mine, but not quite touching me. He reaches up, grabbing the box I can't quite get and tucks it under his arm. He doesn't step back when I turn around, and when I look up, he's looking down. He keeps looking down, as his head lowers and his eyes close.

The back of my neck prickles and my palms sweat. "I don't want you to kiss me!"

My intention is to say it calmly. Coolly, even. A casual "No, thank you, I'm not interested," like an adult. But what actually happens is I accidentally yell it at him so loudly he jumps, immediately snapping up straight and opening his eyes. His instant reaction is confusion, because I'd guess that he's rarely rejected, but he shakes it off quickly. "I wasn't trying to kiss you, Aurora."

I suppress the urge to argue that he was definitely trying to kiss me, because the sooner we move on from this the better, but I can't ignore the opportunity to be petty. "Sorry, my mistake. You're a great friend, Clay."

The face he pulls when I say the word *friend* could be used to scare off crows in a field. "Sure thing," he mutters, spinning with the marshmallows and hightailing it out of the pantry.

I take my time heading toward the campfire area, not wanting to bump into my great friend Clay on the walk, and when I reach everyone, the kids are all sipping hot chocolate and looking exhausted, winding down from their day of partying.

"Why do you look so pleased with yourself?" Emilia asks as I sit in the camp chair between her and Xander. Russ is chatting to Maya on the other side of the fire, so it feels safe to share.

"Clay tried to kiss me in the pantry, and when I stopped him, he told me he wasn't trying to kiss me."

Xander's laughter is louder than the campers combined and he slaps a hand over his mouth as all the kids begin to look at him. "Sorry," he says. "What did you say?"

"I told him he's a great friend." That sets Xander off again, and I have to wait for him to stop. "I wasn't misinterpreting, I swear. He was right up close with his eyes closed, leaning in. And he'd just invited me to Cabo."

"How lucky are you," Emilia snickers. "You love Cabo."

"I told him my passport is expired."

The kids are all too worn out to want anything, so the rest of the evening is spent with Xander and Emilia laughing, mainly at my expense. By the time the kids are going to bed and we're heading back to our cabin for an early night, I think Emilia and Xander have talked about every silly thing I've ever done.

It's weird hearing those stories now and how a little effort and the right setting can make you feel like a different person. I'm not saying I'll never do anything irresponsible again, but being at Honey Acres makes me feel at home. Being disconnected from my phone most of the time keeps me present, and I have so much to feel thankful for. It's more difficult to remember that when I'm reminded of the things I don't have every time my dad lets me down.

Emilia heads into the bathroom to clean up and I change into an oversized T-shirt. I think I imagine the knocking at first, until it happens again, followed by the sound of whining. As smart as Fish is, she can't knock on doors, so I'm not surprised to find Russ at the bottom of the porch steps with her when I open the door. Illuminated by the light, he rakes me up and down with his eyes, setting every inch of my exposed skin on fire.

I should stay in the doorway.

There's no reason to walk out to him. I can see and hear him perfectly fine from the safety of my cabin. But of course I move to stand right in front of him. There's glitter on the bow of his top lip; I fight to keep my hands by my side. "Hello."

"Hi. I wanted to check that you were okay." My eyebrow quirks. "Xander."

That little gossip.

He's as bad as Leon.

"I'm okay. It's no big deal." He nods, shuffling in place. I can't imagine Xander reported that I needed checking on, since I wasn't upset. "Why are you really here, Russ?"

His hand rubs the back of his neck, something I haven't seen him do in a while.

You, sir, are nervous.

"I don't know, Rory." He sighs, and his hand reaches out to move my hair from my face. "I wanted to see you."

I lean in toward him, the faint smell of sandalwood and vanilla hanging in the air. I watch the flicker of uncertainty cross his face before he takes a step closer to me. My voice lowers. "Are you jealous?"

"Of course I am." He says it so candidly that it catches me a little off guard. "I sort of want to punch him and I don't understand why."

It takes every scrap of self-control not to throw myself at him. I'd love to push this, wind him up, see what he does. But jealousy is only fun when you can do something about it. "You don't need to be jealous and you don't need to punch him. Mainly because that's silly, but also because you need this job, remember?"

"I do need this job." He nods once, then twice like he's having a debate in his head I can't hear, and on the third nod, he takes a step away from the porch. "Do you want to go on a hike tomorrow?"

"I have to work."

"Xander said he'll swap with you so we can have the day off together."

"When you say hike, do you mean hike hike? Or do you mean I complain while walking uphill to our spot and then we hang out in the sun?"

His dimples appear as he smiles, melting me from the inside out. "Our spot."

"That'd be good, but, like, only if he doesn't mind."

"He doesn't." He takes another step away and I really, really wish he'd kiss me good night. "Good night, Rory. See you tomorrow."

"Good night, Russ." He waits until I'm back in my cabin so I don't have to watch him leave, like he does every time without fail.

Emilia's drying her hair with a towel when I get back inside. She nods toward the door. "What'd I miss?"

"I think I'm having my main character moment."

"Freaking finally," she says, turning on her hair dryer.

Chapter Nineteen

RUSS

"You've gone rogue, my man," JJ says proudly. "I support it."

I hadn't intended to start my day on a video call with JJ, but at this point, it can't make things worse. Right? I didn't mean to tell him everything, but for once it felt nice to choose to share because I'm excited about something.

"I don't know what I'm doing, JJ," I groan. "Faking confidence can only go so far. I'm supposed to be staying out of trouble; I've made this massive deal about how much I need this job and now I feel like a hypocrite."

"This woman likes you, right . . ."

I massage the tension out of the back of my neck where it accumulates. "I think so. I might be wrong."

"Nah, that wasn't a question. This woman likes you and it doesn't sound like you're faking anything. You asked her to hang out with you today because you like her, too. Are you faking anything when you hang out alone?"

Thinking about it, the answer is easy. "No. I feel like I can be myself with her."

"Listen, buddy," JJ says, clearing his throat. "I know you've got your whole home life bag going on, or whatever is happening there, and I know you like to keep your head down. But don't miss an opportunity to have fun and actually be happy because you're too busy staring at the floor, trying to go unnoticed. You know you can always stay here if you need to avoid family drama until college restarts."

"Thanks, JJ."

"I'm pissed I had to graduate for people to realize how wise I am," he grumbles. "Think about how much better everyone's lives would've been if I was listened to."

"I've always listened to you," I argue. "I've been faking confidence for weeks."

"Well remember, we're not faking now. You are confident. You're a tall, hot, well-educated hockey player. Women will look past every red flag for a man over six two. So stop waiting for something bad to happen and go have fun."

"I don't think I have any red flags . . ."

"Oh, my sweet summer child." He laughs. "You're a straight white man. That's your red flag."

"That seems totally fair, actually. Thanks for chatting with me, man. I appreciate you."

"Love you, brother. Speak soon."

ONE DAY AURORA WILL TAKE her clothes off in front of me and I won't have to recite presidents in my head.

She kicks her shorts onto the T-shirt she's already taken off and pulls a sock from each foot, adding them to the pile, and lies down on the picnic blanket. We're more prepared than we were last time, with towels and an actual lunch to see us through the afternoon. "It's so warm today," she says, adjusting the material of her bikini.

I've seen what's beneath the fabric, so I don't know why I feel so intimidated by it.

"There's going to be a thunderstorm later. It'll cool down tomorrow."

"Ugh, I absolutely hate thunder and lightning. Emilia is working tonight as well." I crouch down to her clothes, folding them and adding them to mine. She sits up, resting on her elbows to watch me. "Why do you always fold everything? I feel like you're constantly tidying up."

This is the part where I ask her a question about herself. Where I deflect, where I'd keep her talking about herself until she was distracted enough to remember she asked me something in the first place. But the anxiety from trying to control a conversation in that way is exhausting, and I'm tired of forcing my guard to stay up with her.

I sit cross-legged next to her and take a deep breath. "Sometimes my dad would come home in really bad moods and he'd pick at every single thing—the house was messy, dinner wasn't ready, my brother and I hadn't done our homework yet—and I fucking hated waiting for him to come home, never knowing what mood he was in."

She sits up and moves in front of me, crossing her legs, too, so her knees are resting against my shins. It's such a simple thing to do, and when her hands rest against my calves, I want to keep going.

"I tried to do everything before he had a chance to complain about it. Keeping everything tidy just became a habit after that. I like being helpful, and neatening things is an easy way to help people."

"I'm sorry for being so untidy." She offers a coy smile. "I have a habit of leaving a path of destruction in my wake, both literally and metaphorically."

"Like a wildfire."

She nods, bringing her knees to her chest and wrapping her arms around them. "I don't mean to be."

My fingers trail patterns on either side of her ankles while she rests her chin on her knees. "This is the bit where you tell me something about you so I don't feel awkward for being the only one sharing." I'm only half joking, but she smiles. "That's how this works, right? A secret for a secret."

"I love that you think I'm sharing to make things even and not because I'm totally incapable of keeping my thoughts in my head when I'm around you. What do you want to know? I'm an open book, Callaghan."

"You keep mentioning little things about wanting to change. What's the deal with that? I think you're perfect, so I don't get why you'd want to."

Lifting her head, she stares at me for what feels like forever. Pools of the most beautiful emerald green look right at me, but for once, she's totally quiet.

"I've told myself for years how self-aware I am and how I'm my own person, but I'm not," she says eventually. "It's really hard admitting you're the person standing in the way of your own happiness, but I realized I was the problem a while ago. I just didn't know where to start. You ever feel like you've made something your entire personality? So much so you don't know how to disconnect yourself from it?"

"What do you mean?"

She rests her head back on her knees, slowly shrinking herself before me. "I know I'm messed up, right? And it's like, if I'm the first person to say it, then people can't use it to hurt me. If I'm the first to say how much emotional baggage I have, then people can't use it to push me away, because I'm the one who knew it was there. Does that make sense?"

"Yeah."

"And I know I struggle with rejection, so I don't give people the chance to reject me. I search for physical connections with people, to feel validated, because I need someone else to prove to me that I'm wanted. So I call myself self-aware because I know those things about myself, but in reality, I don't know anything about myself. I say I'm my own person, but every choice I make is because of something someone else did. That isn't being my own person."

"You are wanted, Aurora. You're incredible and you can be your own person."

"There's something about Honey Acres that makes me feel good," she says quietly. "It feels so fragile right now, but I'm starting to remember what I like about myself. I want to make choices that make me happy. And I'm scared that when I go back to Maple Hills, I won't want to try so hard anymore. That I'll be surrounded by so much external noise I'll forget this feeling."

"I won't let you forget, don't worry." My words hang in the air between us like question marks, because neither of us has mentioned that when the summer is over, we'll be heading back to the same place. I spent two years at college before meeting her, so it's not unreasonable to think I could do another two without seeing her since the college is so big.

Aurora rolls onto her stomach, arms tucked under her head, her hip pressed up against me. Her touch makes me feel settled, a feeling I can't say I'm used to. It's familiar and safe, like there's an unspoken agreement between us as her skin presses into mine. We ease into a natural silence, something becoming common between the two of us, where I don't question it and she doesn't fill it, and for the second time, I drift off to sleep beside her.

THE TREES HAVE CREATED SHADE over me when I wake up sometime later alone.

Alone.

My heart sinks, skin prickling uncomfortably as I stare at the empty spot beside me. I want to be surprised, but deep down I've been preparing for this moment for weeks. The moment where I go too far, share too much, and it's too much to handle. I can't be mad at her for running, when I knew this would happen if I opened up to someone.

I push myself up from the blanket, and the second my head rises I spot her, floating on her back in the water, and my heart doesn't know what to do. I think I've given it whiplash from how fucking quickly I'm flitting from despair to happiness.

I'm such a dick.

I'm six feet away when the water ripples let her know I'm there and she stops floating. "Hey, sleepyhead," she says softly, gazing at me. Gently gripping her waist, I pull her closer, feeling better when she instantly wraps her arms and legs around me the way I want her to. "You look sad. What's wrong?"

I bury my face into her neck, letting my arms wrap around her, breathing in the smell of peach and sunblock. "I thought you'd left."

She tightens her hold. "I'm sorry, I needed to cool down. Are you okay?"

I nod, loosening my grip on her so she can lean back to look at me. Her hand brushes my hair from my face and my eyes flick to her lips. "You don't need to apologize. I thought I'd finally scared you away. I overreacted; I'm fine."

"I might not have the exact same circumstances, but I can relate to your feelings, Russ," she says carefully, running her fingers across my temple and down to my jaw. "I know how it feels expecting more from someone who lets you down. You're not going to scare me with your feelings or your experiences, I promise. I know it's not going to undo the other stuff, but I'm choosing to be here, and nothing you say to me is going to make me change my mind."

I swallow as her fingers skim down my neck and along my collarbone. "Thank you."

The moment of panic and relief has passed, but I still don't want to let her go. We work like this, just the two of us away from everyone else. Where she wants to be wanted and I want to be put first. Where we both ignore the reality that her closeness to me is through forced proximity and under normal circumstances this wouldn't be happening.

Her stomach brushes mine as she sighs deeply, her teeth sinking into her lip while she works out what to say. "Being vulnerable is scary. Sharing the things you think no one else will understand is scary. But if there's one thing I'm good at, it's ignoring all the normal signals to stop talking. I can teach you, but I've got to be honest, it's a lot easier drunk."

"I don't think us being drunk together is a good idea. I actually don't really drink. The party was an exception. I was trying to be confident and I thought it would help." She shivers as my fingers trace her spine; her thighs squeeze around me. She pinches her lips tight and I wait for the laugh she's fighting. "I didn't come across as confident, did I?"

She shakes her head as she giggles. "Did you know you rub the back of your neck when you're nervous? You do it all the time. The tips of your ears turn pink, too; it's adorable." I try to float away as I feel the heat rush to my face, but she doesn't let go as she laughs, pulling me closer. "I'm sorry, I'm sorry, I'm sorry!"

"Adorable," I repeat back to her, her face inches from mine. "Like a puppy."

Her eyes flick down, then back to mine quickly. "Adorable like a guy who isn't a total dick to get into someone's pants at a party."

My face moves closer. "Nobody has ever said those words in a sentence before now."

"I'm happy to be the first," she whispers. "I stand by them."

Neither of us noticed the sky begin to darken or the clouds move to block the sun, and once again, I can't help but feel the universe is intervening as the rain begins to hit the water around us—and somehow neither one of us closes those last few inches.

Chapter Twenty

AURORA

"WHAT'S A GIRL GOT TO do to be kissed around here?" I grumble as I help Emilia load a serving tray with hot chocolate. The rain has been on and off since it started this afternoon, unusual for this time of year in California and wholly inconvenient for me, since it forced Russ and me to run back to camp. According to Alexander I-Know-Everything Smith, it's something to do with a remnant of a tropical storm being dragged north and we're set to have terrible weather for the next twelve hours. I hate thunder and lightning, so knowing Emilia will be watching the kids tonight and I'll be in our cabin alone fills me with dread. Therefore, I've spent the past twenty minutes complaining to my entirely unbothered best friend.

"What happened to sticking to the rules, so you get to sleep peacefully at night knowing you didn't contribute to someone getting fired?"

"I don't think I said that."

Her eyes narrow as she tries to intimidate me into a confession. "I know for a fact you don't remember everything your rambling ass says, but I do. You definitely said it at least five times. I think I preferred when you were wild. I heard about it less."

Flicking her forehead with one hand, I throw a marshmallow into my mouth with the other. Emilia can complain all she wants. I've liked one guy in our entire friendship; she has been single collectively for about four days in as many years, and I've lived through every stage of every relationship.

She owes me after I had to deal with one obsessed girl who turned out to be a drug dealer with scary friends.

"I don't know how to feel my feelings. It's like the opposite of the feeling scaries. What do I do?"

"You *like* him, like him? You don't just like that he gives you attention? And because you know he likes you, too, and therefore won't reject you?"

"I *like* him, like him. I think he's a nice guy and he makes me laugh. He makes me feel seen and I don't want to fuck it up because I don't know how to be a functional adult. Why haven't you made me go to therapy yet? You're a bad friend."

"What happened to 'I don't need to pay a therapist to tell me I have daddy issues'?" she says, rolling her eyes. "Okay, you want my advice? You're not going to like it . . ."

"I'm ready. Tell me."

"You need to wait until we're back in Maple Hills. See how you feel when you get your freedom back and the camp goggles are gone."

"Ugh," I groan. "That's terrible advice. Why won't you just enable me?"

"Because I love you. Now move," she orders, picking up the hot chocolate tray and nodding to the other one. "If you're going to be annoying, at least be helpful."

I try to be helpful, but my mind is working overtime this evening. Between the storm and Russ, I have too much nervous energy. I swear time is moving slower than normal, so I decide to do the one thing that can zap my energy like nothing else.

Leaning against the wall beside the communal phone in the main building so I don't have to go outside in the rain and get my cell phone from my cabin, I count the rings as I wait for my mom to pick up. I've tried to remember to call weekly, but the days are so busy here and a week passes in the blink of an eye, so I haven't been great at remembering.

She's pissed about it. She makes it clear she's upset she's not a higher priority every time I do remember to call. The rings are running out and I know this call is close to going to voice mail because she's screening me. She thinks she's making a point, but in reality, I don't care if she doesn't answer because at least I can say I've tried.

"Hello?" She says it like she hasn't gotten every number associated with this camp saved in her phone.

"Hi! It's me." I force as much enthusiasm as I can into my voice. "Just checking in."

"Oh," she says casually. "Hello."

"How are you?"

"I'm fine. Now isn't a good time for me, Aurora. I'm very busy."

It's a Thursday evening and there's a storm. What could she be busy with? She doesn't go outside when it's raining; she doesn't like risking ruining her blowout. "What are you doing?"

"Oh, now you're interested in talking to me, are you?" I can feel all the nervous energy from earlier being drained. Like somehow this very predictable interaction has recalibrated me. "I can't just drop everything because you're suddenly free to talk to me."

"I totally understand, Mom. We can catch up another time." There's shuffling on her end of the phone and I hear something purr. "Wait, is that a cat?"

More shuffling. "Yes, it's a cat."

I feel like I'm being pranked. I look around the empty room, checking to see if Emilia is somewhere in the shadows waiting to jump out on me. "Whose cat is it?"

"It's my cat."

"You don't have a cat. Do you even like cats?"

"I like this cat because it's mine. I rescued him."

A vision of my mom becoming a cat lady and filling her massive house with them comes into my mind. "From where?"

"He joined me for breakfast on the deck one day. I gave him some of my smoked salmon, because he looked hungry, and he kept coming back, so I let him in the house. I've decided to keep him."

I rest my forehead against the wall, the phone pressed close to my ear. "Did he have a collar?"

"Yes, but it wasn't very nice. I got him a new one from Louis Vuitton. You can meet him if you decide to do that long, hard drive you love to complain about."

I reserve the right to always complain about LA traffic, and she can't guilt that out of me. "Mom! You've stolen someone's pet!"

"I rescued him, Aurora. He's perfectly happy here with me." The purring on the other end of the line increases, and part of me considers she's tricking me into visiting her just to see if she's actually stolen someone's cat.

"You need to check the old collar for a number! I know the only thing you like to listen to is the ocean and Chuck Roberts slander, but somewhere in Malibu, if you listen very closely, there's a child crying for their beloved family pet."

"You're being very dramatic today, darling. Are you on your period?"

Give me strength. "No."

"Did you see that your father is spending summer break on the yacht with the weather girl and her family?" she says casually. "Elsa is very unhappy about it all. She wanted to go to Monaco."

"Mom, where exactly would I have seen that? I'm in the middle of nowhere with next to no service trying to keep twenty kids safe," I say with a huff. I'm not surprised that's what he's doing, and the way it doesn't tear me up immediately is liberating. I wouldn't go so far to say I hope they have a nice time, but I'm perfectly happy where I am.

"I don't know what you do with your time, Aurora. You don't tell me anything. I really do need to go, it's time for Cat to have his dinner."

"You called him Cat?"

"What else was I supposed to call him? He's a cat. Good-bye, darling. Don't forget to call again."

I walk back in a daze to where everyone is watching a film, and by the time Emilia and Xander are rounding up the Brown Bears for bed, I still haven't processed my mom replacing me with a stolen cat.

Temporary respite from my mom's attention happens occasionally when she finds a new interest. Wine tasting, Pilates, a property developer called Jack—but never a pet. As weird as it is, I'm kind of happy she isn't in that house alone anymore.

"What if I just sleep in your bed with you?" I ask Emilia.

"What if you just sleep in your bed alone?" she counters. There are two bedrooms attached to the kids' cabin for the counselors doing night duty, and as spacious as the kids area is, the same cannot be said for the adjoining rooms. "It's a storm. You'll survive. You know what I won't survive? Sharing that tiny bed with you."

"You can sleep in the world's tiniest bed with me, Ror," Xander teases. "I volunteer because I'm such a good friend."

I roll my eyes at him, knowing full well if I ever took him up on that offer he would run for the hills. "Hard pass, but thanks."

It was here during a particularly bad storm that my fear started. Dry lightning caused a wildfire not far from Orla's land and we almost needed to be evacuated. Thankfully, the fire service got it under control. I was so young, and ever since then, they've always freaked me out.

I'm helping Freya into her raincoat when the doors open and Russ strolls through them in sweatpants and a Brown Bear sweatshirt. He shakes the rain from his hair and scans the room, his eyes eventually landing on me. He smiles as soon as he spots me and I can't stop the wide grin on my face. God, I need to get a grip. Freya coughs loudly, dragging my attention back to her. "Is Russ your boyfriend?"

If this is Leon's bullshit again I swear he's going to get locked outside next time I'm on night duty. "No. He is a boy who is a friend. He isn't my boyfriend."

"Then why do you always spend your days off together?"

"Do you like spending your time with your friends?" I ask her, pulling her hood over her brown curls. "Because I do, and that's why I spend my days off with them."

"I'm not a baby, you know," she says. "And I can keep a secret."

"There aren't any secrets here, silly girl. Now, go and get into the line, please."

"Okay," she says, a hint of defeat in her voice. "But Russ looks at you the way my dad looks at my papa when he isn't looking, so I think he might love you."

"Good night, Freya," I groan.

It's an unwritten rule at camp that you will be terrorized by your campers about potential love interests. I know that because I was once the person doing all the terrorizing.

The smart thing to do is forget about it, because who would trust the opinion of a small child? And yet here I am, wondering exactly how Freya's dads look at each other.

Thankfully, no other kids decide to pry into my life, and Russ stays far enough away from me that he doesn't give Leon and his rumor mill any more material. I haven't seen Russ since our almost-kiss, swiftly followed by running from the rain earlier.

I really thought he was going to do it this time. We were so close and his hands on me felt right, but I suppose unlike me, he knows how to exercise restraint. I wasn't expecting to have a wild summer filled with hookups, for obvious reasons, but surely no one will die if we have one tiny little kiss.

If he wants to fuck me against a tree, I could also be convinced to get on board.

God, I wish I'd brought my vibrator.

"You look like you're thinking hard about something," Russ laughs, filling the empty spot beside me. "What's up?"

"Forgot my vibrator." I freeze and make the smart choice not to look at him and see the aftermath of my words. His ears are definitely pink; I don't even need to look at him to check. I just know. "I didn't mean to say that out loud."

"Want me to walk you back to your cabin?" he says, thankfully ignoring my comment. "The weather is crappy."

"No, it's okay," I mumble, looking out at the black sky. "I'm going to stay here until everyone goes to bed."

"Do you mind if I stay, too?"

"I'd really like it if you did."

THE THUNDER IS LOUDER IN the cabin than it was in the movie room and I'm considering taking Xander up on his offer. Three-person night duty can become a thing, right?

I've tried music on my headphones. I've tried calming meditation. I've tried distracting myself with a book, but the weather is so bad not even sexy billionaires with a theme park are enough to distract me. Every time the thunder booms, I swear the cabin shakes. I've talked myself out of heading to Russ's cabin three times. I was like someone from a movie when they stand up, walk to the door and put their hand on the handle, before dramatically shaking their head and walking away.

Nothing good can come from me going to see him—and yet the idea sticks. He can't make the storm stop and I can't go into his cabin, so there's no point in my venturing out in the dark.

Knowing my luck, I'll step outside and get struck by lightning.

I'm arguing with myself for the fourth time when there's a knock on the door. What are the chances that Russ has been having the same argument with himself? When he finally closes those final few inches and kisses me?

Pulling back the door, I realize the answer to that question is zero.

Zero chance.

"Wow, you two are messy," Jenna complains, poking her head through the doorway. She looks at the clothes on the floor and frowns. "How do you guys move around in here?"

"Can I help you, Ms. Murphy?" I grumble, not even attempting to hide my disappointment that she isn't a six-foot-five hockey player with pretty blue eyes and a tendency to blush.

"Wow, she's grumpy today. Still not over the storm thing, I see." She reaches into her bag and pulls out a flashlight. "In case the power goes out."

The power might go out. Fantastic. "Remind me, why did I choose working for you over hanging out on a yacht or something equally douchey, but cool?"

"Because you love me," she says proudly. "And sure, yachts are cool, but you ever had to deal with so much rainwater everywhere floods? You can't get experiences like that in Dubai."

"Living the dream, Jen."

"You know it," she says, grinning. "Okay, you're my last delivery. I'm going to bed because I don't have to work tonight and this weather fucking sucks. Don't stress, okay? It'll be over by morning."

When has telling someone not to stress ever helped them not stress? Climbing back into bed, I try again with the book before giving up after five minutes. For the first time in my life, I'm not feeling romance books.

As someone who's perpetually single, I think it's probably more shocking that I like them to begin with. It's a bit of a conundrum now that I think about it, how I have such faith in fictional happy endings, but have never considered what my own might look like.

Another knock comes. Pulling back the door again, I find Orla on my doorstep. Now I definitely know the universe is fucking with me. I mentally recap everything I've done since I got here that could have landed me on Orla's radar, but nothing stands out. I've only been slutty in my head, not in real life, and she can't read my thoughts, so she has no idea I'm desperately pining after getting to first base like an absolute loser.

"Hi, sweetie. I think I'm in the wrong place." She pulls out her cell phone to check her messages. "There's apparently a leaking roof and I need to take a picture for the repair records. I swear there are no perks to being an old lady these days. Getting sent out in the rain and all kinds of nonsense."

She hands me the phone while she takes off her glasses, cleaning the fog and water with the collar of the jacket beneath her raincoat. "This says twenty-seven, not twenty-two. Twenty-seven is next to the main lawn. I think it's opposite the Hedgehog cabin."

Orla tightens her hood around her face, accepting her cell phone back and putting it into her pocket. "Thank you, sweetie. Sorry to have bothered you, sleep tight."

I'm staring at the ceiling listening to the rain slowing down, trying to fall asleep, when the thunder booms, sounding like it's happening right above my freaking cabin.

"Okay, we're doing this. It's happening," I mutter to myself, rolling out of bed and reaching for my sneakers. Flicking on the lights, I search around Emilia's and my things—Jenna was right, we are messy. Where the fuck is my raincoat?

Admitting defeat, I pull on my Brown Bear sweatshirt, which paired with my shorts looks like I'm cosplaying as Russ from earlier.

This is probably a bad idea.

"Bad ideas are character building," I say to myself out loud, just as the lights in my cabin go out. "Fuck my life. This is not a sign."

I keep repeating that it's not a sign in my head as I fumble around for the flashlight Jenna gave me earlier and slowly navigate my way to the door in the dark. As soon as I'm outside, I can see there are lights on in other buildings. It's just my row of cabins whose lights are out.

Of course it is.

The fact I've never googled the chances of someone being struck by lightning feels like a mistake as I run down the path in the direction of the lake.

There's a real risk he's going to turn me away.

What am I doing? Old Aurora would be booing and collapsing through sheer horror if she could see me now.

I'm thankful for my flashlight as I approach the row of cabins and count the numbers until I read the sign that says 33. My heart is in my throat as I climb the porch steps to Russ's door.

The worst he can say to me is to go back to my own bed. At least I think that's the worst thing. I know I shouldn't be here, so there's no reason to be surprised if he doesn't want my needy ass right now.

The lightning cracks in the sky, stunning but terrifying, and I knock on the wooden door. Light peeks through a gap between the curtains, but he doesn't answer the door. I knock again and wait, rationalizing he might be in the bathroom or something, but he doesn't answer.

Dejected and a little embarrassed, I admit defeat and exit the protection of the porch back into the rain. It was a silly thing to do anyway and I really shouldn't have been doing it. Maybe I have been misreading things. I'm sure I'll have a great time overthinking this night for the rest of my life. When I'm old and gray, I'll wake up in a cold sweat obsessing about how I went out in the rain in a sweater featuring a freaking bear and got ignored by the man I couldn't stop thinking about.

Turning the first corner away from the cabin, I stop abruptly when I spot Russ walking toward me. His head is down, but after a few more steps he looks up at me and stops, too. "Hey," he calls into the darkness. He's as soaked as I am, wearing the same sweater and sweatpants as earlier, now darker from the rain.

"Hey."

"I went to your cabin," he says softly. "I thought you might be scared; I wanted to check that you were okay."

I don't know how to respond to what he said with words, so I move toward him, he moves toward me, and I'm so mesmerized by him that I don't even flinch when lightning lights up the skies over Honey Acres, because he finally closes those last few inches and kisses me.

Chapter Twenty-One

AURORA

I now understand why there are so many songs about being kissed in the rain.

Russ presses me into the wall of his cabin, my legs wrapped tight around him like they have been so many times before, except this time his fingers are tangled in my hair, pulling to keep my head to the side to kiss, lick, and suck the length of my neck.

It's different from last time; he's more confident, more sure of what to do to make me arch off the wall and whimper. I tug at his sweatshirt, impatient to see his body again and feel it against mine. He helps me pull the wet material over his head, immediately pulling mine off, too. Our damp stomachs stick together, heat spreading across my skin like wildfire.

"You're so fucking beautiful," he whispers at the shell of my ear. "I can't believe it took us so long to do this again."

Preach. We deserve some kind of medal for the amount of self-restraint we've shown when we know how good we make each other feel. "Some of us like to respect the rules, Callaghan," I tease. His hands sink into my ass and my entire body feels like it's going to burst into flames at any minute.

Moving us to his bed, he gently lowers me down onto the mattress, the soft material a welcome contrast to the roughness of the wall. He pulls down his pants and boxers and I have to stop my jaw from falling off my face. Time has dulled my memory of how impressive he is, and after several weeks of working here with only myself in the shower, I fear I may be a little out of practice.

"Do you know how big my ego gets when you look at me like that?" he says, kneeling on the bed between my legs totally naked.

I'm pretty sure it's a rule somewhere that it's rude not to look at someone's face when they're talking to you, but in all fairness, they haven't seen how pretty Russ's dick is.

"I'm doing a risk assessment of the likeliness of you splitting me in half."

He snorts and leans over my body to kiss me slowly. "Are you sure you want to do this?"

"It's all I've thought about for weeks," I admit. "I'm not afraid of a little risk."

Unbuttoning my shorts, Russ pulls them down, then slides my panties off, spreading my legs wide in front of him. Without a little alcohol in my system, this is the bit where I'd normally feel self-conscious. Not with him. "What do you need?" he asks, massaging my inner thighs.

Everything. "I want to feel close to you."

He moves to lie on the bed beside me, rolling me onto my side so our stomachs are touching. He hikes my leg over my hip and tucks an arm under my head. "This good?"

"Perfect."

Russ takes his time to rub his hand over the curve of my waist, along the bottom of my back until he's palming my ass. His mouth and tongue move against mine as his hand slips from my ass to dip between my legs. "Fuck, Aurora," he groans, pressing his forehead to mine. "You're so wet."

His dick twitches against my stomach. "Can I touch you?"

"You can do whatever you want to me." He moans when I wrap my hand around him, stroking up and down slowly. He pushes a finger inside of me, followed by a second one, stretching me. My heartbeat speeds up, breathing falling into an unsteady rhythm as I move the hand wedged between us in a rhythm he loves. "You're so fucking good, sweetheart."

He's patient, watching my every reaction to learn exactly what I like. My leg over his hips begins to shake, the building feeling in my stomach feels like it's in my bones. "I'm going to come." His thumb finds my clit and all I want to do is pull him closer. Closer how, I don't know, but my free hand grips the back of his neck and I moan into his mouth. "Oh fuck, Russ. Oh my God."

"That's it. Let me see that pretty face when I make you come."

My body bucks and writhes on his fingers, my hand still wrapped around him. He pulls his fingers out, his hips thrusting up into my hand a few times before he stops, wrapping his hand around mine to stop me. "I don't wanna come yet."

"Where are your condoms?"

I watch the expression on his face sink into horror. "Shit."

"Please tell me you're saying shit because you're upset that you'll have to be away from me for the two seconds it'll take for you to get them."

"I haven't got any," he admits sheepishly. "Don't look at me like that, I wasn't expecting to have sex!"

He rolls onto his back, using my leg to pull me on top of him. His dick is like a freaking rock, conveniently positioned flat against him but between my legs. I gently rock my hips and his eyes roll back, hands immediately gripping my hips to keep me in place as he mimics my actions by thrusting up.

Everything is swollen and aching and wet, which is clouding my problem-solving skills. I can hardly blame him for not bringing condoms when I didn't, either.

"We could just not use one? When was the last time you were tested?" I ask. "I'm on birth control and my most recent test was clear. I always use them. One of us can go into Meadow Springs to buy some this week."

"I was tested a few weeks before I met you and it was clear. You're the only person I've been with since, but um, I'm not comfortable not using a condom. I won't enjoy it if I'm worrying about the statistics of how effective your birth control is."

"That's totally fine, I respect that." We probably should have had this conversation before we got naked, but at least we're having it. He looks a little embarrassed, but he has no reason to be. Pulling him to a sitting position, he leans back on his hands and I wrap my arms around his neck, pecking him on the lips. "There's plenty of other ways I can satisfy you. Let's keep count of th— Oh my God, I bet Xander has some."

I don't think I've ever moved as quickly as I do rushing toward Xander's side of the cabin. Russ puts his feet on the floor, perching on the edge of his bed. "Rory, I don't think we should look through Xander's things."

He's got a point—not one I'll be considering, but a point all the same. "Do you think if Xander knew you needed a condom he would be mad?"

"Fair observation."

I check the obvious places like his bedside table, his toiletry bag, his sock drawer, the wardrobe, but I don't find any. If I were Xander, where would I hide condoms? Dropping to the floor, I check under the bed, and while there's a real chance I'm about to find something furry with claws, I immediately spot a duffel bag.

"Jeez, Aurora," Russ groans, and he physically sounds pained. My ass is in the air, chest close to the floor, and it doesn't take a genius to work out what might be on his mind right now. I pull the bag toward me and find exactly what I'm looking for. Holding up the foil packets in the air like a freaking prize, I try not to run back to his bed. I've never seen Russ move as quickly as he does ripping the foil and covering himself.

Still on the edge of the bed, he grips the back of my thighs to move my legs to either side of his hips. I'm careful as he aligns himself and I sink down onto him. I'm so full that it stuns me, stretching me, making me freeze. "Take your time," he murmurs softly, kissing my chest. His hands hold my waist, guiding me as I lift up and down tentatively, taking a little more of him each time. "That's it, good girl. You feel so fucking good, Aurora. You're making me lose my mind."

The praise makes the sex better and I'm not embarrassed to admit that.

Russ Callaghan can call me a good girl anytime.

We fall into a perfect rhythm. His hands move to my ass, helping as I bounce on him, while his mouth explores my neck and chest. My fingers rub frantically between my legs and I squeeze him tighter. "I'm close," I pant.

His hands keep guiding me and I crash my mouth into his, our skin flush in so many places that we feel like one person. It feels like light bursting through my body and I cling to him tightly, riding out the high, pulsing around him.

"You good?" he whispers.

"Thighs are burning. Worth it."

Russ lifts me off him, laying me down on his bed again and lying behind me. His arm slips under my head, his chest flat to my back, and it seems like we're about to spoon, until I feel his dick poking me from behind. "Lift your leg a little, sweetheart."

"You can't put it in my butt."

Goose bumps spread across my body as he laughs into my neck. "I wasn't planning on that, but thanks for letting me know."

He slides back inside of me with one thrust and everything feels different from this angle. I lower my leg and the arm around my neck crosses my chest, letting him swirl his finger around my nipple. His other hand dances across my stomach before slipping through my legs and I immediately know he's ruined anyone else for me.

His hips rock back and forth gently, combined with his hand, and he whispers sweet things into my ear. He's everywhere all at once and I know I'm going to be falling over the edge again soon. I feel valued like this, worshipped. Like his one mission in life is to make me feel beautiful and wanted. I force my hips back as he drives his forward and we fall into a crazed pattern, chasing a high together.

"That's it, show me how much you want it," he says into my neck. "You're worth any risk, Ror."

The sound of our bodies slapping against each other drowns out any sound of a storm. Shit, I don't even know if there is a storm anymore. Russ is taking over my every sense. I'm moaning, he's moaning. I go harder, so does he. My pulse in my neck is hammering against his mouth and his thrusts start to become sloppy and rough. He pants my name and his fingers rub me faster and I'm there, falling with him.

I'm exhausted, sore, and completely satiated.

We lie there totally still, him still inside of me. He blows out a sigh. "I think I might be obsessed with you."

It's like another orgasm. "That's the sex talking."

"It's not."

He pulls out slowly, kissing me gently as I wince a little. He visits the bathroom to get rid of the condom, and for the first time I don't expect the guy I just slept with to close the door and wait for me to leave.

Lying back down beside me he leans over to see my face, brushing my hair out of the way and kissing me on the forehead. "Do you want anything? Drink? Shower? Something comfortable?"

"I'm good." He pulls the duvet over me and gets in beside me. "Thank you."

Russ kisses my forehead again and rolls my body toward him, putting his arm around me. Spooning after sex is not something I've ever done, but I feel so safe and happy it's borderline overwhelming. He picks up a book from beside the bed and dims the lamp. I want to ask him what he's reading, but my eyes are already closing. I'm about to fall asleep when his voice stops me. "Will you still be here when I wake up?"

"Yes, I promise."

Chapter Twenty-Two

RUSS

I CAN'T REMEMBER THE LAST time I slept for more than a few hours. The closed curtains are blocking out any indication of what time it is, but I know I slept heavily last night; I can feel it.

I'd reach for something to tell me the time, but Aurora is asleep on the arm curled around her and the other is resting against the soft skin of her stomach. As I peck a kiss against her shoulder she stirs slightly and wriggles against me, her ass brushing against my dick, making me groan.

She does it again, this time clearly more intentional, although she's pretending to be asleep. I push my hips forward deliberately, leaning forward to whisper into her ear. "I know you're awake, Rory."

She laughs, and it's my second favorite noise in the world. The first being her moaning my name, obviously. "What a way to wake me up," she says through a yawn.

I'd wake her up however she wanted if it meant she slept next to me at night.

Reaching behind, her hand brushes my knee, then my thigh, slowly climbing higher and higher, pausing to gauge my reaction occasionally, until her arm is folded behind her back and her fingers gently brush past my balls and along my dick.

"Is this okay?" she says, wrapping her hand around me and doing a testing stroke.

"Yeah," I manage to choke out, moving my hips in time with her hand to make things easier for her. "You're so good at that, sweetheart."

She suddenly stops and I immediately panic, thinking I've done something wrong, but then she rolls over to face me. She's still sleepy, her wet hair now dried into waves, and she's looking at me in a way that makes my heart fall out of rhythm. I wish I could save this moment; bottle it and protect it from whatever outside forces are going to try and ruin it.

Aurora leans over and kisses me, and I immediately don't care about anything else but right now. She breaks away, then kisses my collarbone, my chest, slowly moving lower and lower, until I'm holding my breath with anticipation and that sleepy look on her face has been replaced with one that's a lot more mischievous.

She kisses the inside of my thighs, my hip bone, everywhere except the place I want her to. I tuck her hair behind her ear, nudge her chin so she's looking at me. "Are you trying to make me beg, Aurora?"

Those green eyes are staring up at me so fucking innocently, like she doesn't have my cock next to her lips. She kisses the base, keeping her eyes on me. "Nope." Another kiss slightly higher. "You don't need to beg me to do something I've been desperate to do for weeks."

Joining my fingers on top of my head, I pull on my hair as my stomach flexes, my breathing fighting to stay steady. "This is going to be the best seven seconds of my life."

"Don't make me laugh when I'm trying to seduce you," she groans through her laughter.

"You don't need to try, you've achieved it. Consider me seduced.

Obsessed. Consu—" Her lips wrap around the end of my dick and I forget how to speak. I was joking about the seven-seconds thing, but now I'm not so sure it was a joke. "You're unreal, fuck."

Her hair falls around her face as she lowers and takes more of me; I brush it away, collecting it into a ponytail in my fist. She likes that; she lets me know as she moans happily, taking me to the back of her throat.

I like it, too.

I'm scared to blink in case I miss one moment of it. The nails of her free hand gently scrape against my abs while her other works in coordination with her mouth to tip me over the edge. My hand tightens in her hair, muscles tense, and the red-hot feeling starts to build.

She watches me from the spot between my legs, eyes green and dewy and so fucking focused on me right now. "I'm almost there."

My words spur her on; a little bit more and I'll be right there, and that's when the cabin door opens and Xander strolls in from his night duty with the dogs, killing any chance of me ever getting hard again.

"Fuck!" we both scream, him reaching to shield his eyes, me reaching to cover Rory's naked body with a blanket.

"Sorry, sorry," Xander yells, backing out of the cabin quicker than I've ever seen him move. "Do people not put a sock on the door these days? Jesus Christ."

Horrified is the only word to describe how I feel right now.

Looking to Aurora, I expect to find the same mortified expression, but of course I don't, because it's Aurora. Her hand is pressed to her mouth as she tries her best to stop a laugh from bursting out. "I'm sorry," she whispers. "I'm not laughing, I swear. Are you okay?"

The blanket I haphazardly threw on her is partially draped over her head and she's kneeling naked between my legs, while my dick is definitely no longer hard. Dragging a hand down my face, I burst out laughing, which gives her the permission she needed. Tugging her to me, I kiss her forehead as she snuggles closer. "We didn't even last six hours before getting caught."

"We'll be smarter next time," she says, dragging her finger across my skin. "I need to get back to my cabin before someone realizes I'm not there. Sorry you didn't get to finish."

Aurora says "next time" so casually that I don't really know how to answer it. I don't want to have to give her up, but I also don't want to get fired if we get caught. But I *really* don't want to have to give her up. She's the one thing in my life that hasn't been ruined in some way by all the other things. She makes me hopeful, and I'm not ready to say good-bye to that feeling yet.

"We will be more careful," I say, kissing her forehead again.

Climbing over me, she starts to get dressed, frowning when she picks up her still-damp clothes from the floor. "You didn't fold my clothes, Callaghan," she says. "I'm proud of you."

Tugging on my boxers and shorts, I sit on the edge of the bed and watch her grimace, pulling her still damp sweatshirt over her head. She's putting on her sneakers when I pull her toward me, making her stand between my legs. Her hands settle on either side of my face and she smiles down at me while I rub my hands up and down the backs of her thighs.

There's a knock on the door, followed immediately by it creeping open. "Not to spoil this beautiful union, but I'm here because I really need to take a shit. So if you two can wrap this up so I don't have to go in the woods like a fucking bear, that'd be swell."

Aurora looks over her shoulder toward the gap, not taking her hands off my face. "You know there are other bathrooms, right? Your next option isn't the woods?"

"Is a man not allowed to have a preferred place to poop these days? Is that where we're at as a society?"

"I'm leaving, drama queen," she shouts back before kissing me good-bye.

I want to drag her back to bed and lock the door, but it's probably a good thing we were disturbed; I had no idea what time it is and I doubt I could have found the motivation to care anyway.

The dogs come rushing in as soon as Rory opens the door and Xander tries to high-five her as she passes him, but he stops when she jabs him in the ribs playfully. "I stole from you, sorry. Bye."

"It's always the rich girls!" he calls after her. The grin on his face is unmissable as he comes in and closes the door behind him and I can't help but grin like a fool, too. "I'm gonna crap and then we're going to talk about what the fuck happened."

I occupy myself with the dogs while he's gone, and when he comes back, the same—no doubt goofy—grin is still on my face. Neither Xander nor I are working today—the second of my days off and his first after switching with Aurora yesterday—but without even talking about it, I know we're going to be hanging out with everyone all day helping out.

Don't get me wrong, the kids can be exhausting, but it's a good kind of exhausting. It keeps my mind busy and I enjoy helping them find their confidence. In a weird way, when I was younger, I kind of put the wealthy kids on a pedestal because I believed that I would never have any problems if my family was rich. That didn't change much as I got older, especially when I started at a college where it felt like everyone around me was more financially privileged.

Working here is starting to heal that inner child, I think. I see these kids with the same insecurities and worries as I had and I realize how silly I was all those years ago.

And yeah, maybe a tiny part of my motivation to help out today is to see Rory.

Xander throws himself onto his bed, narrowly missing Trout, who is chewing on one of his socks. "Can I guess what Miss Sticky

Fingers stole? Was it a condom by any chance?" I nod and his grin widens. "I'm glad you kids are being safe and I don't have to give you the birds and the bees talk."

I'd rather be attacked by birds and bees than have that conversation with Xander. "You know we're the same age, right?"

"Kids these days . . ." He avoids the shoe I throw at him. "Reflexes of a cat, my guy. But seriously, I'm happy for you. I'm jealous as fuck, but I'm happy. You get to do the whole summer love thing. You're living the dream."

"Thanks, man. What're you doing today?" I ask, changing the subject before he asks me to share too much.

Old habits die hard.

"First thing I'm doing is going back to sleep. Jax decided to tell horror stories before bed, the douche bag. And I know it's not cool to call a ten-year-old a douche bag, but he really is a bit of a dick. Loads of tears and drama, all very annoying. I won't ask what you're doing because I know the answer is hanging around your girl and pretending it's because you care about team sports."

I want to correct him and say she's not my girl, but I like how it sounds. "Pretty much."

He yawns, tugging the blanket over him and Trout, who immediately begins to chew it. "Your secret is safe with me, man."

BY THE TIME I'M SHOWERED and heading for breakfast, last night's rain has disappeared. I'm halfway to the food hall when I hear a "wait up" from behind me.

Freshly showered and now sporting her Brown Bears T-shirt, Aurora smiles as she jogs to catch up to me. Her hand gently brushes past mine, not lingering long enough to be suspicious if anyone was to spot us, but long enough for goose bumps to spread up my arm. "Hey."

"Hi."

"Hi," she repeats awkwardly. "I just wanted to say . . . Well, I've been thinking, and, well, I know I made you break the rules last night and I promised I wou—"

"Rory," I say softly, interrupting her. I stop, moving from her side to in front of her. I'm not used to the look of doubt on her face, or the lack of confidence in her voice. Even when she's rambling to fill the silence, there's an air of confidence to it, but right now, she looks like a woman grappling with uncertainty. "You didn't make me do anything. I went to your cabin, too, remember?"

"I know, but this job is important to you and it's important to me, I love it here, but I also have the impulse control of a hungry raccoon. I don't want you to think that the things that are important to you aren't important to me, when I know they're important to you. Does that make sense?"

"I think so. I don't regret it." Fuck, I want to kiss her. "I promise. I'm trying to relax a little, not be so worried about everything."

"It would be good for you if you could do that. I think you'll be happier."

"So . . ."

How do I say this?

"So . . ." she repeats.

"I like you. Aurora. A lot. I'm really happy last night happened."

Her mouth opens and closes, then opens again a little, much like a goldfish. She clears her throat and nods, forcing out a croaky "Me, too." She clears her throat. "I really like you, too."

"So . . ."

"So . . . we should get breakfast before they send a search party for us," she says, breaking the odd silence hanging in the air. "I went to explain why I was going to miss flag raising and be late for breakfast before I went for a shower, and for some reason Orla was there. I had to lie and say my alarm didn't go off because the power went out and didn't charge my phone and I'd be as quick as I could."

We start walking toward the hall again and I nod with approval. "That's smart."

She scoffs. "It wasn't. Turns out, it came back on two minutes after I left to find you and it had nothing to do with the storm. It was the guy trying to stop the leaky roof issue turning off the wrong switch somewhere."

"Well, they can't prove you're lying."

"Emilia can, she definitely already knows. She gave me the look." She sighs heavily as we approach the doors, stopping and turning to me. "I'm sorry, I haven't had someone tell me they really like me before and it means more than they just like having sex with me. It threw me for a minute. I don't want to go back to college and not see you every day, Russ. Seeing you is the best part of my day. And if you're happy to wait and be patient while I work out what that means, then maybe we can have something special."

Now I'm the one who's thrown. It feels too easy, too natural to be real life, but it is my real life. "I'd wait forever for you, Aurora."

Chapter Twenty-Three

AURORA

I'VE HAD BUTTERFLIES FOR DAYS.

At first I thought I was sick, but it wasn't quite nausea, more like a tingle in my abdomen. It would calm down at night when Emilia and I were in bed, so I thought it was over, but then it'd start again the next day. I questioned if it was an allergy, but I didn't actually feel sick, just different.

It took three days of questioning for me to finally realize it's butterflies.

"So you're not dying then?" Emilia croaks, putting the last life jacket back into the storage chest. She's lost her voice again after a particularly competitive volleyball tournament yesterday. Losing your voice from shouting all day is normal, but it's not something I've suffered. My vocal cords refuse to be silenced, much to Emilia's disappointment.

We've been kayaking this afternoon and had a bit of solitude—well, as much solitude as you can get at camp—and it helped me work out that I have feelings, and those feelings are floating around my stomach making me feel weird.

"Not dying. Confirmed."

"Just malfunctioning over a man, got it." She doesn't look at me, so she doesn't see the finger I'm giving her, but like any good best friend, she knows. "God, you're so easy to get a rise out of. I like this new you; you're floating around like an animated woodland creature; it's super cute."

"Sorry, did you say something? I can't hear you." Looking across the shore, I watch the man in question lifting kayaks and putting them back onto the rack with ease. Woodland creature isn't the worst thing I've been called, particularly by Emilia. "I miss Poppy. She balances out how annoying you are."

"Oh, trust me, she's going to love hearing about this, my little cartoon bunny." She clears her throat aggressively and starts waving her arms. "Hey, Russ! Could you come help us, please?"

She doesn't sound like herself when she says it, but it's just loud enough to capture his attention. Although I'd bet he has no idea what she said. Putting the final kayak away, he weaves through the campers as Clay leads them away to wash up for dinner. "What are you doing?" I grumble under my breath so he doesn't hear as he gets closer.

"What's up?" he says, stopping in front of the two of us.

God, he's pretty.

Emilia points to the box dramatically. "I really have to use the bathroom. Could you help Rory put the chest back into the storage shed, please?"

"Are you doing okay?" he asks, definitely on behalf of the two of us. "You're acting odd."

"You never know who's listening. You're welcome."

"They wouldn't be able to hear you, even if they tried," I say.

It's her turn to give me the finger as she runs off to follow Clay, and now that she's gone, the butterflies are flapping full force.

Definitely not allergies.

The past few days have been a mixture of loaded glances and hand brushes, hushed voices and knowing smiles. I did worry that after weeks of getting closer, once our mutual itch was scratched the excitement would wear off. But then he pulled me into an empty hallway and kissed the life out of me, and I know that's not something to worry about.

Mostly I can't believe there's a guy who genuinely wants to spend time with me and have a connection with me beyond one that happens when we're naked. I know that the bar is low for me when it comes to men, which frequently makes me mistrust my own judgment, but I can trust my judgment about Russ.

Russ nudges the chest with his foot, watching it move an inch. He picks it up, his biceps bulging with the weight. "I can do this alone, you don't need to help."

Oh Lord. I am a weak, weak woman. "I want to."

It isn't far to the shed, which is less shed and more storage building, and within a minute I'm flustered from walking behind him, watching his back muscles flex, and holding open the door for him. He drops the chest onto the floor in the dark room, and thankfully there's no need for us to do anything else. I shouldn't head in, too, and let the door close behind me—but I do.

There's a light in here somewhere, but I have no desire to find it. Small streams of sunlight pour in from some upper windows, and we don't say anything as his hands find my shoulders and move up to my neck. I place my hands on his waist and move them up to link behind his neck. His mouth finds mine, sweet and slow, like he's trying to memorize the moment his tongue moves against mine. Pushing my body close to him, I sink my fingers into his hair, stretching onto my tiptoes to try and be even closer.

I'm about to complain about his hands leaving my neck, until he grips the back of my thighs, maneuvering my legs around him, sitting me on the nearest solid surface. Every touch is perfect, but it's not enough and I still want more. I feel drunk on him; drunk on lust and secrecy and the forbidden.

His mouth travels along my jaw and down my neck. "I want you so badly."

"You can have me."

He's hesitating going further, rightfully so, but it doesn't mean I don't want him to rail me against whatever my ass is perched on. This is not the place I want to be found with my panties down. The kids aren't allowed in these buildings and I watched them all head back to their cabin. Neither of us would ever risk that.

Every other member of staff is the risk.

Which annoyingly makes it, like, ten times hotter than it would be because we might be caught and those familiar feelings I'm used to chasing start to return. The ones that flood your system with endorphins and make your nerves feel like live wires. It's addictive and problematic, but even with all of the different alarms going off in my head, I still want him to test the steadiness of whatever is under me.

"We shouldn't," he whispers.

"We definitely shouldn't," I whisper back. "But if you happen to want to, then just know I can be super quiet."

Russ's laugh is low and husky, dirtier than normal, and I start to throb. That's where I'm at: throbbing at dirty laughs. "You're so smart," he teases, and I swear this man is trying to end me. "But I love it when you're loud."

His mouth is back on mine and I use my legs to pull him closer to me, groaning when his erection presses into the apex of my thighs. I'm ready to say fuck it and get on my knees, but that's when something falls, scaring the shit out of both of us.

He kisses me again, slow and gentle this time, rubbing his hands up and down the back of my thighs, and then there's definitely something moving.

"What the fuck is that?" I ask, reluctantly unhooking my legs and putting my feet back on the floor. He helps me down as I pat around the wall to find the light switch. I flick it on, and the whole room lights up the boxes and shelves full of equipment.

"I can't see anything . . ." he says, as confused as I am.

"I don't thin—" That's when the biggest possum I've ever seen in my life scurries in front of me, and I scream so loud I'm surprised the building doesn't tumble down.

RUSS IS CONVINCED THE UNIVERSE sent a possum to stop us from acting like sluts and make us get back to work.

He's also ashamed that the school system, or my many summers at this very camp, didn't teach me that possums aren't dangerous. If they're not dangerous, why do they have such pointy teeth? And no, he didn't really use the word *sluts*, but whatever he said went straight over my head because his hand was hovering on my lower back and I was still uncomfortably wet and horny.

Fucking possums.

I'm keeping myself extra busy tonight being camp counselor extraordinaire; no dance too hard, no hot chocolate too many. Anything to keep me busy and away from the hockey player who has me acting irrationally. Irrational isn't unfamiliar to me. Being irrational because of a crush . . . that has never happened before.

I'm helping Jade plop her curls when Emilia throws herself down beside me. "I need to go to bed. I'm getting my period and I feel like simultaneously crying, throwing up, and fighting. The guys said they'd cover me tonight, is that okay? I'm sorry."

"Of course it is. Do you need me to do anything for you?"

Jade looks over her shoulder to where we're sitting behind her. "My mom makes all my sisters drink peppermint tea."

"Good shout, sweetie. Emilia, go to bed. I'll bring you some tea when I'm done here. Do you want chocolate?" She nods. "I won't be long."

After I'm done with Jade's hair, Clay promises to help round everyone up for bed while I grab the things to help Emilia feel better. By the time I'm approaching the kids' cabin a short while later, it's alarmingly quiet.

Pushing the door open, I'm immediately greeted by Clay, Russ, Xander, and Maya, all staring back at me, panic in their eyes. All the kids are settling down nicely, the odd one still puttering around getting ready for bed. I look across at the four of them. "What did you do?"

"I'm out, man," Xander exclaims, keeping his head down as he slaps Russ on the arm.

"I love you, Aurora, but I'm not strong enough for this," Maya adds.

"God speed, brother," Clay says, following the other two out of the door, not making eye contact with me.

Russ runs his hand down his face and blows out a strained sigh. "What did I miss?" I ask cautiously.

"Hi, Ror," he says happily, sounding totally fake and forced. "I'm covering Emilia and I thought that might be nice for us, y'know. I had a cute plan. It involved snacks and—"

"Russ, did you lose a camper or something? Why are you being so strange?"

He sighs again, and I'm honestly preparing for him to tell me something dreadful—and he kind of does. "You look really pretty today."

"What aren't you telling me?" I drawl, gradually losing my patience.

"Kevin took the biggest crap I've ever seen in my life and he's blocked the entire toilet system." He gags a little. "And when you try to flush it, all the others fill up, and I'm sorry, but it's horrible. I know we're only supposed to call maintenance for things we can't fix, but I don't know if anyone can fix this."

"Oh my goodness." I can't help but roll my eyes. "Okay, come on, drama queen. Lead the way. Surely you're used to this? Didn't you live in a frat house?"

"I don't know any grown man capable of replicating this," he says, totally serious.

Isn't this romantic? Nothing helps people get to know each other better than bonding over the rim of a toilet. I can smell the problem before we're even in the very large bathroom. To accommodate the number of campers in the building, the attached bathrooms have multiple toilets and private shower stalls, and somehow Kevin has managed to clog all of the plumbing.

Standing with my hand on my hip, I nod toward the offending stall, and there's a look of panic on Russ's face as he realizes I'm asking him to do something. "You're the engineer, Callaghan. Engineer us a solution."

"Board up the doorway and never return. There's my solution."

"I'm going to flush it and hope for the best."

"I've already tried that . . ." he says, holding my hips to stop me from walking into the cubicle. He pulls me until my back is resting against his chest, his hands stay on my hips, and my stomach flips. Damn bugs. "Maybe we should call maintenance now."

I step out of his grasp, because we're not having this cute-as-hell moment resolving a poop issue. "Calling maintenance is admitting defeat."

"I admit defeat." He holds up his hands as a gesture of surrender and moves to sit against the counter. "I was defeated before you even got here. Let's call maintenance."

"I'll just flush it once to see what happens."

"Aurora, don't . . ."

"It'll help me figure out what's wrong," I say, covering my nose as I step into the stall.

"Ror, you're going to flood everywhere."

"No, I'm not. It'll probably just go down."

I press the lever down and the plumbing makes a sound I've never heard before.

I CAN FEEL RUSS'S EYES on me from across the kitchen counter, but I'm not giving him the satisfaction of looking at him.

"I did tell you," he says smugly.

"Shut up. I don't wanna hear it."

After I flooded the bathroom and we had to evacuate the kids, we finally have them resettled in the main building. Thankfully, because we do movie nights in here, there were already mats for them to use, and Cooper, the senior working tonight, was able to guide us to the sleeping bags.

I'd like to think that the kids sensed the stress radiating off me, because none of them have tried me and they all lay down on their makeshift beds straightaway. There's a kitchen attached to the main room where we make drinks and snacks in the evening, and that's where I spend the next fifteen minutes guzzling whipped cream straight from the can.

Russ moves around the table until he's standing beside me. He nudges me with his hip gently, so I nudge back, and before I know it, I'm on top of the counter with a huge man between my legs.

"What can I do to make you feel better?" he asks, tucking my hair behind my ears on both sides.

"Build a time machine and go back to before I flushed that toilet."

"I could do that. Might take me a little bit of time, though."

I point the can toward him and he opens his mouth, letting me squirt whipped cream onto his tongue. "If you could go back in time and change something, what would you change?"

It's a question I think about a lot, which is silly because it'll never happen, but for some reason I love to torment myself with how I'd have done things differently.

His hands rub up and down my thighs gently and he concentrates on watching that instead of looking at me, until he eventually shrugs. "Nothing."

"Nothing? You wouldn't change mistakes you've made or even, like, exams you could have done better on or something?" He shakes his head. "Seriously, nothing?"

"Have you heard of the butterfly effect?"

"I am familiar with butterflies, yes." There are currently one hundred of them living in my abdomen and they all come to life when you're near me. However, I think he's probably talking about the movie. "What effect do they have on my time machine?"

"Not butterflies, the butterfly effect. If I change one thing in my past, it'd cause a ripple effect, and I wouldn't chance not meeting you."

Make that two hundred butterflies, all flapping at once.

My throat feels dry, but I force out the words anyway. "You know you don't have to sweet talk me to get into my pants, right? You've already done that bit."

"I'm not sweet talking you, but I'm never going to get bored of seeing your cheeks flush pink."

It's an overwhelming feeling, watching Russ step into the guy he clearly is deep down when you ward off the insecurities. I feel so fucking lucky that I'm the one watching.

My kiss catches him off guard, but he settles into it quickly, and I hope to God that nobody steps on a butterfly.

Chapter Twenty-Four

RUSS

AURORA HANDS ME MY SECOND coffee of the day as we watch Xander and Emilia argue.

Several weeks ago, the words *talent* and *show* were mentioned in the same sentence in what I hoped was a joke. Then Aurora told me how important it is to her—emotional blackmail some would say—and because I can't help but do whatever she wants because I'm obsessed, I'm now waiting to be taught to dance.

I knew that if I let her down after missing the first practice she would never learn to trust me, so I've been in our designated rehearsal spot before everyone, ready to go.

What Aurora didn't mention when she told us we had to be prepared enough to do a good job is that we would have to decide on our talent as a group.

I know what my and Aurora's talent is, but it wouldn't be appropriate to do it on a stage with an audience.

She stands beside me, occasionally bumping me with her hip, while Maya and Clay stand on my other side, and the four of us watch our two other counselors argue. Again.

"It's a talent contest, Xan," Emilia snaps.

"And I am brimming with natural talent," he argues back.

"I'm a professionally trained dancer."

"You can't teach what I have."

Maya folds her arms across her chest, tilting her head. "Should we intervene?"

"Nah," I say, taking a swig of my coffee. "He'll wear himself out eventually."

"Emilia won't," Aurora says, taking my mug out of my hand and sneaking a sip. "She'll never back down to a man."

The kids were getting antsy about not having enough time to practice since we keep them busy all day, so we switched things up to give us all the morning before returning to regularly scheduled programming this afternoon.

I assumed Aurora was exaggerating when she said it's a big deal, but she wasn't. Everyone takes it super seriously, which makes me worry even more.

Rory steps closer to me, seemingly absentmindedly; her arm rests against mine as she continues to watch our friends fight like siblings. God, I'm pathetic for enjoying something as simple as her gravitating toward me.

"Hey!" she shouts at Xander and Emilia, making them both look at us all watching them. "How about you come up with something and you can just teach us when you know? If I wanted to watch two people fight over something pointless, I'd spend time with my parents."

"Fine," they both snap, immediately returning to arguing with each other.

"Go enjoy your day off," Aurora says to Clay and Maya. "There's no way they're agreeing on something in the next two hours."

"You're a real one, Roberts," Maya says, yawning and waving as she disappears in the direction of the cabins.

"I don't mind hanging around here for a bit longer to help," Clay says, sticking his hands into his pockets and shrugging lazily.

His smile is odd today. It's forced and awkward, and it's making me want to stand in front of Aurora and shoo him. I can't, obviously, because that would be rude, not to mention slightly unhinged.

"There's nothing to help with," she says, her tone sharper than I've ever heard. "You deserve a break, so go enjoy it."

Clay's eyes flick to me and I instantly realize I'm missing a piece of the puzzle. Clearing my throat, I put on my best fake smile to match his. "Enjoy your day off, dude. There's nothing interesting happening here."

He finally concedes, looking embarrassed as he heads off toward the cabins behind Maya.

"Why's he being weird?" I ask Aurora quietly as he gets farther away from us.

"Dunno. Can you make sure nobody gets eaten by a mountain lion for five minutes?" She takes the empty mug from my hand and grabs our water bottles from the picnic table. "I'll get us some water and some deck chairs and we can just sit and watch everyone, okay? Should I get us some paper for origami? Yeah, I should. Find us a strategic spot."

She's disappearing toward the main building before I even have a chance to answer her. I watch her leave before ambling toward Emilia and Xander who are, unsurprisingly, glaring at each other. "Why is Clay being weird today?"

Emilia's eyebrow immediately rises. "Why are you saying 'today' like he isn't like that every day?"

"Rory was snappy with him and he looked embarrassed."

"He's been like that since he tried to kiss her," Xander says casually. "You just haven't noticed because you don't pay attention to any of us because we don't have blond hair and suck your dick."

"You sound jealous," Emilia snorts.

"I am. I'd look fucking great as a blond," he says back. "Not into dicks, though, sorry, dude. Tried once, not for me."

"Back up." My fingers find my temples to try and process the past ten seconds. "He tried to kiss her?"

"Yeah, I told you!" Xander argues. "You went to her cabin to check that she was okay and ended up volunteering me to work."

"You told me he was annoying her and invited her on a vacation, but you didn't say he tried to kiss her!"

"Oh, my bad," Xander says casually, like my brain isn't now full of the image of Clay kissing Aurora.

"Who's trying to kiss who?" says Jenna, appearing behind me, catching the end of what I said. The last couple of days have been exceptionally hot, so Jenna kept the dogs with her to make sure they were staying cool. Fish circles me excitedly, while Trout immediately tries to eat my shoelaces and Salmon paws at me to be picked up. "Gentlemen, no more treating the pups like babies. The carrying stops."

"Feels unreasonable, but okay," Xander grumbles, pouting.

"It's for our talent show performance, Jen," Emilia immediately says, lying, as I crouch to the dogs' level to fuss with them all. "We're workshopping a plot."

Jenna looks between the three of us. "Where's trouble?"

"She's finding some deck chairs for us to sit on and keep an eye on everyone," I say, concentrating on the dogs. Being around Jenna, knowing I'm doing something I shouldn't be, makes me really fucking nervous. I don't understand the rush everyone mentions when they talk about sneaking around. I don't feel that at all; all I feel is guilt. It's just not quite enough guilt to make me stop.

"I doubt she'll be able to reach them, they're on the top rack in the equipment cupboard. I'll go hel—"

"I'll go," I say quickly.

Jenna's looking at me like she wants to call me out on something, but before she can, Emilia steps in. "Jen, will you help settle an argument, please? We can't decide on a performance piece."

She immediately launches into the options, which gives me the chance to run for it. I instantly almost fall down because Trout doesn't let go of my laces, but I finally get free and jog toward the main building. This place is covered in random storage rooms and buildings, so I check two before finding Rory in the third, balancing on her tiptoes on a stool, reaching for the deck chairs.

"Jeez, Rory!" I rush toward her, gripping her hips so she doesn't fall and break something. "Why didn't you come and get me to help?"

"I didn't want to be annoying. I can get it, if I reaaaach—" I grip her hips tightly and lift her higher until she can comfortably grab two chairs, then lower her back down safely onto the stool. I keep a hand on her while she passes me the chairs to set on the ground. Turning carefully, she gives me a sweet but mischievous smile as she sets her hands on my shoulders and I look up at her. "Told you I could reach."

"Please don't do things that might get you hurt."

She jumps down, landing next to me. "You don't need to be worried. I've been surviving my questionable choices for twenty years."

"I do worry," I argue, sitting on the stool and pulling her closer. "Don't do it."

She moves her legs over mine until she's straddling me, and I suddenly can't remember why I'm worrying. Her arms wrap around my neck and she leans in until her mouth is close to mine. She lowers her voice when she says, "You know, telling me not to do something makes me want to do it."

I brush my nose against hers. "What can I do to convince you to behave?"

"Hmm. I can think of a few things."

"Here?"

"I don't see any possums," she says, leaning forward to tug at my lip with her teeth. "And I really do need to be convinced to behave."

Kissing Aurora is intoxicating. Every inch of her molds to me perfectly, and we fit together like we've done this hundreds of times. It's hard to worry about getting caught when she's grinding herself against me, but it isn't impossible. "Is there a lock on the door?"

"Nope," she says, running her mouth along my jaw. "We'll have to make it quick."

Groaning, I hold her hips steady. "I don't have condoms."

She leans back, smiling sweetly. "That's okay, it was probably a silly risk anyway."

She goes to stand but I hold her in place. I unbutton her shorts and she watches me, teeth sinking into her bottom lip as she tries to steady her breathing. "You can't be loud," I whisper, sliding my hand into her panties. Fuck, she's always so ready for me.

"I refuse to be held accountable for my actions when you look like that."

There's something about how much she compliments me that makes me feel untouchable. She isn't shy with it, telling me how hot I am even when I'm doing the most mundane tasks. It gives me the confidence that she's as attracted to me as I am to her, and makes me want to risk everything to watch her say my name as her eyes roll back.

She's not hard to please like this. Kissing, pressure, consistency, and the most important thing, telling her how incredible she is. I'm addicted to the way she clings to me as her body rocks against my hand, and when I feel her tighten and pulse around my fingers, I crash my mouth into hers, absorbing the sound of her chanting my name.

This is my favorite part, when she's satisfied and clingy, trying to get as much of her skin on mine as possible. I carefully remove my hand, pulling her close to me as she sags against my body.

"I'm going to put myself in danger more often," she laughs.

"I can't lie, I was motivated by jealousy, not chivalry. Why didn't you tell me Clay tried to kiss you?"

"Because I thought Xander told you. You came to my cabin and said you were jealous," she says, frowning.

"Yeah . . . that was about something far more petty than a kiss."

"Never had you down as the possessive type." There's nothing hurt or sad in her tone. "It's always the ones you least suspect."

"You get that way when you know how fucking special someone is. How they have no goddamn idea how much brighter they make everything. You're like sunlight, Rory. I want to bask in everything you have. And I absolutely don't want to share that with Clay. Not even for a minute."

Her body stiffens as she leans back, putting distance between us. "I'm not those things."

I hate that she doesn't see it. "You are."

"I don't want to be sunlight, Russ." She shakes her head adamantly. "If you stand in the sun for too long, you get burned. I don't want to be another person who burns you. Let me be moonlight."

The look of vulnerability on her face steals my breath away. "What if we get caught in the rain? You don't get rainbows at night."

"You don't need rainbows when you have the northern lights," she says softly. "And last time we got caught in the rain we did just fine. Incredible, in fact."

I want to say something sweet and funny, but looking at her scrambles every thought in my head. Nothing seems good enough. Nothing quite tells her how mesmerized I am by her. "If you're moonlight, does that make me the sea?"

I'm cringing at myself as she leans in and kisses me. Slow, soft, meaningful. She doesn't laugh at my terrible attempt to be sweet. "You want me to talk about sharks again, don't you."

Just like that, the tender moment slips away as we both begin to laugh, but I don't mind. "We should probably head back before someone comes looking for us."

Scooping the chairs under my arm, we walk hand in hand toward the door. Rory turns the lights off as I pull the door open, and that's when Jenna appears.

My voice hasn't cracked since I was fifteen years old, but it does now. "Jenna, hi!" I clear my throat a few times. "Sorry, dusty in here."

"I wanted to check that you weren't lost, you've been forever. Where's Aurora?"

There's a split second where we have to telepathically decide which avenue to take.

Or more accurately, which lie to tell.

Thankfully, Aurora steps out from behind the door and huffs. "Maybe if the storage in this place was labeled or made any freaking sense we wouldn't have to check everywhere for some chairs."

"Okay, attitude," Jenna snaps, and it reminds me how like siblings these two are. "Sorry for caring about your well-being. What a terrible boss I am."

If Jenna suspects anything, she doesn't let it show as we all walk back toward the kids. After grabbing an extra chair for her and some paper for Rory, I position them in a line in a shaded spot where we can watch all the different groups practicing.

I shouldn't feel this on edge considering we didn't get caught doing anything, and sitting here together isn't illegal, but taking into account I can smell Aurora on the hand I'm leaning against while Jenna asks me about college, it feels pretty illegal.

Chapter Twenty-Five

RUSS

YOU KNOW WHEN YOU FEEL like everyone is staring at you while you're doing something but you tell yourself it's your imagination?

That. Except I look up from my breakfast plate and everyone *is* staring at me.

"What?" I mumble with my mouth full of scrambled egg.

Aurora looks ready to start a fight, but she was perfectly content an hour ago when I managed to find us a private spot for two minutes and press her against a very large and discreet tree to make out.

Emilia looks like her usual, perfectly normal self, but Xander looks as pissed as Aurora.

"Do you have something to tell the group?" Aurora says dramatically, leaning back in her chair and folding her arms across her chest. I've hated getting into trouble my whole life, but the way she's staring at me is kind of sexy.

"No? Am I supposed to have something to tell the group?" There's so many fucking traditions in this place that it's perfectly plausible I've forgotten something ridiculous.

"Your birthday, Russ," Aurora snaps, "is tomorrow."

I concentrate on my eggs, but Aurora kicks me under the table so

I look back up. If I stare at her for too long she'll pout or smile and I'll agree to something that makes me the center of attention when I don't want to. "Is it?"

"Did you ask him?" Jenna asks no one in particular as she walks up to our table.

"Oh God, ask me what?" I groan.

"What type of cake you want for your birthday," Jenna says.

"I don't need a cake. I'm not really into birthdays, so please don't feel the need to do anything."

Jenna sits beside Aurora and steals a piece of toast from her plate. Aurora is too busy glaring at me to notice. Jenna takes a bite and turns her attention back to me. "Aw, don't be like that when it's your twenty-first."

"Your twenty-first?" Aurora squeaks. "And you want to spend it here with no birthday cake and no party? I love this place, but that sucks, Russ."

Jenna scowls at her. "Uh, family legacy? Rude."

"You're the farmer equivalent of a nepo baby, calm down," Aurora grumbles. "Can we all have time off to go to Vegas?"

"You're not even old enough to enjoy Las Vegas," Emilia tells Aurora, only to be met with an unimpressed glare.

"I don't want to go to Vegas," I add, even though I don't think anybody in this conversation cares about what I want.

Aurora looks appalled. "Why not? We can take our camp counselor riches and put it all on red."

I'm back to studying my eggs, wondering how I can say I don't gamble without it creating more questions I'd rather not answer. Thankfully, Jenna saves me. "Can someone tell me what cake I'm buying? Ideally the birthday boy himself."

Xander is the first to reply. "Chocolate."

Followed by Emilia. "Lemon."

And finally Aurora. "Ice cream."

They're all looking at me again. "No cake."

"Y'all are impossible," Jenna moans as she stands from our table. "I'll be at the cabin in twenty minutes to do the inspection. Who's not working today?"

"Me and Russ," Aurora says casually.

"I'm so glad I work so hard on all your programs for you to all switch it around whenever you feel like it," Jenna drawls, rolling her eyes. Jenna has been nice about us switching, even though it ruins her spreadsheet and she has to reprint it. Aurora told her we're the only ones who like hiking and that's why we're spending so much time together. "I'm just going to put you two on the same day off from now on. I'm wasting so much paper."

I don't know how people sneaking around at other camps do it considering so many of them offer hardly any time off. Aurora and I struggle for privacy, but we're lucky Emilia and Xander are flexible and like each other enough to swap with us so we can be alone.

I feel like I'm sweating beneath the pressure of being around Jenna, but Aurora looks perfectly cool as she changes the topic. "Do you want anything from the ice cream shop in Meadow Springs?"

"I thought you were hiking," Jenna asks, and I'm definitely sweating.

"Jen, how do you feel about having a huge food fight tonight instead of a pajama party?" Xander says, quickly changing the topic.

"I do not feel good about it," she replies, instantly turning her attention to my roommate.

I take the attention being elsewhere as an opportunity to inhale the rest of my breakfast, while Aurora has already made a quick exit, saying she needed to do something.

"I'm mad at you," she says as we approach my truck.

"I know, sweetheart."

I open the passenger door for her, holding her hand to help her climb in. The summer dress she's wearing rises, the lace of her underwear just visible as she bends over to climb in, and when she looks back at me, I realize this is supposed to be a punishment. "Really mad at you."

"I accept and encourage you to continue reminding me how mad you are," I say, closing the door.

MEADOW SPRINGS IS A TINY little town not far from Honey Acres that's popular with the staff.

I've been saying I'm going to visit since I got here, but there's only so many hours in the day and I prefer spending it wandering around after Aurora.

Many of the other counselors like its one bar and come here for drinks when they're not working, but bar hopping—would it be a bar hop since there's only one place to drink?—is not on our agenda.

Despite her repeated declaration that she's mad at me about my birthday, the second I open the truck door to help Aurora down she wraps her arms around my neck and kisses me. The amount of self-control and concentration I have to exercise on a daily basis not to touch her in front of other people is ridiculous. She sinks into me, her body smooth and soft and warm.

"Are you excited?" she asks, squeezing my hands as she climbs out of the truck.

She flattens her dress and straightens the straps, and she looks so fucking good I'm considering if we should go back to Honey Acres at all. "That depends, are we going to the famous tea cozy museum? The only one of its kind, and the *Meadow Springs Gazette*–awarded tourist attraction of the year 1973?"

She throws her head back as she laughs and I just soak it all in. "I'm not sure you'll be able to handle the excitement."

Threading Rory's fingers through mine, the realization hits me that we don't have to pretend here, I can hold her hand and kiss her and don't have to worry. She realizes it at the same time as I do, squeezing my hand tightly and looking at me with a soft expression on her face.

We're not even out of the parking lot before I'm pulling her to me. My hand cups her face, tilting it up to mine so I can kiss her again. "You look so beautiful today."

She huffs playfully, placing her hands on the front of my T-shirt, keeping my body close to hers. "You say that every day."

"Because I mean it every day."

She lets me go, rejoining our hands and pulling me in the direction of the stores. "You just like me in this dress."

The fire station comes into view and it's the size of my house. "I like you in everything," I say honestly. "And also in nothing at all."

She gasps dramatically, stopping abruptly just before we round the corner. "You can't say that here, Russ! You'll outrage the townspeople."

She tuts and I realize she's joking. "There aren't any here right now to hear me."

"People will just know. There's a nosy old lady somewhere with her spidey-senses tingling because she knows you want to rip this sundress off and do disgusting and deviant things to me."

"That's exactly what I want to do to you."

"And you will, later. But for now"—we turn the corner—"welcome to the Meadow Springs shopping district."

On first appearances, it seems that the shopping district is just two rows of family-owned stores running parallel from a fire station to a police station. I know they're family owned because the words appear at least three times on every store. "Wow, it's exactly like being on Rodeo Drive," I say, looking at the three different bowling ball stores. "How do they have three different places to buy bowling balls, but not a drugstore? And how can that possibly be economically viable?"

"Ooh," she squeaks. "Big drama. So it was one family business—"

"Surprising."

"—and when the dad died, the three sons couldn't agree on how to run it, so they split into three stores and they all directly compete with one another. It's a great source of stress for the people who just want to respect the sanctity of bowling and not get involved in family feuds."

"Sanctity of bowling?" I'm amazed and confused—and unusually invested. "How do you know all this?"

She stops outside a bookstore and I realize we've walked the full length of the street in a couple of minutes. "Jenna keeps me updated. She goes to the Meadow Springs Committee of Commitments to Town Improvements and Other Important Announcements. We call it MSCCTIOIA for short."

She sounds it out like misk-tea-eye-owe-ah, but it just sounds like a sneeze. "I honestly feel like you're fucking with me."

She gives me her brightest smile as she pulls me into the book-store. "My favorite thing is the fact I'm absolutely not fucking with you."

The bell rings above our heads, the smell of stale coffee and dust immediately assaulting me. The store is small, the same dim brownish glow throughout, but there's plenty to choose from. I'm browsing the classics when Aurora's nose scrunches at the old anthology I pull out. "I freaking hate poetry."

"You're an English major, how can you hate poetry?" I push the anthology back into its slot.

"Just get to the point, y'know? If you love someone, say it with your chest. It's why I like contemporary romance; I know where I stand," Aurora says, running her fingers along the spine as we walk between two rows of shelves. "I don't trust poetry. You think you're reading about an intense love story but then you find out it's actually about a shoe."

She stops in front of the mystery section and I move behind her to hold her waist, resting my chin on the crown of her head as she scans the spines of the books in front of her. She reaches for one, reading the blurb before putting it back. "I have a friend in my major called Halle. She runs the book club at The Next Chapter bookstore in Maple Hills and she's super sweet, but she does wholeheartedly believe my indifference to Jane Austen should get me kicked out."

"What's your beef with Jane? Poetry and Austen hater? I'm beginning to agree with your friend Halle," I tease.

"I don't have beef with her; I just think Darcy is a dick." I can't help how loud the laugh is that launches out of me, because of all the things I was expecting her to say, it wasn't that. "You're laughing, but I'm right. Any man who says, 'She is tolerable, but not handsome enough to tempt me,' deserves to be thrown from his horse into a pond, not to get the girl."

Aurora spins to look at me, and even under these terrible lights she's mesmerizing. "I could never say that about you, sweetheart."

I will never get tired of being able to bend down and kiss her freely. It's that feeling of instant relief that has me thinking about how soon college is restarting and the fact that we're going back to the same place when camp ends. I stroke my thumb against her cheek and enjoy the feel of her pulse against the palm resting on her neck.

"Why? Because I'm so handsome?"

I shake my head, running my thumb along her bottom lip as she pouts up at me. "No, because I could never describe you as tolerable."

Her jaw drops instantly, hand reaching for the closest book to hit me with as I laugh, fighting to pull her close to me. "No, get off," she snaps as I bury my head into her hair and kiss her neck. "I'm mad again."

I totally forgot someone runs this store until they clear their throat behind me. Aurora and I both turn, her hair ruffled and cheeks flushed from our play fight. "Sorry to interrupt," he says. "Can I help you with anything?"

I'm about to say no, but Aurora beats me to it. "Hi, yes, you can actually. My husband and I are looking to open a strip club here in Meadow Springs. Do you happen to have any books on business?"

"I THINK I'D LIKE TO own a bookstore one day," Aurora says as she eats another mouthful of chocolate chip ice cream. "Maybe that's what I'll do when I finish college."

After terrifying the bookstore owner with Aurora's elaborate strip club plans, ones that were so well thought out I'm not convinced they were thought up on the spot, we've ventured to the other side of the street to The Little Moo, a cute ice cream shop.

"Move here, open a rival bookstore, join the community commitment to nonsense, or whatever it's called, sell dirty romance books, and scandalize the townsfolk."

"I love scandalizing people," she says proudly. "And what are you going to do while I'm running my bookstore and corrupting the masses?"

"I'll open a rival bowling ball store to rival the rival bowling stores, obviously."

Aurora snorts loudly, immediately slapping her hand over her mouth and nose. "You're going to get us kicked out of the MSCCTIOIA."

"We'll start a rival one." I shrug.

"You've gone mad with power. I'm so glad you've thought this all through, though, because I don't think Meadow Springs is on the NHL roster."

I scrape up the last of my ice cream, immediately eyeing hers. "I don't want to play professionally anyway."

Her eyebrows practically shoot into her hairline. "What, why? I thought it was every athlete's dream to play in a major league."

Aurora's response doesn't bother me, because it's the one I get every time the topic comes up in conversation with someone. "I have no desire to be famous and I don't love hockey enough to give up my privacy."

"But why?" she says, her face more serious.

I can't tell her it's because I'll always be worried someone will dig into my family or that the money I'll have will make my dad more relentless. I shrug, but I can tell she's waiting for an answer from me.

"I don't know, Ror. I appreciate a low-key life, I suppose. I love my teammates, and of course I love hockey, but I'm not sure I'd have even tried to play at collegiate level if it wasn't the thing that got me a full ride." She spins her spoon in her ice cream bowl and I know instantly I've said something wrong. "What? Why do you look like that?"

"My family is well-known, Russ. Like, famous-level well-known. Elsa is essentially a socialite, she's in the tabloids all the time, and my dad is known all over the world because of Fenrir, so there are quite a lot of people who know who I am. Plus, my parents had this super messy public divorce."

I didn't realize it was anything to do with Aurora when I first met her, but I do vaguely remember my mom following along with court proceedings many years ago. "Oh. I'd never thought of it like that."

"Yeah . . . oh. I'm not saying I've got paparazzi in my face all the time. I mostly get left alone, unless I'm purposely drawing attention to myself, but I could never guarantee privacy to the person I'm dating. I can't even guarantee it to my friends."

Of all the ways I overthink, I can't believe I've never thought about this. My brain is scrambling for a response and doesn't find one, but luckily I'm saved when the ice cream store owner who served us earlier approaches our table. "Are y'all the folks opening a strip club?"

Chapter Twenty-Six

RUSS

"I'VE NEVER KNOWN SOMEONE WHO'S definitely getting head today look so fucking miserable."

I don't realize I've zoned out until I hear Xander say the words *head* and *fucking miserable*. "I'm not definitely getting head later, but I will try to cheer up. Sorry, man."

After the whole food hall sang "Happy Birthday" to me this morning, Xander announced we were spending our day off seeing what Meadow Springs has to offer. I told him I already know the answer and it's not a lot, but he was insistent, saying now that he and Rory have joint custody of me I couldn't not go with him when I went with her yesterday.

It's a nice sentiment, but there's only so much mini golf two men can play.

Normally, I'd spend my day off hanging around to see Rory, but after our conversation about fame and privacy yesterday, a bit of distance for a few hours is letting me think clearly. I can't think properly when I'm around her, and I need to start using my brain again because I haven't been recently.

Stopping at the Drunk Duck, the one bar available, Xander and

I decided to grab some burgers before heading back to camp. I've spent the entire meal half listening, half trapped in my head.

"I'm pretty sure birthday head is in the Constitution," he jokes, causing me to choke on my soda. "Ha, got you to laugh, you miserable shit. What's going on? Tell Uncle Xan."

"Did you just call yourself Uncle Xan?"

"Well I can't call myself Daddy Xan, can I? I know how to read a room. So go on, what's jumped up your ass?"

My knee-jerk reaction is to turn the conversation around and make it about Xander, but I think it'd be good to get his opinion. We've been sharing the same space for weeks now, and he's a genuinely good guy, so I decide to chance it. "I'm wondering if I should call it a day with Aurora."

"You're fucking lying," he says, watching for my reaction. "Say you're joking right now."

"We almost got caught this week. I opened the door just as Jenna showed up. If she'd arrived two minutes earlier she'd have caught me— Well, it doesn't matter, but she would have caught me doing something that would get me sent home."

"Two people sneaking around almost get caught. Yeah, that's how it tends to go, bro. It's half the fun, and do you even care about going home anymore? We're almost done anyway, and your friend said you could always crash with him if you need to. You're too smart to think I'd believe this is about getting caught. What's the real reason?"

I have to give it to Xander, he has a point. I've definitely been more relaxed after my friends encouraged me to risk getting fired and JJ gave me somewhere to go if I needed it until I have the excuse of college assignments and hockey to keep me unavailable. "Have I ever told you I'm not trying to go pro?"

He puts his burger down, wiping his hands and mouth on his napkin, and leans back against the booth, focusing on me. "No, you haven't mentioned it. Why not? What's that got to do with Rory?"

"I don't want to be famous. I don't want to have strangers potentially poking around my life or get attention in the public eye. It's my worst nightmare, and I don't love hockey enough to give up my privacy like that."

"Okay, and . . . ?"

"And she's already famous. I googled her last night and there's so much about her family, there's even photos of Emilia. It's just a lot. I knew about her dad, but I don't really feel like I knew the full extent of it if that makes sense. Because she's Rory and she's the way she is and I forget that outside of camp she has a whole other life."

"A whole other life that she came here to escape." Xander takes a long sip of his beer, and it's the most serious I've seen him. "I need to know if you know what you're saying is wild and you just need my reassurance, or if you genuinely believe it. Because I can deal with a little it's-getting-too-real crisis, but if you actually think you should break things off with her, I don't know how to help you, bro."

"You think I'm being a dick, don't you?"

Xander shrugs, and it's the yes he wants to say, but won't, because he's a good friend. I probably am being a dick, but I also know that things don't go well for me in life. It's hard not to get wrapped up in the good things, since they happen so infrequently in comparison.

Xander sighs and I feel it in my bones. "I think you're finding an issue where there doesn't need to be one. Think of any famous person with a nonfamous girlfriend, boyfriend, best friend, whatever. Tell me something outrageous about them. Think of their deepest, darkest secret, the one thing in the world they wanted nobody to know but came out anyway." I'm totally blank. "You can't, because people don't give a shit. You thought about dropping your friends that just went pro? Your now-famous friends?"

I'd never want to cut out Nate or JJ. "Never even crossed my mind."

"Isn't your brother in a band, too? What happens when he gets mega famous? You'll be Aurora-less and in the exact same situation. You clearly really like her and she stares at you like you hung the fucking moon. So just be together and don't stress for once."

It's like being doused in cold water. I'd never want to give up the way she looks at me. "You're right, man. I dunno. I think I'm just in my feelings."

"That's okay. Feelings are good." He pulls out his cell phone, glancing at the screen briefly and immediately putting it back into his pocket. "Nothing good comes from bottling shit up. For the record, I think you're being a fool because your chemistry is wild. She's great. You're great. I bet the se—"

"Watch it . . ."

"So protective, jeez. But my point stands. What could you possibly do or have done that's so bad you'd give up someone who makes you happy. It's not like you're getting married, but I get it, it's not something that's going to go away in the future. But when did she stop being worth the risk?"

"I never said she wasn't worth the risk. I want her. I like her so fucking much and I can't work out how the hell this happened. But just because I want her doesn't mean I deserve to have her. I'm just . . . I don't know. I don't know what I'm saying."

Xander downs the rest of his beer and I sip on my soda, feeling irritated with myself. "Do you think you're good enough for her?"

"What?"

"You heard me," he says, resting his elbow on the table and leaning against his hand. "Something's got you into this funk because you just said *deserve*. Is that what you're worried about? You two get serious in the future and there's an international debate to try to decide if you deserve her?"

"Well, I wasn't even thinking about that until right now, Jesus Christ." Another thing to now worry about.

Xander rolls his eyes. "Answer my question, dude. Do you think you're good enough for Aurora?"

Wanting her, having her, and feeling like I deserve her are three very different things. "No, I don't. I'm a fuckup."

"That's your problem; you're such a fucking pessimist. Let me tell you right now, Callaghan, no bullshit, no protecting your feelings—you are good enough. The sooner you start believing that, the sooner we get to pretend this little crisis you're experiencing never happened.

"You gotta trust the universe to let you be happy, man. But if you're not and you're going to let Aurora down when shit gets too scary for you, then yeah, you should bow out now while it's just starting. She doesn't deserve to have that happen to her."

"And if I fuck everything up first?"

He rolls his eyes again. "I swear you just enjoy punishing yourself, bro. You're not a fuckup. You're twenty-one and you're one of the nicest, most levelheaded guys I know. We're friends, so you get to be in your head right now and I won't hold it against you, but she will if you call it a day and change your mind when you realize you fumbled the bag."

Well shit. I rub at my jaw nervously, feeling like more of a dick than I did before this conversation started. "Did they put a birthday lecture in the Constitution, too?"

"Stop acting like a goof and I'll stop hitting you with my wisdom. Come on, birthday boy, drink up. The woman who's obsessed with you texted to tell me to get our asses back to camp."

I down the rest of my drink. "I didn't know Fish could text."

I MULL OVER XANDER'S WORDS as we drive back to Honey Acres with the radio loud enough that we don't have to chat.

After we sign back in at reception, Xander starts telling me about one of the lifeguards—who he's 75 percent sure checks him out when we take the kids on the lake—as we head toward the entertainment area where the evening activities take place. He keeps up a steady stream of anecdotes, which isn't necessarily unusual for Xander, but this is different and it makes me stop suddenly.

"There's a cake, isn't there?" Xander stops, too, a sheepish look on his face as he shrugs.

"Why would there be a cake? Maybe there's cake, maybe there's not cake. I don't know! I'm just here to keep the kids safe; I don't know about kitchen operations." He blows out a breath, putting his hands on his hips. "There might be a cake."

"Thanks for being so clear and concise, buddy."

We're almost there when he throws an arm around my shoulders. "She gives you the puppy eyes. You don't know how scary she can be to the rest of us when she chooses to be."

I can cope with a cake on my birthday if it makes Aurora happy. Having a birthday during summer break has always meant people are busy, and my mom's attempt at a birthday celebration always turned into some kind of drama, so I stopped making an effort.

I haven't checked if anyone has tried to reach me today to wish me happy birthday, but last night when I used it to google the Roberts family—which feels embarrassing to admit now—I had no missed calls or messages from my family. I haven't heard from anyone since Dad was in the hospital, and even though I made it clear I didn't want to be contacted, I'm still surprised they listened. I don't even have any money requests from my dad, which is more suspicious than surprising.

Xander clears his throat, dragging me out of my head. "Listen, I need to blindfold you, and I really need you not to punch me."

"Please tell me you're joking. Why could I possibly need a blindfold?"

"Does this feel like the kind of thing I'd joke about? Maybe Clay's going to jump out of your cake and strip, I don't fucking know." He pulls one of the blindfolds we use for the kids' games from his pocket. "I'm not tough enough to fight you, big guy. Let's not make this difficult. She was very clear that you need a blindfold."

He places the material over my eyes as I huff. "You knew this was coming and you still let me moan about my feelings?"

"Told you, you're a fool." Letting Xander navigate me while blindfolded is now my personal hell. It's totally silent as we come to a stop, and part of me worries he's about to push me into the lake or something. "I'm taking the blindfold off. Remember to act surprised about your cake," he whispers as he unties the material at the back of my head.

I squint beneath the sunlight as my eyes readjust and everyone shouts happy birthday all at once. I'm immediately piled on by multiple bodies, and it's not until they free me from their clutches and step back that I realize who's in front of me.

Henry's pushing Nate away from his personal space, while Robbie maneuvers himself out of Kris's and Bobby's way. JJ's arm lands on my shoulder, and my jaw still feels like it's on the floor. "Happy birthday, kiddo."

"The girls and Joe send their love," Robbie says. "We wanted to video call them, but you weren't joking about the service here."

"What the fuck is happening right now?"

Two of my campers, Sadia and Leon, push their way through my friends and hold out a huge handmade birthday card. Sadia frowns. "You can't say curse words in front of us."

Crouching down, I try to drag myself back into work mode as I gratefully accept the card. "You're right. I'm sorry, I'm just very, very surprised." There's a painting on the front, but I can't tell what it is. It looks like it lost a fight with a paint gun. "Give me a clue, guys."

Leon points to blue blobs. "It's you crying about Kevin's turd."

"Your friends are really noisy," Sadia says, looking around at them. They *are* being noisy, cheering and shouting as they try to control their excitement. Each of them has a yellow lanyard around their neck with the word Visitor printed on it.

"Being slandered by an eight-year-old," Mattie says quietly to Robbie.

"I slander you all the time, Liu," Nate snorts.

They're not quiet enough, because Sadia hears everything. "It's not slander if it's true—my mom's a lawyer."

"Okay, legal eagle," Jenna says, making her way through the people crowding around me. "We've had Russ to ourselves for lots of weeks. Why don't we let him have one more minute with his college friends and then we can start his party."

"Party?" I repeat, swallowing.

"You really thought she was going to let you get away with not celebrating?" Jenna says. There's something in her tone. Something that tells me maybe she knows what I don't want her to know, and, weirdly, it makes me feel better, because she hasn't fired me. "Fat chance of that. She got everyone here in under twenty-four hours. She goes all out for people she cares about."

Looking over the shoulders of my friends, I spot her talking to Emilia near the stage. I don't know why she's hanging back, when all I want to do is wrap my arms around her. "I'll be back in one minute," I say to the guys, immediately heading toward her.

Her face lights up as I approach, and it takes every fiber of my restraint to hug Emilia first, so it doesn't look suspicious. I let Emilia go and hold out my arms to Rory until she wraps her arms around my waist and I bury my head into her hair.

Aurora is glowing as she leans back and smiles up at me. "Happy birthday, Callaghan."

"You're incredible."

"Happy birthday, Russ," Emilia says, slapping me on the arm, as she leaves Aurora and me alone.

I don't want to let go, but I know I have to. She knows, too, which is why she takes a step backward. "You didn't give me any time to get you a birthday present." She grabs a small paper gift bag from behind her. "So it isn't very good, but please know it caused me a lot of stress and took so freaking long to do because I'm out of practice."

Reaching into the bag, I pull out my present: a yellow origami dog. "Oh my God, is it Fish?" She leans over to peek into the bag, reaching in and pulling out two smaller yellow dogs, placing them on my palm, too. "This is incredible."

"I tried to make possums, but nobody could tell what they were supposed to be." I let her hold the origami as I pull out something else from the bag. "Okay, so I can't lie, I stole this one from the old library that nobody uses and it's older than both of us combined."

I read from the cover. "Learn all thirty-seven presidents: for ages six to ten."

"I know how much you love naming presidents." She gives me a look that makes me want to say *fuck the party*. "There's one more present, it's probably at the bottom."

Digging in the bag, I pull out the final present. It's a piece of pink card the size of a hockey ticket. When I flip it over, it's unsurprisingly nothing to do with hockey.

One Birthday Wish Coupon
Eligible for redemption by Russ Callaghan at any time
From Aurora Roberts

"You don't have to decide what you want now," she says softly. "I'm sure you're overwhelmed. I know I went a little overboard . . ." I look around at the banners, balloons, streamers that I didn't even notice before. "But you deserve to have nice things."

"I wish I could kiss you."

"Give me your coupon and we can make that wish come true. I mean, we'll cause camp-wide outrage, which isn't very birthday celebration-y, but a deal is a deal."

I wish I could go back to earlier and slap that Russ. I wouldn't have spent the day worrying about whether we're a good idea.

Aurora Roberts will always be a good idea.

Handing her the coupon, I watch her eyes widen in surprise. "I want to take you on a date. That's what my birthday wish is."

"A date?" she says.

"Yes. A real date."

"With me?"

"With you."

"Even though I gave you origami golden retrievers and an old moth-eaten book on presidents for your birthday?"

"Especially because of those things."

The hardest part of being on everyone's radar is going to be having no opportunity to sneak off tonight. She takes the coupon from my outstretched hand, her green eyes sparkling, and nods. "Consider your wish granted."

BEING THE CENTER OF ATTENTION is exhausting, and I'm ready for it to be over.

I pick at the frosting of my second piece of cake, soaking in the quiet now that all the campers have been taken to bed. Well, as quiet as it can be with my friends around. As soon as the cake was cut, presents were handed over, and "Happy Birthday" was sung, I finally got the rundown of how my birthday party came to fruition.

Before we headed to Meadow Springs yesterday, Aurora got JJ's number from Emilia, and between them they coordinated this very last-minute surprise. They set off this morning, arriving just in time to make the friendship bracelets now decorating my arms.

Henry said Honey Acres is worse than he thought it would be, and Bobby is upset Jenna is both uninterested and unable to remember him, while JJ is just happy to be reunited.

Orla agreed to the guys visiting on the condition they wear the visitor lanyards and they're not left unattended anywhere on site.

"Should I be expecting you to move her in?" Robbie says, sitting beside the fire with me and Nate. "That room alters brain chemistry, clearly."

"Why are you acting like Lola doesn't sleep in your bed five nights a week?" Nate snaps back.

"You try telling Lola what to do," Robbie argues back. "See what happens."

Aurora has made herself scarce this evening, keeping herself busy making sure everyone is having a good time. I wish I could sit her beside me and let the guys get to know her, but it'd look suspicious, and I think if she wanted to do that, she would. A few of them have caught her on her own for individual chats, but I have no idea what they've said to her.

"She's not moving in, don't worry. We haven't labeled it, so I suppose we're technically friends who like each other." The words feel weird coming out of my mouth, but what else am I supposed to call her? "She's great, though. I really like her."

They both start laughing at the same time. Nate smirks as he leans back in his chair. "I remember thinking Stas was my friend."

"She actively disliked you and then she got Stockholm syndrome," Robbie snorts. "She was never your friend."

"Still got the girl, didn't I?" Nate shrugs. "Y'know, Aurora offered to pay for everyone's flights if it got us here. She was ready to hire a private driver. Either she's about to be the best friend you've ever had, or you're about to be the relationship Henry complains about living next to."

Forcing away all the insecure feelings from earlier, I answer honestly. "I want both."

The pair of them laugh, and I've never noticed before now how similar the two are, like an old couple who mirror each other's mannerisms. Robbie sips his hot chocolate and Nate does the same, and they both give me identical smug grins. "Young love."

Chapter Twenty-Seven

AURORA

"I TOLD YOU HE'S A good guy."

Henry doesn't say anything else as he drops into the seat beside me with his breakfast. Russ's friends stayed in a B and B in Meadow Springs last night, but Orla said they could visit before leaving as long as they still had their visitor lanyards and it was during the morning cabin inspection, so the kids would be busy.

I concentrate on my toast, suddenly feeling nervous to have one-on-one time with Russ's best friend. I mean, technically we've had one-on-one time before, but that was when I was unknowingly ditching Russ post hookup. "I know you did. I never thought he wasn't."

We both watch Russ at the table across from ours while we eat in silence. He's laughing with Robbie and Mattie, two of the guys who made it their mission to get to know me better last night. I've tried to keep a safe distance, not wanting to smother him or overcrowd him when his friends are here, but it's hard when I naturally just want to be near him.

The loud buzz of multiple conversations fills the silence until Henry slices through it, catching me off guard. "My room is next to

Russ's room in our house. It isn't soundproof, so please don't treat it like it is."

I almost choke on my veggie bacon. "Sorry?"

"I imagine you're going to visit a lot. I'd rather not hear you come, sorry." I expect him to start laughing or give me some indication he's joking around, but he looks entirely serious.

"I, um . . ." I am not a girl who stumbles over her words. I am a rambler. I am an oversharer. I am lost for words. "I promise to try my hardest to not put you through that."

"He told me you know how shitty his dad is to him."

"Yeah."

"You know more in six weeks than some of our friends have found out in two years." When he puts it like that, it makes me value even more how much Russ has trusted me with. "He doesn't know how much everyone loves him. He only ever assumes the worst and jumps to the worst conclusions. Sometimes you'll need to spell the good out to him."

I don't say it to Henry, but I know exactly what he means. Russ and I would have started on a much more friendly foot if he hadn't wrongly assumed I'd feel uncomfortable around him. "You're a good friend, Henry."

"Russ deserves good friends."

We spend the rest of breakfast talking about some photographs Henry took of their B and B and the surrounding landscape for him to try some new painting techniques when he gets home. By the time everyone is leaving, I feel like Henry will remember me as the girl who likes his friend and not the girl he bumped into that night.

Even hours after the guys left, the aftermath of having seven painfully attractive strangers here for a few hours has disrupted the normal order of everyone's day. All the staff are acting horny and a little chaotic after seeing so many new faces. I'm okay, though, because a painfully attractive man makes me feel horny and chaotic daily, so I'm used to it.

Maya and I work hard to keep the kids busy and burn off all their excess energy by swapping our morning schedule of arts and crafts for a treasure hunt—much to Jenna and her program spreadsheet's dismay—but Russ and Clay lose our map with all the treasure locations and the whole thing takes three times as long.

The hunt does the trick, and by the time our post-lunch quiet hour arrives, everyone is a lot more chilled than they were a few hours ago. Maya is losing her voice from shouting all morning. My voice remains undefeated.

I'm hanging out with the other counselors in the shade on the picnic bench outside the Brown Bears cabin when Xander clears his throat. "I have an announcement to make." I think he's waiting for some kind of dramatic reaction, but nobody says anything. "Emilia and I have decided to part over creative differences."

"Gimme a clue," Maya says, squinting at him as she shields the sun from her eyes.

"You're so goddamn dramatic," Emilia groans. "The talent show. Xander is going to do his own thing because we can't agree on anything."

"Is this because she said you couldn't win *American Idol*?" Clay asks. "Nobody sounds good singing campfire songs, bro. Don't take it to heart."

My jaw drops. "No. Absolutely not. We're a team." Every other counselor group has said they're going to work out an act the day before, because it's not that serious. Fuck that, I want my group to be the best. That's why I've been trying to get everyone organized for weeks. It's not my fault I'm not creative enough to come up with an idea myself. "You can't do it on your own, Xan. That's super sad and lonely. You need us."

"I'm not. I have Russ." He pats Russ on the back and Russ looks up, suddenly alert.

"Sorry, what's happening?"

"Creative differences. Talent show. Dog tricks. Come on, man, I told you like an hour ago," Xander says, blocking out Emilia with his hand when she starts laughing at dog tricks.

"I didn't realize you wanted me to join you! If Xander gets to leave the group, can I just not participate?"

"No!" Xander and I snap at the same time.

"You promised," I remind him.

He rolls his eyes. "Was worth a try."

Several high-pitched screams ring out from the kids' cabin, and Maya and Clay jump to their feet. "I swear to God, if Michael has brought in another frog, I'm going to make him sleep by the lake," Maya grumbles.

As soon as they're gone, Russ moves closer to me, leaning against his hand at an angle that blocks out Emilia and Xander from our conversation. "I won't go with Xander if you don't want me to. I know how important this is to you."

I want to kiss him. I always want to kiss him. Sighing overdramatically, I place my hand on the table next to his elbow so I can gently brush my finger against his arm. "It's fine. I don't want Xander to be on his own and I don't want you to be unhappy. It's not a big deal. Now that Emilia has no opposition, we'll definitely be dancing."

"I'd be happy if I was dancing with you," he says quietly. "You'd make it worth it."

The butterflies in my body all flap at once. "Go with Xander."

"You're the best," he says, nudging me with his knee. "Are you doing anything tonight after we clock off?" I shake my head, mind immediately running with a thousand different possibilities. "Don't make plans. We're going on a date."

———

THE EVENING IS PAINFULLY SLOW in comparison to the afternoon, and I spend my entire night clock watching, waiting to see what my first-ever date is going to be.

Shortly after the kids are ushered to bed, Russ appears looking concerned, which immediately puts me on edge. I'm in comfortable clothes, like he told me to be when he left earlier, but having zero idea what's going on is not my idea of fun. "We have a slight problem," he says as he approaches me, stopping far enough away so we don't look overfriendly.

"What is it?"

"We need to sign out at reception, and it'll look suspicious if we're both signed out together."

"We've done it before," I say.

"Not at night. You gotta admit that looks suspicious."

He's right, as much as I don't want to admit it. I don't even know what he has planned, but I'm nervous and excited and I don't want him to say we can't go. "There's a path that starts near the back of the kitchen that leads to a dirt track a few minutes' drive away. I could sneak out, but you have to promise to not snitch on me, because unlike you who's breaking the rules left and right, I'm trying to repair my image."

He rolls his eyes and his dimples appear as he fights a smile. "Is it safe?"

"Yeah, it's an evacuation route that they put in decades ago. I'll need a flashlight."

He throws his truck keys at me. "I don't want you walking in the dark. Don't check the back or you'll ruin the surprise."

The excitement and nerves eat away at me as I keep a straight face signing out at the front office. When I'm safely in Russ's truck, that's when I give up fighting it. I keep the headlights on as I wait the five minutes it takes for him to find me, and as he jogs up to the fence line, I try not to drool when he jumps over it with ease.

Is everything he does hot, or am I just easily impressed? One of life's great questions.

Opening the driver's door, he slides me along the seat and positions himself in front of the wheel. "I don't even want to know how you know that barely there path leads to here, trouble."

"Am I trouble or am I an explorer?"

He throws an arm over the back of the seat as he looks over his shoulder to drive in reverse up the dirt track back to the road. Again, hot or easily impressed? His hand twirls the ends of my hair and the definitive answer is hot. Definitely, definitely hot.

"Trouble. One hundred percent."

There's no one else on the roads this late at night, but Russ concentrates as he drives, one hand resting on my thigh, tapping to the song on the radio. The next song is by an up-and-coming rock band Poppy likes, which is starting to get radio play. I bought Poppy and Emilia tickets to their LA show in a few months, but before I can tell Russ, he changes the station. "You don't like Take Back December?"

"Not really." He lifts his hand from my thigh to rub along his jawline. "It's my brother's band."

Oh my God. "Your brother Ethan is Ethan Callaghan? How did I not notice that before? Emilia's girlfriend loves TBD."

"Yup." He doesn't sound very pleased about that fact, and after what I've learned about his relationship with his family, I'm not surprised.

He takes a right down an old dirt road, looking at me for a split second before putting his hand back on my thigh. "Your brother is famous, but you don't want to go pro because you don't want to be famous? As someone with a family always in the press, I know you sometimes have no choice."

"You're not the only person to point that out to me recently, funnily enough. Ethan isn't really famous, though." He squeezes my thigh, which I think is supposed to be a comfort, but I feel it every-where. "Should we tell everyone we're only children?"

"Definitely, but I'm a bit concerned it won't matter anyway, since you appear to be taking me somewhere to murder me and bury my body in a field . . ." The truck throws us around a little as we drive over the uneven ground in the direction of an old, derelict building. "Where the hell are we? I am not fucking you in that haunted house if that's your plan."

He snorts as he puts the truck into park. "I thought you knew every inch of Honey Acres, Ms. Explorer," he teases, taking the keys out of the ignition.

"I do. This is not Honey Acres. We are almost definitely tres-passing."

We both climb out and I walk around to his side, still totally confused about what we're doing here. As soon as I'm close enough, he bends to kiss me, reviving the butterflies that are now a perma-nent addition to my body. "I thought trespassing would be exciting for you."

"Trespassing in a hotel to make yourself a midnight snack, yes. Trespassing in a field is how you end up with a gunshot wound."

"We're on Orla's land, I promise. I found this place on a run and I checked when I got back to camp. We're not that far away, it just takes longer to get here by vehicle, since I can't drive through fences." He laughs and takes my hand, walking us to the back of his truck. "I just realized people don't kiss at the start of a first date."

"You can drive through fences . . . but people yell at you when you go to apologize and they make your parents pay for the dam-age." His eyebrow rightfully rises. "Anyway . . . I haven't been on a first date before, so I don't know the rules. Which is probably a red flag for you, because why would I be undated at twenty unless it's because I'm really annoying, which I am, and, well, we might get charged at by cows tonight or eaten by wolves or something, so I'd rather kiss at the start than not kiss at all. I need to stop talking. I'm doing that thing that you make me do where I j—"

He stops at the back of the truck, nudging my chin up with his knuckle to close my mouth. "I know you're the English major, but undated isn't a word, sweetheart."

"I feel like it is." He ignores me and opens the tailgate, pulling off a white sheet, revealing cushions and quilts, an ice chest, and the battery-powered projector we sometimes use for outdoor movie night. "Oh my goodness."

Lifting me onto the tailgate, he leans in and kisses me again. Slow, gentle, perfect. "I haven't been on a first date before, either."

I'm stunned into silence as Russ helps me shuffle back to get comfortable on the makeshift bed, handing me a thermos labeled hot chocolate and a bag of popcorn. He positions the projector on top of the truck, pointing it at the side wall of the creepy house, and that's when it hits me how much effort he's put into this.

I'm not a crier, but this man might just make my eyes water a little. He throws another blanket on top of me and finally sits down, getting under the covers, too. "Comfortable? Warm enough?" he asks.

"Everything is perfect." The wall turns blue as the Disney castle appears, followed by the Pixar lamp, and as soon as Gusteau's restaurant appears on the tiny television, my heart just about explodes. He's thought of everything. "*Ratatouille!* Russ, you're perfect. Like dream-guy perfect. You're too good to be real."

My honesty catches him off guard, and beneath the glow of the moon, I watch all the emotions run across his face. I've always known I need validation like I need air and, although I don't think he's exactly the same, we are very similar.

People have made us feel like we're less than we are, and those opinions are buried deep in us both, like weeds. Every drop of self-doubt waters the soil, and once they start to grow it feels impossible to stop. But it isn't impossible, it just takes someone to rip them out by the root, over and over if needed.

We're so different, and yet so similar, and part of me is starting to believe that's the perfect mix.

He reaches toward me, brushing a strand of hair from my face. "Tell me a secret."

"I don't want to go back to reality next month. I want to stay here with you and the dogs and throw our cell phones into the fire." He laughs quietly, his hand massaging the back of my neck while I ramble. "I'll open my bookstore and you can open your bowling store or build robots or whatever engineers do—they can protect us from the possums and the wolves, I guess. But you'll choose me and I'll choose you and we'll be happy without anyone else ruining it."

"You are the brightest thing in my life, Aurora," he says. "And you're a living reminder of the good things that can happen when I allow myself to be happy."

Part of me wonders if I'd let someone in before now, could I have avoided a lot of the unhappiness I've dealt with, but I think the answer is no. I'd have still been doing the same reckless things as before, bouncing from one emotional overload to the next, desperately seeking something more. I'd never have made someone happy, and chances are that after the initial buzz of their attention wore off, I'd be lost again.

Russ makes me feel content, the one thing I didn't realize I needed.

We shuffle closer, sinking deeper into the blankets, facing each other, totally ignoring the cartoon rat being projected onto the wall. "You tell me a secret," I whisper.

"It's not a secret because a lot of people know about it, but can I tell you about something bad that happened to me? Something I really hate talking about?"

"Of course." I'm patient while he awkwardly chews the inside of his cheek, clearly delaying things. His leg slips between mine, his hand rests on the curve of my waist and, just when I think he's about to start talking, he leans in and kisses me instead. Breaking us apart, I rest my forehead against his. "I'm still going to be here to kiss you when you're done sharing," I say softly.

"Did you hear about the hockey rink getting trashed at the start of the year?"

"I think so, maybe? Didn't you guys have to share the other rink or something?"

"Yeah. Well, it was my fault."

My jaw almost unhinges. "You trashed a hockey rink?"

"No! Of course not. I, um, I met this girl, Leah, at a party, and she was nice to me. I'd gone with some guys I lived with. Leah kissed me, we messed around a bit, not all the way."

Someone tell me why I'm jealous. "Then every party I went to, Leah was there and we ended up hooking up a few times. I liked her and I thought maybe, just maybe, sophomore year wouldn't be trash and I could have some happiness. Next thing I know I've got her boyfriend in my DMs threatening me. They'd been fighting or whatever, she'd been using me to get back at him."

"I'm so sorry she did that to you."

"Oh, it gets so much worse." He laughs, but it's humorless. "This thing between her and her boyfriend was super toxic, one of those relationships everyone loves to hate. So when she found out she was pregnant, she told her older brother, who's a hockey player at UCLA, that she'd been ghosted. I'd blocked her when I found out about the boyfriend. She wouldn't give them my name, just that it was some-one on my team, thinking that'd be the end of it. But it wasn't. They trashed the rink."

"Oh, Russ."

"I wanted to drop out because of it, I was so embarrassed. If Nate hadn't held my hand through it, I would have. It was bad enough when I thought the rink had been trashed because of her boyfriend, but this was so, so much worse. Everyone was talking about it; I had to go to meetings about it until it was proven I hadn't done anything. It was a fucking mess."

"You have no reason to feel embarrassed! You're the victim in all of this. You didn't do anything other than hook up with a girl at a party, and there's nothing wrong with that. You could have hooked up with every girl at that party, it still doesn't make someone using you as a scapegoat okay."

"That's what Stassie and Lola say, but I haven't been able to shake the guilt. When I'm on campus, I'm wondering if people are thinking about it when they see me. I hate having to play UCLA knowing that's what they'll all be thinking about."

"I hate that this has been eating at you. When something happens it feels so huge to you, but that's because it's happening to you, but in reality, most people don't know or care. If everyone was talking about it like you feel like they are, I'd already know everything. I just heard there was some damage. Nothing about you."

"You really didn't know?"

"No! I promise I didn't. But someone took advantage of you, Russ. You gotta stop punishing yourself for it." I stroke his face with my thumb and he kisses the palm of my hand. "If you overthink it, you won't be able to move on. So what, a rink got trashed? It's not like somebody died! Do you know how much stuff I've trashed by accident?"

"Some fence lines, I'd guess."

"That wasn't an accident." I roll my eyes, leaning in closer. "But my point remains. You're a great person, your friends love you, and the dogs love you. That's all I think about when I think of you. How easy you are to l—like."

"I don't know why I'm bringing it up now. I'm sorry, have I fucked up our first date already?" His eyes shut and he sighs, sinking further into the pillows.

Sometimes I want to shake this man, because he doesn't realize how happy his handing over those pieces of himself he keeps so tight to his chest makes me.

"You voluntarily sharing something that's personal to you makes this the best date, Russ. I promise. Thank you for trusting me with the full story."

His eyes open slowly. "Can I have that post-sharing kiss you promised now, please?"

I can't help but smile as I lean in. "Of course."

Chapter Twenty-Eight

RUSS

I HADN'T INTENDED TO TELL Aurora about Leah when we got here, and on reflection, it's probably not the most suitable topic of discussion for a first date, even if she says it is.

But Aurora makes everything feel lighter.

A few sentences about something that's been plaguing me for almost a year and I feel better. All she did was listen and tell me that if everyone was talking about it she would have known, and the slightly more dramatic "It's not like somebody died."

I don't know why I decided to tell her right now. Maybe because she called me too good to be real and I know I'm not. That's one of the stories that proves I'm not, and by my telling her, she's not being misled about who I am.

Sharing things you've kept so close to you is exhausting. "Can I have that post-sharing kiss you promised now, please?"

"Of course," she says softly, leaning in.

My hand cups her cheek, thumb brushing gently across her skin as her lips meet mine. She tastes like hot chocolate, and when I pull her body closer to mine, she immediately complies. "I love this," I whisper against her mouth.

"Making out?" I guide her leg over mine until she's straddling my hips. Her hands pull the duvet around her shoulders, then link around my neck, cocooning us. My hands slip beneath her sweatshirt, tracing my fingers along her spine with one hand, maneuvering her flush to me with the other.

"Having you to myself."

Aurora brushes her nose against me, lightly pressing kisses against various parts of my face: the corner of my mouth, my temple, the tip of my nose. "Considering how many times a day you remind the kids to share, it's pretty funny you're so bad at it."

She rests her forehead against mine and my arms wrap around her waist, holding her tight. "I'll happily share everything but you."

I'm forced to let go when she sits back, letting my hands sit on her hips instead. She looks at me with an uncertainty I'm not used to seeing from her. "They're pretty words, but do you really mean them?"

As needy as it sounds, I hate the small distance between our bodies right now, but I hate how unsure she looks in this moment more. Being so candid with someone would usually make me anxious. I just shared a big thing with her, voluntarily I should add, so it's a lot for me to continue to put my thoughts and feelings out there. It isn't a secret I'm not amazing with women, and under normal circumstances, I'm pretty sure I'd be sitting scared, waiting for them to be stomped all over.

I don't feel like that with her; I want to be close to her.

"Your attention is a gift, Aurora. I have no intention of not valuing the time I get with you."

"God, Callaghan. Why do you have to be so freaking sweet?" she mumbles, looking down at her hands fiddling with the hem of my sweatshirt.

"I'm only like this with you. You're the only person who's ever made me want to be like this, Aurora. You'll never have to question if you're wanted. You'll never have to question if you're my first choice." My heart is hammering in my chest as the words pour out of me. The duvet is still draped over her shoulders, making it easier for me to pull each side, pulling her body down to mine again. "You are."

Whatever else I was about to say doesn't happen because her mouth crushes against mine, her hands settling on either side of my face as her hips roll against me, sending electricity shooting up my spine as I groan, flexing my hips into her. I'm burning beneath her touch, and as all the blood in my body rushes south, I'm so happy I told her how I feel while I could still focus on speaking.

"I don't want to share you, either," she says, her mouth traveling along my jawline. Her teeth nip at my earlobe, while her warm breath tickles my neck. I roll us over until she's pinned beneath me with her legs crossed at the bottom of my back.

I grind myself into her, enjoying the way her eyes roll back and her breathing hitches. We're both still fully dressed, but the flimsy cotton separating us does nothing but prove how perfectly I fit between her thighs. Her tongue moves against mine, back arching to push her breasts into me. "My perfect girl," I mumble as I move to kiss down her neck.

Aurora's hands reach down, pushing clumsily at the waistband of my sweatpants with one hand and doing the same action with her leggings. "I want to feel you," she whispers.

It takes all my mental strength to lift myself off her enough to remove her leggings and a tiny piece of lace she claims are panties, but it's so fucking worth it. I push my pants and boxers down over my hips, shuffling them off in a way that doesn't make the truck shake. Pumping my hard dick in my hand, I let Aurora pull me back down to her, both of us now bare from the waist down. I kiss her, groaning into her mouth when her hand reaches between us and she grips me gently. My hips have a mind of their own as I start to thrust into her hand slowly. "I won't put it in, okay?"

"Okay."

She guides me closer to her and I hover at the right distance, waiting, holding my breath to see what she's going to do next. That's when she opens her legs a little wider and slides the tip of my dick against her clit gently. It feels fucking perfect. She's gentle but deliberate, going further, changing pressures, and when she starts to lose her rhythm, I take over, replicating what she was doing.

It's easier for me to grind against her, allowing me to kiss her, too. Her fingers dig into my shoulders as her tongue rolls against mine. "You feel so good," she moans, arching her back. Her hips rock against me, the wet sound music to my fucking ears. "Condom?"

"Not yet." That gets her attention, but I ignore her confused look in favor of pulling up her sweatshirt, exposing what is supposed to be a bra, but is also just a scrap of lace. "Did you wear this for me?"

I pull down the material carefully, closing my mouth over one of the already stiff peaks. She instantly gets louder and louder as I try to pay attention to every inch of her. My dick is throbbing; I'm desperate to be inside of her, but watching her come from this makes it worth the wait. "I asked you a question, Aurora."

"I need you inside of me," she mewls, tightening her legs around me.

I switch to her other breast. "Did you wear this for me?" She nods frantically, eyes pinched shut as her jaw slacks. "Why?"

Her nails sink into my skin and her breathing changes. "Because I want you to fuck me. I'm going to co—"

Aurora buries her head into my neck as she moans out a sound I'll be able to hear for the rest of my life. Her body works perfectly with mine; it's addictive. Reaching into the cooler beside our makeshift bed, I pull out a box of condoms I bought earlier.

I bought the condoms before I found anything else for this date. Which normally wouldn't be a great sign, but there was no chance

I was receiving the same disappointed look I've had multiple times now when I've been unprepared.

Ripping the foil with my teeth, I sit back on my heels, quickly rolling it over me.

"You have a really pretty dick, y'know," she says, pushing herself onto her forearms. "It's kind of visually perfect."

I just rubbed against this women until she came, and I can feel myself blushing because she called my penis attractive. I really need to unbox that at some point.

"I don't know how to respond to that. Thanks?"

"You're welcome. Will you be gentle with me, please?" She rolls over onto her stomach, her legs only slightly separated. "And lie on top of me?"

"Of course." I position myself behind her, my legs over hers, guiding myself between her parted thighs until I feel myself start to sink into her. There is no better feeling than this. None. "You are the best feeling in the world, sweetheart."

It's really fucking deep like this. I lie down, my front on her back, trying my best to give her the closeness she clearly needs while not crushing her. I kiss along her shoulders, up her neck; I can even reach her face from this position. I cover every part of her I can reach with kisses, all while rocking myself into her in a steady rhythm.

I intertwine her fingers with mine and pin them to the bed on either side of her head. "Harder," she whispers, and it's taking everything for me not to come, especially listening to her little moans. Her hands tighten around mine as I do as she asks.

The sound of my hips slapping against her ass is making me lose my mind, and when she starts pushing back against me, I know we're both close.

"You're so deep. I can feel you everywhere."

"You take it so well, sweetheart. You're such a good girl."

Praise is key to getting this woman off, and as soon as *good* and *girl* come out of my mouth, it's only a matter of time. I'm nearly there, I can feel like a tugging sensation and I'm desperately trying to get her there first. I let go of her right hand and slip mine along the front of her body until I find the spot between her legs that makes her throw her head back.

"Oh God."

"That's it, sweetheart. Show me how beautiful you look when you come for me."

Her body starts to thrash, but she has limited options given my body is covering hers.

"Russ," she moans as she squeezes me so fucking tight I'm coming right there with her. It lasts for so long that when I pull out of her slowly, I'm still going.

Collapsing next to her, I'm fucking beat. She snuggles closer, kissing me again slowly.

"Are you going to judge me for putting out on the first date?"

I snort, once again never knowing what's going to come out of her mouth. "Technically you put out before the first date. Loophole."

"Thank goodness, my virtue won't be compromised in that case."

Rolling onto my back, I do my best to get rid of the condom in the most practical way and lie back down, pulling her under my arm so we can stare up at the stars. The movie has long finished, but I kind of prefer only to listen to her soft breaths. "Thank goodness. What would you do without your virtue?"

Chapter Twenty-Nine

AURORA

"Sit down, please, Aurora."

My face scrunches, confused, as I side eye Emilia, who hasn't been given strict instructions to sit down by Xander. I take a seat on the picnic bench in front of him, resting against my hands as he paces in front of me dramatically. "Done."

"Thank you, Aurora."

"You're welcome, Alexander. Your wish is my command, clearly."

He stops pacing. "Is this a joke to you?"

"This? What's happening right now?" He nods. "Yes, it's very much a joke to me. I have no idea what's going on. Can you move a couple of inches to the right, then a couple of inches forward, please? The sun is in my eyes."

The three of us were supposed to be filling water bottles for the kids ahead of rock climbing, and somehow I've ended up with Xander wearing his most serious expression. I thought it was weird when he insisted on helping, and I should have known he was up to something.

He kisses his teeth, his hands settling on his hips as he stares me down. "This is serious."

"I'm sure whatever is happening right now is very serious to you, Xan. Still don't know what's happening, though."

I look across to Emilia, who shrugs, watching our friend with interest. "The way you act sometimes makes me glad I don't date men," Emilia says.

"I'm going to pretend you didn't just say that to me. I have two words—"

"*Attention* and *seeker*?" Emilia says at the same time I say, "*Over* and *dramatic*?"

"Basketball tournament." He glares at me. "*Overdramatic* is one word. Get your head in the game, Roberts. You're an English major."

I'm really struggling not to laugh. He's caught my interest now and I'm excited to see where this whole thing is going. "Is the game spelling or basketball? Because I'm confused."

"Basketball tournament," he repeats, a little louder this time. "We can't lose."

I once again look at Emilia, mainly searching for confirmation that we're both experiencing the same thing and I'm not having a weird hallucination. Her perfectly sculpted eyebrows are nearly touching she's frowning so hard.

I decide to be the nominated speaker for the both of us. Clearing my throat, I look back at Xander. "Uh, okay?"

"I don't know what sordid and creative sexual wizardry Callaghan has promised you to throw the game, but I need you to forget about it. My reputation is on the line here and I need you to be a team player."

"Rory is very popular with the Titans basketball team, Xan. You don't have anything to worry about," Emilia says, stepping just out of my reach when I try to punch her in the arm. "She loves being a team player."

"Shut up," I snap at her. "Xander, I can't lie. I have zero idea what you're talking about. I'm not throwing anything, there's no promises of witchcraft and/or wizardry that I'm aware of, and, sweetie, I really don't think it's that serious. The tournament is supposed to be a bit of fun."

Somehow—and I truly believe that Xander is probably the one who started it—we've ended up involved in a staff basketball tournament this evening. Teams were picked at random using colored pieces of paper in a hat and, much to his absolute delight, Russ is on a team with Clay, while Emilia and I are with Xander and some of the lifeguards. Poor Maya has never played basketball in her life, but says she doesn't care because all the people on her team are tall, and in her book that automatically makes them good.

"Russ told me you'd agreed to help them cheat."

That little sneak. "Russ is just getting under your skin, buddy. That's what you guys do when you play, right? Shit talk each other. I haven't even talked to him properly since this morning."

My favorite thing is when Russ stops by my cabin on the way back from his morning run before people are up. I sit on his knee or beside him, depending on how sweaty and gross he is, and we watch the sun rise. I'm always half asleep, but I'd definitely remember making a diabolical plan to betray Xander.

"You know you could have just said *don't cheat*, right?" Emilia says, looking at her watch. "Could have saved us so much time."

"If there's sexual wizardry on offer, I might cheat, Xander. I'm just being honest with you; it is very likely that I'll be influenced. I don't even know what it entails, but I know that I want to be a part of it. I'm sure you can respect the difficult position I'm in."

"I can't and won't. I'm not losing to Clay because you're horny, Aurora," Xander says sternly.

"If we lose to Clay, it's because I have to play basketball when I have no hand-eye coordination." I'm super lazy when it's on the Brown Bears' schedule because I just let Xander or Clay take charge. "You need to relax. It's not going to count against you next season, y'know."

Xander and Clay both worked here last year, but in different groups, so they weren't strangers when they were put together this year. But last month, on one of the rare occasions I checked my phone, I saw Ryan had texted to tell me he signed with the LA Rockets.

The guys overheard me tell Emilia and it started a conversation about the NBA. Which then started a further conversation about how Xander and Clay know Ryan because they've played against him and, just to add another level, the pair plays against each other.

I've heard them make subtle digs at each other sometimes, but I've brushed it off as guy nonsense. What I didn't realize is that Stanford and Berkeley are bitter athletic rivals, and apparently that expands to informal-just-for-fun summer camp basketball.

Ridiculous.

"I've seen you play paint dodgeball. I know there's nothing wrong with your hand-eye coordination, you Judas."

"Serious question," Emilia says, picking up the water bottles we put down when Xander insisted we stop for an important discussion. "Why are you the way you are?"

He doesn't answer her, instead opting to explain all the rules of basketball to us while we walk to the water machines and back. By the time we return to our group, I'm surprised the kids haven't passed out from dehydration.

I hand Russ's bottle to him as his eyebrow quirks. "What took you so long?"

He puts the bottle to his lips, taking a big drink. When his mouth is full, I say my two new favorite words to him: *sexual wizardry*. Some of the water sprays out of his mouth, the rest causes him to choke. He bashes his palm against his chest, covering his mouth with his forearm until he eventually stops spluttering. "Need me to put you in the recovery position, Callaghan?"

His eyes are watering and his face is pink, but it doesn't stop him from beginning to laugh. "I couldn't help it."

"I feel like you could definitely help it."

"Sweetheart, you don't understand," he says quietly. "He was being so annoying. He asked me if I was excited to play a real sport. He's normally so laid back, but competition makes him vicious, and I have to live with him."

"Oh no." I pout playfully. "Did the nasty man who chases men for a ball insult you? A man who also chases men for a ball, but on ice?"

"I know you're just trying to mock me right now, but let me say, you're really fucking cute when you pout at me like that. But I'm going to need you to confirm for me that you know there isn't a ball in hockey. I mean, I'm the goalie, so I don't technically chase anyone, but if we could start with the ball thing first, that'd be great."

He's staring at me, and given the fact his face hasn't recovered from the choking, it's pretty intense. Just past him I can see some of the boys starting to get into the rock climbing harnesses, and they're definitely not the right ones. "Boys," I yell, looking past Russ. "Not those ones! Let me help."

Stepping around a still-perplexed Russ, I head toward my campers, only getting halfway there before I hear Russ shouting at me. "Ror! I just need to hear you say you know it's not a ball! Just once!"

"Sorry, Callaghan! I don't negotiate with my competition!" I yell back over my shoulder, smiling to myself when I see Xander immediately start to stomp in Russ's direction.

THERE'S A REASON I'VE ALWAYS liked basketball players, but rarely attended basketball games: they're boring.

Someone—probably Xander—organized the tournament schedule, and at this point, I can't remember how many games we've played. I have no idea if we're winning or not, and although my legs are sore, it's mainly from running up and down the court while Xander hogs the ball and scores all our points.

The kids are having a blast, cheering and shouting enthusiastically throughout every game, but I have definitely lost interest. I want a hot chocolate. I want to watch a movie. I want to hold a dog while Russ's hand rests on my thigh under a blanket.

Basically, I'm ready to get my evening back on its regular schedule.

"What if we just refuse to play?" Emilia says, stretching beside me.

"He doesn't actually need us, so I don't think that'd work."

"Protest?"

"Pointless."

"Fire?"

"Extreme," I sigh. "I already thought of that one."

"You know if we went on vacation like I suggested, we could have avoided this," she says.

"I know," I say, sighing even more dramatically than the last time. "I already thought of that, too."

The only perk to this whole circus is that Russ is pretty good at basketball, and every time he demonstrates that skill, Clay and Xander look really confused, and it's very satisfying to witness. When we play it with the Brown Bears—of course, I say *we* lightly since I don't do anything—Russ is concentrating on making sure the kids are all having fun.

Now that he's playing for himself, he doesn't need to hold back, and I don't need to pretend I'm not staring at him because everyone else is, too.

Xander sits in the empty space beside me and I hear Emilia groan before he's even opened his mouth. He looks around me to my best friend, scowling. "Next time you need something off a top shelf, don't bother asking me for help. Try growing."

Emilia cackles. "Ooh, someone's feeling feisty."

He ignores her, instead turning back to me. "Roberts, how do you feel about flashing?"

"Being flashed? Big no. Not a fan. Being the flasher? I ordinarily wouldn't be against it if it's for something important, like a summer camp amateur basketball tournament where there is no prize or real incentive to participate, but it isn't possible with minors around. Sorry."

He sighs. "That's true. Damn kids. I wish Clay had a mascot you could steal."

"I steal one pig a million years ago and suddenly I'm a risk to mascots." I roll my eyes. As for my various reputations over the years, this is probably the most annoying one. "Would it help if I told you it's not the winning that counts, it's the taking part?"

Xander pins me with a look so icy it reminds me of my mom staring at my dad. "Grow up, Aurora."

What feels like a dozen games later, it's finally time for us to play Russ. I've been purposely avoiding him since this afternoon, instead sending him intimidating looks, occasionally dragging my finger across my neck when I catch him staring at me.

He approaches me as soon as we step onto the court, holding out his hand to shake mine. "Isn't this the bit where you proposition me with something debased and scandalous to help you cheat?" I say quietly, trying to look casual given our huge audience.

"Sorry, Roberts. I don't negotiate with my competition." He lets go of my hand, moving on to shake everyone else's so it doesn't look weird.

Xander is at my side immediately. "What did he say?"

"He said he'd organize a threesome with someone on the hockey team if I help him cheat. I said no. Told him I'm committed to my team."

"Okay, you could have picked something believable if you were going to lie to me." Xander snorts, and it's the most Xander he's been all day, which gives me hope this super intense version of him will pass. "That boy isn't sharing you with anyone, ever. Is your head in the game?"

"My head is always in the game."

The game starts, and in a very predictable turn of events, it's the Xander-versus-Clay show. Emilia and I are jogging up and down the court trying to keep up, but they all have such long legs and everything moves so quickly. They battle for points, which is fine, until Clay and Russ find their rhythm, making it harder for Xander and the other people on our team to keep up. Harder, but not impossible.

We're neck and neck, and honestly, I'm more than ready for this to be over.

"Roberts," Xander hisses as he runs past me. "Distract him."

I don't need him to expand on who him is. Rolling my eyes, I move to the other side of the court, the side Russ seems to favor. The only good distraction methods I have involve nudity, and as previously established, I can't do that here. He looks over his shoulder at me as I approach him, and I feel really freaking silly because there's no way I can do what Xander wants.

I watch Clay battle with Xander, then turn, looking for Russ, and I realize it's my shot. The ball is heading right for him and I get as close as I can. "Can we have a threesome?"

Russ's head snaps to me instantly and the basketball hits him right in the stomach. He grunts, making me feel sort of bad.

Even in his winded state, he half lunges for the ball, but I'm quicker, and as soon as it's in my hands I freeze.

Oh shit, I didn't think beyond the distraction.

"*Go,*" about fifty people shout at me at once.

Bouncing a ball and moving my feet at the same time is not as easy as it looks, and somewhere in the distance I can hear Xander screaming at me to pass, but it's too late, because there's a body on mine. Russ being this close to me in front of so many people feels scandalous, but even with his heavy breath on my neck making my nipples go hard, he's really freaking determined to get the ball back.

"We can both play dirty, sweetheart," he huffs.

I'm surprised I can hear him, considering how loud the kids are being on the sidelines. The whistle blows and Russ takes an extra second to unwrap himself from around me. I tut at him, bouncing the ball once while our teammates argue over God knows what in the background. I can only assume what we just did breaks some kind of rule, but I'd be lying if I said I had any interest in finding out which one. "I have a proposition for you."

"If it's another threesome offer, I respectfully decline."

I can't help but snort. "If I pretend to hurt myself, wanna go find the dogs and drink hot chocolate?"

"Of course I want that. Basketball is shit."

"Not all balls are created equal." Xander gestures for me to throw him the ball while he continues to bicker with Clay about something. "You're allowed to favor your own."

Russ is staring at me with his hands on his hips. His hair is messy, brushed back off his face in the way I love. It's a real struggle not to tell him how pretty he is every minute of the day. "I know we sort of laughed about it, but I need to hear you say you know what a hockey puck looks like and that you know it's not a ball."

"Of course I do." He breathes a sigh of relief. "Like a little baby car tire."

"What? No, it—"

I turn to walk away from him, pretending to trip over my own feet and fall to the ground before he can say anything else, shouting, "*Ouch!*" at the top of my lungs. Russ crouches beside me, pretending to check my knee for injury. "You'd be a terrible actress, y'know."

"I'm in so much pain," I say casually. "Please take me to the nurse, my hero."

The rest of our team jog over, staring down at me on the floor. "What happened?"

"She fell over her own feet," Russ says, holding out his hands to help pull me up. "I should take her to the nurse to be on the safe side. You guys carry on without us."

Clay immediately tries to protest, but Xander beats him to it. "Yeah that's fair, then we're both one person down. Feel better, Roberts. Good effort, etcetera."

He mouths "Good job" as I pretend to hobble away with Russ, and I love that Xander immediately thinks I did this for him and not myself.

When we're far enough away from the basketball court that the kids' cheers are just a quiet hum, Russ pulls me off the path and pushes me against a tree. My heart rate instantly spikes, excitement growing as he presses into me, caging me in with his arms. I know everyone is at the basketball court, but this is bold, especially for him.

"If I knew you wanted to take me against a tree, I'd have fallen down so much earlier."

"Take you?" he echoes. "No, I need your undivided attention while I talk to you about hockey pucks."

Chapter Thirty

AURORA

WHAT'S THE WORD FOR WHEN you find yourself exactly where you're supposed to be?

I feel at peace with myself and my life for the first time, and there's nothing that can derail that. Today is finally visiting day. A lot of families leave camp for the day and only come back for the evening barbecue and games; some families don't visit at all.

I hated visiting day when I was a camper. Some years my parents didn't come because Elsa wanted to visit our grandparents, so they'd use the child-free opportunity to take a vacation and try and save their unsavable marriage. Other years only Mom came. The worst year was when Mom, Dad, and Elsa came and they made me so miserable Jenna gave me an extra bowl of ice cream when they all left.

All our kids are expected to be taken off-site today, meaning we've all got the easiest day ahead. Emilia forgot about the camera Poppy bought her to document the summer and has therefore documented nothing, so today is our do-over day.

"Do you think we need outfit changes as well?" Emilia asks as I throw different hair accessories into a purse with my cell phone, headphones, and a paperback about a princess and her hot bodyguard.

"I love you and I love Pops, but I am not stripping behind a tree for either of you. It's a uniform and it has a bear on it; why would we ever want to wear anything else?"

I'm not saying I'm an expert at candid shots, but I am. We set up camp at a picnic bench not far from our cabin and I give Emilia my best work, changing my hairstyle so the photos look like different days. While I'm pretending to laugh at Xander, whose back thankfully is to the camera, we realize this isn't going to be easy.

The dogs are more photogenic than the guys, which is no exaggeration.

"Russ, stop grimacing," Emilia yells at him. She stomps over, showing me the camera, and he honestly looks like he's sitting on a wasps' nest.

"You're too pretty to be this bad at being photographed," I say, flicking through the pictures. I hand the camera back to Emilia and ask her to go back to where she was so I can try something.

"And what about me?" Xander asks, picking Salmon up to cuddle.

"Put the dog down!" we all say at the same time, which is met with a grunt and an eye roll.

"You're pretty, Xan," Russ says, flinching as I try to force his face into a more relaxed position with my hands. "What are you doing?"

"I'm relaxing you."

"This is not relaxing, Aurora."

Looking around, I check that there isn't anyone hanging around near us before leaning in and kissing Russ. I wasn't expecting him to respond so enthusiastically, but his hand grabs the back of my neck, keeping me in place.

Xander loudly heaves, which is when Russ lets me go. "It's kinda selfish for you guys to do that when I haven't had sex for two months. Just saying."

I wish I could bottle the way I feel after Russ kisses me. I reluctantly drag my eyes from Russ to scowl at our friend. "You saw Clay naked, surely that counts for something?"

"You two are disgusting," Emilia says as she approaches us, handing over her camera again. "I miss my girlfriend."

I lean over so Russ can see them as well, starting with his grimace ones, clicking all the way through our kiss to the ones from a few seconds ago. I never understood the phrase "My heart skips a beat" until right now, when I see how Russ looks at me when he thinks I'm not watching.

Russ kisses my shoulder and goose bumps travel down my arm. "You're so beautiful," he whispers.

This is what being wanted and valued feels like.

This is the feeling I want forever.

Emilia is taking pictures of the guys throwing a football, something they both protested, but much to the delight of the dogs. Emilia snapped that there was no way for her to combine basketball and hockey into a sport she could photograph and to get over it.

I'm flicking through my book when my cell phone starts vibrating in my purse. I don't know where the noise is coming from at first; I brought it out as a photo prop and I've kind of forgotten it exists after so many weeks hardly touching it.

Reaching into my purse to retrieve it, I almost drop it on the ground when I see the Man Who Pays the Rent staring back at me.

"Hello, Dad" I say, fully anticipating he may have butt-dialed me.

"I've been trying to reach you for more than twenty-four hours."

There's that Roberts charm I love so much. "Sorry, Dad. I'm at camp, the service here is terrible."

He huffs, like somehow my inability to control whatever makes cell service a thing is inconveniencing him. "I need to share some news with you. I proposed to Norah over the weekend and she said yes."

"That's . . ." not a surprise, "incredible, Dad. Congratulations to you both."

Maybe that's why he's so frustrated about not being able to reach me. He was worried I'd find out from someone else. Dad has had tons of girlfriends over the years, but as soon as he started letting Norah post about him online, I knew it wouldn't be long until there was a wedding.

I'm not Norah's biggest fan out of principle. But if he's going to marry someone, I'm at least glad he's marrying someone closer to his own age and not dating the women closer to my and Elsa's ages, like he was doing for a while.

Mom called it his midlife crisis.

"You being at camp has made it difficult to organize a bridesmaid dress. Your mother told me you're home on the fifteenth, correct?"

I don't know which thing to follow first. The fact I'm wanted as a bridesmaid or the fact my mom and dad have talked. Norah has her own kids, so I wouldn't have expected to be included in the wedding party, and I can't imagine Dad advocating for my involvement. "Yeah, Dad, the fifteenth."

"I'll have Brenda change your flight home; email her the details along with your current measurements. You'll need to fly straight to Palm Springs for this to work out."

Palm Springs? "For what to work out?"

I hear him sigh. "The wedding, Aurora. Are you listening properly? We would like a short honeymoon before summer break ends and I have to go to Europe for the Dutch Grand Prix."

My words catch in my throat. "You're getting married so soon?"

"Yes, Aurora. And I need you in Palm Springs. Do you understand?"

His snippy tone should hurt me more than it does, but my brain is scrambling as I realize he's waiting for me to be free instead of just doing it without me. Jesus Christ, the bar really is on the floor. "I understand, Dad. I'm excited to see what dress Norah picks for me. Thanks, um, thank you for letting me be a part of it."

"Of course you're a part of it, Aurora. You're my daughter." I'm stunned to silence. It's such a basic statement from a parent. It's not even something particularly kind, but from my dad it's major. Weirdly, I feel like my recent happiness caused this. Put good energy into the universe and get it back. Silly, but comforting all the same.

I want to tell him how much that small statement means to me. How it's everything I've ever needed and how I desperately want to have a good relationship with him, but I don't get a chance to, because he starts talking again. "And it'd look strange in the photos if you're not there. I'm not having Norah's moment stolen by the media's obsession with giving you and your sister attention."

My heart sinks. "So you only want me there for the photographs?"

"Is there something wrong with you today? What aren't you understanding?" he snaps impatiently. "Norah has arranged a magazine exclusive. Yes, you need to be there for the photographs. I'm not having our day overshadowed by rumors of a family divide because of you."

I feel numb. "Okay. Do I get a plus-one?"

"Do you need a plus-one? Who is it? Emily?"

"Emilia," I correct him. "But no, not her. I met someone. He's cal—"

"Met someone where, exactly?"

I don't know why my hands are sweating, but they are. "At camp. He's cal—"

"Don't be ridiculous, Aurora. I'm not letting you bring a stranger to a private family occasion." He interrupts me again and I can feel my heart pounding as my frustration grows. "You won't even remember who he is after you stop playing make-believe at that farm. Be realistic for once, for Christ's sake. It's my wedding, not a children's birthday party."

My throat is completely dry, but I force the words out anyway.

"He's important to me, Dad. I'd like to bring him. We go to the same college, it is realistic, we like each other."

He sighs, and I feel it all the way in my bones. It's like acid. "I'm sure your fling is very important and special, but I said no. Can I trust you to be there alone, Aurora? Yes or no?"

Fling. "Yes."

"Good. I'll see you in a few weeks. Bye."

The call disconnects before I can say bye back and I sit in the same spot frozen, trying to process how my day was bulldozed by a three-minute phone call.

I don't know what I thought would happen when I answered his call. I could have stopped talking at "you're my daughter" and been blissfully unaware. I'd have spent the rest of the day floating around feeling untouchable. But I went too far, asked too much.

If I wasn't so desperate for something I'm clearly never going to get, or if I grew up and stopped being pathetic about the fact he doesn't care, maybe I wouldn't feel like I'm being run over when I talk to him.

I need to get away from here, and that's the thing I repeat over and over as I somehow get myself from the picnic table to my cabin. Sitting on my bed, I lean against the wall while I replay the conversation.

I think about what I said and how he responded, then what I could have said instead and how he might have responded to that. I keep going and going and going, until there's an endless stream of dialogue spinning around my head and I can't do anything to get the outcome I want.

The outcome where he changes and I feel like he wants me in his life for more than just media purposes.

My hands are shaking as I pull my suitcase from the wardrobe and open it on my bed. I love Honey Acres, but pretending it's my home when it's not is silly. Dad's right, it's all make-believe. They're just people who were paid to look after me and probably took pity on me.

I don't know why I brought so many things with me, knowing I'd hardly wear any of them. It's just making it harder to get out of here quickly. I don't know why I believed I'd last the summer. My shorts won't fold. Jenna knew deep down I wouldn't last. No matter what angle I twist and turn my clothes in, they look messy and uneven in my suitcase. I wonder if Emilia thought I'd fail, too. Russ is great at folding my clothes.

I could go to Bora Bora and turn off my cell phone.

I don't even need a cell phone. Fuck, I might just throw it into the trash.

Why won't these shorts fucking fold properly?

I need to tell someone to make sure Freya remembers to put on her bug spray and that Michael doesn't eat anything with sugar after 6 p.m. I'll miss the talent show, but Emilia can make it work without me. Everyone will be fine. Opening the drawer in my bedside table to empty it, I spot the origami dove Russ made for me next to my collection of friendship bracelets from the kids.

I sink to the floor beside my bed as my chest constricts, and years of hurt that I've buried beneath reckless actions and self-deprecating jokes finally race to the surface as a sob. It's like the dam breaks and I just let the tears fall because there's nothing else to do and no one else who can fix it.

I'm not sure how long I'm sitting here before I hear his footsteps. "Ror?"

The cabin door opens and I can only imagine how chaotic it looks in here. Suits me, though, I suppose. Russ sinks to the floor in front of me, immediately reaching for my face to wipe away the tears. "Going somewhere, Roberts?" he asks softly.

"I have to go. I need to leave."

"Okay, let me pack my bag, too. I'll come with you."

My breathing is uneven, and my eyes begin to sting. "You can't. You have to stay here. You need this job. And you need to make sure they pass the cabin inspection and check Sadia's bunk for spiders. Xander doesn't do it properly. I haven't changed; I'll just disappoint you, Russ. I don't want to disappoint you."

He crosses his legs and picks me up, nestling me in his lap. Everything about feeling him touching me makes me feel better. After kissing each of my eyelids, then each of my cheeks, he kisses both of my ears and my breathing begins to fall into a rhythm with his.

"You could never disappoint me, Aurora, and you don't need to be anybody but yourself. I know you're hurting and I want to make it better, but if you want me to stay and check for spiders, you need to stay, too, because if you go, I go. We all need you and we all want you here."

"My dad is getting married," I whisper, almost choking on the words. "And he only wants me there for the magazine exclusive, so we don't look like we're a family at war."

"Fuck your dad." His hands cup my face as he leans back to look right at me. "You don't have to let him keep burning you, sweetheart."

My bottom lip wobbles. "I just want to be wanted."

"You are. Let's both stay. Let me show you how wanted you are."

"I like who I am when I'm with you, but what if you leave, too? Who am I going to be then?"

"Do you trust me?" he asks, still cupping my face gently.

Even with the tears still running down my face, I nod. I do trust him. I'm also scared.

"I'm not going anywhere, but you don't need me, Aurora. You're strong and sweet and funny. You're smart and affectionate and you're all those things without me. You don't need anyone but yourself, but you can have me anyway. I worry I'm going to fuck this up, too, but we have to trust ourselves as much as we trust each other."

"I can't fold my shorts like you can."

"Exactly," he says, resting his forehead against mine. "So don't go. Don't run away from the place that makes you feel at home. From the family you chose."

Russ's lips meet mine, soft and gentle, like I might break if he's too rough with me. His fingers dance up my spine, and bit by bit, the tension eases out of my body. I wrap my arms around his neck, sinking into him, rolling my hips against where we're joined.

"Please show me how much you want me," I whisper. "I need to replace all the bad feelings. You make me feel good."

If I wasn't so distracted by my crumbling life, I'd have more time to be impressed by how easily Russ stands from the floor with me around him. My suitcase crashes against the floor as he knocks it off the bed, lowering me carefully onto the mattress, climbing on top of me.

The weight of his body on mine does more to kill the anxiety rolling through me like waves than anything else. He tugs off his T-shirt and waits while I run my hands down his chest, feeling his heartbeat beneath my palms. Mine comes off next, followed by my shorts and his. There are layers of fabric between us, but the pressure of him between my legs makes goose bumps spread down my body.

He kisses my forehead. "I want everything about you, Aurora." My nose is next. "I want your smiles." Then my jaw. "Your laughs." My collarbone. "I want the way you ramble when you're nervous." The top of my breast. "I want your big reactions and your little ones." The center of my stomach. "I want to watch you get frustrated at origami but carry on anyway because it makes you so happy." My navel. "I want to protect you from possums and sharks and, sometimes, when you need it, yourself." Finally, my hip bone. "And I want to want you because you're worth it, sweetheart. And you make me feel good, too."

He sits up when I do, letting me smash my mouth into his, pouring as much into it as I can. His hands grip my neck, keeping me in place.

And that's when Jenna shouts my name from outside of my cabin.

And the door begins to open before I can shout wait.

Chapter Thirty-One

AURORA

THERE HAVE BEEN MANY TIMES in my life when I've been caught doing something that I shouldn't.

When I was seven at my grandparents' house when I pushed Elsa into the pool for telling me I was left behind by aliens.

When I was twelve and I was supposed to be in detention for punching the kid punching other kids, but I went to hang out at the mall because it felt like an unfair punishment. That one was double bad because I wasn't allowed to go to the mall yet, either.

When I was fifteen and got high for the first time in the pool house, a very poor choice of location, especially as Mom was home and found me immediately.

When I was seventeen and the paparazzi took pictures of me stumbling out of a nightclub I was too young to be in, totally wasted, with Connor James, the son of Dad's work nemesis.

Basically anything I did with Connor James, I shouldn't have been doing. Yacht crashing excluded, because I still maintain that one wasn't my fault.

As bad as those times were, nothing really happened. Eyes were rolled, disparaging looks and maybe a short lecture on personal safety were given, but I knew nothing would happen and that's why I did it and why I continued to do it.

Jenna's eyes widen as she fills the doorway.

"Oh shit," is all Russ manages to say as he reaches for something to cover me up. When really, he should be more concerned about the huge erection pressing against his boxers.

The door handle is still in Jenna's hand, which makes it easier for her to immediately close it again. There's so much to consider as my mind rushes between panic and confusion.

"Fuck fuck fuck," Russ chants as he scrambles for our clothes. "It's going to be okay. Don't panic."

"I'm not panicking," I reassure him, pulling my shorts up my legs. "I was talking to myself."

His hands are shaking as he tries to put his sneakers back on and I navigate him to sit on the bed. I should be in more of a rush; so far I've only managed to get my shorts back on, but Jenna can stew in her anger outside if it means I get to soothe Russ.

I know he hates getting in trouble because of his dad, and this situation is the one he was trying to avoid since day one. Considering I'm the one who was having a meltdown five minutes ago, it seems all that was required to snap me out of it is for Russ to be looking at me like the world's ending.

"It isn't really bad. We're consenting adults, there are no kids in our care right now, and we had already had sex before we got to camp, which Jenna knows.

"Russ, listen to me. The very worst-case scenario is we leave a few weeks early. Hand in hand. Nothing happens, we don't even need to tell anyone, we can hide out anywhere in the world. Doing something wrong does not make you a fuckup. Your dad is a liar; you aren't anything he says you are."

It feels funny being the one handing out dad advice, but it's what makes Russ so important to me. We're both a little bit broken, both trying to be a bit better, and both just desperately searching for someone to want them for who they are.

"Why is she here?"

"I honestly don't know." Stressing over that is a problem for when I'm fully dressed.

Jenna is crouched on the porch fussing over Fish when we finally emerge from the cabin. She doesn't say anything as she stands, brushing the dog hair from her pants. It's like a standoff of who will go first and I'm about to shoot, but Jenna beats me to it.

"Your parents are here," she says.

Russ and I look at each other, confused. He clears his throat. "Whose parents?"

Jenna folds her arms and boy, does she look pissed. "Both of you. Your dad is here, Russ, and so is your mom, Aurora. They're both waiting in reception."

Confused doesn't even cover how I'm feeling right now as the three of us walk in silence toward our parents. The color has drained from Russ's face, and I wish I could comfort him, but I don't feel like making things worse with Jenna.

Mom is already outside the building when we get there. I don't get a look at Russ's dad. Jenna and Russ continue walking and I feel like I'm being pulled between them.

"Russ!" I shout, causing him to stop and turn around.

Running up to him, I wrap my arms around his torso, squeezing tight. "If he's horrible even for a second, walk away. I'll be waiting for you when you get back."

He kisses the top of my head and says nothing. He continues after Jenna and I turn to my mom.

"Are we going to talk about why you're here unannounced?"

Mom hates the outdoors and she's dressed like she's going on a shopping trip in Saint-Tropez, not whatever she plans to do here.

"It's visiting day. I thought we could go for a walk," she says casually.

I'm immediately suspicious. "You came all the way here from Malibu unannounced because you want to go for a walk with me?"

"That's what I said, Aurora."

What's the worst that could happen? "Okay then."

Our choice of walking route is limited because Mom decided to wear Louboutin pumps instead of sneakers, so I take her down to the lake where she can walk barefoot in the sand. Mom makes small talk with me for the first twenty-five minutes, and I'm growing more tired and frustrated. My mom is not a walk-in-the-woods mom; she's more a let's-go-buy-your-first-Birkin mom. Minute thirty passes and my suspicion and confusion have reached their max capacity. I stop at two deck chairs that have been left out and sit down.

"I need to know why you're here because you pretending to like walking is stressing me out."

"I love walking on the beach. It's one of my favorite things," she says defensively.

"Yeah, at home. Or maybe the Caribbean. Not dodging sticks and God knows what else."

"You're always so suspicious of people's intentions. You definitely get that from your father. He was always the same."

The lightbulb practically illuminates above my head.

"You know, don't you?" I say as she sits beside me staring out at the lake. "That's why you're here. When he asked when I'm home, he told you he's engaged, didn't he?"

In the whirlwind that has been the past hour, I'd forgotten why I was so upset in the first place. She threads her fingers through mine. "I thought you might be upset. I wanted to be here for you. I didn't want to leave it to Emilia."

"You knew what he was going to say to me?"

"No, but I assumed there would probably be something." Her thumb rubs against my hand gently. "Your dad is an asshole, Aurora, and it's a well-earned title. The chances of him saying something cruel were higher than me arriving and you being on cloud nine."

Dad has always been a thorn in the side of our relationship. I question if it's frustrating for Mom to watch me fight for the attention of someone she dislikes so much. He isn't something we ever really talk about at length, and to her credit, she only tries to be horrible to his face. "Why doesn't he like me, Mom? He doesn't treat me like a daughter."

"Your father is . . . I don't know, darling. When you marry someone, you believe you know everything about them, but people change. Your dad changed. Small things at first—how he talked about certain topics, how he spoke to other people. Then Elsa was born and he went back to being the man I married. He was wonderful with her and she idolized him for it."

I'm itching to start packing my suitcase again. "Must be nice."

"It didn't last long and he went back to being the man who was rude to everyone, picked fights over nothing, and came home late with no reason. Our marriage was strained and I was tired of feeling like I was constantly at war." She shuffles in her seat and I squeeze her hand to urge her to continue. She's never been this candid about her relationship with Dad and I'm desperate to hear everything. "You know this part, but we left Elsa with your grandma and took our trip to see the northern lights, finally disconnected from the outside world, and we were happy again. A few weeks later I found out I was pregnant with you and he was so happy."

"Oh, so there was a time when he was happy I existed. Prebirth."

"You were like a tiny little doll when you were born. You were absolute perfection. You never cried, you slept constantly, and you just loved being held. I was obsessed with you. But Fenrir was taking up all of your dad's time and I didn't want to travel while you were so small, so we were apart a lot. As you grew, you didn't look like any of the Roberts family and your father became even more distant."

"Distant? Why?"

"It was subtle at first. He'd comment on how blond your hair was getting when Elsa's was dark brown, your eyes started to turn green. Everyone in that family looks alike and you were the exception. You looked exactly like me."

I feel sick and it all starts to make sense. "He thinks I'm not his daughter."

"He didn't outright say it, but for a while I was convinced that was the answer. I pushed it aside at first because I thought when you got older, you'd be able to bond and bridge that gap he'd created." Mom brushes her cheek with the back of her hand. "I wish that had been the answer. I could have fixed that with a DNA test and a hefty round of couples counseling. But then he started to treat your sister the same way and I realized I was searching for answers that would make sense to me, something I could work with, when the reality is the problem was him the entire time.

"We fought and fought over it. I couldn't stand that I'd started a family with a man who could treat his children like they were an inconvenience to him. I felt like I was grieving the loss of my husband, but he hadn't died. He just wasn't the man I knew. You noticed; even when you were very little, you knew things weren't right. Elsa started acting out to get his attention, which would work, so you copied. I thought it would get better when we traveled together, but if anything, it made you both worse."

I sit in silence, scared to say anything and interrupt all the answers I'm finally getting.

"It was harmless at first. 'Daddy watch me do this,' and you'd wait expectantly, but the less it worked the more you did. And I couldn't even reprimand you, scare either of you into behaving, because it wasn't your fault. You were little girls who didn't know what they'd done wrong. Who didn't understand—" Her voice cracks. "I'm so sorry, Aurora. I'm so sorry you feel the way you do about yourself because we weren't better parents. I left him when I realized he'd never change, but it was too late. The damage was done."

"So the answer to my questions is something that I already know? That he isn't a good person."

"I've never claimed to be the perfect mother. I know we have our differences, but I love you enough for both me and Chuck." She stands, brushing off invisible dust from her pantsuit, her pumps in her hand looking wholly out of place. "You're an adult, Aurora. I cannot tell you what to do and you wouldn't listen to me even if I did but, legally your father has to pay for your education and living costs until you have access to your trust. It doesn't mean you have to see him. Do with that information what you will."

I feel like I've had a lifetime's worth of information in such a short time and I'm exhausted.

Like Mom, I've been searching for a reason. Desperately looking for answers that might explain things, give me something I can cling to and fix. I don't think I can fix a serious character flaw.

I stand, too, following Mom's lead back toward the main path, helping her step back into her pumps when we reach the gravel. "Are you going to stay for a little while? Emilia will be around here some-where."

"I can't, darling. I need to get home for Cat. He'll be wondering where I am."

I forgot about the damn cat. "Is this cat real? Or is it some kind of ploy to get me to come over?"

She rolls her eyes as she reaches into her bag to pull out her cell phone and there, on her phone background, is a picture of a scruffy black cat lying in a sea of pillows on— "Why is he on my bed?"

"You have your own place, Aurora. You can't claim every bed you sleep in forever."

"Are you kidding me? You were asking me to move home two minutes ago!"

She huffs as she stuffs her phone back into her purse. "I'm sure if you bring some smoked salmon with you on your next visit he will consider sharing with you."

I'VE LEFT MOM WITH EMILIA and Xander is under strict instructions that he's not allowed to hit on her. Xander made some jokes about becoming my stepdad as soon as he realized my mom just looks like an older version of me, and I'm taking no chances. I gave Emilia permission that if Clay even looks in Mom's direction, she's allowed to beat him.

I know as I approach Jenna's office that I'm going to hate every second of this conversation.

Honey Acres has been part of my life for longer than it hasn't been, and I know that being fired means I'll never be welcomed back here. Really, I should have considered that before I started things with Russ. I can't lie, I've never truly believed that the fraternization rule was enforced, but after being given the cold shoulder earlier, I'm not as confident.

But some risks are worth it, and given the time again, I wouldn't change it. Russ told me he wouldn't change anything in the past because he wouldn't risk not meeting me, so if getting fired from the place I love most in the world is how it goes for me, at least I get to keep the butterflies.

Rapping my knuckles against the door, I know from the *Mamma Mia* soundtrack blasting that Jenna's in there. I've never knocked before entering Jenna's office, so I don't know why I'm starting today. Maybe it's because I know not pissing her off further will help my cause. I knock again a little harder and she finally shouts for me to come in.

Her expression when she realizes it's me practically cuts me open. I can tell she's not angry, she's disappointed.

"Jenna, I'm sorry."

"Don't tell me you're sorry when you're not, Rory. You knew exactly what you were doing when you broke the rules, and you've knowingly put me in a difficult position."

"Please don't fire him, Jen," I say desperately, sitting on the other side of the desk. "He doesn't deserve to lose his job because I convinced him to break the rules."

"You're both adults and you're both responsible for your actions." Shit. "When did it start?"

I want to lie. Like maybe if I tell her it was today because I was sad it'll make it easier for her to process and she won't be as harsh. But Jenna means a lot to me and I don't want to betray her even more than I have. "When we had the storm."

She shakes her head as she leans against her hands. "You fucking horny so-called adults are driving me up the wall. I can't wait for you all to go back to college and be someone else's problem. I'm so annoyed with you, Aurora."

"I'm so sorry, Jenna. I will leave with no drama, I swear. But please don't fire Russ. He will be crushed if he loses this job. He doesn't deserve it, I promise."

"Can you stop with the pity party, please? You're giving me a headache and my head already hurts after seeing a half-naked man crawling all over you today and then having to look your mother in the eyes."

"I'm so—"

"Stop apologizing and go do your job, please. No, bring me a lemonade. Then go do your job." My eyebrows raise in surprise. She huffs, folding her arms across her chest and leaning back in her chair. "What? You think you're special? If we had to fire every member of staff who fooled around together, we'd have no staff."

"But I thought . . ."

"I saw him the night of the storm, Aurora. I knew you'd be scared, so I went back to your cabin. I watched him hover around the steps to your cabin in the rain, presumably arguing with himself, until he finally knocked. That's when I knew."

"Knew what?"

"I knew he cared about you." She sighs. "And I realized you weren't just doing it to give your middle finger to the rules."

"I care about him, too."

"We're your family, Rory. You will always have a home here, even if you do things that make me want to strangle you. I'm not going to report it like I'm supposed to, but that doesn't give you a free pass to do what you want until you leave, all right? Keep sneaking around until you are out of my hair. I don't wanna hear a peep out of either of you."

Family. "I love you, Jen."

"And I love you. People don't always let you get away with things because they don't care. I let you get away with things because you deserve to be happy. You deserve to feel and believe you are wanted, and enjoy being loved, because so many people love you, Ror."

"I had a really great heart-to-heart with my mom today. A lot of things make sense now, especially about my dad."

She stands and walks over to me, wrapping her arms around me. "*Dad* is a word. It doesn't mean anything unless there is action and intention behind it. He's really just an asshole who you happen to share DNA with. That's it. We don't need him. You don't do fine without him, you do better."

Jenna kisses the top of my head before moving back to sit at her desk. "Okay, heart-to-heart is over. Scram. And so you know, you're mucking out the horses for the rest of the week. Take lover boy. You're both pains in my ass."

This is not at all how I would have predicted this going, and I'm walking out of here feeling totally confused, but thankfully I'm not leaving and neither is Russ. If I have to deal with some horse crap but Jenna isn't truly mad at me, I'll definitely cope. Pulling the office door open, I have one last question before I head out and prepare for the end of visiting day. "Wait, who else has been hooking up?"

She runs her fingers across her lips, zipping them shut. "You've lost your gossip privileges. Should have kept your panties on."

As much as she's right, I'm glad I didn't.

Chapter Thirty-Two

RUSS

WE'VE BEEN SITTING ON THIS picnic bench for five minutes and neither of us has spoken yet.

He looks better than last time I saw him, but not being in a hospital bed covered in wires will do that to a person. I knew it was too good to be true. I knew the silence wouldn't last long, but I must admit, I never expected him to turn up here.

"I don't know where to start, Russ," he says.

I can't remember the last time we sat in a normal setting together. I wish I knew how many minutes it is until he leaves so I can count them down.

"Why don't you start by telling me why you're here," I say harshly.

I'm not someone who often gets angry, but there's something about being around my dad that makes me emotional. It's like I have to become a different person to be able to cope with being around him.

"A lot has happened since we last saw each other. Your mother went through my cell phone and saw how much I've been hiding from her. She understands now how bad things are, how terribly I've been treating people, treating you. She kicked me out."

I'm stunned. "Why don't I know about this?"

"Because she said we should allow you to enjoy your summer without us ruining it. Me ruining it. I wanted to call on your birthday, apologize for everything I've done, but she told me not to. She said that you deserve time and space to heal from the damage that I've done to our family."

I don't say anything at first. I don't know if it's because he's caught me so off guard I'm not sure what to say, or if my instincts are telling me to wait for the other shoe to drop. For him to reveal what his true intentions are.

"So why are you here now? I don't have any money for you and you can't stay with me. There isn't anything I can give you."

"I don't want anything, Russ," he says. "I'm just here to talk. I think we can agree that I've taken enough from you already. I've made a lot of mistakes in my life, burned a lot of bridges. I regret a lot of things, but there's nothing that I regret more than the hurt I've caused you, your mom, and your brother."

I know all humans have flaws, and my dad lives every day knowing he's shown every single one of his.

I know my experience isn't the blueprint. It isn't the cookie-cutter version of how things go. I've listened to the people whose parents were so attentive, so loving, so riddled with guilt for their actions that they never knew anything was wrong. My anger isn't toward people with addiction issues. I've looked at the statistics, read the case studies, heard the heart-wrenching personal tales of struggle, and I've felt empathy. See, logical right?

My heart has always told me to say fuck logic. My dad shouldn't have let it beat him; he should have fought harder. Not because he's better than anyone else fighting invisible demons, but because he's my dad. He's mine and I needed him and he didn't try and he didn't even care. He served himself, his desires, and his impulses and he kept serving himself until the anger and the regret and the resentment came like a tsunami—and when he let the waves engulf him, he dragged us all down with him.

I clear my throat, staring him directly in the eyes. I'm not a scared kid anymore, I don't need to shrink in front of him. "I still don't understand why you're here, Dad."

"The last time you saw me, you told me to sort my shit out. I wanted to see you in person to tell you that that's what I'm going to do. I know that you probably don't believe me, or maybe things are so far gone that you don't care. But I am going to fix things. I don't want to live like this anymore. I want my family back. I want my life back. I want to be someone you can look up to again."

I should be excited that he's finally saying the things I've wanted to hear for so long. That he wants to change. That he knows things are bad. That he knows he's hurt people. But all I can think about is how it's a lot of words, said in the right order in a way that makes them feel real, but he's always been good at that. That's why it's taken until now for Mom to see the light.

There's a fine balance between dedication and desperation sometimes, and that's how I know Dad's at the place the books call rock bottom. Addiction is a disease, a losing game. Everyone knows the house always wins. It might not be this hand, or even the next one. It might take one horse race or twenty. It might be that one last roll of the dice, but eventually the house will come to collect, and when they cash out there will be nothing left.

I don't think Dad has anything left, and the realization makes my anger subside a little. "I hope you get it back, Dad. I do, honestly. But you can't just declare you're going to change; you have to act. You have to make a conscious effort to seek help and remove the temptations from your life."

"I will," he says adamantly.

"How?"

"I don't know."

Rubbing my fingers against my temple, I try not to sigh because I don't want him to think I'm dismissing him. "There are programs for people like you; I've read about them. They're anonymous and they're free. You should look into it; there's always fliers on bulletin boards around town."

"I will. I'll look as soon as I get back. Look, Russ, I know I haven't been the person you deserve. You've had to work harder, sacrifice more, struggle alone all because I wouldn't fight my demons. I can't change the past, but I can make sure it doesn't happen again. If there's help out there, I want to find it."

I think he's waiting for me to make a huge declaration of how it's all going to be okay and how I trust and believe he's going to get better, but I'm not going to believe it until I see it with my own eyes. I hope with everything that he's serious, but it feels too good to be true right now. A small part of me worries that I'm too far gone to forgive him, that everyone will move on and I'll be stuck in the past, still hurt beneath the surface.

Can a person really get everything they want? I've spent years struggling alone, and in such a short time things have changed so much.

Sharing my feelings has worked so far this summer, which encourages me to be honest with Dad. "It would be nice to feel like a family again. If you could get better, I wouldn't find it so difficult to be around you. Your unpredictable moods make me anxious."

He nods, his eyes watering. He looks like he's going to say something more, but instead he taps his fist against the table twice and stands. "I'm going to get out of your hair. This place is beautiful. Are you enjoying working here?"

I nod. "I love it."

"I'm proud of you, Russ. You're building a great life for yourself despite what I've put you through." He looks like he's going to lean in and hug me, but he doesn't, instead holding out his hand for me to shake. "I'll see you soon, son."

"Bye, Dad."

I SIT ALONE AT THE picnic table for another twenty minutes. Thinking, processing, wondering if this could really be the start of the change I've been desperate for.

Eventually, I remember myself and head to find Jenna. It feels like there's been more drama today than there has been the whole summer combined.

I know I fucked up and I know that Jenna has every right to fire me for what she saw, but I hope she won't. Earlier, I thought being caught was the worst thing that could possibly happen to me at camp. But then my dad made an unplanned visit, and suddenly that was the worst thing that could possibly happen to me at camp. Facing Jenna now feels a hell of a lot less scary.

As I knock on the door to her office, I realize a smart person would've kept out of the way and hoped for the best. I don't appear to be a smart person anymore. But I'm not going to be able to function if I'm waiting around, wondering if I'm about to get told to pack my bags and leave.

"Nice to see you with your clothes on," she says when I walk into her office.

The heat immediately rushes to my cheeks and ears. "I've been trying to think of something I could say that might explain why I knowingly ignored the rules, but I don't have a good enough excuse and I don't want to waste your time." She folds her arms across her chest and sits back in her chair, staring at me with a look of defiance. "I never expected someone like Aurora to even look in my direction, but she has, and I'm going to cling on to that with both hands. I know you love her, Jenna. All I want to do is make her happy."

"You can't make her happy and also keep your pants on?" she says. "This is a place of work, not a frat house."

"I've spent my life trying to stick to the rules. I've kept my head down, kept my stories and secrets and done my best to carry around my baggage alone. She makes me not want to be alone anymore. I'm sorry I broke the rules, but I don't regret it, and I'd do it again if it meant I could do it with her. I'm grateful for the opportunity your family has given me, but I'm more grateful for her."

"Y'all stress me out so much, I swear." Jenna rubs her temples and groans loudly. "Every day I want you to think about what you're grateful for in life. Every single day. If she's ever not on your list, I want you to work out why and fix it. If you're not treating her like she's the best thing to ever happen to you, you don't deserve her. Do you understand?"

"Yes."

"She has a big heart, but it's bruised. When you spend a long time self-destructing, sometimes your pieces don't fit back together quite right. She's gonna need time and patience."

"I understand."

"Good. Now get out. Go do your job so I can forget about this."

"I'm not fired?"

"For now." She waves me off with a hand. "And Russ, I have a million places to bury a body if you break her heart. We have acres you don't even know about. They'd never find you."

Jenna is kind of terrifying and I wholeheartedly believe her. "Noted."

Chapter Thirty-Three

RUSS

EVERY DAY I THINK ABOUT the things I'm grateful for like Jenna told me to.

Most days it's little things, like all the kids having fun or a good night's sleep. I'm grateful when I check the group chat with my friends and see that they're excited to see me soon, or when I see that another day goes by and I don't have a cash request from my dad.

Every single day I'm grateful for Aurora, for getting to see how happy she is letting the kids push her into the lake for the millionth time, or hearing about the cat her mom may or may not have stolen from a neighbor. I'm grateful for the smile I get from her when she first sees me in the morning when I stop by at the end of my run or the kiss we manage to steal away from the group.

I'm grateful to Jenna for not sending us home and I'm grateful to Xander and Emilia for doing what they can to help us successfully continue to sneak around.

Taking the time to look at my day and appreciate what I have and what I'll be taking away with me is helping me not be sad that it's time to leave.

But today on the stage in front of everyone at Honey Acres, I'm grateful that the talent show is nearly over.

I'm used to hearing people cheering and applauding, but usually I'm on the ice surrounded by my teammates and it's easy to zone out. It's not that simple when it's just me, Xander, and the dogs on a stage where Xander is showing no sign that he plans to get off it soon.

I know my face is bright red as I hop down, whistling for the dogs to follow me, hoping that it'll force Xander down. Without Aurora's determination to do a good job, Xander and I didn't attempt to put a plan together until yesterday. Now that we're done and I can stop worrying about it, I'm grateful that Fish, Salmon, and Trout will do anything for bacon.

To their credit, they did every trick perfectly, and I'm convinced nobody will know how unorganized and chaotic this thing has been all summer.

"Nailed it," Xander says as we throw ourselves into our seats at the back of the seating area. "Told you we would. Tell me I was right."

"You were right," I grumble reluctantly.

All the Brown Bear kids smashed it and now that I'm not the performer, I can appreciate how fun this is and what a good way it is to end the summer.

The cheering starts again as the rest of our group takes the stage to do their performance. Aurora is wearing the sundress I love: the yellow one with little flowers and narrow straps that are easy to peel down. Her hair is curled and pulled back off her face with a ribbon and she looks beautiful.

Maya takes her place behind Emilia and puts her hands on her waist and when Clay takes his place behind Aurora and puts his hands on her waist, the music starts, but all I can hear is Xander laughing.

"I wish I could take a picture of your face right now." He tries to stop it by covering his mouth, but when I give him the dirtiest look I can manage, it only makes him worse. We cheer along for support, but every time Clay's hands are on her, Xander starts laughing again, irritating me more. "I'm sorry, man. It's just too funny. Did she not tell you?"

"Would you have told me if you were her?"

I've asked how her practices were going a couple of times, but she just said, "Stop trying to copy, Callaghan," and we'd move on. If it was anyone other than Clay I wouldn't be jealous. Trout climbs onto my lap and up my body, settling on my chest to sleep. He's so big and heavy now he covers a lot of my torso when he's sprawled out. Another thing I'm grateful for, because it's stopping me from dragging Aurora off the stage like a caveman.

She looks like she's having so much fun and I concentrate on that and how cute she looks trying to keep up with Emilia, who is clearly the only person on that stage with a shred of professional training, or you know, rhythm.

The song comes to an end and the rest of the audience is clapping and cheering, but Xander leans over from his seat beside me, wearing a smug grin. "They cheered louder for us."

I know there's no real reason to be jealous—of the touching, not the clapping—but the dance ends with Aurora in Clay's arms and I'm officially feeling grumpy. She's smiling broadly as she comes off the stage, heading straight for me. I force a smile onto my face as she approaches, but she immediately tries to smother a laugh when she spots me. "You good?"

"That is the fakest smile I've ever seen, Callaghan," Emilia says, collecting our water bottles. Maya and Clay come up behind her, Clay looking pleased with himself. Emilia is trying not to laugh. "We're going to grab drinks. Does anyone want anything?"

"No, thanks," I say as they disappear off toward the main building.

Aurora takes the empty seat beside me, leaning in. "You jealous?"

"Nope," I say, concentrating on the next act on the stage. "But know you're getting it from me next time we're alone."

"I'm going to the bathroom," Aurora says in a strange tone, standing and moving directly in front of me.

"Okay," I say, but she doesn't move.

"I really need to use the bathroom," she says again in the same unnatural way.

I'm officially confused. I repeat what I said before. "Ohh-kay?"

"I'm desperate," she says, eyes widening.

"Oh—"

"Jesus Christ, my guy," Xander snaps, lowering his voice so people around us can't hear. "She's trying to tell you to follow her to the bathroom. Probably for sex, I don't know." He looks to her. "Sex?"

She nods. "Probably."

"Fantastic," he groans. "I'm so glad I could be part of this conversation. I'll just sit here and die alone."

She presses her lips together as she shakes her head at me, trying not to laugh. Xander glares at me as she walks away in the direction of the lake where our cabin is. "Stop staring at me. You think I have any idea what I'm doing here?"

"Unbelievable. Go on then, fuck off to your loving relationship. Where's my summer romance, hey?"

I try to be discreet as I stand and casually stroll in the same direction as Aurora. I want to sprint, but not only would that be embarrassing, I'm trying not to get caught again.

She's sitting on my bed flicking through a book from my bedside table when I walk in. Her face lights up when she sees me, and within a second, she's on her feet and on tiptoes to kiss me. I lift her and her legs wrap around my waist, something we're well practiced at anytime we're alone. Pressing her into the wall beside my bed, I move my hands beneath her summer dress and over her hips, snapping the band of her panties against her skin before traveling up to her waist.

She breaks our kiss and rests the back of her head against the wall, a smug smile on her face. "You're doing your grumpy pout."

I ignore her, kissing down her neck as my hands move further up to the curve of her breasts. It's easy to pull the material of her bra down and roll her hardened nipples between my fingers. Her body reacts the same way it always does when I touch her, by grinding into me in search of friction. "Are you going to fuck me against this wall because you're jealous?"

"No. I'm going to fuck you against this wall because being inside of you is the closest thing there is to heaven," I murmur as her breathing becomes slow and shallow.

Her teeth sink into my bottom lip and she tugs. "And you're jealous."

"I'm not." I slip my fingers back beneath the band of her panties, moving them to the side, and she's soaking wet already. "I love how responsive you are."

"Because I love it when you touch me. Especially when you're jealous."

She smiles triumphantly because she knows she's got me. So I rub my thumb over her swollen clit and watch her eyes roll back. I don't do it again and she grinds into my hand. "Don't be petty because you're jealous."

My dick is throbbing in my shorts and we've hardly done anything. I can't deny the sneaking around has been hot. The stolen kisses, secret touches, the looks only we understand. But when all I want to do is lock the door and keep her until the only name she can remember how to say is mine, being back in my own house is starting to look really good.

"I don't need to be jealous when I'm the one who gets you this wet."

"You're the only one," she says. "Nobody else matters but you. Put me down and let me show you."

Walking over to the bed, I lower her down. She moves to her knees and sits in front of me, eyes staring up at me as she unbuckles my belt and pulls down my shorts. My boxers go next and she immediately grips the base of my dick with one of her hands, tongue out flat to lick the precum from the end.

Her free hand slips between her legs beneath her dress as her lips slide over the tip. "Fuck, Aurora," I groan, sinking a hand into her hair. "You feel so fucking good."

Green eyes stare up at me through thick lashes. I take a mental picture because there is nothing prettier than seeing her on her knees in front of me. Brushing her hair out of her face, I collect it into my fist, holding tight the way she likes it. I'm working so hard not to come on the spot, but she's moaning as her hand works with her mouth to satisfy every inch of me, and I can see her hand frantically moving between her thighs.

Her tongue swirls around me before she takes me to the back of her throat again and my eyes roll to the back of my head. My hand tightens the closer I get, my stomach flexes as my balls tighten, and right when I'm on the edge, she pulls me out of her mouth and grins up at me.

Despair is the best way to describe the feeling until, saying nothing, she turns around and lowers her chest to the bed so her ass is in the air right in front of me.

I don't think I ever truly appreciated how magnificent summer dresses are until now. Quickly grabbing a condom from the drawer, I put it on and tug her dress up over her ass. She watches me over her shoulder as I peel her panties to the side again.

"I'm fucking obsessed with you," I groan, sinking into her slowly. "Obsessed."

"Show me."

It's quick and hard. I slam into her and she pushes back. My hands pin hers to the bottom of her back, the yellow material of the dress I love so much entangled in my grip. I watch her face twist with pleasure as she moans my name loudly.

"Harder."

"Can you take it?"

"Yeah, please, Russ. Go harder." My grip on her tightens, her nails dig into my palm as her back arches even more to take me. Her mouth hangs open as her eyes screw shut and I can feel her begin to tighten. "Please, don't stop."

"Fuck, Rory." Stanley Cup winners. Name some Stanley Cup winners. "I'm gonna—"

Aurora's cry interrupts me, and her entire body tightening and shaking tips me over the edge. I come so hard I'm struggling to stay standing, but she's too busy writhing beneath my hands to notice.

I let go of her hands, gently leaning over her to kiss between her shoulder blades, then beneath her ear, and finally on her cheek. Her eyes open again. "Told you I could take it."

She's unreal. "Well done, champ." I'm teasing her, but she holds up a wobbly hand, indicating for me to high-five her. "We're really good at this, aren't we?"

"I'd argue we're the best at it," I say, pulling out gently.

She hums thoughtfully. "I'd argue that, too."

By the time I'm heading back to my seat, I know I've got a smug grin on my face. It might be a permanent fixture, because I can't imagine ever not being this pleased with myself.

"I feel like I don't tell you I hate you enough," Xander says to me when I sit.

"I'm going to miss you as well, buddy."

TONIGHT IS OUR LAST NIGHT all together and I can't believe how quickly time has passed. We'll be helping the kids leave tomorrow, then spending the rest of the day putting all the equipment and furniture away, before the rest of us leave on Sunday.

After much deliberation, Aurora is still going to go to her dad's wedding when she leaves here. I've been listening to her go back and forth repeatedly, but she says she's finally decided.

When she told me everything her mom said, it was all still so raw to her and she was explaining to me how much lighter she felt finally understanding that it isn't something she's done wrong. She was so emotional, the relief and the years of pain rolled into one, that I couldn't bring myself to answer her questions fully when she asked about Dad.

I still feel guilty about downplaying why he showed up at camp. She is always a completely open book about all her thoughts and feelings, and I held back the full truth. I told her he'd had a fight with my mom and he was trying to get me to help, which is only the tip of a very big iceberg.

She's asked me to tell her everything multiple times. Always in the same way, nervously, with the promise of patience and understanding. When she asked on the day of Dad's visit, the whole truth was on the tip of my tongue, but after hearing everything she'd had to shoulder, from the phone call from her dad to her mom's impromptu visit, I couldn't put my problems on her.

I knew if I told her everything she'd have spent all her energy trying to help me navigate my feelings, instead of concentrating on dealing with her own. I will tell her eventually, but the more that time passes since Dad's visit, the more my willingness to share decreases. Every day I don't get a cash app request it feels a little less urgent, and when being honest with myself, I still don't think I'm truly ready.

Aurora loves when I share. I love making Aurora happy. But wanting to give her what she wants because I'd give her everything if I could is not the same as being ready.

I know one day I'll feel comfortable enough to talk with her about all my dad's issues. Now that I've had time to process his visit, there's a tiny shred of hope growing in me that he might be about to turn things around. It's a lot to cope with, especially as an outsider, and I'd rather talk to her about it when I know what's going to happen. If nothing's going to change, I want to know that instead of being embarrassed when I share my hope and he lets me down.

My family is such a huge emotional burden and I just want to save her from that, especially after she's worked so hard over the past couple of months.

She says that for her this summer was about making choices for the right reasons, and choosing to go to the wedding because she wants to be at an important family event is her right reason. It isn't a knee-jerk reaction, it isn't derived from hurt feelings or bad choices—she wants to go.

If she decides she doesn't want to go, she doesn't have to, because she's in control.

I can't bring myself to remind her that one conversation with him had her spiraling, ready to pack up and leave. I want her to do what makes her happy, and she's an adult who can make her own decisions. But I think she's going out of fear of closing the door on their relationship and not because she actually thinks their relationship is salvageable.

But, saying all of this would make me a hypocrite, so I tell her I'm proud of her and that I'll be there for her, no matter what.

It's going to be weird being so far away from her while she's at the wedding. I'm heading to JJ's in San Jose for his official housewarming party, and as much as I wish she was coming with me, I'm excited to hang out with everyone.

Aurora has learned more about me in these last couple of months than my friends have learned in years, and I feel better every day simply because I have her. Even if Dad does get better and stops the gambling—and hopefully the drinking, too—it's going to take time for me to work through the years of embarrassment.

And I'm grateful I'm not going to be alone when I start that journey.

Chapter Thirty-Four

AURORA

THERE'S A SAD ATMOSPHERE IN the air as kids march past the window in the direction of the camp bus.

Orla runs departure day like a well-oiled machine with scheduled pickups to ensure everything is as organized as possible. It's emotional to say good-bye to people you've been with for over two months. When I was here as a child, I would spend the last day in tears, usually clinging to Jenna.

Thankfully, our kids seem to be more mature than little me, and although they're sad, most of them are excited to see their families. This morning was a circus as we made sure everything had been packed into the right bags and suitcases were ready to be collected. I'm happy to be kept busy, because while they might be ready to go, I'm not ready to say good-bye to my gang, which I've successfully kept alive and mostly free from injury.

If I think about the fact they're not going to be around tonight I might start crying.

Freya and Sadia are cutting off the circulation to my legs as they both perch on my thighs, wiggling around to get a good view at

Emilia's cell phone screen as we wait for the Brown Bears' turn to be collected.

Poppy is showing us Big Ben and the Houses of Parliament, and the girls are enthralled. They both know Emilia's girlfriend has a surprise for her, but they don't know what and they're super excited. Trusting two small children with a secret is like trusting the guys to be around when someone's sick or there's a blocked toilet—a terrible idea.

The rest of the campers are outside playing flag football with the guys, but Emilia and I are tired after working the night shift with twenty overstimulated kids last night.

I've been excited for this reveal for weeks, since I was the one who organized it. I know how much Emilia has missed Poppy this summer, and I'm certain there were times when she was playing her millionth game of tetherball, dealing with homesick kids, and trying to work out if there's an animal in the kids' cabin, when she wished she'd gone to Europe, too.

She's been so supportive of me pursuing things with Russ, which made the whole sneaking-around thing so much easier. Thankfully, she actually likes spending time with Xander. She's even planning to invite him to visit us when we're all back at college.

The sky is totally gray in London, despite the fact it's August, which doesn't set the greatest scene for Poppy's news. Her smile is practically taking over her whole face as she announces the surprise. "You're coming to London!"

"What!" Emilia shouts. "When?"

"Tomorrow!" Poppy shouts back.

Emilia looks like she's going to burst into tears, so I usher the girls to their feet, taking them back outside to give Emilia and Poppy some privacy.

They sit beside me on the bench while we watch the football game. Russ is cheering on Billy, a more introverted kid who hated team sports nine weeks ago, as he scores a touchdown. He high-fives him, praising him as the kids who I presume are also on Billy's team jump on him.

Somebody make my ovaries shut up.

"Will you and Russ go to London?" Freya asks, plaiting the ends of my hair.

"No, sweetie. Russ is going to visit his friend JJ at his new house, and I'm going to a place called Palm Springs because my dad is getting married."

"So when will you see each other again?" Sadia is next to start messing with my hair.

Little girls are like monkeys when it comes to hair.

"We go to the same college, so we're going to see each other when we're back at school." It isn't a lie. Russ and I haven't fully talked about what happens when we're both back at UCMH. We still haven't talked about what we are, which is pathetic at this point considering we've spent sixteen hours a day together for ten weeks. We just know that we're both going to be there and we're both not ready to say good-bye to this. "Why don't you go ask him to tell you a secret?"

The girls sprint toward Russ, grabbing him as he tries to ref the game. He crouches to their height and they lean in whispering the message. He looks right at me through the space between them, smiling, and even though I can't see much of his face, I just know I'd be able to see his dimples if I was close enough.

God, I was never supposed to be this obsessed.

I watch him whisper a reply and they giggle before running back to me. Sadia reaches me first. "He said he's excited to see you at college and to ask you for one."

"Hmm." I tap my lips and pretend to think. "My secret is I have a really big crush on Russ."

I expect them both to squeal and laugh and get excited, the way they do over basically everything. Freya's hands go to her hips. "That isn't a secret. Everyone knows that."

"Yeah," Sadia echoes. "You love him. Tell us a real secret."

I didn't expect to get called out by children today. "Okay, okay. My secret is I want to do this all again next year."

They run back and I watch them almost crash into him. He smiles, looking over at me briefly, before saying something. The girls run back over to me, panting after all the back and forth. Freya sits down beside me. "He said 'where you go, I go.' These aren't secrets, you two should just talk to each other."

She has a point. "Brown Bears," Jenna yells, appearing with her clipboard. "You're up!"

How long would I be able to get away with refusing to let them go?

"Go grab your jackets and backpacks, girls," Emilia says as she reappears from the main building. We watch them run toward the rest of the group; Emilia wraps an arm around me. "You okay?"

"What if I just keep them all?"

"I think their parents will have an issue with that," she says softly. "Three of them asked me yesterday if you'll be back next year. They really love you, Ror. They were scared to ask you in case you said no."

"I love them all. Even Leon. Even though he's an asshole."

The counselors here were such a huge part of my childhood that hearing my kids like me and want me to come back has a huge impact. I needed to come back to heal part of me that was just a little bit too broken. I'm going back to LA feeling like a new person, and I truly don't think I could have achieved that anywhere else.

"Poppy told me what you did."

I can't help but roll my eyes. Poppy and I had a very serious conversation where I warned her if she told Emilia I paid for and arranged her Europe trip that I'd put spiders in her bed until we graduate. "Please tell Poppy she brought what comes next on herself."

"You didn't have to do that, Ror." Gift giving is this awkward thing between Emilia and me that we dance around. Usually I go too far and she has to give me a lecture about me not needing to buy her love, and how calling something a love language doesn't give me a free pass to do what I want. "But thank you so much."

"You've been very understanding this summer while I've been . . . preoccupied."

"Sorry, do we need to recap all of my relationships you've held my hand through? The late-night pickups? Not judging me when I got back together with Sawyer for, like, the third time?"

"We don't have enough time to recap; you have to catch a flight to London tomorrow morning."

She hits my arm playfully. "You deserve someone who looks at you like you're the only thing on this entire planet. I would move a million days off if you got to be happy. You needed someone to prove to you that you're worth it, and for what it's worth, I'm glad it's Russ. Even if he is a man."

"Jesus Christ, Emilia. You know being sad makes me horny."

"You are so fucking weird sometimes. Come on, my little love-bug. Time to say good-bye to Honey Acres for a year."

THINGS ARE EERILY QUIET AS we all sit around the fire next to the lake, full from eating the pizza Orla bought for us to say thank you for all our hard work. The chefs at camp are excellent, but there's something about a veggie pizza from Dom's Pizzeria in Meadow Springs that can't be beaten.

After we waved off our campers, we got to work putting away the various equipment around the site for next summer. Emilia and I had to do double the work because Russ and Xander spent an hour having an emotional good-bye with Fish, Salmon, and Trout. I think it got to the point where even the dogs were over it before the guys were.

After Orla's closing meeting earlier, we're officially not employees anymore, and she finished by saying she didn't want to find any beer bottles tomorrow morning. My eyebrow quirked and Jenna immediately rolled her eyes at me before mouthing "free pass."

The beer run is done in record time, and while I'd normally be the first person to grab a drink and initiate a drinking game, I'm perfectly happy curled up on Russ's lap in our camping chair, trying to eat the last of the gelatin-free marshmallows without covering us both in graham crackers.

"Are you boring now?" Emilia asks, sipping her beer from the chair beside us. I know she's joking, but it doesn't stop me from giving her the finger.

"Forgive me for not wanting to be hungover when I face my dad tomorrow," I grumble, rolling my eyes. "And what happened to 'don't be peer pressured by your friends'? Stop peer pressuring me to be irresponsible with you."

Russ kisses my shoulder and continues to rub his hand up and down my shin. He doesn't need to say anything, but I know he's proud of me because it was fifty-fifty whether I was going to go off the rails today.

Nobody batted an eyelid when I crawled into Russ's lap earlier and he kissed my forehead. I was a little offended by their lack of surprise, before Emilia pointed out I'm naturally as discreet as a blaring fire alarm. But then I saw Clay's jaw drop, someone who has spent most days with us for weeks—and my ego got a boost.

Fire alarm, my ass.

He's stayed away from us this evening, opting to get drunk with Maya and her hometown friends instead. Can't say I'm mad about it, because I love my little trio and it means I don't have to turn down Cabo again.

"Should I transfer to Maple Hills for fun?" Xander says, swigging his beer. "It doesn't feel right for me to separate the dream team. How will you all get anything done?"

"Who's the dream team?" Emilia teases.

"We're the dream team, Emilia. You know what, forget it. I'll stay at Stanford."

I lick the chocolate and marshmallow that's spilled out of my s'more from my fingers, and Russ buries his head into my neck, whispering "stop it." I ignore him, wiggling a little to pretend to get comfortable, only to feel his fingers dig into my side, making me squirm and giggle. Xander frowns as his eyes flick between us both. "Are you two even listening? Disgusting. God bless the no-fraternization rule. I'd have thrown myself into a septic tank if I had to watch this every night."

"I'm listening," Russ says, clearing his throat and wrapping his arms around me. "Doesn't your dad work at UCMH? Didn't you tell me that when we first met? You don't wanna play basketball with your brother, right?"

"Oh, so you do listen to me then. First, he's my stepdad—let's not disrespect Big Phil by making him share dad status with that jackass. Dave has an obnoxious fucking job title; I can't remember what they call him." Xander snaps his fingers a few times as he tries to remember. "He's head of athletics, but they don't call him that."

Russ sits up so quickly he almost flings me into the fire. "Your stepdad is Skinner? Are you fucking kidding me? We have shared a room for ten weeks and you are just now telling me that your dad—"

"Stepdad."

"—controls my entire college career?"

"Skinner?" I say again. "Why does that sound fami— Oh my fucking God." I'm dead. Nobody revive me. It's over. I almost fall off Russ's knee. "Is your brother Mason Wright?"

"Stepbrother." He swigs his beer without a care in the world. "You two are very animated suddenly. I share one snippet of information and suddenly you're interested in something other than pawing at each other. Interesting."

"You're related to my archnemesis!" I can't process this. "I feel violated."

"By marriage," Xander says. Russ tucks me closer to him, wrapping his arms around my waist. Xander shrugs at us both. "I don't share DNA with them so I can't be held responsible for their wrongs."

Emilia can't stop laughing beside us since she knows how much I hate Mason. "I can't believe this has been the big reveal of the night and not you two being revoltingly happy together."

"What a plot twist," I mutter, leaning back onto Russ, who tucks my head under his chin. I've never really done this cuddling thing before Russ. I've never stuck around long enough for it, but one thing I've learned this summer is I'm a big fan.

The rest of the night goes by without any more bombs being dropped and the heat of the fire is sending me to sleep. I don't want this night to end for so many reasons, but mainly because it's been the best summer of my life. Even though I know I'm going to be miserable as soon as I touch down in Palm Springs, I don't care anymore. I'm going to count down the days until I'm back at college and keep myself out of trouble and off my dad's radar.

I know why he doesn't have a relationship with me now, and there's nothing I can do or stop doing to change that. I don't have the urge to battle for his attention anymore, or to act out, so I at least get reprimanded, which obviously never happened.

His opinions don't matter to me anymore and it's freeing.

My jaw cracks loudly because I yawn so wide, and Russ hears it. "Come on Sleeping Beauty, let me take you to bed."

"I think she's more like Sleepy from Snow White than Princess Aurora," Xander muses, Emilia nodding beside him. I look at him, confused. "You think I've been looking after eight-year-olds for two months and don't know my princesses? Get outta here."

"Good night, see you in the morning," I say through another yawn.

Russ and I walk hand in hand along the path toward my cabin and I still haven't lost that feeling that it's against the rules. I'm too tired for small talk, so I listen to him talk about how excited he is to go to San Jose to visit JJ tomorrow. I learned Russ has been getting pep talks from JJ and I don't think I've ever been more infatuated with him.

We finally reach my cabin and he audibly gasps when we walk through the door. "It's so tidy. Is it bad I'm more attracted to you now?"

I throw myself down onto the bed, kicking off my sneakers and lying down. "Yes."

He sits me back up and pulls my T-shirt over my head. "You told me earlier to make you shower before bed because you won't have time to wash your hair in the morning. I don't even really know what that means, but I know you should have a shower."

Another huge yawn. "Ignore me. Earlier me didn't know how tired we are. She was optimistic and foolish."

"Come on, Roberts. Into the shower."

I fold my arms across my chest defiantly, pouting for as long as it takes me to yawn again. "Make me." My yawn turns into a hiccup of surprise as he throws me over his shoulder and marches us toward the bathroom. "You're cruel."

He slaps my ass and that wakes me up a little. "Shush."

Russ is methodical as he strips us both of our clothes, and five minutes ago I would have said I'm too tired for sex, but the ass slap and the bossiness might have changed my mind. The shower starts to fill the bathroom with steam and he checks the temperature before ushering us both in.

He stands behind me; I'm not ashamed to say I'm waiting to be bent over. He doesn't, though, he just reaches for my shampoo and squirts some onto his hand, lathering it up between his palms.

I don't need to be bent over. I can definitely come from him washing my hair for me.

"You are perfect," I groan as his fingers massage my scalp. "Why haven't you been washing my hair for me this entire time?"

He chuckles as he begins rinsing out the suds. "I promise I'll do it anytime you need when we're home."

Home. We still haven't talked about what that looks like for us. I've been waiting for the opportunity to bring it up in a cool and casual way. A way that doesn't apply any pressure, in case the sweet things he's said to me have been in the moment. "Tell me a secret, Russ."

"It's a physical and emotional struggle to not stare at your ass all day." I spin to look at him, his wet chest pressed against mine as he continues to wash my hair gently.

"A real secret."

He pauses and thinks about it, rubbing the back of his neck. I'm glad he's nervous, because so am I. "I think you know most of my secrets."

"Can I ask you a question?" He nods, and I clear my throat as I scramble for the easy intro I've been looking for. "What happens when we go back to school? What are we?"

He cups my face, and when I look up at him, he appears as nervous as I feel. "We're whatever you want to be, Aurora. I'm a little worried I'm going to scare you away, but I think I've been pretty clear I don't want to let you go."

What I want is the next big question. As soon as I'm with him I forget everything I've ever said about other people's baggage, relationships, men. But the thoughts still linger when I'm alone; I can't help it. Emilia is right when she says the bar is so low for me that

I'm impressed by mediocrity, and I get attached easily to someone who gives me hit after hit of the things I crave like attention and validation.

Nothing about Russ is mediocre.

"I want to be together," I say quietly, suddenly feeling ten times more exposed than I did when he stripped me of my clothes. "I've never been in a relationship before, but I want to see where this can go. I want to be your girlfriend."

He bends to kiss me, and even under the hot spray of the shower, goose bumps spread over my entire body. "Good," he murmurs against my lips. "Because I want to be your boyfriend."

I'm exhausted by the time we're dried and I'm climbing into bed. "Why don't you sleep in here tonight?"

"I haven't finished packing yet, sweetheart. I got distracted saying bye to the dogs."

"But you're great at folding shit. You'll do it in no time."

"Go to sleep, Ror," he says softly. "I'll go when you've fallen asleep."

I tug him to lie down beside me over the covers, and with the weight of his arm draped over me, I fall straight to sleep.

I'M SO GLAD RUSS CONVINCED me to shower last night, because Emilia and I both overslept this morning.

I don't know what time she came to bed because I was already asleep, but apparently neither of us thought to check that the other was setting an alarm.

I said my good-byes to Jenna, even though it's not really good-bye because she's visiting us in September, and we're now waiting with our bags for the guys. Xander is first to appear with his things and I'm feeling impatient. "Where's Russ?"

Xander drops his bags by our feet. "You can't even pretend to be excited to see me for two minutes, Roberts? Immediately hit me with the 'Where's Russ?' I am underappreciated in this friendship."

I throw my arms around him. "I miss you already, Xan."

"That's more like it. Your man was getting a shower when I left."

Emilia and I need to leave to catch our flights. "I'll go make him rush."

I jog—something I strongly disagree with—down to his cabin, letting myself in. His things are all lined up neatly on his bed, his keys and cell phone on the top of his bag. I can still hear the shower running, and as I'm about to go make him hurry up, his cell phone lights up with a call from an unknown number. The call ends after a couple of rings and I can see he has twenty missed calls from the past few minutes.

The phone lights up again in my hand, the same number as before. Clicking the accept call button, I lift it to my ear. "Hello?"

Chapter Thirty-Five

RUSS

I ALMOST JUMP OUT OF my skin when I open the bathroom door and Aurora is standing in the bedroom.

When she hears the door open, she turns to face me, and that's when I spot my cell phone in her hand. My stomach sinks, because the look on her face tells me everything I need to know about who's on the phone.

I should take the phone out of her hand, end the call, something. But instead, I stand frozen in the doorway staring at her. "I'll tell him," she says quietly to the person on the other end of the phone. "Bye."

I need to say something, but every terrible possibility runs through my head at once.

"I shouldn't have answered your cell phone," she says. "I'm sorry. I didn't think. It was your brother. He said he's been trying to reach you because your dad has entered an addiction program. They want you to come home to make amends."

It's like being bulldozed with several emotions at once: surprise, hurt, optimism, anger. I knew I'd have to tell her eventually, but I wasn't ready to share now.

She's staring at me with pity, like I fucking knew she would, and the frustration builds. "You shouldn't have answered my cell phone."

"I know, I'm sorry. I didn't think! It was ringing over and over and the number wasn't saved in your phone . . . You know what the service is like, maybe if I hadn't answered it would have disappeared again. I don't know, Russ. I thought something might be wrong, but I shouldn't have answered it. I'm really sorry."

Dragging a hand down my face, I blow out a sigh. I want to scream. "The bathroom is right here. You could have gotten me, you could have yelled for me, you could have done anything."

"I'm sorry, Russ," she says, her voice strained. "I thought it was urgent. I didn't think."

"I've told you before, he does it to make me pick up. You know he rings over and over until I get pissed off enough to answer."

"I forgot. The number wasn't saved, and I didn't think. It was a mistake and I'm sorry."

It's too much to process all at once. I can't think straight when I'm around her. "You should go."

"I said I'm sorry," she stresses, walking toward me. "I'm really, really sorry. I know this must be a lot for you. Why didn't you tell me your dad has problems with addiction? I thought we'd shared all our secrets . . ."

"Because I didn't want you to look at me like you are right now, Aurora," I say flatly. The embarrassment fucking stings. "Because I wasn't ready to tell you, and now I don't have any choice in the matter."

The words are so sharp and I hardly recognize myself as I hear them back. I hear him in the way I'm talking to her; my worst nightmare playing out before my eyes. He found a way to ruin her and he doesn't even know she exists. I throw myself down on Xander's bed, far enough away from her that I feel like I can still think, even though my head is swimming and none of my thoughts make sense.

"You get to be mad at me, but you don't get to shut me out," she says. Her voice wobbles with every word, and when I look up at her, she looks devastated. I caused this. I'm the one that's fucking this up. "I'll wait while you call your brother back. Hear it from him. I can hold your hand and I won't listen if you don't want me to, but I'll be here for you."

The last thing I want to do right now is call Ethan. Part of me questions if it's even true, or if it's just another one of his ploys to trick me into going home and he's not there. Another day where I get left on my own to pick up the pieces of our family and break off a few of my own in the process.

"I don't want you to." I thought I'd be happier about hearing my dad has taken steps to get real help, but now all I can think about is this. What does she think of me?

"Russ, please don't shut me out. I've told you everything about my family and you know I get it."

"You don't get it," I snap. "It isn't the same thing."

My head drops into my hands; my stomach churns as my thoughts spiral.

This isn't how this summer was supposed to end.

It's incredible how shame fills the cracks other people create. For every fracture my dad's actions have caused, humiliation has glued everything back together.

Ethan's call took a sledgehammer to it all.

"I think you're madder at me than I deserve," she says, crouching down in front of me. "Yell at me, Russ. Let's fight about how angry you are at me and I can yell back that you kept this huge thing from me for months and we can scream at each other until you realize

I'm not scared to carry your baggage. And we'll make up. And I can support you the way you support me."

I don't want to yell at her. I don't want this to be something she has to carry, especially knowing she has to face her own family today. "Just go," I say. "You don't want to miss your flight."

"I won't be able to stop overthinking until I know we're okay." Her hands shake as she rests them against my knees. "Please don't burn me," she says, voice barely above a whisper.

I feel like I'm burning everyone at this point. "Just go, Aurora. Please."

She kisses my forehead as she stands, and I feel her tears drop onto my skin. I want to reach out and hold her to me, but I don't deserve that. She takes a sharp breath, but I can't look at her. "For the record, I really hope your dad gets better and you can heal from this. I'm sorry I found out before you were ready to tell me."

It feels like she's taking half of me with her as I finally lift my head to watch as she walks out, and I finally get the answer to the question that's been plaguing me all summer.

It's harder to watch her walk away than it is to wake up and find she's not there.

I KNOW I'VE FUCKED UP before I even head out of my cabin with my bags, and I fucking hate myself.

I couldn't get good enough service to call Ethan back in my room, so I've decided to do it from the road. I'll call JJ, too, let him know I'm not coming anymore. As much as I don't want to, I know I need to head home and face whatever is waiting for me. I miss Aurora, and that makes no sense, because I'm the reason she isn't here and I fucking hate myself for that as well. I'll call her from the road, beg for forgiveness, pray I haven't hurt her too badly.

I've sent her to see her dad believing I'm mad at her and that she's done something wrong, when it's my fault because I don't know how to process things without clamming up like an ass-hole. I can't even enjoy the walk through camp back to my truck, despite being the happiest I've been in my life during the last ten weeks.

I just keep thinking the same thing: of course she answered the phone. She's my girlfriend and it wouldn't be a problem for a normal fucking person. But I'm not normal. I've let the shame and embar-rassment eat at me for years, scared that if I let someone in it'd ruin things. I didn't let her in, not fully, and I've managed to ruin us anyway.

I keep my head down as I pass the people I've worked alongside, hoping they don't notice me or want to say good-bye. Thankfully nobody stops me, my keys are in my hand, and I'm ready to get out of here as quickly as I can.

I'm watching my feet scrape against the dusty parking lot when I hear her clear her throat, forcing me to look up. Her bags are litter-ing the ground around her and she's biting her fingernails, anxiously tapping her foot.

"I've never begged a man before," she says, and as confident as she sounds, she doesn't look it. I know how big this is for her. I know what kind of courage this took. "But you're the first of many things for me."

"Rory . . ."

"I don't want you to be my first heartbreak." Another piece of me breaks off. "Either we get into the truck together and for the next four hours we talk, or we can sit in silence, and when we get to Maple Hills we go our separate ways. You can tell me as little or as much about your dad as you want. You're in control of what you're ready to share with me." She picks up her bags. "But you can tell me everything about how you're feeling. You wanna be together? This is how we're doing it. We're not miscommunicators, Russ. We share our secrets."

"I'm so sorry, Ror." She drops her bags as I speed toward her, crushing her in a hug. I instantly feel better having her in my arms again. "I was going to call you and grovel as soon as I was on the road. I don't deserve you."

"Yes," she says harshly. "You do. I don't need you to grovel. You don't need to punish yourself for being overwhelmed. I just need you not to push me away."

Word by word, I feel her gluing me back together. "What about the wedding?"

"You're my first choice, Russ," she whispers, burying her head into my neck. "Where you go, I go. You don't have to face this alone."

"But your dad—"

"—will survive. I think we both know by now he doesn't really care anyway. I can try to twist it in lots of different ways that make me feel in control, but let's be honest. I probably wouldn't be invited if there wasn't press there." She shrugs. "If he wanted me to listen to his demands, maybe he should have held me accountable all the times I broke the rules."

"I'm sorry for how I acted earlier. I'm so fucking lucky to have you." Her mouth crashes into mine, frantic and desperate, and I can't help but match everything she's giving to me. I'm still scared about what we're heading back to, but I know she's by my side.

It doesn't take long for me to load our things into my truck and get on the road. I know that anytime now I need to start talking. Going our separate ways isn't an option for me, and if she leaves, the only person I'd have to blame for that is myself. I'll have been the one who pushed her away when she was trying to pull me close.

She sits quietly beside me while I call JJ to tell him I'm not visiting him. He's understandably bummed, but as soon as I drop "family drama," he tells me not to worry and he'll see me next time he's in LA.

"He's a bit like a brother, isn't he," Rory says quietly when the call ends.

"Yeah, he's kind of like the older brother I wanted but didn't have."

She nods. "Like Jenna for me."

There are so many things in our lives that mirror one another, and I need to trust that if anyone is going to understand and help me, it's going to be her. She's turned my world upside down, and there's no reason she won't now.

"My dad has an addiction to gambling," I say, not taking my eyes off the road. "Horses mainly, because it's easy to do, but he loves casinos and poker. He left me sitting outside a casino in the car once for hours when I was younger. That's when Mom realized he had a problem. He drinks, too, but it's always because of the betting. Celebrate or commiserate kind of thing, y'know?"

"Yeah."

"I'm embarrassed, and that's why I didn't want to tell you. What type of parent would pick a slip of paper over their kid? What does that say about me if I'm not even worth more than some shitty odds and a horse?" I can't help but laugh. "I told you the horrible things he's said to me. Those were times he was drunk or I wouldn't send him money. When you hear something enough times, you begin to believe it, Rory. I didn't want you to think the things about me that he does."

"I could never," she says instantly, rubbing the back of my neck with her palm. "Because they're not true."

"All I've wanted is for him to get better. When he turned up here that day we got caught and I told you he'd had a fight with my mom, he actually told me my mom had thrown him out. He said he was going to get better, but I didn't want to get my hopes up that he would. When you told me what Ethan said, you're right, I felt overwhelmed. Overwhelmed because you finally knew. Because it's what I've wanted for years. Because it doesn't feel real. It's like when you wish for something so much, but when you get it, it seems too good to be true. He's let me down so frequently that I'm scared to trust that this is the time where things change."

"You told me expecting change is like repeatedly putting your hand in a fire and expecting it not to burn you," Aurora says. "I want to hold your hand so you don't have to put it in the fire, Russ. Recovery isn't easy for anyone, not just the addict; for you, too. It sounds like your dad has taken the step to try to get better, but nobody is going to force you to forgive him. I will physically fight your brother for you if he tries."

"What if he burns you, too? My family is a mess."

She laughs, and I swear her smile could fix anything. "Fire can't burn fire. I will raze Maple Hills to the ground before he gets a chance to make you feel shitty about yourself again. Also, family mess? Hello? The poster child for daddy issues right here."

I take her hand and press the back of it to my mouth. "You never have to feel embarrassed with me, Russ. Maybe the universe wasn't trying to fuck us over. Maybe it knew we needed each other, because I do need you. You're the best thing to happen to me, and more important, I want to be there for you through this in whatever way you want me to be."

"I don't even know what recovery entails. I don't know what make amends even means. How the fuck is he going to do that? It's been such a long time."

"Why don't we call your brother so you can hear it from him, and anything we don't understand I can google? I won't even call him an asshole."

"Thank you, Aurora."

She leans over and kisses my cheek. "Thank you for not making me sit here in silence for four hours."

I WALK INTO MY BEDROOM hand in hand with Rory and instantly get déjà vu.

That Russ, the one who was pretending to be confident, would not have believed that this would be the situation we're in a couple of months later. Not one to dance around the obvious, Aurora struts straight around me and sits on my desk.

"Wanna role play us doing it?" I roll my eyes as I walk over and step between her legs, gripping her under her thighs and throwing her onto my bed, making her squeak. "Hey, you weren't this rough with me!"

"Yeah 'cause I was fucking terrified," I say, throwing myself down beside her. "I don't get girls like you and I was very worried I'd watch you come and it'd be game over for me. In my pants."

"Confident you could then," she says, teasing, rolling to lie on top of me. "How'd you know I wasn't faking it?"

"I'd have suffocated between your legs before I'd let you fake it."

The guys are at JJ's for the housewarming party, and after the day I've had, I think taking out my stress in a healthy way is a good idea. I spread her legs over my hips and run my hands along her thighs until I'm under her sundress, then her cell phone starts ringing.

"Are we destined to be interrupted forever?" I groan. "I thought this would end when we left Honey Acres."

"You know who it'll be," she says, climbing off me and reaching for the phone. She holds up her screen to me and the caller ID reads Man Who Pays the Rent.

We haven't really talked about the fact Aurora is supposed to be in Palm Springs right now. I was too distracted with my own problem, and I guess she didn't want to talk about it. I didn't have anything to add when she said that he's never punished her before.

She presses the accept call button and puts it on speaker, but even before she says hello, she does something I haven't seen her do in weeks: she forces a smile onto her face.

"Hi!" Her voice is unnatural, not the voice of my girl, and I hate it.

"Where the fuck are you, Aurora?"

Six words and my blood is boiling.

"I'm not coming, Dad." She chews on the inside of her cheek and I pull her along the bed, letting her sit between my open legs with my head resting on her shoulder. "Something came up, I'm sorry."

"That doesn't answer my question. I asked where the fuck are you?"

"I'm in Maple Hills."

"Get your ass in your car right now. I am so serious, Aurora. I'm not playing your games this time, do not ruin this for everyone."

I hold her a little tighter. "I said I'm not coming."

"I'm coming to get you."

"I'm not at home."

Leaning around her I press the mute button so her dad can't hear us as he launches into a rant about how selfish and immature she is. "I'm so fucking proud of you. You're so strong, Rory. Don't let him bully you into doing something you don't want to do. You're worth more than some photographs in a magazine. If you have to force a smile you deserve better."

She takes us off mute as he finishes yelling. "I don't care that you're upset with me, Dad. I don't like who I am when I let you dictate how I act." I hold her a little tighter. "I've spent a really long time being reckless to get your attention, because at least then you'd remember I existed. You make me feel like I'm not worth sticking around for. I'm not letting you burn me anymore because I have people in my life who do like me for me."

"If you arrive in the next two hours, we'll pretend this conversation never happened," he says, not an ounce of emotion in his tone.

"I hope your marriage is happy, but I won't be there. I'm not faking smiles for you. Good-bye, Dad."

She disconnects the call and I expect her to burst into tears, but she doesn't; she sinks into me and pulls my arms tighter around her. "I'm going to crush you if I hug you any harder."

"I don't mind."

"How do you feel?"

"Supported," she says.

"That isn't what I mean, sweetheart." I kiss her neck and she's quiet for a moment, something I'm still not used to.

"I feel lighter, like I made the right decision for once, and I know it'll help me move on now that I've told him. Maybe if it makes him change we can work on our relationship. Maybe it'll be the thing that wakes him up."

"I hope it does."

We sit in silence for five minutes and she doesn't let me loosen my grip until her phone starts ringing again. I feel her freeze in my arms, only relaxing when she lifts the screen and sees it isn't her dad. She presses accept and the screen fills with a woman with dark brown hair sporting a huge grin. There's no resemblance between her and the woman in my arms until she raises her sunglasses, placing them on the top of her head, and I spot the exact same eyes I'm used to.

"Oh, so the boyfriend thing is true then," is the first thing Elsa says. Aurora moves the camera down so less of me is in the shot. "Mum said she has a cat and you have a boyfriend. I thought she was mixing prescriptions with wine again."

I can't lie, the British accent catches me off guard at first.

"Hello to you, too." Aurora shuffles in my arms. "What are you doing? Why are you calling? Feel free to answer any other questions I might have missed."

"You stand up to dear old Dad one time and suddenly you have an attitude," she tuts. "Hold on, I'm just getting to a dress fitting."

We hear Elsa talking to someone rapidly in a language I don't recognize and Aurora sits up a little straighter. "El, who are you talking to in Italian?"

"I'm in Milan at a dress fitting for Fashion Week next month."

Aurora's jaw hangs open. "You're not going to the wedding?"

Elsa's nose scrunches, and it's the same expression Aurora pulls when she's horrified. "To the weather woman? Christ no. I'm not being photographed in something that can be made in three weeks."

"I thought you might be calling to convince me to go."

Elsa scoffs, and Aurora lets go of a breath, relaxing a little more in my arms. "I'm calling to congratulate you on finally growing a backbone. I'm proud of you, little sister."

"Uh, thanks, I think," she mumbles quietly. "Does he know you're not going to Palm Springs? He's going to be really mad at us. I know he's mad at me."

"I have no idea, nor do I care. You definitely shouldn't care. I've set up a reroute so when he calls me, he's forwarded to a therapist's office in London. I suggest you do the same. Lord knows the man needs it."

I can't help but snort, but I try to smother it by hiding my face in Aurora's hair. "I haven't forgotten about you, mysterious, faceless boyfriend," she says, making me freeze. "You're lucky I have to go get pins stuck in me, but at some point, I will interrogate you."

"She won't," Aurora says. "She'll forget."

"Stay mad at the patriarchy, Ror. *Ciao.*"

Aurora throws her phone onto the bed beside us and turns

around, climbing over each leg until she's straddling me with her head pressed against my chest and her arms wrapped around my waist. I stroke her hair, not saying anything. Another five minutes of silence pass and I can't remember a time where she's ever been this quiet.

Eventually, she pushes herself off my torso, sitting up to face me. "So, that was Elsa."

"That was Elsa," I repeat. "She's . . ."

"She's very Elsa."

"How do you feel?" I ask again.

She trails her hand down the side of my face, brushing her fingers across my jaw lightly. "Still supported."

Chapter Thirty-Six

RUSS

"YOU'RE REALLY ANNOYING TO SLEEP beside, do you know that?" I say, pulling a T-shirt over my head.

Aurora looks up at me as she starfishes in the middle of my bed, her blond hair sticking in every direction. "You've slept beside me before."

"I think having no room in that camp bed kept you in line. Now that you've got the space you're a pain. You kicked the shit out of me at one point; I felt like a soccer ball."

"I'm sorry," she says sarcastically. "Would you prefer if I left when you were asleep?"

"Asleep or in the bathroom?"

"Ouch, too soon to joke," she says playfully.

"You know what, Callaghan, I'm going to Cabo to see my friend Clay. I bet he won't bully me."

"Are you trying to make me jealous?" I slip my feet into my sneakers and grab my keys from my dresser. "Because it's working."

"I'm trying to make you fuck me." She sits up and her hair falls over her shoulders. She really is the most beautiful woman I've ever seen. I can't believe she's mine. "I'm kidding. I'm just trying to make you laugh so you're in a good mood for today."

Bending to kiss her good-bye, I force myself not to crawl into bed with her. "We can do that later. I need to leave before I change my mind."

"Are you sure you don't want me to come? I can sit in the car outside."

"I'm sure. I want to keep you to myself for as long as I possibly can."

"Say no more," she says, throwing herself back against the pillows. "I'll be right here waiting for you when you come home. Remember you can leave anytime, and if you're too overwhelmed to drive, call me and I'll get you an Uber."

I never realized how important it was to have someone to share my concerns with until now. I thought being able to tell her about stuff that's already happened was the biggest relief, but it's experiencing it together. Knowing that she's going to be here waiting for me, in whatever state I come back in, is a bigger comfort than her waiting outside of my parents' house.

"What're your plans while I'm gone?"

"I'm going to video call Emilia and Poppy, and then I was thinking of maybe seeing if my mom wants to go to Café Kiley for a coffee."

Aurora's mom texted her last night with the message *proud of you, sweetie*, so Aurora presumes her dad made a call after she told him she was done.

"And I might hide my things in your room, so you can't bring girls who give you lap dances up here when college restarts."

"Wait, what?"

"I'm going to hide notes in the pillowcases. The pillowcases are suspicious all on their own; wait until you throw them down and something crinkles beneath their head."

"You're unhinged," I say with a chuckle, bending to kiss her one last time. "Thank you for trying to distract me."

"Yes." She grins. "It was definitely a distraction . . ."

I sigh, because I have to go but I could go back and forth with her all day. It's weird having no kids interrupting us or constantly worrying we look too close. It's fucking exciting that we're already so happy together and the real part of our relationship is only just beginning. I kiss her again, telling myself again that it'll be the last time because I'm leaving. "Can you be good while I'm gone?"

"Usually with the right motivation."

"And what will motivate you? Me thinking you're good?"

She shakes her head. "You already think I'm an angel."

"Not true. You've the opposite of angelic most of the time."

"I want a Callaghan jersey. If I'm about to become a hockey girl, I need all the jersey chasers to know you're mine."

Mine. "Done."

"Good luck. I'm proud of you, and please remember to call me if you need me."

"I will, I promise. Bye."

AFTER TALKING TO ETHAN YESTERDAY on the drive home, I feel slightly better equipped for what I'm walking into. He's promised me it's an informal family discussion where we air things in a healthy way, and Dad has the opportunity to apologize for his past actions. It's an opportunity for us to rebuild and heal, just like I've wanted.

There's a rental car in the driveway when I pull up outside my parents' house, so I know he's already here. His band has a small break between shows, which is why he was so insistent it had to be now. Pulling the keys out of the ignition, I kind of wish Rory was here, but at the same time I'm glad she's not.

Pulling out my phone, I send her a text, smirking again at what she's saved herself as in my phone. She said she wanted me to know which one is her, given all the girls I'm going to attract with my new-found confidence.

RORY (THE HOT BLOND ONE)
Is it weird that I miss you?

Who is this?

You're funny

I miss you too

Good luck x

Ethan bangs on the window beside me, frowning at me, and it's like looking in a mirror that ages you. "Hurry up," he says impatiently. "We're waiting for you."

My first thought is should I start the truck and drive away. I've wanted my dad to change for so long that I'm scared to start things. Anxiety is rumbling through me like a storm, but I'm trying to tell myself that things can't get worse. I wanted change, and now it might be happening.

Ethan doesn't wait for me to respond before walking back into the house, and I slowly climb out and follow. I've never liked this house, and it's never felt like home. My parents sold my childhood home to buy this smaller one in a worse area, telling everyone they were downsizing after Ethan moved out and I was preparing for college.

In reality, they took the equity to pay off dad's gambling debts, which just led him to start the borrowing process all over again. I feel like a stranger walking inside, even though my face lines the walls.

Everyone is sitting in the living room and there's a tension in the air, which isn't exactly unusual for my family. Mom is the first one to act, by standing and giving me a tight hug. "Hi, Mom."

"I've missed you so much," she says, sounding like she's tearing up. "Take a seat. I'm so glad you're here."

"We'll let you two talk," Ethan says, moving to usher Mom out of the room with him.

"Wait, what?" My heart starts to thud. I was told we're having a family discussion, not Dad and me one-on-one. "This isn't what you said, Ethan."

He ignores me, and my first instinct is to get up and leave. Dad looks better than he did a couple of weeks ago when I last saw him. The bags around his eyes are no longer dark, his face is less gaunt, I can see his things scattered around the living room. "Have you moved back in?"

He nods. "I'm sleeping in the guest bedroom. I was staying in a motel, checking in with your mom each day. We've talked a lot. I feel like all I do is talk at the moment, but it's good. I'm glad to clear the air and work on getting better."

"I don't know what *make amends* means, Dad. I've read about it and heard about it, but I don't know what it means for us."

"I want to start by saying sorry, Russ." I don't say anything. I can't say anything because I'm scared of opening my mouth. "And I want to say thank you."

I can't hide it, the thank-you has caught me off guard. I'm so used to my dad pushing the blame onto everyone but himself. There was always a reason he was in a bad mood or was having a bad day, and it revolved around how we all weren't doing good enough.

"That day in the hospital when you told me how I made you feel, I thought that was my rock bottom, but it wasn't because I didn't change. I was humiliated that I'd made my own son believe vile things about himself—and why wouldn't you? I'd been living for myself for years, not caring about anything or anyone. But I still didn't change."

"But why? Why wasn't that enough?"

"Because I had further to fall. And I did, until your mom kicked me out and I truly hit rock bottom. I didn't want to admit I had an issue. It's easy to hide a gambling addiction because there's no physical signs. It's not drugs or alcohol, nobody sees what's going on. You convince yourself it doesn't affect anybody but you." He leans against his knees, his hands shaking as he holds them together. "But that was my turning point. From there things started to get better. I don't want to be someone you hate, Russ. I don't want to be someone who hurts you."

"You're an expert at lying, Dad. Why should I believe you're not just dragging us all along for you not to change?"

"Because pride stopped me getting help before. When I was gambling, I was always a bad loser, but I stayed optimistic the next bet would be the right one. I'm taking that optimism and I'm applying it to my recovery."

"When you were gambling?"

He nods, rubbing at the back of his neck, a habit I've never noticed him do before. "I haven't placed a bet since I saw you at your camp. I know it's not long, but it's the longest I've gone in fifteen years. I've been attending Gamblers Anonymous meetings and I'm going to be starting counseling to try and process some things I need to."

I'm overwhelmed with information, and it all still feels too good to be true. I know what a big deal this is and I know I'm supposed to be happy, but there's a small nagging feeling in my brain that tells me not to get my hopes up and to continue to hold him at a distance.

"Do you have any questions to ask me?" he says.

I have millions, but none of them come to mind. "No."

"You must have some."

We sit in silence for a full minute and I try to think of what I want to ask him. I've spent so many years trying not to engage with him that I can't remember how to do it now. It's like trying to use a muscle you haven't used in a really long time. "I don't."

"Well if you think of any, you can ask me anytime. Part of my recovery is to make amends with the people I've hurt through my addiction, and I know I've hurt you. At GA they say the best form of apology is changed behavior, and I hope over time you'll see me become someone you want to be around again."

"I hope so, too."

"Your brother put me in touch with a debt charity and they're giving me advice on how to get my finances in order. I've been hiding things from your mother for a really long time. I want to pay back the money I took from you."

"I don't care about the money," I say instantly.

"That may be so, but it's your money and I never should have asked you for it in the first place. It was wrong of me and it shows you're a good person to be so generous."

I wonder if I hit my head and I'm hallucinating. Before I'd mentally checked out of my family drama, when things were really bad, I used to have pretend conversations with my dad in my mind. I'd practice what I'd say, how he'd react, and then by the end of it, he'd be better.

"I want to be part of this family again, Russ. I know it's my fault I'm not, and I know it's my fault you don't feel welcome around here, but I hope over time you can trust me enough to see I really do want to get better."

"I'm glad you're getting help, Dad. I truly hope it works."

I HAVE TOO MANY THOUGHTS in my head.

After our heart-to-heart, Mom insisted on us all having lunch together. I cannot remember the last time we sat down as a family to eat. Thankfully, Ethan talking about his band's new record deal manages to take up the majority of the conversation, leaving me free to listen and observe.

Ethan doesn't bring up speaking to Aurora on the phone, which I'm grateful for. She feels too precious to risk bringing her into this environment. I know she's strong and resilient, but I want to look after her, and given the situation with her own dad, she doesn't need to be made to get to know mine.

If her dad was to make strides to improve like mine is trying to, she'd be first in line to give him another chance. Yesterday marked the first time she told him how she felt, much like me in that hospital room all those weeks ago. I hope it sparks the same kind of reaction I've gotten.

Ethan walks me back to my truck in silence after lunch. His eyes are red and glazed, and he's thinner than he was the last time I saw him, in an unhealthy way. If I had to guess, I'd say he's high. "Are you okay?"

"Worry about yourself, little brother," he says, opening the truck door for me.

"You look strung out, Ethan." I've never seen him smoke a cigarette, never mind take drugs. "What's going on with you?"

"Nothing," he says, rubbing his jaw with his hand. "You wouldn't understand anyway."

"Try me."

He ignores me, diverting the conversation. "You good? You have everything you need for school? I've got some money heading my way with this deal, so, y'know, I can help out more now."

"I have everything I need," I say, closing the door and rolling down the window. "But thanks."

"This is what I've been working so hard for, this deal. All the shows, all the traveling. We're gonna fix everything. Money buys resources, Russ. Things will be good again real soon," he says.

"Bye, Ethan." He pats the side of the truck before heading back toward the house, and I make a mental note to call him to check in soon.

———

LETTING MYSELF INTO THE HOUSE, I find Aurora in the backyard huffing over some fabric on the ground. "What're you doing?"

She squeals and looks at me over her shoulder. "Oh my goodness, announce yourself before you sneak up on a girl. I nearly had a heart attack."

She continues to pull at the material even as I walk toward her. "What're you doing?"

"I found a tent in your wardrobe!" she says happily, looking up at me from the ground. "But I don't know how it works and there aren't any instructions. I thought we could camp outside next to this fire pit."

"Ten weeks in the great outdoors wasn't enough for you?" I say, smiling. I sit cross-legged on the grass and pull the tent farther away from her. "If you put it this close to the fire it'll melt."

"Why do you know everything?" she groans, moving all the pieces to the new spot.

"Why do you not know that you shouldn't put plastic near fire?"

Crawling along the ground in my direction, she climbs into my lap and immediately brushes my hair back, kissing my forehead. "This is my formal invitation to talk about how your day has been."

"I still need a little time to wrap my head around it before we talk about it. Is that okay?"

She hugs me closer. "Is there anything I could do that might help you feel better?"

"You can explain to me how you think my six-five ass is fitting in this tent with you."

Her eyes freaking light up as she grins at me. "We always make it fit."

Chapter Thirty-Seven

AURORA

THE TENT WASN'T ONE OF my better ideas, and somewhere around 2 a.m. I got so annoyed with the noise it made when I moved around that I dragged us both back into the house.

I thought the tent would be romantic, but for the first time, we really did struggle to make it fit. It was stuffy and annoying, and I entirely misjudged how cute it would be. There was also a massive spider that Russ claimed he removed, which I truly believe he did not, and now I'm worried I ate it in my sleep.

I hear the sound of the front door opening while Russ is in the shower, and I know that I have a short window to join them as the water shuts off. Pulling on some shorts under the Callaghan jersey I stole from Russ's wardrobe, I head downstairs to what I hope is going to be his favorite surprise.

It feels weird wandering around Russ's house like I live here, when the people who actually live here just arrived. Bobby and JJ are fighting over the Happy Housewarming Party banner that appears to have been edited with a Sharpie to say Happy Housecoming Party.

"Housecoming?" I ask as I reach the bottom step.

"It's the closest we could get to homecoming on such short notice," JJ laughs.

Bobby holds it up. "You could have made it say 'homecoming,' you just didn't want to."

A smaller woman I recognize from all the pictures steps in front of me and reaches out for a hug. "Hi! I'm Stassie, it's so nice to meet you. Nate told me all about you, but he has hockey stuff and can't leave Vancouver. He's really sad he's missing out."

"Maybe he should have stayed on this side of the border then instead of moving and moaning about it every two seconds. Hi, I'm Lola. I am already obsessed with everything I know about you and I'm planning for us to be friends."

"Russ has told me really nice things about you both," I say honestly. "It's really nice to meet you, and thank you for getting everyone here." Why am I being so formal?

"If muffin is saying nice things about me, then I'm not working hard enough to scare him," Lola says, looking confused.

"You definitely are, babe," Robbie says. "You're doing a great job with everyone."

"Rory?" Russ calls from upstairs, and everyone instantly goes quiet. "Are you talking to someone?"

"Yeah," I call back upstairs. "The ghosts."

"Okay! That's not at all creepy and unhinged, thanks. I'll be down in a minute."

The guys move in silence to quickly pin the banner to the wall at an angle that is definitely not straight. Henry produces a massive bag; when he empties it balloons flood across the floor. Our half-assed decorations look like the world's saddest birthday party, but in reality, it's the sweetest thing his friends could have done for him.

While Russ was at his parents' house yesterday, I received a call from an unknown number that turned out to be Stassie. She hadn't talked to Russ herself, but she knew if he was missing JJ's house-warming party because of family trouble it was likely going to be bad. She wanted to know if it was okay for them to come here and throw Russ a homecoming party.

And so the housecoming party was born.

"I feel like all my kids are home," JJ whispers proudly as we hear Russ's bedroom door open.

"You don't live here," Robbie whispers back.

My heart feels as loud as Russ's footsteps, and the farther he descends, the more we see of him through the banister: ankle, calf, knee, thigh . . .

"Is he naked?" Mattie whispers, panicked.

"I did not sign up for seeing anyone's dick today but my own," Kris mutters.

Upper thigh . . . boxer shorts. Thank God. The group releases a collective sigh of relief, and when he gets far enough down the stairs that he can see into the living room, he freezes.

"Surprise," Henry says in the most unexcited way possible.

Russ's jaw drops. "What the fuck?"

I'VE HEARD ABOUT THE GUYS' trip to Miami so much I feel like I was actually with them.

"We should all go next year!" Mattie says excitedly.

"No," Henry and Russ say at the same time.

"I think I'm going to go back to Honey Acres next year, so I'll have to politely say no," says Russ.

"If they'll have you," Henry says, taking a bite of a chicken wing. "You got caught breaking their number-one rule, and it's not like you two will grope each other less in a year's time. We learned that one from Nate and Robbie."

Russ, who is currently resting his head on top of mine with his arms draped over my shoulders, ensuring as much physical contact as possible, scoffs. "Nate and Robbie groping each other?"

Stassie's eyebrow quirks. "That sounds about right, yeah."

They all launch into different stories, stopping to explain the significance to me so I don't feel excluded, and Russ's arms tighten around me. "You okay?" he whispers into my ear. I nod, continuing to listen to a story about the time Robbie and Nate fell out of a ski lift.

This group dynamic is new to Russ, too, but I can see why it's so important to him. This group is a family more than they're friends, and they're so welcoming that it's impossible not to fall in love with every single one of them.

That's what we both desperately need, I think. To be surrounded by people who make us feel loved and wanted. We've spent the summer getting used to it with Xander, Jenna, and Emilia . . . and the dogs, of course. My relationship with my mom feels like it's healing, and Russ is on a path with his parents that I hope will give him peace.

All the pieces of our lives are fitting together like a jigsaw, and I finally have the inner pieces.

Bobby finishes telling a story about an away game that left him locked outside the hotel naked, getting screamed at by their hockey coach, which gives me the opportunity to ask a question I've been wanting an answer to for weeks.

"Guys, why do you all call Russ muffin?"

Robbie opens his mouth to answer me immediately, but then closes it and frowns, looking at Kris. Kris has the same confused expression as Mattie, and one by one they glance at one another with the same look of uncertainty before JJ finally answers. "I literally have no idea."

I turn in Russ's arms to look up at him and he's hiding a grin. "Do you know?"

"Yeah. Long story short, I used to work in a bar and Stassie was there one day on her own. These horrible customers were harassing her, and I didn't really know her at this point, so I pretended to be her boyfriend. Basically I fake-dated Stassie for an hour, and that's the nickname she gave me."

"I love fake dating."

"Fake-dating? That is the most ridiculous thing I've ever heard," Henry says.

"It was cute. Very creative under pressure, I'd say," Stassie adds.

"One night I picked Stassie and Lola up from a bar and she was super drunk. She called me muffin in front of everyone and it, um, stuck I guess."

The group goes quiet at the same time, and I watch all their faces still sporting the same look of confusion. Mattie clears his throat and reaches for his beer. "Yeah, that is not what I thought. I thought you just liked muffins a lot, I don't know."

"Rory, did Jenna ask about me after we visited?" Bobby asks, giving me a wink.

When the guys visited Honey Acres for Russ's birthday, we realized that Bobby and Kris would have been at camp at the same time as me. We didn't remember each other, thankfully, which I'm extra grateful for because I was probably being annoying and dramatic. Character traits I'd like to not reveal to them until they already like me.

"Would you like me to lie to you so your feelings don't get hurt?" I ask carefully.

"Yes. If that's an option, I'd like you to always take it," Bobby says.

Before I even have a chance to answer, Henry beats me to it. "You're really good at hockey."

The guys play-fight, and while everyone's distracted, Russ kisses my neck and whispers into my ear. "You're doing so well. They love you."

Calm quickly resumes, and Bobby looks back at me for confirmation. I nod enthusiastically. "She absolutely asked about you."

When I told Jenna about Bobby's long-lived crush on her, her response was less than happy. "Fantastic. I love it when people return as adults and want to fuck me like I didn't literally look after them as children." She made a loud and dramatic retching noise. "I hate men."

"Maybe I really will work there next year," Bobby says, much to the disapproval of his friends.

"I hope you're better at fixing toilets than Russ," I laugh.

LEARNING HOW MUCH RUSS LIKES to touch me when there aren't any rules prohibiting it has been my favorite discovery since coming back to Maple Hills.

My brain is frazzled trying to suppress my natural instinct to overshare, and despite being a somewhat confident person, the pressure to make sure the people Russ loves so much like me is intense.

The homewarming—or housecoming, whichever one it is—party is less of a party and more of a chilled day hanging out together. It's needed after a dramatic couple of days, and I love seeing Russ ease me into it all.

I take a break from the action to video call Emilia and Poppy in the backyard. They're both big fans of my tent and can't believe I convinced Russ to sleep in it with me. I'm pretty sure Russ would sew a tent from scratch if he thought it'd make me happy.

The back door opens and JJ appears, spotting me on a deck chair on my own. He ambles over, hands in his pockets, and sits down across from me. "Pops and Emilia send their love," I say.

"I saw Emilia's story. They look like they're having fun."

"This feels very formal," I say awkwardly, shuffling on my seat. Shielding my eyes from the sunlight, I try hard to focus on JJ's very serious face. "Are you about to give me a lecture? A pep talk? Life advice?" Oh God, the rambling is back.

"A thank-you. This is the happiest I've seen Russ in the two years I've known him."

The butterflies that live in my stomach dance around happily. "He makes me happy, too. Thank you for teaching him to fake being confident long enough for him to talk to me that night."

"Thank you for letting him see himself the way we see him."

"This got really fucking deep," I say. "I think I prefer you making me do Jenga dares."

"Yeah, it was a bit unnecessarily emotional, wasn't it. I'm trying this mature thing out, don't think it's going to stick." He stands, holding out his hand to me to stand, too. "Are you interested in being introduced to drunk Hungry Hippos?"

Walking back into the house, JJ announces he wants to play the new game and disappears to find what he needs. Walking into the kitchen, I spot Russ getting two glasses out of the cupboard. "Stop, thief." He puts the glasses on the counter, turning to lean against it with his arms folded across his chest.

"I'm the thief?"

"You look familiar. Have you burgled here before?"

He reaches out and pulls me closer, nudging my chin up with his hand, kissing me in a way that makes my knees go weak. I don't need to search for validation or attention, because I have everything I need right here with this man.

"Tell me a secret, Callaghan." He brushes my hair out of my face, staring at me like I'm the only thing he sees in this world.

He doesn't even hesitate. "I'm falling in love with you, Aurora."

Ten million butterflies. "I'm falling in love with you, too."

Epilogue

RUSS

Nine-ish Years Later

"I think I'm going to be sick." Aurora holds her stomach, groaning dramatically. I drape my arm across her shoulders, tugging her closer until I can kiss the top of her head. I've spent the last six weeks reassuring her, and now I'm just giving her affection because she doesn't listen to me anyway. "This was a horrible idea. Why did you let me do this?"

"What happened to 'Aurora Callaghan doesn't have bad ideas' and 'When have I ever been wrong?' or—"

"Okay, okay," she says. "You've made your point." Aurora moves in front of me, leaning back against my chest, as we both stare up at the Happy Ending sign above the bookstore door. "What if nobody wants to buy books from me because I'm not a family business?"

"We are a family business. I'll write it on the window with a Sharpie if you want me to."

"I'm not sure you, me, and the animals count as a family business."

Pressing my lips to her neck, I drown in the sweet smell of her perfume. I hate how hard her pulse is hammering. Nervous Rory is the version of my wife I see the least, but buying the old bookstore in Meadow Springs has given her lots of things to be nervous about.

"I feel like that type of claim is going to land us in front of the Committee of Commitments to Town Improvements and Other Important Announcements."

"Mrs. Brown has been dying to get us back there after she lost the name-change vote," I reply.

Apparently, Happy Ending sounds like an erotic massage parlor, and will only invite misfits and deviants to the town. I wanted to argue that a misfit and a deviant bought the store, but Jenna stressed that the MSCCTIOIA was not a place for jokes.

When Jenna took over Honey Acres from her mom two years ago, the committee of chaos and nonsense demanded she do a business presentation, despite the fact they've known her since she was born and she's been on the committee for the last fifteen years. She made a few jokes about said history to lighten the mood, which, surprisingly, did quite the opposite.

Rory sighs heavily. "I do plan to promote sin; she wasn't totally wrong."

"Wait until she hears about the hot tub delivery," I say, gently pushing her in the direction of her new business.

Moving to Meadow Springs wasn't a difficult decision; it's always been special to us, especially after working three summers at Honey Acres together. What can I say? It really is like a great tea-cozy museum.

Aurora was tired of her job in the sales team at a small publishing house, and desperate to get out of the city. Then I received a promotion at the engineering firm I work for, and the new remote role only requires me to travel a couple of times a month, so we started packing our boxes to start our new life.

After Jenna sold us the land and haunted house where we had our first date, we spent the last eighteen months turning it into our dream home. The amount of land has given Aurora big ideas for all the animals we can now rescue.

Even though I said no to getting a puppy when Aurora told me Fish was having another litter—in my defense, we were fresh out of college—I came home from a work trip one day and found not one, but two golden balls of fur in my living room, appropriately named Tuna and Flounder. She immediately blamed Anastasia, who had apparently talked her into it, after getting their sibling, Bunny.

Since then I've said no to but still ended up owning: Neville, a rescue border collie with a penchant for daytime television; Mary-Kate and Ashley, two black cats that, even though it's been three years since we rescued them, I still cannot tell apart; and our latest adoption, Beryl, a pig that can't decide if she's a dog or a cat, but definitely believes she's not a pig.

Aurora really wanted them all here today for the opening of her bookstore, but I suggested that unleashing three dogs, two cats, and a pig onto her new neighbors maybe wasn't the best idea. She countered that they behaved at our wedding, to which I argued that I'm not sure Jenna officiating on our back deck while Emilia sipped on a margarita can be considered a wedding. Thankfully, I won that argument.

The bell jingles above our heads as we walk through the freshly painted door, and the store that was once dark and musty is now bright and revived. "I know I've said it a million times, but your dad really knocked it outta the park with these," she says, trailing her hand across the new wooden bookshelves.

I nod, humming in agreement. Dad has worked nonstop for weeks to make sure this entire place looks exactly how Rory wants it. He drew her sketch upon sketch, produced sample upon sample, and at one point, I'm pretty sure they made a digital vision board together.

It was strange living with him on the weekdays he was here working, especially since I haven't lived with him since I was a freshman. He'd offered to stay in a local B and B, but Aurora was insistent that he stay with us. I was nervous at first, unsure how things would be despite our relationship being so much better than it was all those years ago. I think the weirdest part for me was starting to miss him on the weekends when he'd go back to Maple Hills.

We said he didn't need to leave, and Mom could come to us, but he's a sponsor now at Gamblers Anonymous, so he likes to be local in case any of the people he's helping work through their addiction need his support.

I think Rory needed a father figure to help her, too, given her own father's absence. I overheard Dad reassuring her more times than I can count while he stayed with us. My parents both love my wife, so much so that I only got yelled at once for our spontaneous, guestless wedding. They were just happy she was finally officially their daughter.

Aurora's heels click against the hardwood floor as she paces up and down the aisles in search of something to panic about. I follow her, strolling slowly with my hands in my pockets, listening to her huff and puff her way around what is a perfect bookstore.

"Sweetheart . . ."

"Don't sweetheart me," she grumbles, spinning to face me. She plants her hands on her hips and pouts. "You did this, Russ Callaghan. You told me I could run my own business. A bookstore, no less. Not even a bar or a strip club or something I might actually be good a—"

Whatever she was about to say dies when I close the space between us, taking her face in my hands and pressing my mouth against hers. Her body melts into me, the tension dissipating with every passing second. Moving my hands to cup the nape of her neck, I rest my forehead against hers. "You are the most capable woman I have ever met in my life. There's nothing you could suggest that I wouldn't support. I will be there to hold your hand through all of it, Ror, but you don't need me to. You've never needed me to be incredible. You. Just. Are. And I love you more than I can put into words."

"I love you, too." Her arms wrap around my neck, her big green eyes staring into mine. "This is our last chance alone all weekend. Tell me a secret, Callaghan."

Secrets aren't really a thing between us. I've spent so many years with Aurora that her ability to overshare has finally rubbed off a little. "I did eat your Cheetos last week. It wasn't Neville. He looked at me with such judgment when I blamed him that I felt guilty for, like, three days."

Those eyes I love so much roll extra-dramatically. "No shit. You had orange dust all over your face. Try again."

It's the *try again* that throws me. Like she's waiting for me to admit something specific, something she already knows, which isn't how this game works. Our friends and neighbors will be arriving soon for the opening, but she's still staring up at me expectantly.

And that's when I realize.

She knows.

"Oh shit." The corner of her mouth tugs up into a smirk. "I invited your mom and forgot to tell you."

"Oh shit is right, because yes, you did."

"How did you know?"

"Because she called me to confirm I'd be serving good champagne."

"I THOUGHT I'D ESCAPED BEING forced into bookstores with Aurora," Henry sighs, eyes scanning the tall mahogany shelves lined with new books. "And yet here I am. Again."

Aurora wanted the kids' corner painted like the northern lights, so she enlisted her favorite—and possibly the only person she knows who can do it—artist to help her. The painting he was good with. It was helping make the hundreds of tiny origami stars to hang from the ceiling that got him.

"Here we both are." I nudge his shoulder with mine playfully. "Thanks for bringing those signed editions, man. Aurora appreciates you being here. We both do."

"It's fine; it means less books in my house. She'd have come, but it's just a bit far with the baby and—"

"What about me?"

We both look at the child perched on Henry's hip, clinging to him like he's her favorite toy—which he pretty much is. "Yes, Mila. We're very happy you're here, too."

She smiles brightly, which reminds me the older she gets, the more it's like staring at Stassie. "Uncle Henry, can I have my ice cream now? It's been the mandatory five minutes."

Henry drops her to her feet and nudges her away. "Go ask your dad for money."

"Mandatory five minutes?" I ask as we watch her crash into Nate's legs, shouting her request up to him. Nate pauses his conversation with Emilia, sighing as he reaches for his wallet, scowling at Henry from across the room as he places some bills in his daughter's palm.

"Mandatory five minutes of socializing," Henry says.

I smother a laugh with my coffee and Mila comes barreling back toward us. "He said I have to get the twins some, too, but they're taking a nap, so I don't think they need any and we should get extra for us."

"That sounds reasonable. Come on, kiddo." She reaches up to take Henry's hand and the pair of them head in the direction of the ice cream shop, The Little Moo, leaving me to fend for myself. I still don't love being the center of attention, and I'm thankful today is about Aurora. A mixture of customers and friends are scattered around the room, each scanning the shelves, chatting with each other. I can see JJ and Alex talking to my parents, Stassie rocking a double stroller as she talks to Jenna, Mrs. Brown intensely inspecting the romance section. What was an old, forgotten bookstore not that long ago now feels full of life.

I know my mother-in-law is in here somewhere, so I'm avoiding our inevitable meeting for as long as possible by keeping myself busy, taking candid photographs of everyone like Aurora taught me. That's when I take the best one: Aurora, behind the cash register with the biggest smile on her face, selling a huge pile of books to someone. The light pouring in through the windows is making her practically glow. I'm immediately overwhelmed by her beauty, and the feeling of pride that she did all of this herself.

She spots me watching her while her customer looks down, patting around their body to find their wallet. I mouth "I love you" and she mouths it back. I mouth "I'm so proud of you," and she mouths back something that looks like "I'm proud of how hot you are." It's the moment that all the moving, all the renovations, all the working in my boxers because I couldn't find the box with our clothes feels totally worth it. Everything brought us here, to being this blissfully happy.

After another hour, I realize that I won't be able to work from the store like I was planning to. I'll get absolutely no work done if I'm staring at my wife all day. Rory is a natural, like I knew she would be, and every customer makes her relax a bit more.

When the opening party starts to wind down and she steps away from behind the register, someone, likely JJ, shouts, "Speech!" We all watch in awe as she accepts a glass of champagne and throws it back quickly. Sarah tuts disapprovingly, but Aurora is an expert at not listening to her mom's complaints. "It's for courage." She laughs. "Um . . ."

I make my way through the people who have gathered around her so she can see me front and center. Her shoulders relax, and her eyes lock on me.

"Thank you everyone for being here today. Really, thank you. I can't believe it. I know a lot of you have traveled a long way, and I've promised those of you staying with us pancakes in the morning, and this is my way of telling you that I'm really terrible at making pancakes." She really is. "Thank you to the people of Meadow Springs for welcoming us into your community. I know it wasn't easy at first, but Russ and I feel so at home here. For everyone else who might not know, many years ago, I made a joke about opening a strip club here. Apparently nobody forgot."

Everyone in the room laughs, and out of the corner of my eye I spot Mrs. Brown muttering something to John from one of the bowling stores. "Thank you to everyone who helped get the store ready. My wonderful father-in-law for spending all his time making sure things were perfect; my friends for helping get rid of that awful magnolia color, and for helping to make hundreds of tiny stars. Thanks to my mom for sending me carefully curated lists of books I should buy.

"God, this is turning into an Oscar speech. I'll wrap it up. It's no secret that I love books. I love stories about people I don't know, and places I haven't been to. I've lived a thousand lives between a thousand pages, but no story, no life, no page has ever made me as happy as you do, Russ Callaghan." Everyone awws, and I feel the tips of my ears turn pink. "Before I met you, I hadn't considered what my happy ending might look like. I wasn't sure I'd get one. You're my happy ending, Russ. I fell in love with you in Meadow Springs, and watching you help build our life here has made me fall in love with you a million more times. Thank you for giving me a life that feels too good to be true. Thank you for letting me bring home animals even when you say no. Thank you for letting me live my dreams every day."

I want to rush over there and kiss her until her lips turn pink, but this is her job now and I don't want to embarrass her. Instead, I raise my glass in her direction. "To happy endings."

She raises her glass. "And unlimited pets."

"No," I immediately respond, but it's too late.

"To happy endings and unlimited pets," the room echoes.

Acknowledgments

PEOPLE SAY "IT TAKES A village" about a lot of things, but boy does it apply to this book.

First of all, I need to say thank you to you, reader. Without your overwhelming enthusiasm for *Icebreaker* I wouldn't be writing the Acknowledgments for my second book. To say I never saw it coming is the understatement of the century, but the aftermath of the incredible support you've shown me has changed my life. So thank you, from the bottom of my heart.

Thank you to my husband, for pretending to be an airport. Also, for not judging how much Starbucks I ordered while working on this book.

Erin, Ki, and Rebecca: For listening to me talk nonstop for the past year, for supporting me through the scary but wonderful transition into traditional publishing, and for tolerating seeing me on your FYP far more than you'd all like.

Lauren, for reading this book more times than I have and being supportive for every second of it. You deserve an award for keeping me sane, even when I start dying at three a.m. miles away from home. I'm so lucky to have you on my side.

Kimberly, for helping me navigate this weird new world and always being there when I need you, time zones be damned. You are truly wonderful, and I could not do any of this without you. I am so grateful for everything that you do for me.

Ellie, for your valiant attempts to keep me young and relevant. I'm so lucky you saw *Icebreaker* that day, and I'm so happy we get to work together. I'm proud of how far you've come in the past twelve months, and I can't wait to see what the future brings us.

Nicole, I'm not sure anybody loves Russ and Aurora as much as you do. Thank you for always being there to listen to my millions of ideas and for cheering me on every step of writing this book.

Allie and Kimmy, for taking the time to read my drafts and give me your honest feedback. Your positivity was what I needed and I'm so thankful that I can call you both friends.

Becs and Elena, for telling me I could write this book when it really, really felt like I couldn't at times. I'm so thankful that ten-minute voice notes are the norm in our friendship group.

Becky, for just generally being my favorite bear and Henry's girl.

And my biggest thank-you to the whole Simon & Schuster and Atria team: Molly, Sarah, Sabah, Pip, Kaitlin, Ife, Morgan, Zakiya, Megan, Anthea, Kate, and everyone else behind the scenes who works their butts off to make my books what they are. I could not be prouder to be part of this group and I'm so thankful to each of you who work tirelessly to support me in any way you can.

About the Author

HANNAH GRACE IS AN ENGLISH self-labeled "fluffy comfort book" author, writing predominantly new adult and contemporary romance from her home in Manchester, England. When she's not describing everyone's eyes ten-thousand times a chapter, accidentally giving multiple characters the same name, or using English sayings that no one understands in her American books, you can find her hanging out with her husband and two dogs, Pig and Bear.